Confessions of the
DEAD

James Patterson is one of the best-known and biggest-selling writers of all time. Among his creations are some of the world's most popular series, including Alex Cross, the Women's Murder Club, Michael Bennett and the Private novels. He has written many other number one bestsellers including collaborations with President Bill Clinton, Dolly Parton and Michael Crichton, stand-alone thrillers and non-fiction. James has donated millions in grants to independent bookshops and has been the most borrowed adult author in UK libraries for the past fourteen years in a row. He lives in Florida with his family.

J.D. Barker is the international bestselling author of numerous books, including *Dracul* and *The Fourth Monkey*. His novels have been translated into two dozen languages and optioned for both film and television. Barker resides in coastal New Hampshire with his wife, Dayna, and their daughter, Ember.

A list of titles by James Patterson appears
at the back of this book

Confessions of the
DEAD

JAMES
PATTERSON
& J.D. BARKER

PENGUIN BOOKS

PENGUIN BOOKS

UK | USA | Canada | Ireland | Australia
India | New Zealand | South Africa

Penguin Books is part of the Penguin Random House group of companies
whose addresses can be found at global.penguinrandomhouse.com

First published in the UK in Penguin Books 2024
001

Printed and bound in Great Britain by Clays Ltd, Elcograf S.p.A.

The authorised representative in the EEA is Penguin Random House Ireland,
Morrison Chambers, 32 Nassau Street, Dublin D02 YH68

A CIP catalogue record for this book is available from the British Library

ISBN: 978–1–804–94886–6

www.greenpenguin.co.uk

MIX
Paper | Supporting
responsible forestry
FSC® C018179

Penguin Random House is committed to a
sustainable future for our business, our readers
and our planet. This book is made from Forest
Stewardship Council® certified paper.

Confessions of the
DEAD

Analysis Note: My name is ██████████ assistant direc-tor and special agent in charge with ██████████ of ██████████. I've been tasked with making sense of the events that occurred between the hours of 6:37 GMT-4 on 10/15/23 and 22:16 GMT-4 10/16/2023 at 43.9792° N, 71.1203° W, an area now defined as "Hollows Bend, NH." This report is preliminary. These events are still ongoing. I imagine this text and these happenings will be picked over by many people far more qualified than me in the days and weeks to come, and I hope that action will bring more clarity than I have at this time. That in mind, I need to preface what you are about to read with one simple statement, words spoken by a man far wiser than me:

Midway upon the journey of our life
I found myself within a forest dark,
For the straightforward pathway had been lost.

Let me be clear: I don't know what all this means for the rest of us. If you're looking for those answers, you won't find them here. I also know that if you continue beyond this page, all you thought you understood will unravel and once you tug that string, there's no putting it back.

1

LOG 10/16/2023 20:17 GMT-4
TRANSCRIPT: AUDIO/VIDEO RECORDING

Sordello: For the record, this is Special Agent Beatrice Sordello. We have yet to determine if quarantine is necessary, so until told otherwise, I'm in a Manfred booth, which is a double isolation chamber best described as two sealed Plexiglas cubes positioned against each other. Both have their own self-contained atmosphere, which is being monitored remotely not only to ensure the air remains viable, but also for unknown pathogens. Until cleared, I will remain in my chamber and the interview subject will remain confined in his. Anyone entering either chamber is wearing a full hazmat suit and will undergo decontamination protocols upon entry and exit. It's important to note that we haven't found any sign of an airborne contaminant. This is strictly a precaution. My interview subject appears to be in good health aside from signs of recent physical trauma—primarily cuts and abrasions, which have been treated. At this point, I am switching on my secondary microphone so he can hear me.

[*Audible click*]

Sordello: Can you state your name?

Subject 1: Seriously? You know my name.

Sordello: For the record.

Subject 1: Deputy Matthew Maro.

Sordello: Your full name.

Maro: Deputy Virgil Matthew Maro, but nobody calls me that.

Sordello: What should I call you?

Maro: Matt is fine.

Sordello: Matt. The woman who just entered your chamber is going to apply several sensors to your chest, right arm, and your forehead. These will allow us to record not only your vitals but also your brain wave patterns in sync with this recording. Are you okay with that?

Maro: What, like a lie detector?

Sordello: Strictly for observational purposes.

Maro: Sure. Go ahead. Whatever helps.

Sordello: Okay. I have a vital feed coming in. Transmission seems to be okay. For the record, Deputy Maro has a resting heart rate of 102 beats per minute, blood pressure is 132 over 81. While these appear to be slightly elevated, this is understandable considering…recent events. Blood oxygen and brain patterns are normal.

Maro: You said you were a special agent, but you didn't say with who.

Sordello: We'll get to that. Would you like me to have them administer something to help you calm down?

Maro: No. I'll be fine. I'm just, you know, trying to wrap my head around everything.

Sordello: I'm hoping to help you with that.

Maro: If you want to help, how about telling those guys to lower their guns. I'm not going to do anything.

Sordello: I'm afraid I can't. We need to follow protocols.

Maro: You have protocols for this? Has it happened before?

Sordello: Your blood pressure is rising. Are you sure you don't want a mild sedative?

Maro: I understand the guns, but why is there a priest here?

Sordello: I need you to focus, Deputy. I don't know how much time we have. We need to get everything on the record while we still can.

Maro: Okay. Okay.

Sordello: Walk me through it. Start with yesterday morning. Try not to leave out any details, even if they seem minor to you.

Maro: [*No response*]

Sordello: Deputy?

Maro: With her, right? When she first showed up?

Sordello: [*Subject muted—Audible to technician only*] Can you check his heart rate monitor? He dropped off for thirty seconds, then came back.

[*Audible click—Subject unmuted*]

Sordello: Yes. Start with her.

2

MATT

Earlier

BEING SUNDAY MORNING, SHORTLY after the last of the crisp night fog burnt away, Hollows Bend, New Hampshire, had a buzz to it. Streets deserted twenty minutes earlier were now bustling with vehicles. Most were tourists heading home after a weekend in the mountains or behind the business end of some expensive camera taking photographs of the New England leaves—leaves that by the second week of October were well on their way to deep shades of red and gold and thick enough on the grass of the commons to blot out the green.

The Stairway Diner on Main was the final stop for those tourists. It was also the starting point for many of the Bend's locals, who enjoyed watching them depart, and by ten there wasn't an empty chair in the place.

Deputy Matt Maro sat on his favorite stool at the far end of the counter, his back against the wall, watching Gabby Sanchez zip from table to table in comfortable shoes. With steaming breakfast plates balanced precariously down the length of her slender arm, she moved with this practiced elegance, twisting and bending like a dancer. Even when a customer complained, the smile never left her face. Matt envied her that she never let her anger slip. It was just one of the many reasons he'd fallen for her.

Gabby caught him watching, gave him a quick wink, twisted with a flirty cock of her hip, and turned to the corner booth holding the sizable Lockwood family, all eight of them, paying extra attention to Libby Lockwood, who recently turned four and insisted on placing her own order.

A grunt came from Matt's left, followed by a phlegm-filled cough, and Matt swiveled back around on his stool. The man slouched on the stool beside him would have passed for dead if not for the way he was shoveling in his eggs.

Roy Buxton (Buck to everyone but bill collectors and the nuns back at Saint Mary's) might have weighed 140 on a good day, and for Buck, today was far from one of those. His hair was greased back and smelled like a wet cellar. The filth on his skin and clothing was thick enough to flake off, if not for the layer of sweat holding it in place.

To the amusement of several out-of-towners, Matt had found him last night on Main Street at a little after eleven, bottle of Jack in one hand, shoes in the other, shuffling along barefoot two sheets deep into an argument with himself that might have been about politics or might have been about *Game of Thrones*. Matt'd walked Buck back to the small sheriff's office and set him up in the single cell with a blanket, a pillow, and two bottles of water. It was not his first time in that bunk, and Matt was certain it wouldn't be his last. That particular dance had become ritual, as had breakfast on the county at the Stairway the morning after.

"Pass the ketchup?" Buck held his hand out but didn't look Matt in the eye. He rarely did.

Matt slid the bottle toward him.

Buck worked the cap and held the bottle wobbly over his plate, dribbling his eggs, home fries, even the bacon. When he set the bottle off the edge of the counter—Matt snagged it mid-drop and replaced it safely. "When was the last time you saw a doctor, Buck? Got yourself checked out?"

He dug back into the eggs. "How 'bout we postpone the banter for another thirty? Bacon and lecture don't mix well, tends to give me gas."

"I'm just worried about you."

Buck leaned to his left, lifted his leg off the stool, and let out a fart loud enough to turn several of the closest heads. "You brought that upon yourself, Deputy."

Two stools over, Mr. Wheeler from the deli was staring at them both, his face twisted in a grimace. Matt paused a beat before saying, "You don't let up on the drinking, and your body's gonna give up on you."

"Ain't nothing givin' up. I'm fine." Even as Buck said this, sweat trickled down from his brow, streaking the dirt with salty lines.

"You don't look fine."

Buck stabbed at a potato wedge, missed, and tried again. "I slipped up last night, is all. Won't happen again." He managed to impale a slice and carefully maneuvered it to his mouth. "Didn't mean to burden you with my shortcomings, Deputy."

Matt took a sip of his coffee. They'd had variations of this conversation more times than he could count. Sheriff Ellie Pritchet had taken her share of failed runs at getting Buck some help, and her father before her when he'd been sheriff. The best they could all come up with was to put Buck on the town's payroll doing odd jobs. Try to keep him busy. The truth was, Buck had been putting away his share of drink for the entirety of Matt's twenty-nine years on the planet, and then some, but that didn't mean Matt couldn't try to get Buck to stay sober. "Tell you what. I'm barbecuing tonight at Gabby's place. Burgers, hot dogs, couple of nice sirloins she handpicked down at McKinnon's. Why don't I pick you up, drop you off after? Get another meal into you, maybe watch some football. Between Gabby and her daughter, Riley, I'm outnumbered over there. The place could use a little more testosterone."

Buck choked deep in his throat and took a drink of water. "I don't think your girlfriend wants the likes of me in her home. You best run that by Gabby."

"Run what by Gabby?"

Gabby had slipped back behind the counter. She was scooping grounds into the large coffee maker with one hand while filling a glass with Coke from the soda fountain with the other.

"I invited Buck here over for dinner tonight."

A lock of brown hair broke free from her ponytail and fell over Gabby's right eye. She blew it to the side and grinned at the old man. "Absolutely! We'd love to have you."

"You're awfully kind, the two of you." Buck ate a strip of bacon, then wiped the corners of his mouth with the back of his hand. "Excuse me a minute? I need to use the head."

He eased off the stool, took a moment to steady his legs, then hobbled off. Matt watched as he walked right past the restroom and pushed through the kitchen door at the end of the hallway.

Gabby watched him, too. "He's not coming back, is he?"

Matt shook his head. "He'll sneak out the kitchen and up the mountain, head for home."

Gabby frowned. "I don't get it. He must be so lonely."

Matt picked up his fork and started on his own breakfast. He'd let it go cold. "I guess some people prefer their own company."

"He always seems so, I don't know, sad." Gabby lowered her voice and nodded at a booth on the far side of the diner. "Henry Wilburt told his wife if Buck's trying to drink himself to the grave, he's doing a piss-poor job of it. Then *she* said someone should give him a gun and tell him to stop pussyfooting around."

Matt fought the urge to twist around on the stool for a look. Henry Wilburt's wife ran the bake sale at the elementary school, knitted winter scarves for the homeless, and volunteered two days a week at library story time. "Corine Wilburt said *that*?"

Gabby nodded. "Don't let the gray hair fool you. That woman is malvada."

Matt considered that. "Evil?"

Gabby beamed. "You've been practicing!"

He held up his thumb and index finger. "Un poquito."

Addie Gallagher had come in while they were talking and managed to sidle up next to Matt and drop her purse on Buck's empty stool. "Practicing what?"

At the sound of her voice, Matt twisted a little too fast—coffee spilled over the side of his mug and dripped down his shirt.

"I'm so sorry! I didn't mean to startle you! Let me get that—"

Addie tugged a paper napkin from the dispenser, moistened it in Matt's water glass, and blotted at the growing stain on his uniform. "You've got to get it while it's wet, or it will never come out." She looked over at Gabby. "Do you have any white vinegar?"

Her hand drifted to Matt's shoulder and gave him a gentle squeeze.

Oh boy, Matt thought. *Here we go.* He really didn't want to start the day with some kind of territorial pissing contest.

Back in high school, Addie had been the girl Matt called twenty minutes after dropping his real date off at home. Friends with benefits. Fuck buddies. Nothing more than an alcohol-fueled grab-and-go. When she started getting a little too clingy, he'd put an end to it. And when he found himself dialing her again after partying a little too much, he'd put an end to that, too. They'd completely lost touch when he went off to UNH and she went off to wherever. He hadn't given her a second thought until she reappeared in Hollows Bend last summer, hoping to rekindle things. Matt had made it clear he was with Gabby and those days were in the past. Addie's return had been the fuel behind his first real fight with Gabby and the spark behind the others that followed. Matt didn't keep secrets from Gabby, but maybe that had been a mistake, because sometimes not knowing was better than knowing. Her relationship with her last boyfriend ended when she caught him cheating, and once that taste found its way into someone's mouth, it didn't wash out.

Although the smile was still on Gabby's face, there was no hiding the vein pulsing on the left side of her temple like the thin wisp of steam that signaled a tea kettle whistling.

Matt shrugged out from under Addie's hand. "It's fine. I've got a spare at the station."

Abbie grinned at Gabby. "It's funny, I was gone for so long, but everyone here has just welcomed me back, arms wide open. Feels like I never left, the way we're all picking right back up." Her grin shifted to Matt and widened. "Good seeing you again. Real good."

She retrieved her purse and wandered back through the dining room, her black bra fully visible through a sheer blouse worn over tight jeans. While Matt pretended not to look, Gabby glared at the other woman. "Pregnant women should not dress like that."

It had been about a month since Addie dropped that particular bombshell. She was about twelve weeks along, and she'd yet to tell anyone who the father was. In a town as small as the Bend, it was a hot topic. Addie and Matt's past wasn't exactly a secret.

Matt took out his wallet and set a twenty on the counter. "I best be getting back to the station. Ellie is out on patrol, and Sally's holding down the fort."

Gabby didn't answer. She was still looking out over the dining room, her flushed face gone white as a sheet. The voices behind Matt died away, the clink of silverware on plates vanished. There were several gasps, then silence.

One hand instinctively easing to his gun, Matt turned slowly on the stool and faced the front of the diner.

Standing in the open door, the sun bright at her back, was a girl of maybe sixteen. She wore not a stitch of clothing. Her long dark hair draped over her shoulder, partially covering her right breast. Her bare feet were caked in mud.

3

MATT

SHE DIDN'T MOVE.

Nobody did.

Gabby reached over the counter and clasped Matt's hand.

Somewhere in the room, a throat cleared.

But nobody went to her.

Matt wasn't proud of that fact, and it would haunt him until his dying day. He wasn't the type of person who froze, never had been. Even back in his glory days when he played ball, standing back on his own twenty-yard line with linebackers sailing through the air about to unleash a world of hurt, he didn't freeze. He got the ball off. He sidestepped. He reacted, he acted, but he never froze.

She looked ethereal.

Celestial.

Christ, she looked like a damned angel. There, he said it.

Not any angel, but a fallen angel, and for the briefest of seconds, he was absolutely certain if she turned around there would be tiny nubs at her shoulder blades where her wings had been clipped.

Matt knew how unbelievable that all sounded, hadn't set foot in a church since he was a kid, but there it was. Looking around at the faces around the packed diner, he knew those thoughts weren't solely his own. He even caught Peggy Lockwood crossing herself, and she did go to church. She went at least three times a week.

Matt didn't recognize her. She wasn't a local, and if she'd come in for the weekend with the rest of the tourists, he hadn't seen her before. He would have remembered her.

Matt rose from his stool, and his legs were trembling as badly as Buck's had been. In a fraction of a second, a buzzing in his ears was followed by a feeling like intense air or water pressure. His skin prickled all the way down to a momentary numbness at the tips of his fingers that then tingled with the pins-and-needles sensation of a sleeping limb. In the time it took for him to complete a single step, the world tilted and it was gone. Matt wasn't alone in that, either. All around him, people were rubbing their arms, glancing at each other with a mix of fright and bewilderment.

Someone to his left said in a childlike voice, "I smell ozone. Anyone else smell ozone?" Sounded like Hershel Brown, but also didn't because Hershel Brown was a six-foot-four Black man on the wrong side of fifty who weighed upward of three hundred pounds. His speaking voice was deep enough to rattle the windows, anything but childlike. When Matt glanced at him, the fear in the man's eyes told him all he needed to know.

The girl still hadn't moved. Naked as the day she was born, she stood at the mouth of the diner, one arm bracing the door open, the other hanging at her side. She opened her mouth as if to speak, but no sound came out.

Matt got his shit together.

He crossed the room to the coatrack where he'd hung his

jacket when he first arrived with Buck. Snatching it with enough force to nearly tumble the rack, he draped it over the girl's shoulders, quickly scanned her body for visible signs of trauma—cuts, bruises, abrasions—and found nothing except that she was in some form of shock.

With fumbling fingers, nothing but thumbs, Matt pulled the jacket closed and managed to get the zipper going, brought it up to the base of her neck. She wasn't very tall, maybe five foot two; the jacket reached halfway down her thighs, offering her at least some sense of modesty.

"You're going to be okay," he told her softly, and the moment the words passed his lips, he knew they were a lie.

She took a step forward, enough for the door to close, and Matt looked out over her shoulder at Main Street, the commons beyond that. Her feet were caked with mud, but it hadn't rained in nearly a week.

Matt saw the dark shape rocket down from the sky an instant before it slammed into the diner's glass door about a foot above the girl's head with a thump loud enough to make him jump. It hovered there for a second, frozen on the other side of the glass, then slipped and fell lifeless to the sidewalk.

A black crow.

Its beak had cracked with the impact. One of the bird's dark eyes had ruptured, tinging the surrounding feathers with a line of oily jelly.

Matt inched closer and then another hit—this one on the large picture window above the booth holding Mr. and Mrs. Tangway. Several of the women in the diner screamed with that one, a couple of the men, too, but not as loudly as they did when the third bird hit, or the others that followed.

4

LYNN TATUM

LYNN TATUM STOOD IN the center of the cluttered home office (formerly back bedroom, pre-pandemic) of her house on Morning Glory Road, staring at the note taped to the center of her computer monitor:

> Wasn't sure if you were working today. Didn't want
> to wake you. Went to grab juice—be right back. Kids
> playing in Gracie's room. —J

She looked up at the clock on the far wall—quarter to eleven. She'd overslept, and yes, she was supposed to work today. Shit.

Goddamn dizzy spell got her out of bed. Yanked her from a half-pleasant dream about a vacation they'd taken to Club Med at Turks and Caicos a lifetime ago (before kids) when she was still happy (before marriage) and still had some semblance of a body (before daily double caramel macchiatos). She'd woke with the world tilting, nearly fell from the bed, then managed to get her shit remotely together.

Still half asleep, Lynn dropped down into her chair and squealed as something bit into the meaty part of her ass. She jumped back up again, glaring down at the wood seat—one of Oscar's Matchbox cars. The silver Aston Martin with the missing hood and bent door. She swatted the small car across the room, watched it crack against the wall and vanish behind the white banker boxes stacked precariously in the corner. It left a mark in the drywall. Lynn didn't much care. Let Josh add that to his Saturday project list, the one that never seemed to get started.

Josh's desk sat back-to-back with Lynn's, and while her workspace was relatively free of clutter (there was a coaster for her coffee mug, nothing else, because a coaster was far less unsightly than stains left by unprotected cups), Josh's desktop was buried under accounting books, printouts of IRS code, knickknacks, and God knows what else he needed to keep his daily shit show of an accounting company running. How the man was able to function at all was a mystery. She'd given up picking up after him. Maybe she should hang a sheet across the room, divide the cramped space. Subtle enough hint, Joshy dear? Maybe.

Down the hall, Gracie yelped, Oscar laughed, then the sound of spilling trash. Lynn knew exactly what that was—they'd tipped Gracie's toy chest and dumped the contents across her bedroom floor. Like their father, those two had mess making down to an art form.

Lynn groaned and closed her eyes. She drew in a deep breath and held it for a moment. The Ambien she took last night had filled her head with cobwebs, made her thoughts sticky. She didn't want to work (Sunday, no less!). Lynn hated her job. She should go back to bed, sleep it off. Just this once, take the rest of the morning for herself. Let Josh figure out how to cover the mortgage payment. The utilities. Groceries. Gas in that beater he forced her to drive around. Let Josh deal with the kids. Let Josh—

Another crash from Gracie's room.

She leaned back and shouted over her shoulder. *"What are you two doing in there?!"*

They didn't answer. Of course not. Why would they?

Lynn tugged open her center drawer, took out the three pill bottles, and lined them up on the edge of the desk. She popped the tops and dry-swallowed one of each. The white pill would wipe away the last of the Ambien and help her focus. The blue one silenced the ugly thoughts. And the yellow pill…she wasn't a hundred percent sure what that one did, but her doctor had prescribed it, and that was good enough for her. She needed a shower, but there was no time for that.

Returning the bottles, Lynn leaned back in her chair and closed her eyes again.

Gracie screamed, a gut-wrenching, high-pitched shrill. Lynn felt the blade of it scrape down her spine. She kept her eyes closed. Whatever they were doing in there, Josh could deal with it.

Her computer dinged and a box popped up in the center of the screen, directly behind Josh's note, like her asshole of a husband had purposely placed it in the most intrusive spot he could find. Maybe he did. A little fuck-you before abandoning his morning responsibilities. She didn't for a second believe he'd gone to grab juice. More likely, he went to play a quick game of grab-ass with Nancy Buckley two streets over while her husband was out golfing. That's where she'd found his car the last time he'd gone to get juice.

Gracie and Oscar were laughing again. She heard small feet run down the hallway, thud down the steps. So much for staying in Gracie's room.

Not her problem.

Josh's problem.

His turn to watch the kids while she worked.

Her computer dinged again with another text box. The sound of that ding cut nearly as deep as Gracie's scream.

She pulled the note off of her monitor.

The box on the screen said:

> Lanford Collection Services: 23 calls in queue.
> Log in to earn big bucks on a bonus Sunday!

She couldn't do it. Not yet. Not until the pills kicked in. And why was that taking so long? Because she'd taken them without water? No, that couldn't be it. Maybe she needed to take more? She'd taken two Ambiens last night instead of one, maybe that was it.

Thumping footsteps again, like two small animals racing up the stairs. A moment later, Gracie's door slammed shut. That was followed by shouting. Both Gracie and Oscar screaming over each other, the words so muffled they were meaningless.

Lynn reached over, slammed her own door, and immediately regretted it. The clutter in the confined space seemed to inch closer. They'd discovered mold in the house back when they first bought it. Josh swore he got it all out, but if he did, would she smell that?

A new box appeared:

> Lanford Collection Services: 29 calls in
> queue. You're missing out! Lost seconds = lost
> opportunities!

Oscar yelled. Something about the color red.

Lynn closed her eyes again and pressed the palms of her hands against her ears.

Why weren't the damn pills working?

She yanked open her drawer and eyed the bottles. Maybe one more of each.

Just one.

5

MATT

MATT PULLED THE GIRL deeper into the diner as at least a dozen more crows rained down and slammed against the door and windows facing Main.

They were coming down from the mountains in thick lines, fast and angry. Shrills escaped their beaks moments before they slammed against the glass. The air grew dark as a dozen grew to hundreds and hundreds became a swarm blotting out the sun. A voice in the back of Matt's mind whispered the word *murder*—that's what a large group of crows was called—and as that word echoed, several hit the picture window together. A spiderweb of cracks appeared near the middle. More birds hit that spot dead center, like they were—

"EVERYONE GET BACK FROM THE GLASS!"

Half the diners sat frozen in their seats; the other half dove under their tables, pulling children down with them.

The birds couldn't possibly be aiming, but that's what it looked like. Like small missiles darting from the sky. Black rain. Just beyond the windows, they bounced off the sidewalks. Main

Street. The grass in the commons. The roof of the bandstand, the small structure barely visible less than two hundred feet away. Several car alarms went off. Holes appeared in the convertible top of an Audi A5, then it was shredded, then gone.

Gabby crawled up beside Matt and grabbed his arm, shouting over the sound of it all. "Where did all the people go?!"

A few had jumped inside the cars, Matt had seen that much. Others crawled under. More had run toward the shops lining Main Street, but had they made it? Nobody had come through the diner door, nobody since the girl.

He pulled her close, pressed his lips near her ear, went to answer, when the picture window nearest the Tangways' table crashed down in a rain of glass. Beneath the table, Bob Tangway shifted his considerable bulk around his wife and two kids, enfolded them beneath his navy suit jacket. Streaks of black poured through the opening, circled the interior of the diner, and cracked against the walls, the floor, the tables. Their shrieks and flapping wings mixed with the screams and shouts of terrified patrons. Matt caught a glimpse of Addie scrambling behind the counter, her face streaked with tears.

A few feet to his left, the girl had her head buried in Matt's borrowed coat, her face lost in her hair. One of the crows cracked against the tile floor between them, its neck snapping on impact. Two more directly after. Another landed on the girl's back, pecked at the coat, tore open the fabric, and furiously yanked out white stuffing. The girl didn't move. Matt swatted the bird away. Watched in awe as it climbed right back up. He hit it again, closed fist. It sailed across the floor, thudded against a chair leg, and this time didn't move.

A heavy weight landed on Matt's head, feet tangled in his hair, and pulled. A sharp beak tore at his scalp, and Matt's screams joined all the others as he blindly got his hands around it, tore it free, and slammed the bird against the floor until it stopped squirming. He killed five more before it was over.

6

LYNN TATUM

GRACIE AND OSCAR WERE screaming now. Fighting about God knows what.
Lynn Tatum dug the palms of her hands into her ears and
hummed in hopes of drowning them both out, little good that did.
It was like they knew what she was doing and yelled louder to com-
pensate. Where the hell was Josh? Why weren't the pills working?

On her computer screen, another box popped up:

> Remember—you're not a bill collector, you're a
> friend! If not for you helping each person you speak
> to, their credit rating would be negatively impacted.
> You're doing them a favor! You're a solution to their
> problem! 31 calls in queue. 31 people waiting for
> your help! What are *you* waiting for?

Lynn sucked in a breath, held it, then let it out slowly, just like
her doctor told her to.

Work.

Earn.

Get it over with.

Before she could change her mind, she slipped her headset on, scanned the text on her screen, and clicked the Connect button. "Is this Gordon Woolley?"

Landford's system auto dialed, and when a live person picked up, it placed them in the queue with a recording asking them to hold. If they hung up on the recording, it dialed them back from a different number. Once the system had you, it didn't let go. Gordon Woolley had hung up twice in the past minute, according to the time-stamped log.

"Who the hell is this?" The voice was gruff, full of gravel.

"My name is Tamera," she lied. "Am I speaking to Gordon Woolley?"

"What do you want?"

Lynn forced her eyes shut again. "I'm calling on behalf of First Encore Auto Loans. Are you aware that you are three months behind on your car payments and facing repossession on your 2016 Toyota Tundra?"

"Yeah? How is that any of your goddamn business?"

Lynn swallowed. "I've been authorized to make you a one-time offer. If you make two payments with me today, not only can I stop the repossession, but I can cut your third payment in half to get you caught up. How would you prefer to make those payments? I can either take a credit card or your checking account information."

The man on the other end of the line said nothing. He hadn't hung up, though. Lynn could hear him breathing. She added, "Of course, if I cut the third payment in half today, the balance will be due at the end of your loan period."

"If I had the money, don't you think I would have paid it by now?"

Lynn's heart thumped. "If you don't have the funds immediately available, I do have the ability to offer you a low-interest loan against your next paycheck. To do that, I need you to take a photo of your last pay stub and send it to me. Would you prefer to do that in order to bring your account current today, or will a credit card be easier?"

"Fuck you, you ignorant cunt. Don't ever call me again!"

The call disconnected with a hard click. The hang-up didn't sting as much as that particular word did. She hated that word.

Shut it out.

Ignore it.

Don't let it get to you.

A new box filled her screen:

> Congratulations! You earned $1.37! And we've got better news—For the next 30 minutes, you could earn 20% of whatever you collect! Yay, bonus Sunday! 34 calls in queue. Don't miss out!

The pills made her numb. The pills made it all doable, kept these people from creeping under her skin. So why weren't they working? She looked down at the drawer in her desk. Take another? No. She couldn't take three.

A crash came from down the hall, behind the various closed doors. This wasn't the toy box; this was something bigger. Lynn started to rise from her chair, then dropped back down.

No.

She wouldn't do it.

Whatever mess they made, that was on Josh. He could deal with it. He could clean it up.

A thick rubber band sat on the corner of her desk. Lynn scooped it up, wrapped it around her wrist, and snapped it. Allowed the sting against her skin to work up her arm before she rolled her mouse over the Connect button on her monitor again and clicked the next call. "Is this Klara...Pacheco?"

"Yes."

Lynn snapped the rubber band again. "I'm calling on behalf of Springton Medical Group in regard to your outstanding invoice of..." Although she'd read the details only a few seconds ago, she couldn't remember the exact amount and had to look at the screen again. "$23,681.43."

"My husband passed away last week. Do you think this can wait?"

Lynn went quiet and studied her screen. Lanford's system used sophisticated voice recognition software to analyze what was said and provide several approved responses. Scripts vetted by legal. Because it was fairly repetitive, Lynn had most of those responses memorized. Her mind went blank, though, and she waited for the computer to update. When it did, she scanned the text, then read, "I'm sorry for your loss, Mrs. Pacheco. This particular invoice is nearly a year old. Because it's a medical debt, I can bring it current with a payment as little as one percent. Would you prefer to make that payment with a credit card or from your checking account?"

Please don't cry.

Please don't cry.

Lynn could deal with the name-calling, had no trouble forgetting the ones who hung up on her, but the people who cried? They were the worst.

"That's when the cancer first appeared," the woman said. "A year ago. Springton was Lou's first treatment center. First of four."

Down the hall, Oscar shouted, and that was quickly followed by a scream from Gracie. Lynn cupped her hands over her headphones and pressed them against her ears. Her blood felt hot and itchy under her skin, carried by ants too large for her veins.

Her screen updated with a new response, and Lynn wasn't

sure she could read it. She could hang up. Let the system call this woman back and connect her to someone else. Maybe she should do that. When Lynn hesitated a little too long, a new message box appeared:

> This call is eligible for the 20% collection bonus!
> You got this!

Lynn closed the message box and scanned the system's response again. If she didn't do it, someone else would. Someone would collect that 20 percent. Why not her? She snapped the rubber band again, did her best to block the emotions roiling in her gut, and read the computer-generated text. "Unfortunately, Mrs. Pacheco, you guaranteed payment to the treatment center with the title of your home. If you are unwilling to make a payment with me today, you'll be at risk of foreclosure. I can prevent that with a payment of $236.81. Do you have your wallet handy? Any major credit card is acceptable."

"And when would the next payment be due?"

Lynn checked the system. "One week."

"One week."

Lynn pulled the rubber band back as far as it would go, let it snap down on her wrist with a *crack!* and then did it again. "Yes. How would you like to cover it, Mrs. Pacheco?"

The woman's voice began to break. "Do you have a family? Are you married?"

"No," Lynn lied. Beneath her desk, her left foot was tapping like a jackrabbit. Her leg bouncing with it, smacking the underside of the drawer. She willed it to stop, and that was worse, like she shut off a tap and the anxious energy had no place to go, pressed against her insides, inflated like a balloon. Maybe ten seconds passed before her foot started again.

"Of course not. You couldn't do this for a living if you did.

If you cared for someone or had someone in your life who cared about you. There's no way you could treat other people this way."

Lynn didn't respond to that. She knew better. She'd been trained to ignore the bait, stick to the script.

Down the hall, Gracie screamed again, and this time she didn't stop. She held it out for nearly a full minute—one long, high-pitched shrill. Lynn smashed down her Mute button somewhere in the middle of it. If the woman heard, she didn't say anything. She was going to pay, Lynn could feel it. She snapped the rubber band again, barely felt it this time. "I need your credit card number, Mrs. Pacheco."

"You're a horrible person. I hope you burn in hell," the woman replied and slammed down the phone.

New message box:

Congratulations! You earned $1.37!

Lynn didn't remember taking the pill bottles from the drawer. She certainly didn't remember opening them and lining up one of each next to her keyboard, but there they were. For one brief second, she thought maybe she forgot to take them when she first came in. She'd been half asleep.

Gracie's marathon scream finally came to an end, and both kids went quiet.

Lynn shoved all three pills in her mouth and swallowed. This time, she felt the effects immediately. Maybe her imagination, maybe not. Maybe she had taken the pills earlier…maybe not. She didn't remember and didn't much care. The warmth, numbness… that would come next. That would get her through—

Another scream—Oscar this time.

"*Stop!*" Lynn shouted out, yelled it as loud as she could. "*Shut the hell up!*"

The silence that followed was harsh and sharp, abrupt.

Lynn mashed her mouse button down on the Connect link and took another call. "Am I speaking to Louis Martinez?"

Her words came out fast, spilled from her mouth.

Heavy breathing filled the line, nothing else.

"Mr. Martinez?"

No response.

"Mr. Martinez? You're seriously delinquent on your—"

"I told you if you called me again, I'd come to your house and gut you like a pig. You remember that?"

"We've never spoken, Mr. Martinez. I'd like to—"

"You'd like to what?" he spoke in a low drawl, the hint of a Southern accent. "How 'bout this? How 'bout I pay you a visit? You know how you people spoof the caller ID? I bought this gizmo that gets around that and gives me your real number. You're in… where the fuck is Hollows Bend, New Hampshire? Huh, lookie there, it ain't that far. I can be there in a few hours. Maybe I'll do that, and you and I can have ourselves some time together. How you like that? Bet you'd like that lots. You ever take it in the—"

Lynn tore off her headset and dropped it on the desk, ran her hand through her oily hair.

New message box:

Congratulations! You earned $0.29! 41 calls in
queue ready to talk to you!

Her hands were trembling. Heart pounding like a hammer. Her pajamas clung to her skin with sweat. Whatever she thought she felt from the pills, that was gone. This was something else, and it wasn't good. Overdose? No. Not from…how many had she taken? Just give it a minute. She'd be okay. Pins and needles crawled over her skin, the room swooned, and Lynn closed her eyes as dizziness washed over her. A light show of pinks, reds, and purples against the inside of her eyelids. It all passed in a moment, but it didn't go far. The feeling lingered like a stranger standing on the opposite side of a closed door waiting for the lock to click open.

How long did she sit there like that? Lynn wasn't exactly sure, but her children had gone oddly quiet in those moments. That was either really good or really bad, and she was leaning toward the latter.

She leaned her head back and shouted, *"Josh!?"*

No answer.

"Gracie and Oscar—what are you two doing?"

Nobody answered. If she'd heard them yelling, they certainly heard her.

She shouted again. Still nothing.

Forty-three calls in queue now.

A new message box:

> **Moving a little slow today? Feeling stressed? If you'd like one of our mental health specialists to call you back, click HERE. Don't let the negative people of the world get you down! We're in this together!**

"Fuck you."

Lynn rose, and the fact that she had to hold on to the edge of the desk to pull herself up wasn't lost on her. She stood there for a moment, long enough for the room to go steady. Her nerves felt like tiny firecrackers, pins poking at every inch of her skin. It only grew worse as she stepped out into the hallway, the silence slapping at her.

7

LYNN TATUM

LYNN OPENED THE DOOR of her daughter's room to find both her children on the floor covered in red.

Red everywhere.

Their clothes. Hair. Skin. The carpet. Gracie's walls and bedsheets—the quilt her grandmother had made her sat in a heap on the floor with her pillow, stained, ruined.

Unmoving and horribly pale against the crimson, they looked up at her with petrified stares.

Gracie's upper lip twitched. "Oscar wanted to paint a dog. I told him not to."

Still dressed in his Paw Patrol pajamas, Oscar's face twisted from fear to rage. "That's not true—I wanted to watch TV!" He somehow stretched the word *I* into no less than four syllables. *Eyeeee.* "Gracie said she wanted to paint."

"He's lying," Gracie quickly fired back. "He got the paint down from the pantry shelf even when I told him we weren't supposed to. Then he opened the red, even though dogs aren't red, and when I told him he had the wrong brush he used his fingers, so I tried to put the blanket down and he wouldn't let me, and when he got it on the floor he tried to mop it up with clothes from my hamper—he used my favorite Elsa shirt, Mama!"

The shirt was in the corner of the room, covered in so much paint Lynn could barely make out the faded image of Elsa from *Frozen* standing in a field of ice. The shirt was a 5T, too small for a seven-year-old, but Gracie wore it several times each week anyway.

"Clifford's red," Oscar muttered, as if that made everything okay.

Along with open bottles of blue, green, and yellow, the red was lying sideways on the floor between them, soaking into the carpet. It was acrylic and would probably come out, but Lynn had no intention of touching it—that was Josh's problem.

"I can't reach the paint," Oscar added.

"Can too!" Gracie shouted. "From the counter. You climb up with the stool!"

Oscar yelled something in response, but Lynn didn't hear it. The buzzing in her ears drowned it out. The rush of hot blood. Her heart was pounding so hard she felt it in her teeth.

They were arguing again. Screaming. This muffled mess of words tripping over each other. Lynn covered her ears again, but it did little good. "Stop."

They ignored her.

Gracie smacked the paint bottle with the palm of her hand, and it cracked against Oscar's chest, sending red spittle everywhere.

"STOP!"

Both kids went quiet.

Down the hall, her computer dinged with another message box. Probably one telling her she'd be fired if she didn't get on the phone. She thought of the pills in her drawer, and her mouth watered. "Both of you, take off your clothes and get in the bath."

Gracie glared at her, horrified. "I'm not taking a bath with him! I'm too old!"

Lynn wanted to grab her by the shoulders. Shake her. Throw her from the second-floor window. Anything to shut her up. She sucked in a breath between clenched teeth. "Take off your goddamn clothes."

Gracie's jaw began to quiver, and her eyes glistened.

"NOW!"

Fighting tears, Gracie stood and pulled her shirt up over her head, dropped it on the floor in the puddle of paint, and shed the rest of her clothes.

Lynn yanked at Oscar's pajama top, and when it caught on his elbow, she pulled even harder, nearly lifted him off the ground before something tore and the top came free. Oscar yelped and started crying. He cradled his arm as she tore away his pants and the pull-up diapers he still wore at night. The smell of stale pee lofted out, filled the room. Josh hadn't bothered to change him before running off. Of course not. Why would he?

Lynn was shaking nearly as much as her kids when she jerked her finger toward the hallway and pointed. "Bathroom. Now."

8

MATT

IT ENDED AS QUICKLY as it began. The fluttering of wings and screaming birds vanished, replaced by muffled sobs and broken shouts as one by one the diners crawled out from under tables and chairs.

Matt had pulled Gabby so close their bodies might have been one. Every inch of her trembled. Her warm breath brushed his neck in short gasps. He nestled his face deeper into her hair and whispered, "You okay?"

She didn't answer. There was only a rushed nod. Her fingers tightened around his and squeezed.

He managed a sitting position, lifting Gabby with him, holding her against him. He didn't want to let go.

The strange girl was about five feet to their left, also sitting, hugging her knees against her chest. She watched him from behind her long dark hair, ruffled and partially covering her face. A curiosity behind her eyes, this strange tunnel vision, as if they were the only two people in the room and unspoken words passed between them. She looked from him to Gabby, then her gaze jumped across the diner to where Addie huddled under a table near the old Wurlitzer jukebox in the far corner, then back to Matt, and when their eyes met that second time, there was something else there.

Matt's heart thumped.

She knows.

When the corner of her mouth twitched up, he was certain of it.

Matt forced himself to break away and cleared his throat. "Is anyone hurt?"

"Got some scrapes and cuts from the glass over here!"

That came from Henry Lockwood. He was under the table at his booth, his meaty arms wrapped around his two youngest children. Both were crying. A few tables over, Helen Hardwick had a napkin pressed to her husband's temple.

"I'll get the first-aid kit from the back." Still shaking, Gabby pulled free of Matt's arm and hustled off toward the counter, carefully stepping around the broken glass and dead birds covering the tile floor.

The birds were everywhere.

Matt stooped to get a better look at one of them.

He'd never seen crows this large. Maybe twenty inches from beak to tail feather. Probably weighed two or three pounds. Its talons looked more like those found on a hawk or raven, and its dark beak twisted at the end in a sharp hook.

This deep into fall, it wasn't uncommon for strange birds to appear in Hollows Bend. With flocks migrating south, Matt had seen his share of oddities, but never anything like this.

He took out his cell phone, snapped several pictures from different angles, and texted them to the sheriff.

About half the diner's large picture windows had shattered, Henry Wilburt was standing near one of the few remaining. He straightened the wire frame of his glasses, cleaned the lenses on his shirt, then put them back on. He had to squeeze the supports around the bridge of his nose to get them to stay in place. When he turned to look out the window, Matt noticed a thin cut on the back of his pudgy bald head. It wasn't bad, but the blood had made it to the collar of his usually pristine white pharmacist's jacket. "Oh, my lord."

Avoiding eye contact with the strange girl still sitting on the floor, Matt crossed over to him and looked out.

The open field of the commons across Main Street was blanketed in dead birds. The pavement and parked cars had fared no better. The Audi Matt had spotted earlier looked totaled—the top was gone, shredded away. Birds stuck out from the leather upholstery at odd angles, beaks and heads embedded in the seats as if they had made no effort to slow or stop as they approached the ground, but instead had sped up like the kamikaze pilots of World War II, hell-bent on destroying some target at the cost of their own lives. Other cars had sizable dents. Most of the windows were gone.

People began to emerge from the businesses along Main, walking slowly and staring up at the sky in some kind of stunned silence. They stepped around the carcasses. A few turned in slow circles.

Addie Gallagher walked by him and placed her hands on the door.

"You shouldn't go out—"

She ignored him. Addie pushed the door open and stepped outside, shattered glass crunching under her shoes.

Gabby returned with the first-aid kit. She placed it on the Lockwoods' table and went to work on the children. As far as Matt knew, she had no formal medical training, but she moved with the skill of a professional, carefully plucking out small shards of glass with tweezers before applying some kind of ointment and bandages. The work seemed to help calm her nerves. She was no longer shaking. She whispered to the children as she went, the familiar warm smile returning to her face.

Outside, Addie stepped off the curb and crossed the street to the commons. A crowd was forming near the bandstand. All locals, from what Matt could tell. Most, if not all, of the tourists had gotten out before it happened. Whatever *it* was.

Matt gave those in the diner another look, then stepped through the door to the sidewalk.

"What do you think?" Henry Wilburt asked as he joined Matt on the sidewalk. "Some kind of freak electrical storm?"

Matt only shook his head.

A heavy scent of ozone filled the air, as if a storm had passed through. There had been no rain, though, and certainly no lightning. The sky was clear blue, save for a small white cloud wrapped around the peak of Mount Washington in the distance.

"I remember reading that birds use some kind of radar, almost like a radio, to communicate with each other," Henry said. "They latch on to the seven or eight surrounding them and are able to move as a single unit. That's how they fly in formation."

"Isn't that bats?"

"Pretty sure birds, too," Henry replied. "I'm thinking something disrupted those signals, confused the leaders, and the others followed." He rolled his hand through the air, then dive-bombed toward the ground. "Like flying lemmings. One hell of a thing. Miracle nobody got killed out here."

He was right about that. Looking around, Matt saw his share of cuts and scrapes, but nothing serious. Whatever this was, it seemed to be focused on Main Street, a radius of maybe three hundred feet. He could see where it ended on the opposite side of the commons and down both legs of the road.

"Do me a favor, Henry. Open up the pharmacy for a few hours. I know it's Sunday and all, but people might be in need of supplies."

"Sure thing." Henry nodded back toward the diner. "You might want to do something about her. Now's not the time to be running 'round all barefoot."

Matt turned to find the girl standing in the open doorway, oblivious to all the glass around her feet. He opened his mouth to say something when his cell phone rang—Sheriff Ellie Pritchet.

9

LYNN TATUM

"THE SOAP'S IN MY eyes, Mama!"

Gracie's fingers were covered in suds, and she was drilling both her palms into her red eyes.

"Well, stop doing that!" Lynn slapped her hands away and yanked the handheld from the wall. "Here, let me rinse them—"

She twisted the diverter on the faucet and water sprayed out—too late, she realized she was holding it in the wrong direction. Icy water soaked her, hit the wall and vanity, and grazed the toilet before Lynn managed to turn it on her daughter.

Gracie yelped and jerked away. "It's too cold, Mama!"

Through all this, Oscar hadn't stopped screaming. He'd started back in Gracie's bedroom and only grew worse as Lynn dragged the two of them into the bathroom and filled the tub with random toys, bubble bath, and water. He kicked, flailed, and managed to scratch her three times before she got him in. The worst one was across her cheek—his nail sliced her right open.

"Mama, too cold! Too cold!"

Lynn cursed and twisted the dial a little too fast. She yanked it back in the opposite direction, but not before scalding water and steam shot out.

Gracie pulled to the side and cracked her head against the tile. She went quiet, her mouth rolled into a slow-motion silent *oh*. Then the crying came—a bawling sob that picked up with each hitched breath.

"If you'd just sit still—".

Lynn thumbed off the handheld and reached for Gracie.

Gracie smacked her away, splashed her with soapy water stained pink from the paint.

Lynn grabbed both her daughter's wrists and held them above her head. When she tried to pull free, Lynn squeezed.

"Mama, you're hurting me! Stop!"

Lynn didn't, though. She squeezed harder. She looked Gracie dead in the eyes and squeezed—she squeezed like a goddamn vise. She squeezed those tiny wrists as hard as she could, and it wasn't until Gracie's face twisted from pain to fear that she finally let up and released her. And damn, did that feel good. That brief satisfaction was quickly followed by guilt and shame, but those only lasted for a second, because her pills had finally (yes, finally!) kicked in, and they did what they were supposed to do—they swatted those feelings down and coated them with a nice thick blanket of numb.

Lynn looked around the bathroom, half expecting to find Josh standing in the doorway all high-and-mighty, ready to accuse her (not for the first time) of being a shitty mother. Captain Righteous. Mr. If-I-Wanna-Get-My-Juice-from-the-Sexpot-Neighbor-I-Can. No Josh, though. No nobody.

When she turned back to Gracie, her daughter had inched to the far side of the tub and gone quiet, and was rubbing her wrists. A look passed between them, one that clearly said, *I'll do it again if you give me more shit*, followed by Gracie's narrow-eyed *I know you will*, but neither said a word. Let her run to her father later; Lynn didn't care. She was done caring. Maybe next time he'd think twice before running off and leaving her with both kids *and* work. It only happened because he wasn't pulling his weight with his bullshit accounting business. She'd make that very clear if it came up. And hell, she wanted it to come up. She was ready for this fight. It had been a long time in the making.

Gracie might have received the message loud and clear, but her brother had not. Oscar was not only still crying, but he was busy throwing his toys from the bath one at a time. At least half were already on the floor, and soapy pink water trailed down the bathroom walls where many of them had struck. Even the ceiling was wet. As if to show her how he did it, Oscar scooped up a rubber tugboat and heaved it underhanded, straight up. It bounced off the exhaust fan, released a spray of filthy water, and landed near the door with a thud. When he picked up a toy golf ball and craned his small arm back to heft it toward the mirror, Lynn smacked it away. She hit his arm so hard, it twisted back and made this sick popping noise at his shoulder a moment before the golf ball struck the tile wall behind him and vanished in the water.

That quieted him, but only for a second. Shocked, stunned, whatever—his little mind seemed to process what just happened on some kind of delay, came to some sort of conclusion, then followed up with Oscar's go-to—he started screaming again, dialed the cry up to eleven, and let loose as only five-year-olds can. He dropped the plastic robot he'd been about to throw and grabbed at his injured arm.

Lynn waited for some sense of guilt to wash over her, but it didn't come. The pills were in overdrive now, and things like guilt, anxiety, fear, depression—those things were off the table. Until the pills wore off, those things would be stored away in the closet, and that felt good. That felt really good.

Cry all you want, she thought. *Both of you.*

Water started to cascade over the side of the tub, and Lynn realized Gracie had stuffed the overflow drain with a washcloth and turned the faucet back on. Maybe she did it to distract Lynn from Oscar, or maybe she did it because she was a little fucking monster—Lynn didn't care. Rather than turn it off, she reached over and twisted the knob to full. She also turned off the cold water and opened the hot valve completely. When Gracie started to stand, Lynn glared at her. "Don't you dare get up. You sit right there."

Down the hall, Lynn's computer dinged. Some other message box. Probably one telling her she was slacking, she should be on the phone. Missing out on all kinds of earnings. Fuck them. Fuck all of them.

Water pooled around her, soaked the rug, rolled across the floor toward the door.

Oscar's shoulder had swollen up to an angry knob nearly twice its normal size. Dislocated? Maybe. She reached for him, stroked his hair. Held his head still. Gave him a gentle push. "It's okay, baby. Mama's gonna make everything all better."

10

MATT

"**WHAT THE HELL AM** I looking at, Matt? Are those crows? In the Stairway?"

Sheriff Ellie Pritchet was studying the pictures he had sent her by text.

Matt pressed the phone to his ear. "Am I on speaker? I can barely hear you."

There was a click. "That better?"

"You're still fading in and out."

He turned up the volume on his phone and stepped off the sidewalk. The town's only cell tower was halfway up Mount Washington, and service was sometimes better with line-of-sight.

"I can hear you just fine," she replied through a wall of static. "Just tell me what happened."

Matt quickly rattled it all off, his voice picking up steam with each word. When he finished, his gaze was back on the front of the diner. Through one of the broken windows, he could make out the silhouette of the strange girl; he couldn't see her face, but he felt her eyes on him.

"Did she give you a name?"

"She hasn't said a word."

Ellie Pritchet came from a long line of local law enforcement. Her father had been sheriff before her, her grandfather before him. And while the sheriff's office was an elected position, for the past twenty-six years, Ellie ran unopposed all terms but one, in 2010. A lawyer from Conway had thrown his hat in the ring, and if rumors were to be believed, he'd received only three votes—his wife's, his own, and a cousin's. A Pritchet on the ballot was considered a lock, and nobody since had been willing to suffer the embarrassment of a loss against such a legacy, a legacy coming to an end. Ellie had never married, and at sixty-one years old, any chance of producing an heir was long gone. Most locals considered Matt next in line. He still wasn't quite sure how he felt about that.

A thick roll of static, then Ellie said, "Do you think she was raped? That would explain the missing clothes. She in shock?"

"That was my first thought, too, but I don't know. Doesn't seem like shock to me. Breathing is normal. Pupils aren't dilated…"

"So not drugs, either."

"I don't think so," Matt said. "She doesn't appear confused or anxious. Aside from not speaking, she seems…normal."

"Normal people don't wander the streets in their birthday suits."

Matt crossed Main Street to the commons. The pump on the large fountain was off for maintenance, but it was still full of water. Dozens of dead birds floated lazily on the surface. Wings spread on some; others folded against their lifeless bodies.

"I've found Buck wandering in his skivvies once or twice," he pointed out.

"I said normal people," Ellie replied. "She look like a car thief?"

"Why?"

"I'm out on 112 near Lower Falls. Found a red Honda in the ditch. Door open, keys in the ignition, no driver." She paused for a second, and when she came back, her voice was distant and then grew stronger. Sounded like she had him on speaker and was holding the phone as she walked around the vehicle, raised it back to her mouth. "No real damage to the front end, it rolled into the ditch slow, like it coasted. Manual transmission, stalled out in third. Didn't run out of juice; still has a half tank. Driver-side window is shattered. No paperwork in the glove box. No tags. I'm thinkin' a joyride gone bad."

"She barely looks sixteen. How many teenagers you know who can drive a manual?"

"Good point."

Matt reached into the fountain water and tentatively poked one of the birds. He pushed it below the surface with his index finger and watched it float back up. His finger came away sticky—the tip had some kind of black residue on it. He rubbed his thumb and index finger together, blackening both. "Huh."

"What?"

"Do you know of any kind of oil or chemical leak around here? The birds are covered in something." He looked back at the water. "It's washing off in the fountain at the commons, staining the water."

"Staining how?"

"I don't know. Like black food coloring."

"Oil is lighter than water, it would float on the surface. Wouldn't mix."

Not oil, then.

Ellie clucked her tongue again. "Take your girl over to the station and run her prints. Then tell Sally to try to find someone to take her up to the med center in North Hollow for a rape kit. Best to rule that out. Maybe a blood panel, if she doesn't start talking. General once-over. Ask for Dr. Joshi, he'll know what to do."

Half the town seemed to be out on Main, taking in the carnage. Most were snapping pictures with their phones; others were staring up into the blue sky. "Do you want me to tape all this off?"

"Birds die, Matt. Get Buck out to help clean up. It's Sunday, I'm sure he can use the double time. I'll wrap up here and meet you back at the station. I'm—"

Another rush of static poured from the phone, drowning her out. The call dropped, and when Matt dialed her back, he got voicemail. He wiped his finger on his uniform pants and crossed back over to the diner. The girl stepped aside as he came through the door, folded into the shadows next to the jukebox. Gabby was still at the Lockwoods' table, patching people up. Matt knelt beside her and kissed the side of her head. "Ellie wants me to take our friend over to the station and wait for her to get back. Are you okay here?"

Gabby finished wiping a minor scratch on Bobby Lockwood's arm with peroxide and tapped the boy's nose. "Bobby here agreed to help me out in exchange for a milkshake, so we'll be just fine. Isn't that right, Bobby?"

"Yes, ma'am." He nodded firmly, then told Matt, "I wanted to pick up the birds, but Ms. Gabby said not to touch them."

Matt looked down at one of the dead crows. The tile around it glistened with the same black film he had found in the fountain. "Ms. Gabby is a wise woman. I wouldn't touch them, either." He turned back to her. "I'll get back here as soon as I can and give you a hand."

"If you happen to find yourself near my house, can you stop in and check on Riley?" Gabby asked. "She's not answering her phone."

"The cell tower is acting wonky," Matt told her. "I'm sure she's fine."

"You're probably right."

There was a hint of worry behind her eyes, and considering she was helping all these people rather than running home to check on her daughter, it was the least he could do.

"Sure, I'll stop by." He kissed her again. "You got it."

She smiled. "And I'll see you tonight?"

"Absolutely."

11

MATT

THE HOLLOWS BEND SHERIFF'S station was a squat brick building about a half mile from the Stairway Diner on the opposite side of Main Street. Matt parked his cruiser out front and led the girl inside.

A wall of sound hit him when he opened the door—ringing phones, fax machine, garbled chatter on the radio. Sally Davie was manning the front desk, phone receiver in one hand, pen in the other. Her curly gray hair was a wild mess, papers littered the floor, and there was a giant puddle of coffee along with the remains of her favorite mug near the center of the room.

The moment Sally saw him, she stood and held up a finger. "Hey, Pat? Matt just walked in. I'm putting you on hold for a second." She pressed the Hold button and rested the receiver on her shoulder, let out a flustered breath, and pointed at the mess. "I'm a jackass—got spooked, slipped, and took half my desk to the floor on my way down. Nearly busted my butt bone. Watch your step."

Matt started toward her. "You okay?"

Sally was three years past retirement, two short of seventy, probably one of the toughest women Matt had ever met, but a fall at her age could be dangerous.

"I raised four boys, two by my lonesome after they put my husband in the ground. Takes a lot more than a crack on the linoleum to put me against the ropes."

Matt never met her husband. Jack had died in a hit-and-run in Portsmouth before he was born. He'd been standing next to his truck, unlocking the door, when someone sideswiped him. There were two witnesses, but neither got a plate, and the driver had never been found.

Another line started ringing. Sally mashed down a button. "Sheriff's office, be right with you." She put the caller on hold before they could reply. "Phones are going insane. What's going on out there? I've never seen—"

When she spotted the half-naked girl standing behind Matt, her mouth fell open. "Oh, my. What we got here?" Sally twisted the phone cord around her finger. "You pick up a stray?"

Matt told her what little he knew. "Think you can find something for her to wear in the lost and found?"

Sally nodded and studied the girl. "What's your name, sweetie?"

When she didn't answer, Matt told Sally, "She hasn't said a word. Not yet, anyway. You recognize her?"

Sally chewed the inside of her cheek, her eyes narrow, then shook her head. "You get to be my age, and you feel like you've run into everyone on the planet at least once, but nope. She doesn't look familiar."

"Ellie wants you to try to find someone who can run her to the med center. We need to get Buck out to clean up the mess in the commons, too."

"Thought Buck was with you?"

"He bolted after he got some food in him. Back home, would be my guess."

One of the lines on hold started to beep. With a roll of her eyes, Sally picked up. "Sheriff's office, sorry for the hold. What can I do for you?"

As she listened, the lines on her face grew deeper. She motioned for Matt to come over, then put the call on speaker. "Josh, I need you to calm down. Ellie's not here, but I've got you on speaker with Matt. Can you repeat what you just said?"

Matt looked at Sally and mouthed, *Josh...Tatum?*

She nodded.

The voice on the phone sounded nothing like the man Matt knew. He tried to speak between broken sobs. "...wasn't gone that long. Twenty...thirty minutes, maybe. Oh, God...you need to get over here..."

Matt leaned in closer. "Josh, what happened?"

"Lynn...Oh Jesus, Gracie and Oscar...oh my God, oh my God...please..." His voice trailed off. It sounded like he dropped the phone.

"Josh? You still there?" Sally said.

He hadn't hung up, they could hear him crying, but he didn't respond.

Sally bobbed her head toward the girl. "I got her. Go."

12

NORMAN HEATON

NORMAN HEATON FELT DIZZY, then he didn't. Came on like a breeze through the crack of a window left open, swept over him, then vanished. As with most aches, pains, spells, and general fuckery that visited a man's body after breaking seventy, he acknowledged its presence, remained still until it passed, then confirmed he was still breathing on the other end of the ride.

"You gonna want more eggs?"

Eisa Heaton was standing at the kitchen sink in her favorite threadbare muumuu, her back to him when she spoke, but her voice sounded much farther away than it probably should, more like she was in the other room rather than five feet from him. Like he had water in his ears or was on an airplane dipping down toward its destination.

"Eggs?"

Norman noted his own voice sounded off, too.

"Yeah. Those things from chickens that you're not supposed

to be eating, like all that bacon and the half gallon of syrup you drowned your pancakes under. Eggs."

Her voice came back full steam about halfway through that sentence, and all was right again with whatever came over him. No longer dizzy. Hearing all good. His ticker...Norman paused as if he could mentally assess his heart pumping away, found nothing abnormal, and decided that was all good, too. He'd been reading the *Hollows Bend Gazette* when it started, and the corner of the sports page was now nothing but a crumpled mess in his sweaty palm. He unfurled his fingers, flexed, and smoothed the paper back out. His wife hadn't seen any of it, and that was all right by him—any time Eisa sniffed even the hint of a health problem, she insisted he make a trip over to Doc Billets for a once-over, and he had no intention of missing the Patriots trounce the Raiders this afternoon.

"Norman?"

"Huh?"

"You done with breakfast or you want more? You didn't answer."

Before he could respond, she returned to the table, loaded up the length of her arm with leftover food and dirty dishes, and carried everything over to the sink.

"Yeah, I suppose I'm done," he told her.

Before the dizzy spell, Eisa had been going off about the women in her bridge club. Something about Bernadette cheating again and Julie wanting to drop her from the group or suspend her, or some nonsense. Norman heard about every fifth word and tuned out the rest. He learned long ago the key to staying married for forty-seven-plus years wasn't necessarily listening but knowing when to listen and when to not listen because hearing all of it would drive a man batshit crazy.

"...even if she agrees to put an end to it," Eisa said, taking his half-empty coffee mug away. "Does that make sense?"

"Yep," he replied, finishing off his juice before she ripped the glass from his hand and carted that away, too.

Eisa was a talker. Always had been. She had no trouble carrying their conversations, and most days he had no trouble letting her. It was all fine when she did the talking, but sometimes she felt the need to rope him into the conversation, and today was one of those days. Usually about every three or four sentences she'd poke him, force him to answer before she'd go on. Norman had taken to calling them her needy days, and he downright hated the needy days.

Norman made a show of shaking out the creases from the newspaper and burying his face in the sports page again. He started the article about Jackie Bradley Jr. for the third time. No way the Red Sox would take him back, but the hack who wrote up the story was making a half-assed case.

Still blabbing away, Eisa crossed over to the refrigerator, took out two steaks, and carried them over to her cutting board. She tore away the packaging and began beating on them with a mallet. She was a good three minutes in before she stopped long enough to ask him, "You're okay with steak tonight, right?"

Norman cleared his throat, shook the paper again, and gave a solid five-count before replying. "Yep."

She did that all the time, too—asked him for his opinion when his opinion didn't much matter anymore. He had half a mind to tell her he didn't want steak just to see what she'd do with the two hunks of meat already beaten to death and the packaging in the trash. Norman knew they were having steak tonight whether he wanted it or not, so did Eisa, so why bother asking?

Talk. Talk. Talk.

Whatever happened to *silence is golden*?

Norman looked down at his hand. When had he picked up a butter knife? He was squeezing it hard enough to leave a red line across the bridge of his thumb, not hard enough to break the skin (good luck doing that with a butter knife), but still.

"...I suppose I could ride down with Julie if they ban Bernadette, but I'd rather not. Would you believe she's still smoking? She thinks her husband doesn't know. Her car smells like an ashtray, and she smells like an ashtray that's been dipped in watered-down Estée Lauder. Two minutes in her Prius, and I feel like my lungs are coated with tar and my clothes need to go in the trash heap. Mary said she'd pick me up, but she lives on the opposite side of town, so she'd have to go out of her way to get me and..."

Norman did the math. Hollows Bend was maybe seven square miles soaking wet. You could walk one end to the other in less than an hour, so was a mile or so in the opposite direction really such a deal-breaker? More bullshit. More of Eisa spouting out words for the sake of spouting out words.

He squeezed the butter knife again, pressed his thumb down on the blade with all the force his arthritic hand could muster. He found himself looking up at Eisa as he did it, at the tender spot on the side of her neck. No need to beat that with a mallet to soften it up, a knife would cut right through like...

He looked at the butter knife in his hand and grinned.

Just like butter.

"Norman? I asked you a question."

He almost hid the knife, which was stupid. She was still facing away from him. Also stupid, because it was just a goddamn butter knife and there was nothing wrong about handling it at the kitchen table. Not like he was holding one of his chisels from the garage or his bowie knife. Now that would do some damage. He loved that bowie knife. If he pressed his thumb on that blade like he was the butter knife, his thumb would be on the floor right now. He could cut Eisa's head clean off with the bowie and probably not even work up much of a huff. Start by burying it in that soft spot right above her shoulder, give it a good twist and a yank, and he'd be off to the races. Bet he'd be done in less than—

"Norman? Are you wandering again?" Eisa asked before

bringing the hammer down on the steaks. "You think I tell you these things because I like the sound of my own voice? I want your opinion."

Oh, you love the sound of your own voice. You can't kid a kidder, you cackling old—

Norman cleared his throat and gave the sports page another rattle. "I'm trying to get up on the game before it starts."

"Sure, because that's important." Eisa smacked the hammer down again. She put some oomph behind it; the cabinets rattled with that one.

Norman felt a tickle at his temple and realized he was sweating. He wiped it away with the back of his hand, caught his reflection in the butter knife as he did. For a brief second, he didn't recognize himself. It was his eyes. Not like looking in a mirror, the blade distorted his features slightly, stretched them out, he got that, but those eyes were not his own.

"Maybe you should drive me," Eisa said, breaking the momentary silence.

"Drive you where?"

Smack!

Christ, those poor steaks.

She said something under her breath, all he caught was "…never listen."

Why the hell was it so hot in here? Did Eisa forget to shut the oven down? Norman's shirt was sticking to his back and chest. "Can you open the window?"

If Eisa heard him

and she most certainly did

she made no move for the window behind the sink. Instead, she beat the steaks with three quick hits—*Smack! Smack! Smack!*—in rapid succession.

Norman found himself staring at that soft spot on her neck as she did it. The loose flesh bobbed and quivered like a—what was that dog called?—a Shar-Pei, that was it. A fucking Shar-Pei. He remembered what that neck looked like forty-seven years ago, and it certainly wasn't that. No loose, flabby skin back then. No cackle. No blah, blah, blah, run-off-at-the-mouth. Then a crazy thought entered his head—well, not that crazy; it actually made a lot of sense—if he cut deep enough, if he got under that flabby skin and sliced it away, would he find the woman he married?

A butter knife had no will of its own, no thoughts or feelings, but Norman was fairly certain the knife grew warm in his hand, became excited, anxious. The knife sent him some kind of signal, as if saying, *I like where your head's at, Norman. Not only do I think you're right, I think you're a goddamn genius for figuring it out. Count me in. Let's do this. I know I'm not sharp, but I'll do my part, just put some elbow grease behind it.*

"The window, Eisa," Norman heard himself say in a voice that wasn't his anymore, this one belonged to the eyes he saw in that reflection.

This time, she did reach for the window. She unlocked it, tried to lift the sash, but the window didn't budge. "I think the wood is swollen again. It's stuck." She grunted.

Norman set the newspaper down carefully, avoiding the dirty and wet spots on the table. He fully intended to finish that story about Jackie Bradley Jr. later, and there was no reason to muck it up more than it already was. He rose and felt a strength rush through his limbs he hadn't felt in a long time, maybe half a lifetime ago.

The knife firmly in his grip, Norman eased up behind Eisa, both eyes on her neck as he reached around her for the window. "Let me give it a try."

13

MATT

THE TATUM FAMILY LIVED about a third of the way down Morning Glory Road in a square white-sided house with black shutters that might have fit perfectly in a Hughes movie back in the eighties, but hadn't been renovated in all those years and was in dire need of some work. Two shutters were missing from the front windows, another was hanging precariously, as if contemplating a fall. The lawn hadn't been mowed in some time; weeds sprouted up at varying heights among what was left of the grass. A child's bicycle was off to the side, most of the purple paint lost to brown rust.

Matt hadn't even shut off the motor when Josh Tatum bolted from the front door, flew down the walk, and yanked at his door handle. His door was locked—a habit Ellie had beat into him within a week of putting on the uniform—and the locked door caused Josh's face to go beet-red. He smacked the window with the back of his fist.

"Get the hell out of the car, Matt!"

There was a wild look to his eyes. Hysterical. Puffy and red.

His pupils weren't dilated, but his gaze was erratic. Jumping around everywhere. As far as Matt knew, Josh wasn't a drug user, but the last time Matt had seen that look on someone's face, it was a kid up for the weekend with his friends, and he'd tried meth for the first time.

"Step back from the car, Josh!"

Josh glared at him through the glass, and for a quick second, Matt thought Josh might put his fist through the window. He didn't, though. He shook his head and took a couple of stumble-steps back.

Matt unlocked the door with a deliberate slowness, and when he climbed from the cruiser, he did so with one hand on his gun. He spoke in a calm, disarming tone, "Keep your hands at your sides, visible. No sudden movements, okay?"

Josh's face corkscrewed from anger to confusion, then back again. "What the hell, Matt? You gonna shoot me?"

"Do you have any weapons on you?"

"What? No. Of course not!" Josh was trembling. He reached up and wiped snot from his nose with the back of his hand.

This wasn't anger. He'd been crying.

"Tell me what's going on."

"It's Lynn and the kids..." He tried to say more, but his words turned into a garbled mess. He choked them back and nearly tripped over the bicycle running back into the house.

Matt reached for the microphone clipped to his shoulder and pressed the Transmit button. "Sally, I'm at the Tatums', going inside. You don't hear from me in the next few minutes, send Ellie."

"Copy."

His hand still on the gun, ready to draw, he followed the stone walkway to the open front door.

Josh was standing in the middle of the living room, facing the staircase to the second floor.

The hair on the back of Matt's neck stood up as he cautiously stepped inside, sweeping the empty room. The air was still, smelled stale. The windows were all closed, drapes drawn, no HVAC circulating. No voices. Eerily quiet. So quiet, Matt heard the refrigerator compressor kick on in the kitchen.

"Josh, where exactly are Lynn and the kids?"

At first, he didn't move. When he finally did, his arm rose in a slow sweep, as if it weighed a thousand pounds. He pointed upstairs with a quivering finger.

14

NORMAN HEATON

EISA STIFFENED AS NORMAN pressed up against her from behind. For once in forty-seven years of marriage, she finally stopped talking. At least for the handful of seconds it took for her to realize what he was doing.

The butter knife still in his hand, Norman reached around her to the window, gave it a good tap with the back of his fist in all four corners, then lifted. It fought, then rose with a thin squeal.

Eisa plucked the butter knife from his hand and dropped it into the soapy water with the other dirty dishes. Then she did something Norman didn't expect; she backed up slightly and ground her butt against him. When he didn't move, she let out a soft gasp and pressed harder.

Norman couldn't remember the last time she'd done something like that and didn't much care. Her breath smelled like denture paste and orange juice, and if he was happy about any part of this, it was the silence. Her not saying a single word. If he had to take one for the team to keep her quiet, so be it.

"Don't speak," he said softly. He whispered it right into her ear, like he used to do back in the days when their intimacy was as common as breathing, and heaven help him, he pressed into her the way he did back in the day, too. Her body responded to him as effortlessly as it did that very first time in the bed of his '62 Ford pickup parked out at Hollows Bluff overlooking the valley—Norman knew that's where her mind was—those two kids fumbling over each other's bodies under the crisp night sky with nothing but a ratty old flannel quilt swiped from the Carmacks' barn to keep them modest, knowing they had maybe an hour before someone came looking for them. Ray Charles had been on the radio, but for the life of him, Norman couldn't remember the name of the song. "Don't speak," he had said back then, and he said it again now. "We don't need no words."

Norman eased his left arm around her waist and brought his other up around her neck, reached around until he was able to grip her left shoulder. He gave her a tender squeeze. This brought on another one of those gasps, and with that came the smell and Norman held his breath before too much of it found its way into his lungs. He looked down at the soapy water, thought of the butter knife somewhere in there. He didn't really need it, did he? There were so many ways to keep her quiet, to keep her from ending the blessed silence.

Norman tightened his left arm, pulled her waist tight against him. Eisa seemed to like that. Before she could let more stink out into the air with another one of those wretched gasps, he tightened his right arm, brought the crook of his elbow up under her chin, against her throat, and began to squeeze. He did this slowly at first, just a little pressure. It had been years since he put someone in a choke hold, and while some things never really left you, machinery tends to get rusty when you leave it in the barn.

Either in discomfort or because Eisa thought this was something it wasn't, she ground against him again, and that was when Norman tightened his right arm. He did it with enough force to jerk her head back. Eisa stopped grinding. She didn't get a chance to gasp. What choked out of her mouth was a wet cough. Spittle sprayed the window glass and the screen below.

Norman pulled back hard enough to lift her from the ground. He had no idea where the strength was coming from, but it felt good. It brought him back to the man he once was, to the boy of his youth who feared nothing. He caught the reflection of his eyes again, this time in the window glass, and he saw Eisa's, too. While his were confident, hungry, full of life, her eyes were wide and looked like balloons pumped up with fear. They bulged from her skull, threatened to pop.

"Stop…" The word came out of her like a hiss between clenched teeth, stretched out as long as a sentence, and with the sound of her voice, every annoying thing she'd said to him in the sixty years since that night in his truck came into Norman's head all at once. Yap, yap, yap. Jagged nails down a chalkboard. Ice picks jabbed into his ears.

"I said…don't…" Norman yanked back, brought his elbow up, and used the leverage of his fingers wrapped around Eisa's shoulder to tighten his arm like a ratchet sizing down.

Her legs flailed, kicked at him. She caught him good in the left knee with the heel of her foot. Norman's grip loosened, but only for a second. Long enough for the pain to register, but it was just a blip. Whatever gave him his newfound strength also seemed to keep the hurt away. He liked that. He liked that a lot. Damn if he wasn't laughing.

Norman yanked up on his arm again. He put his back into it and pulled Eisa nearly two feet off the ground. Her legs slammed into the cabinet doors below the sink, and her arms waved about, but he knew this was almost over—she smacked him in the head, and it was barely a tap. He found her reflection again in the glass. Her eyes were up in her head somewhere, nothing but white. It was his own reflection that grabbed him—he looked twenty, maybe younger. Not a line on his face. His hair was thick and black, slicked back with Cornwell's Tonic, that greasy shit he used to steal from his dad that made his scalp itch. His reflection wore that brown leather bomber jacket, the one he'd picked up at the thrift store in Portsmouth because he thought it made him look like James Dean. Oh man, he loved that jacket, always had. Where the hell had it gone? He hadn't seen it in maybe—

Norman caught a flash of silver from the corner of his vision an instant before Eisa struck him in the side of the head with the meat tenderizing mallet. It was more of a wild swing than a coordinated attack, but somehow she clocked him square in the temple with enough force that the spikes embedded in his flesh and the hammer hung there for half a second when her hand dropped away before falling to the ground. Norman's head jerked to the side with a resounding deep *boom!* echoing through his skull. He stutter-stepped and lost his grip on Eisa, and she fell from his arm, puddled at his feet.

Norman waited for the pain (that type of hurt always came on a slight delay), but there was none. The echo in his head dulled and vanished. He reached up, tentatively touched the side of his temple. His fingers came away wet and sticky, but he felt nothing. His reflection in the window glass gave him a quick wink.

It took her a couple of tries, but Eisa managed to get to her feet and scramble from the kitchen down the hall, spitting up God-knows-what as she went. Norman let her; she wouldn't get far. He reached down and scooped up the mallet, felt the heft of it. Much better than the butter knife.

The Ray Charles song popped back into his head, and this time he did remember the name, even the words. A few days after their tussle in the back of his Ford, Eisa had bought the record and played it over and over. He started down the hallway after her, whistling softly, the lyrics singing in his head: *I can't stop loving you, I've made up my mind...*

15

MATT

MATT TOLD JOSH TO wait in the living room before ascending the stairs. The stillness of the house grew thicker with each step, and by the time he reached the top, he felt like he was wallowing through some invisible heavy fog. He came upon the daughter's room first, saw all the red, and felt a sinking feeling in his gut before he spotted the open bottles and realized it was only paint. Relief washed over him, but it was short-lived—every inch of his being knew something was wrong, told him to get out. His throat was as dry as sandpaper.

There were four other doors off the hallway, three of which were open. Matt quickly moved in and out of each of those rooms, confirming what his gut had already told him; they were empty. They were behind that closed door, most likely a shared bathroom. The light was on, visible in the crack under the door, but even as Matt put his ear against the wood, he heard nothing but the steady hum of an exhaust fan.

He knocked twice. "Lynn? This is Deputy Matt Maro. Is it okay if I come in?"

Matt desperately wanted an answer—he'd settle for a whimper out of one of the kids—but nothing came.

Gripping the butt of his gun, he flicked away the leather safety strap with his thumb. His free hand went to the doorknob, turned it just enough to confirm it wasn't locked. "Lynn, I'm coming in. If you're near the door, please step back."

He closed his eyes for a moment, drew in a deep breath, and opened the door.

As a law enforcement officer, Matt had seen some horrible things. Gunshot victims. DOAs at car accidents. Two years ago, he'd been called out to the apartment of Robin and Stew Holland. They'd woken to find their three-week-old daughter dead in her crib from SIDS, sudden infant death syndrome. The images of all those things had burned into Matt's mind like vivid snapshots. He saw them when he closed his eyes, when he woke at three in the morning either crying or screaming, all of them fluttered back in moments like this, and as he stepped into that bathroom, he knew what he found would stay with him until his dying day.

Gracie and her little brother, Oscar, were both under the water, resting facedown at the bottom of the bathtub, visible only through breaks in the dwindling bubbles and soapy film on the surface. Kneeling beside the tub, bent over the side, her head in the water, was Lynn Tatum. Her hair fanned out, partially covering the body of her son. The water was as still as the air, not a single ripple, and it was clear all three had been dead for some time. Lynn Tatum was wearing pajamas and was soaking wet. There was water all over the floor, partially up the walls, streaking the doors of the vanity and the side of the toilet. Obvious signs of struggle.

A single thought rushed into Matt's mind—only one member of the Tatum family survived whatever this was, and he was downstairs.

Matt took out his gun and quietly reached for the microphone clipped to his shoulder. "Sally, this is Matt, come back. Over." When no reply came, he pressed the Transmit button again. "Ellie? Sally? Either of you there?"

He spoke in a low whisper, didn't dare raise his voice any louder. Nobody responded. He took out his phone and dropped it back in his pocket when he realized he had no signal.

A cold sweat filmed over his forehead. Matt cleared his throat and called out, "Josh? You still downstairs?" When Josh didn't answer, he added, "I need you to stay down there!"

Matt turned slowly and stepped out of the bathroom. He worked his way back toward the staircase, clearing each room as he passed, knowing that in the coming seconds, there was a very good chance he'd have to shoot Josh Tatum.

16

LOG 10/16/2023 20:31 GMT-4
TRANSCRIPT: AUDIO/VIDEO RECORDING

Analysis Note: While I know little about the subject, I know even less about Beatrice Sordello. I was told she holds a PhD in psychology from ███████████ and completed her undergraduate training at ███████████ with a double minor heavily focused on religious studies. No ring, so either unmarried or she removed it. Mid- to late thirties. Had I been asked, I would have suggested monitoring her vitals along with the subject's. Although she hid it well, she was clearly nervous.

Sordello: Before you continue, I'd like to clarify one point.

[*Silence*]

Sordello: Matt?

Maro: Yeah? Sorry. It's still a little raw.

Sordello: You said you encountered gunshot victims during your time in law enforcement. This wasn't in Hollows Bend, correct?

Maro: No. During training, I did a month in Conway, New Hampshire. It happened there. Drug deal gone bad. Customer tried to rob his dealer; the dealer shot him in the gut. Customer managed to get a round off from this rusty old .38 before going down. It was a mess, both of them on the ground trying to hold their insides in. One of the nastiest things I've ever seen.

Sordello: You left Hollows Bend...for training? Do you remember the exact dates of that?

Maro: I'm sure it's in my file.

Sordello: It isn't.

Maro: Well, it should be.

Sordello: The car accidents. Those happened where?

Maro: Out on 112. Tourists in a hurry to get home, in a hurry to get to the Bend. It's a relatively straight and quiet stretch of road. They tend to go faster than they should. Something darts out in front of them...a curve sneaks up...it can get messy.

Sordello: Accidents, though, not crimes. Correct?

Maro: Correct.

Sordello: Same with the dead baby? SIDS implies death by natural causes. No crime there, either, correct?

Maro: No. No crime. The Bend is usually very quiet.

Sordello: Before you go on, there's one other thing. After the birds, you mentioned the tourists were gone. You only saw locals. Where do you think they all went?

Maro: Home, I guess? I'm not sure what you mean.

Sordello: Did you see them leave?

Maro: I wasn't really watching, but that's what typically happens on Sundays. All the weekenders head home. We're a tourist town.

[*Silence*]

17

NORMAN HEATON

THE SECOND WEEK OF every November, Norman Heaton loaded up his pickup with supplies, and he and Henry Wilburt would four-wheel up to their blind on the far side of Mount Washington. They'd stay up there at least a week or so, until they both bagged at least one buck worth bragging about, then they'd bring them over to North Hollow Meat & Pork to have them butchered. Norman would stomach venison, but he never found it to be a substitute for a good ol' porterhouse. He didn't hunt for the meat; he hunted for the chase. He rarely shot a buck from the blind. Instead, he'd climb down and get up close—sometimes moving so slow it would take him an hour to move fifty feet—close enough to throw his knife and go for the neck or belly, then follow as the animal stumbled around in the woods and eventually slowed, and he'd finish it off. He'd often lose them in the brush and have to rely on his tracking skills to pick up the trail again—drop of blood here, snapped twig there, rustle of leaves. That was real hunting. A good buck could hide in plain sight if it had to, go so still and quiet you could be ten feet away and not know it was there. Eisa would have done well to ask a buck for a few pointers before running out of that kitchen, because she wasn't very good at hiding her tracks.

Norman stood in the archway between the kitchen and living room and watched her fall, twice, trying to cross the space. First she tripped on the corner of the hideous burgundy area rug he'd wanted to toss out way back when the first Bush was in the White House, then she caught the coffee table with her toe. That one sent her face-first into the hardwood, and when she managed to get back up on those peg legs of hers, something had opened up in her nose and blood was coming out like a tap. He stopped whistling long enough to point at his own nose and say, "You got a little something…"

At the sound of his voice, she swiveled her head back in his direction with enough force to send a trail of blood across the room. It slapped against the wall and the brick of the fireplace, leaving a thin line like the start of Pollock painting.

"Norman…why are you—"

"Shhhh!" He shot up his finger. "How fucking hard is it for you to keep your damn mouth shut?" He twisted the mallet between his fingers. "Just once, one Sunday, I'd like to read my paper, enjoy a quiet breakfast…Is that so much? Is that so fucking much?!?"

There was a half-finished jigsaw puzzle on the end table next to the couch—five thousand pieces making up a bird's nest filled with baby sparrows. He grabbed the corner of the table and yanked it up, sending it somersaulting across the room. It cracked against the wall; pieces rained over the floor. Man, that felt good! He made a fist, flexed his arm. The muscles tensed and flexed like a freshly primed hydraulic jack. No sign of the arthritis that had been there as recently as this morning when he crawled out of bed. Aside from that, he hated puzzles. If that was the last one in his life, he'd be perfectly okay with that.

Eisa had taken advantage of his momentary reverie to skitter across the floor and get herself upright on the opposite end of the living room. The blood from her nose covered her mouth and chin and had done a number on her favorite muumuu. That stain would not be coming out. She kept looking at the stairs, then the front door, then back again.

Norman took a step closer. "Make up your damn mind, you indecisive bitch. I'll give you a three-count. Then I'm comin', ready or not."

That did the trick.

Her hand slick with blood, Eisa fumbled with the dead bolt and managed to get the door open. She nearly fell again coming off the front stoop, but once she got her feet under her she crossed their lawn and got to Pollard Street quick enough. It wouldn't be the chase he'd hoped for. Eisa just didn't have that kind of speed in her anymore, but it would be better than tagging a buck from the blind like that lazy prick, Henry Wilburt.

Unlike his wife, Norman had no trouble with speed, or energy, or frail old bones. With each step he felt younger, more virile. He went after her with the vigor of a twenty-year-old, cocking the arm holding the mallet like a shotgun.

18

MATT

MATT SAID NOTHING AS he eased down the steps at the Tatum house, carefully placing his feet as close to the wall as possible to avoid any noisy boards. He pulled back the slide on his gun to chamber a round, cursing himself for not readying the weapon earlier. In the otherwise silent house, there was no mistaking that sound, and he expected to hear something from Josh—movement, the draw of a breath—something, but the downstairs had gone as quiet as the second floor.

When Matt reached the bottom step, he came around the corner into the living room cautiously at a low crouch, hugging the wall, his finger on the trigger guard. Josh wasn't in there—Matt spotted him outside through the open front door, sitting on the stoop with his back to the house.

Matt slipped his finger from the guard to the trigger and tried to steady his breathing. He'd never shot anyone and didn't want today to be the first. "Josh, I need to see your hands! Raise them slowly, put them behind your head, and interlace your fingers!"

Josh didn't do that. Instead, he turned and faced Matt. The man's face was red and streaked with tears. He tried to speak between sobs. "Why…would Lynn do that?!? How could she? I was only gone for maybe twenty minutes! If I'd known…I…I never would have left her alone. Never! You gotta believe me!"

He spotted the gun in Matt's hand and swallowed; quickly started shaking his head. "It wasn't me, Matt! I'd never hurt them!"

Matt kept his finger on the trigger, but lowered the weapon, pointing the barrel at the ground. He reached behind his back with his free hand, took out his handcuffs, and held them out. "I don't know what happened here, Josh, but we'll straighten it out. Until then, I need you to put these on."

Josh glanced at the cuffs but didn't take them. "Lynn was in a bad place. She hated her job, wasn't sleeping well. I finally got her to see a doctor in Portland, and he put her on a slew of medications. I thought they were helping, they seemed to—for a little while anyway. But the last couple days…" He faced Matt dead in the eyes. "If I thought for a second she'd ever hurt the children, I never would have left her alone."

Matt's mind flashed to what he found upstairs—both children facedown, under the water. Lynn crouched over the side, her head submerged. "So Lynn…drowned Gracie and Oscar, and you…" He let that word hang in the air.

"She drowned them, then herself," Josh told him. "When I came home, I found them all like that and I called you. I didn't even go in the bathroom. I could tell they were…" His face twisted, he tried to choke back the tears, but couldn't. Josh buried his head in his hands and sobbed.

Or you drowned all three.

Or she drowned the children, and you killed her.

Lynn's problems were no secret. You couldn't hide something like that in a town this small. But kill her own kids?

She wouldn't be the first.

People did some terrible things under emotional distress.

Matt had known Josh since grade school. Lynn nearly as long. He couldn't picture either of them killing anyone. When they were kids, Josh cornered a mouse in Matt's garage. Matt had a shovel out, ready to bash it into its next life, and Josh had stopped him, trapped it in a bucket, and walked it a half mile up the mountain before letting it go.

Josh was crying again.

Matt holstered his weapon and went to the man, gently cuffing his wrists. "Just until we get to the station, okay?"

"Yeah. Okay."

Josh didn't protest as Matt helped him to his feet, walked him down the sidewalk, and placed him in the back of his cruiser.

He took out his phone and checked the screen—two bars. Not as strong as usual, but better than nothing. He dialed Ellie—she picked up on the third ring, and he told her what happened. When he finished, neither of them spoke for a long time.

"Did you Mirandize him?" Ellie finally said.

"What? No." Matt ran a hand through his hair. "I don't think he—"

"It doesn't matter what you or I think. We need to do this by the book. Are his clothes wet?"

Josh thought about that but wasn't sure. "I don't think so."

"You don't think so," she repeated under her breath. "When you get him to the station, Mirandize him, inspect and bag his clothes. You said Lynn was soaked and there was water all over the bathroom. You can't drown someone like that without making a mess. If there's a drop of water on him, make a note of it. Take photographs before it dries out. Write everything down." Her voice faded a bit toward the end, but not enough to keep him from hearing.

Matt glanced at Josh in the back of the car. "What if he changed clothes before I got here? After he…" He looked up at the house. "I should go and look before they dry out, too. I—"

Ellie cut him off again. "You don't set foot in that house, do you hear me? I want you to lock the front door and tape it off. We need to preserve the scene. We're not equipped to deal with a homicide. I've gotta call someone in."

"Closest FBI office is Portsmouth. That's an hour and a half away," Matt pointed out.

"I'll try the Jackson sheriff's office first. They have a crime lab. If they can't send someone, we'll have to wait on the feds, no choice."

"The kids are still in that bathtub..."

Static rolled over the line, then faded away. When Ellie spoke again, Matt had trouble hearing her at first, then she came back stronger. "I know it's horrible, but the best thing you can do for them is to preserve the scene."

And they're part of the scene, his mind reminded him. He blinked, and the image of those two small bodies under the pink bubbles flashed in his mind. *Getting a conviction is how we make things right by them.*

Through another wall of static, Ellie said, "When you get to the station, I want you to call Harvey Cooper. Tell him what's going on, and tell him I said I want him to come down and represent Josh."

"Josh didn't request an attorney."

"That's good, because we don't have a public defender to give him. We'd have to pull one from county, and that's not happening on a Sunday."

"But Cooper does family law, doesn't he?"

More static, then: "I don't care if he practices tribal law for the wetlands of New Guinea. Can't risk a potential prosecution coming apart because Josh didn't get representation. Cooper can hold things together until the courthouse at county opens tomorrow. Hopefully when CSI concludes their investigation, the findings will back what Josh told you, but if they don't, we need to be ready. Mirandize him, bag his clothes, call an attorney. Got it?"

"Yes, ma'am."

"What a clusterfuck," Ellie muttered.

In the car, Josh had gone quiet. He was staring down at the floorboard. When he looked up, Matt turned away from him and asked Ellie, "Are you still with the abandoned Honda?"

"I was. Figured I'd wait for the tow truck to get here, but Sally just called me and said there's some kind of disturbance at the library. I'm heading over there now."

"The library?" Matt said. "What the hell is going on today?"

19

MATT

MATT SPENT TEN MINUTES sealing up the Tatum house. Several neighbors came out and he told them as little as possible; even Annie Bergen, who was never shy about showing her feelings. She smacked the back window of Matt's cruiser and glared in at Josh. "Did this bastard hurt 'em? Lynn said he was cheating with Nancy Buckley—he tell you that? What did he do to Lynn? Where are the kids?!?"

He told them all to get back in their homes, what little good that did. When he finally pulled away, there were at least ten people standing out there. They knew better than to approach the house—he didn't have to threaten them. They all knew Ellie would string any one of them up if they tried.

Matt made the right off Morning Glory to Sumptner and drove another quarter mile before shifting the rearview mirror so he could see Josh. "Want to tell me about Nancy Buckley?"

Josh sniffled and raised his cuffed hands to wipe his nose. "Nothing to tell. Lynn wasn't well and saw things where there wasn't anything. I do the Buckleys' taxes, that's it. Lynn noticed my car at their house one day and decided I was having an affair."

"And you weren't?"

He shook his head.

Matt knew Nancy Buckley. She graduated a year before him and like most, never left. She married the same guy she dated through most of high school. He worked for a local contractor hanging drywall. Matt recalled seeing her husband's red pickup parked out front of the Black Moose Tavern at closing time at least three times in the past week. Not exactly a sign of a good marriage, but not a smoking gun, either.

He met Josh's eyes in the mirror again. "Where did you go this morning? Where were you when—"

Josh's eyes went wide. "Look out!"

Matt turned back to the road a moment before Eisa Heaton half stumbled, half ran out between houses, tripped on the curb, and fell in front of his cruiser. He slammed down the brakes and squealed to a stop, expecting a thump but hearing nothing.

"Jesus!"

He jerked the gearshift into park and got out, nearly slipping as he rounded the front of the car.

Eisa Heaton was on her back, trying to get back on her feet, a terrified look on her bloody face.

Matt got an arm around her shoulders and tried to steady her. "Are you okay? Did I hit you?"

Her palms were scuffed from the asphalt, but aside from that, she didn't have any visible cuts or bruises. Eisa clenched a hand around her throat, tried to speak, and couldn't, then started jabbing at the air, pointing frantically.

Norman Heaton rounded the Peterson house, stomped through the center of his neighbor's prized yellow roses, and started across the lawn at a fast clip. He was holding something. It looked like a hammer.

Trembling, Eisa pulled out of Matt's arms. She managed two steps before falling again.

"Don't listen to her, Matt!" Norman shouted. "Don't listen to a goddamn word she says!" He raised the hammer and smacked it down against his palm.

The last time Matt had seen Norman Heaton, the man needed a cane to climb the steps at the front of the VFW hall. The fingers of his right hand were twisted with arthritis, and he made this wheezing sound when he breathed; the by-product of smoking a pack a day most his life. He had no cane now, his fingers looked just fine, and his breathing was more akin to a locomotive steaming up a hill than someone with third-stage emphysema.

Matt stood, got in front of Eisa, and spread his arms. "Norman, what the hell are you doing? Drop the hammer!"

The man didn't stop. Instead, his pace quickened and he brought the hammer down against his palm again. "You best stay out of this, Matt. It's family business. Doesn't concern you."

Not a hammer at all. A meat tenderizer.

Matt grabbed the taser from his belt and fumbled the safety off. "Norman, stop! Don't come any closer!"

Norman struck his palm again with a wet slap, and Matt realized he'd hit his own hand with the tenderizer so many times the flesh had turned to pulp. The side of his face was torn up, too. Part of his cheek flapped against his jowl. Yet, the man was smiling as he stepped off the curb to the pavement and brought the tenderizer back up. "You best move, you little—"

Matt pulled the trigger.

The taser jerked in his hand and let out a soft *pop*. Two probes shot out the front and embedded in Norman's shirt. That was followed by a high-pitched crackle as electricity raced down the thin wires from the gun to the probes.

Norman's body went rigid. His head jerked up and his fingers splayed out. The meat tenderizer clattered to the ground a moment before Norman did. Matt held the trigger down until the charge fully dispersed, watching the man flop around in a stiff, electrically induced seizure. When it ended, Norman was finally still.

Matt dropped the taser and crouched, checked for a pulse—found one, and let out a breath. Although rare, tasers could induce cardiac events in those who were predisposed, and Norman Heaton was far from the prime of his life. Not only was he breathing, but he was already coming back around. *Was he on something?*

"Don't move, Norman. You'll be just fine." Matt reached around his back for his handcuffs, found the leather case on his belt empty, and remembered they were on Josh. He had another pair in the glove box. "Stay on the ground."

He ran back to his cruiser and had just opened the passenger door when he heard a raspy grunt.

Eisa Heaton had retrieved the tenderizer and was standing over her husband, glaring down at him. She brought the mallet down on his head with a sickening crunch.

20

SHERIFF ELLIE

SHERIFF ELLIE PRITCHET DIALED the sheriff's office in Jackson for the third time, and for the third time, the call rang twice and disconnected. **Call Failed** appeared on the display. She tossed her phone over to the passenger seat, muttering "Damn it all."

A few years back, some telecom company approached the town select board and offered to put up four more towers to help supplement the one up on Mount Washington. The board shot them down, caving to a handful of locals who felt the towers wouldn't blend with the town's quaint aesthetics. The same group of people complained when the Bend's first traffic light went up on Main and Court Avenue next to town square, petitioned to keep out the fast-food chains, and generally shit on progress of any sort. Well, maybe a good week or two of spotty service would bring them around.

She tried her radio again. "Sally, you there?"

Nothing but a rush of static.

While that was common out on Route 112, surrounded by

mountains of granite, it made no sense in the center of town less than two blocks from the sheriff's station, unless there was some problem with the antenna up on the roof. Maybe one of the birds Matt mentioned had managed to hit it just right. It hadn't been replaced since her father's long stint as sheriff, and even then the job had gone to the lowest bid.

She'd worry about that later.

Ellie was still trying to wrap her head around what Matt found at the Tatum house when she pulled to a stop in front of the Hollows Bend Public Library. Built around 1900, the library was two stories of hand-forged red brick topped by a stone and copper clock tower that had an on-again, off-again relationship with accurately telling time. She noted it was only off by two minutes today, which was fairly impressive considering the last three times she'd checked it had been off by more than an hour.

Ellie was barely out of her car before the head librarian came running over, cradling a fire extinguisher in his lanky arms.

Edgar Newton was in his early seventies, at least six foot four, and thin as a rail, weighing maybe a buck-sixty. He was bald and had a nose well out of proportion with his closely set eyes. He'd worked at the library for as long as Ellie could remember. When she was a kid, her friends had called him the Stork. As she got older, she learned most of the adults called him Bean, which wasn't much better.

"Mr. Newton," Ellie said, careful not to call him either of those names as she looked past him toward the library entrance, fetching her hat from the passenger seat. "What's going on?"

Newton hefted the fire extinguisher from his left side to his right, cradling it under his arm. "Follow me, I'll show you."

He led her through the entrance, past the main counter, and down several aisles to a smoldering pile of books stacked under a framed photograph of Oscar Wilde. Everything was covered in white powder discharged from the extinguisher. The air was still cloudy with it. Beneath the dry odor not unlike baby powder was the pungent stench of some kind of accelerant.

Newton brushed the bottom of his nose with the back of his wrist and sniffed, as if he was trying not to sneeze. "It's Ms. Gilmore; I don't know what's gotten into her. I came in just as she dropped a match on this pile. I managed to get the fire out, then she disappeared in the stacks, pulling books as she went, mumbling some nonsense about filth." He glanced deeper into the library, narrowed those beady eyes, and turned back to Ellie. "She opened this morning. If I hadn't come in thirty minutes early, she might have burned the entire building down." Although he was clearly flustered, he spoke in barely a whisper. Each of his words was articulated perfectly, as if he were giving a speech. Somehow, his voice dropped even lower. "She's covered in lighter fluid, Sheriff, absolutely reeks of it. She was carrying one can, and I saw at least one more in her purse. I've known her for the better part of fifty years, and she's never once acted like this, I'm afraid something in her may be...broken."

Ellie looked around the library. It seemed oddly still. Only about half the motion-activated lights were on. The tall bookshelves made these elongated shadows across the Berber carpet.

"Where did she go?"

Newton pointed through the maze of books to a spot in the back left corner. "She was near Young Adult the last time I saw her."

21

MATT

"EISA, NO!"

Matt lunged from the car to where she hovered over her husband, but not fast enough to keep her from bringing down the tenderizer again. She didn't weigh much, maybe 110 soaking wet, but she put every ounce of herself into that next swing, and Matt knew from the deep thud that resonated from the man's skull as the mallet cracked against his temple that Norman Heaton was dead. Eisa managed to hit Norman two more times before Matt was able to pry the mallet from her grip. She fought, clawed at him, spitting and kicking like some wild animal, then she simply went still. She collapsed on the pavement beside her dead husband like some kind of rag doll, like someone had reached in and pulled out her spine.

Matt quickly checked Norman for a pulse, didn't find one, then snapped his fingers in front of the old woman's eyes. "Eisa, can you hear me?"

There was no reaction. Her eyes were open, and she was breathing, but it was like she couldn't see him.

A woman screamed.

Several neighbors had come out of their houses and surrounded them in the street. The scream had come from Pat Peterson, who twisted and buried her face in her husband's chest. It was nearly noon, but both of them were still wearing pajamas under loosely tied robes.

"Take her back inside," Matt told Stu Peterson. Then he looked around at the others and raised his voice. "All of you, get back inside your houses!"

A couple of them shuffled back a few steps, but nobody left the street. At least half had their phones out and were recording video.

Matt shook his head and quietly told Eisa, "Let's get you in my car."

She made no effort to stand. Her entire body was limp. He got both his arms under her, gently hefted her up, and carried her back to his car.

Without a free hand, he couldn't open the back door. He was about to set her down when Stu Peterson came over and opened the back door for him. When he saw Josh Tatum already in the back, the two locked eyes for a moment, then Josh turned away and faced out the window. Matt eased the woman down on the seat and closed the door gently, as if he didn't want to wake her. He was reaching for his radio microphone when Stu Peterson placed a hand on his shoulder and spoke in a low voice.

"Right before you got here, Pat and I heard gunshots. Three of them."

"Hunters up on Mount Washington?"

Peterson shook his head. "Sounded like a pistol to me. Three quick shots, like a semiautomatic. The mountain adds an echo. I didn't hear that."

Stu Peterson did three tours in Afghanistan, and Matt regularly ran into him at the range up in North Hollow. Former special forces, he kept a large gun safe in his garage and several handguns around his home, all of them properly registered; Matt had helped him with the paperwork.

Peterson looked up and down the street. "Somewhere close. One of these houses, I think. We tried to phone it in but couldn't get through. What the hell is going on?"

Matt didn't answer that. He pressed the button on his microphone. "Sally, it's Matt. I need an ambulance on Sumptner near the Peterson place. Over."

A couple of seconds ticked by, and Matt tried again. "Sally?"
Nothing.

He tried his cell. Sally's direct line rang twice, then disconnected and failed. The same thing happened when he called the coroner.

When he looked back over toward Norman's body, Cliff Stubbs was busy covering him with a blue plastic tarp from his garage.

"Hey," Matt shouted. "You can't do that!"

Cliff tugged the corner down over Norman's foot. "You can't leave a dead body in the middle of the street. I don't want my kids seeing this. You got plenty of witnesses who saw what happened. Hell, you got a camera right there on your dash, probably recorded the whole thing. Get him out of here."

Matt rolled his eyes and tried the coroner again but couldn't get through. Ellie wasn't picking up, either.

"You gotta get him to the coroner's office, right? We could use my truck," Stu Peterson suggested.

"I can't ask you to do that."

"Well, Cliff's an ass, but he's right. You gotta get him out of the street." He nodded at Josh and Eisa in the back of Matt's cruiser. "You've got your hands full as it is."

What Matt needed to do was tape off the street, get Ellie down here, get CSI down here, get someone down here to help him properly investigate and document everything.

A voice in the back of his mind mocked him. *Sure. Right after the Tatum house, the mess on Main Street, and whatever Ellie is currently dealing with at the library. Three gunshots, too—don't forget that. There might just be another body or three behind one of these doors. What you really need to do is get back to the sheriff's office, regroup with Ellie, and figure out what the fuck is happening, then get some help out here.*

Matt's head was spinning. He asked Peterson, "Can you help me get him in the trunk of my cruiser?"

Peterson nodded.

22

LOG 10/16/2023 21:02 GMT-4
TRANSCRIPT: AUDIO/VIDEO RECORDING

Sordello: Did you notice anything odd about Stuart Peterson at that point?

Maro: [*Shakes head*] Stu? No. Nothing.

Sordello: Josh Tatum? Eisa Heaton? Norman Heaton?

Maro: No. None of them.

> Analysis Note: As instructed, at this point, Special Agent Beatrice Sordello reached into a box at the side of her chair and retrieved several files. She placed them in the carrier of the pass-through between both sections of the Manfred booth but didn't slide them through to the subject. Maro took note of the names (which matched the

people she'd just asked him about) but otherwise disre-
garded them. He settled back in his chair.

Maro: Could I have a glass of water?

Sordello: You're thirsty?

Maro: Yes.

[*Silence*]

Maro: Is that some kind of problem? People get thirsty.

Sordello: How often do *you* get thirsty?

Maro: What the hell kind of question is that?

[*Silence*]

Sordello: I'll have a bottle brought to you. While we wait, I want
to know what you pieced together about Hannah Hernandez
and Daniel Jones. Do you know what happened to them?

Maro: [*Nods*]

Sordello: We're capturing audio and video, but it's best you
speak to ensure we have an accurate transcript.

Maro: I know what happened to them.

Sordello: Even though you weren't with them and didn't

personally encounter either of them through this entire ordeal. You know what happened to them?

Maro: [*Nods, then seems to recall previous instructions*] It's just like I knew what happened in the Heatons' kitchen, even though I wasn't there. Same with Ellie at the library.

Sordello: But you *don't* know what happened at the Tatum house? You don't know whether Josh or Lynn killed the children?

[*Silence*]

Analysis Note: Slight spike in Maro's blood pressure and oxygen intake. Unclear if this is deception or something else. His baseline readings do not appear to be atypical.

Along with the files for Hernandez and Jones, Sordello added Edgar Newton and Arwa Gilmore. She hesitated with Malcolm Mitchell, then dropped his folder in there, too.

Maro: I could really use that water.

23

HANNAH

DANNY GROANED AND LEANED over the steering wheel of his Ford Fusion. "Geez, what's up with all the traffic?"

Hannah looked up from the playlist she was compiling on her phone. Route 112 was at a standstill. Cars were stopped bumper to bumper for as far as she could see. "Maybe there's an accident or something."

He slumped back in his seat. "I was hoping to get us to Boston by lunch. Guess that plan is shot to shit."

"So you're going to let a little traffic get you down?" Hannah reached over and stroked his thigh. "You can't be depressed on such an epic occasion."

He clearly had no idea what she was talking about.

Hannah pulled her hand away. "Do you have any idea what today is?"

Danny thought about it. "Sunday?"

"Today is officially our 111th date, Mr. Jones." Hannah went back to her phone and added the latest Lady Gaga song to her growing list. "One, one, one."

They'd started going out about a month after Hannah transferred to Hollows Bend High from Connecticut when her dad took a job with an engineering firm in Barton. Hannah had been a freshman and Danny was a junior and captain of the varsity basketball team, and holy hell, was he good-looking. When he first approached her in the hallway near her locker, she only heard about half the words that came out of his mouth. She'd gotten lost in his green eyes, and for the life of her, she couldn't figure out why this guy was talking to her. The other girls had watched in awe as he asked her out. He smiled when the word *yes* fell from her mouth, told her he'd see her around, and walked off. That had been that, and they had been inseparable ever since.

Danny curled his index finger around a loose strand of Hannah's dark hair and tucked it behind her ear. "One, one, one. You're right, that is a milestone. I can think of at least a dozen ways you can demonstrate your appreciation for me, but you may want to stretch first. I'd hate to see you pull something, Ms. Hernandez."

The brake lights of the Toyota minivan in front of them blinked off, and they started to creep down the blacktop.

"Finally!" Danny took his foot off the brake and rolled slowly forward. They gained maybe five feet before they were forced to stop again.

"Or not."

"Or not."

Hannah tagged "Bubbly" by Colbie Caillat. She loved that song.

Danny rolled his window down and leaned out, then fell back in his seat. "I can't see anything up ahead. I don't know where this ends. We could be stuck out here all day."

Playlist, done!

Hannah connected to the stereo in Danny's car via Bluetooth and hit Play. Jason Mraz strummed his guitar and went into his latest. Hannah listened for a moment, then leaned across the center console and rested her head on Danny's shoulder. "Maybe today's not the day to go to Boston. Maybe it's the day to do something else." She stroked his thigh again and gave him a gentle squeeze.

Danny grinned mischievously and slipped the transmission in reverse. "I like where your head's at, Ms. Hernandez. Hang on."

24

SHERIFF ELLIE

"WAIT HERE."

With a soft grunt, Ellie took the fire extinguisher from Newton and started down the main aisle of the library before deciding it might be better to follow the outer wall and come up behind Gilmore while she was doing whatever it was she was doing.

As sheriff, Ellie had crossed paths with Arwa Gilmore twice in the librarian's seventy-six years, first in 1996 and again in 2008. Her father had a file on Gilmore from 1983. In all three instances, she'd buried a husband. Each had died of a heart attack. The first had been thirty-eight, the second forty-seven, and the third fifty-one. Each man had been wealthy prior to marriage. While her father had no reason to charge her with anything, he always thought something was off about her first husband's death; a heart attack at thirty-eight was rare. The autopsy had found a blocked artery to be the cause, completely natural, but he had trouble letting it go. Said it was Gilmore's reaction that troubled him—he didn't buy her grief. Ellie's father was dead and she was sheriff when husband number two died, and again, the cause was due to a coronary induced by not one but two blocked arteries. Ellie had petitioned to have the first husband's body exhumed and was denied. It took a third man dying before a judge finally signed off on digging up both predecessors and granted a warrant to search the house. All three bodies went to the federal lab in Boston and were tested extensively, but nothing was found. The warrant didn't turn up anything, either. Two days later Ellie had gone to Gilmore's house to confront her, but she wasn't home. Ellie was walking back to her cruiser when she noticed a string of ants eating something leaking from one of Gilmore's trash cans. Ellie removed the lid and found it stuffed with food—milk, cream, three different kinds of butter, at least twenty pounds of thawing cuts of meat, sausage, hot dogs, salami, ice cream...If Ellie hadn't recently undergone a physical, it probably wouldn't have clicked, but her cholesterol was up and the doctor had given her a pamphlet listing foods to avoid. Mainly saturated fats—damn near everything in that trash can.

Had Gilmore killed off three men just by feeding them too much of the wrong foods?

Ellie had never shared that theory because it was fucking crazy, but that didn't mean it wasn't true. It only took some patience. Ellie was patient, too. She kept an eye on the woman, waited for her to remarry, but she never did. Ellie had spied her eating salads for lunch out on the commons a couple of times. That wasn't lost on her.

A loud bang came from the far end of the library. That was followed by the shuffling of feet, then quiet.

There were many times in her life Ellie cursed the fact that she was short, this being one of them. While the bookshelves along the outside walls went to the ceiling, the ones in the center of the room topped out at six feet. That was fine and dandy for someone like Newton, but not so much when you're five foot nothing.

She couldn't see a damn thing, and Ellie knew if she tried climbing one of those shelves, the boards were likely to come out from under her feet and leave her ass-up on a pile of books long before she'd see anything useful.

"She moved to the children's section."

The whispered voice came from behind her.

Ellie banged her elbow on a shelf as she spun around.

Newton was standing there, both palms held out defensively. "I'm sorry, I didn't mean to startle you."

"I told you to wait back there!" Ellie growled between clenched teeth.

"And you're going the wrong way. I'm not going to stand by while you wander about and someone burns down my library."

Ellie rolled her eyes. "Which way is the children's section?"

He held out a bony finger and pointed to the right.

"Okay, but stay behind me."

Ellie heard Arwa Gilmore a moment before she saw her. The woman was muttering softly to herself. Harsh, abrupt words, chopped and cut off as she spat them out. Like some kind of argument with herself.

I'm afraid something in her may be...broken.

That's what Newton had said.

Gilmore was standing among the tiny chairs in the story-time area next to a giant cardboard bunny dressed in a suit. The librarian was holding a book, studying the print on the back. She normally wore her gray hair pulled back in a neat bun. Ellie noticed wiry strands standing out all over her head as if she'd slept with her hair up and hadn't bothered to fix it this morning. Her silver glasses were perched precariously at the end of her nose as she turned the book to its spine, frowned, and flipped through the pages. "Absolute filth," she groaned before throwing the book on a pile at her feet.

Ellie glimpsed the title: *If I Ran the Zoo* by Dr. Seuss.

Gilmore plucked another from the shelf and gave it only a cursory glance before throwing it aside. *The Cat's Quizzer*, also by Dr. Seuss.

The air was hazy and stank of lighter fluid, but that didn't keep Gilmore from taking the small can from the purse hanging off her shoulder and dousing the books, the surrounding carpet, and part of the wall. Even the cardboard rabbit hadn't escaped.

Ellie motioned for Newton to stay behind her, then said in the calmest voice she could muster. "Arwa, want to tell me what you're doing?"

At first, the woman didn't acknowledge her; she seemed to look right through her to her boss. Her eyes narrowed to tiny pin-pricks. "I'm trying to clean up the mess made by that man!" She grabbed another book off the shelf and shook it. Another Seuss book—*On beyond Zebra!* "This garbage has no place here! It's poison to anyone who touches it!" She threw it on the pile and zigzagged the colorful cover with a spray of lighter fluid, which splashed up on her shoes and the hem of her dress. A large box of matches stuck up from her open purse.

Ellie's grip tightened around the fire extinguisher. "I imagine there is some kind of process in place if you'd like to remove a title from the library. No need for you to do this, right?"

"Process…" Gilmore huffed and blew a strand of loose hair from her face. "I've been telling Mr. Newton to remove these books for the better part of a year. I've shown him the supporting liter-ature, the studies, the peer reviews. You know what his answer to me has always been?" She paused and licked her chapped lips. "He said, 'I like Dr. Seuss.' He told me the same thing with all the others." She grabbed another title off the shelf and waved it around. "He even left *Charlotte's Web* in the stacks, of all things! Banned by numerous school boards in 2006! And when parents come in here asking why we still have it, he expects me to defend it!" She dropped the book on the pile and saturated it. "I will do no such thing!"

Newton cleared his throat. "Ms. Gilmore and I have a difference of opinion, which we've discussed at length. When she's running the library, she's more than welcome to exercise those opinions."

Newton was seventy-two and more than likely to die in that library than retire. Gilmore must have come to the same conclusion, because she raised the bottle of lighter fluid and doused him—one quick stream starting at his shoe and getting halfway up his suit jacket before he managed to back away.

"Arwa!"

Ellie tried to slap the can from the woman's hand, but Gilmore was far faster than she looked. Not only did she pull away, but she managed to hit both Newton *and* Ellie with another stream, splashing Ellie's cheek and left eye.

Ellie screamed and twisted away. She nearly dropped the fire extinguisher when she wiped at her face with her uniform sleeve. The burning came on a delay, not as bad as she expected, but bad enough to cause tears to cloud her vision and set her nose running. She spotted a water fountain against the wall and started for it when Gilmore told her not to move.

"Just stay right there," the woman said, and Ellie realized she was no longer holding the can of lighter fluid. She'd dropped that and managed to strike a match.

While Ellie stayed where she was, Mr. Newton did not.

He backed away at a quick shuffle and managed to get behind some kind of craft table. He pulled a phone from the wall and frantically punched in 911. Little good that would do—Sally would get the call at the station, if it went through at all.

One eye closed, the other a hazy mess, Ellie locked on that flickering flame in Ms. Gilmore's hand and tried to keep her voice calm. "You're covered in accelerant, Arwa. Put that out before you hurt yourself."

The woman was staring at the flame, too; her eyes were locked on it. Mesmerized. She watched the matchstick dwindle until it was nearly to the tips of her fingers. "I think you're looking at this all wrong, Sheriff. Fire sets us free. It's nature's equalizer."

Ellie threw the fire extinguisher at her.

It caught Gilmore under the chin, sent her staggering. She fell back and cracked her head against the side of a table. The match tumbled, rolled, and landed on the carpet. Ellie quickly stomped out the flame and crouched next to the other woman.

Gilmore wasn't unconscious, but the two blows had stunned her. A good size knot had already started to form on the side of her head, but she wasn't bleeding. Ellie pulled several zip ties from her pocket and quickly secured the woman to a chair before getting to her feet and staggering toward the water fountain to wash out her eye. Waving a hand behind her back, she shouted at Newton, "Watch her! I need to get this shit out of my eye..."

If the head librarian heard her, he didn't say anything. Didn't sound like he was on the phone anymore.

Ellie pressed the bar on the front of the fountain, scooped the water in her palms, and splashed her face. Her left eye didn't want to stay open so she pried it with her fingers, forced the water in, and kept at it until the burning turned to a dull ache. Nearly five minutes had gone by before she finally stood upright again and blinked away the last of it.

"Mr. Newton, are you—"

She heard a strange *swoosh* followed by a loud *chomp!*

Ellie turned to find Newton still standing behind the craft table. He was staring down at a large paper cutter, the large blade glistening under the overhead lights.

He'd just chopped off four of his own fingers.

25

HANNAH

BACK IN TOWN, HANNAH and Danny were parked in the far corner of the empty lot sandwiched between Lou's Laundry and the muffler shop. Hannah's playlist came from the speakers, not too loud. They had relocated to the back seat of Danny's car, and he had his hand under Hannah's sweatshirt, gingerly caressing her stomach as he slowly worked his way up to the frilly underside of her bra. Hannah nibbled on his ear as he traced the cup, followed under her left breast to the center, and fumbled around for the clasp.

"It's in the back," Hannah managed to get out in a fevered breath.

Danny's hand moved around her in that way all boys did— fast enough to get where it wanted to go, slow enough to make it seem like some kind of accident. *Oh, look what I found. While I'm here, do you mind if I…*

Get on with it, she thought. She wanted this as much as he did.

Hannah loved the fact that Danny still got nervous and took things slow. She loved how he knew to apply just the right amount of pressure, where, and when. She loved the way he kissed her as he did all of it, not sloppy or all tongue, just right. Just enough.

She loved *him*.

"You know that, right?" Hannah said quietly, before realizing she'd said the words aloud.

"Know what?"

She tugged the clasp on his belt open, unsnapped his jeans, and pulled down his zipper. "I love you."

They'd said the words before. That had first happened on milestone date number 43, but this might be the first time Hannah realized she actually meant it. She loved this boy with all her heart.

"And I love you," he told her, finally getting her bra off and dropping it to the floor between them. "One of these days, I'll marry you. We'll get a nice little house down on Colonial with a view of the mountains and have two point four kids."

They'd had that talk before, too. After college. Troy and Ivy, a boy and a girl. But like using the L-word, this was the first time it felt real. There was something in his voice. He wasn't just saying it to get what he wanted. He meant it.

Hannah pressed tighter against him, their bodies entwining. The heat had steamed up the windows, and it felt like they were the only two people in the world. "This is way better than Boston," she breathed, maneuvering her hand down into his jeans.

The two of them rolled over, Danny on top now. He sat up, pulled his shirt off, and tossed it aside, then went still as he looked down at her.

"What?"

A smile spread across his face. "You're so damn bea—"

The window behind his head exploded, and a small black hole appeared in Danny's temple, just above his right eye.

26

SHERIFF ELLIE

WITH TWENTY-SIX YEARS OF law enforcement under her belt, Ellie liked to believe she could handle just about anything. Hollows Bend had never had much crime, but she'd seen enough, dealt with her share of drunks and domestics, the occasional smash-and-grab, usually some out-of-towner. She'd even talked a jumper off the old bank building once, not that the two-story fall would have killed him, but she liked to think she at least spared him a nasty broken bone or two.

At least ten seconds ticked by as Ellie stared across the children's section of the library at Edgar Newton—the Stork, Bean, this man she had known her entire life, who always seemed to smell like he had cheese in his pockets. He hovered over the paper cutter, looked down at his severed fingers, then raised his hand to his curious face and studied the remaining nubs as if he were inspecting some item on exhibit rather than his own savaged limb.

Ellie's training kicked in and she rushed over to him, wiping the last of the water from her swollen eyes.

"I seem to have had an accident," Newton mumbled, still eyeing his hand, his voice oddly calm.

Ellie grabbed a tablecloth from under a display of Harry Potter books, spilling the worn hardcovers across the floor. "Hold your arm up," she told him. "You need to keep it above your heart to slow the blood loss." He did as she asked, and Ellie twisted the tablecloth over the wound. "I need your tie," she told him, already working at the knot. She cinched the tie around the bundle as tight as she could get it, knotting it twice.

"Mr. Newton, you still there?"

Sally's voice sounded disembodied, thin and soft. Ellie realized it was coming from the phone receiver; Newton had left it on the table next to the paper cutter. Ellie scooped it up and it on her shoulder. "Sally? It's me, Ellie."

"Oh, thank God! I've been trying to reach you! Phones are down."

Ellie pulled a plastic evidence bag from her pocket and gently began picking up the fingers from next to the paper cutter and dropping them inside. Her stomach groaned, and she choked her breakfast back down. "How did this call get through?"

"*Mobile* phones are down," Sally corrected. "Radios aren't working right, either, but landlines seem to be okay."

Even as she said this, her voice faded out, the line crackled with the same static Ellie had heard on earlier calls. Then she came back. There was some clicking in the background, steady, one click every three or four seconds.

Ellie quickly told her about Ms. Gilmore and what Newton did to his own hand as she retrieved the remains of his index finger and dropped it in the bag. "I need you to have North Hollow dispatch an ambulance. The cuts are clean—if they hurry, they might be able to reattach them." She needed ice to keep the digits cold.

"You best take him up to North Hollow yourself," Sally replied. "I've been trying to get through to them all morning, and I'm getting nothing but busy signals and disconnects. We got two heart attacks, a stabbing out at the Lecassa house, broken leg from a hit-and-run on Mountain View, two dog bites…God knows what else. Every time someone manages to get through to me, the list gets longer, and that's just the medicals. I've taken three calls for fights, someone vandalized the elementary school—spray-painted Nazi whatnot all over the auditorium…Henry Wilburt said someone broke into his pharmacy and cleared half his shelves—didn't take anything, mind you, just dumped everything on the floor, broke what could be broke. Want me to keep going? 'Cause there's more. I got walk-ins, too. People who couldn't get through on the phone coming through the door. Don't got a single empty seat out in the lobby, and half those people are out there arguing. I had to pull Dave Prath off Lou Passani about ten minutes ago over some bullshit about Lou parking his work truck in the street in front of Dave Prath's house overnight. Crossed the property line by three inches and set him off. On a public street, mind you. Like Prath just wanted a reason to bitch."

Ellie tried to wrap her head around all that. The list Sally rattled off was longer than all the incidents they'd had in the Bend over the last year, maybe the last two. They'd never had much crime. None of this made sense. "What are you seeing on the wire? Is this happening everywhere?"

"Wire system's been down all morning, crashed with the phones. Cable's out, too."

Phones, television, internet…those services all came from a company called BroadNet. They maintained the cell tower, too; maybe they had some central hub down.

"Is Buck out on Main clearing out the dead birds? He might know how to get us back up."

"Haven't seen or heard from Buck, and not for lack of trying, believe you me." She huffed.

Ellie blinked her eyes a few times. Most of the pain was gone, but her left eye still burned. "Okay, has Matt—"

"Are you listening to me?" Sally barked angrily. "I can't get through to anyone! No hospital. No ambulance. No you. No Matt. The fact that we're talking at all is some kind of fluke. You need to get that man to the hospital yourself, then get back here. Matt, too. This town is coming apart, and it feels like I'm here all alone in the thick of it!"

Arwa Gilmore started to come to. She let out a soft groan, rolled her head, and studied the zip ties Ellie had used to fasten her to the chair before finding her across the room. "You need to let me go, Sheriff. I've got work to do."

"You need to sit tight," Ellie replied.

"Sit tight?!? How about I take the rest of the day off? How would you like that?!" Sally shouted back her.

"I was talking to Ms. Gilmore, Sally, not you. I would never—"

"You start shitting on me too, and I'll walk. Don't think I won't."

Ellie was seriously beginning to regret getting out of bed today. "Okay, I'll run Mr. Newton up to North Hollow, then I'll head to the station. If you manage to reach Matt, tell him to come in, too. We'll regroup and figure this thing out. Think you can hold down the fort until then?"

There was a long silence, then: "Tell the med center to send at least three ambulances back with you. We need help."

Ellie went to reply and realized Sally had either hung up or the line had disconnected. She told herself it was the latter. Even when she was aggravated, she'd never known Sally to shirk her duties.

She took Newton by the arm and started leading him toward the door. "Let's get you some help."

"Hey! You can't leave me like this!" Gilmore shouted. She yanked her arms up against the ties hard enough to rock the chair.

Ellie reached down to the pile of books soaked in lighter fluid, plucked out one of the Dr. Seuss titles, and tossed it into the woman's lap. "Read that till I get back."

27

HANNAH

A SPLIT SECOND AFTER the window shattered and the hole appeared in Danny's forehead, Hannah heard the gunshot. A thin *pop!*— nothing like in the movies or on television. More like a firecracker or kid's toy, and that's what she wanted it to be—in that milli-second she tried to convince herself what she heard wasn't the blast of a gun, the hole in Danny's head wasn't real, and this was all some kind of elaborate prank. For that millisecond, everything moved in slow motion. She waited for the half smile on Danny's face to complete, for him to laugh, for him to tell her, *I got you!*

Danny didn't, though. Instead, he fell forward, his head cracked hard against her temple, and he went still.

"Danny?"

Hannah managed the single word, but nothing else came out. There was nothing but her shallow breathing and Ed Sheeran singing "Bad Habits" from the tinny speakers of Danny's Ford. No sound came from Danny, and that's when she realized it was real.

"Oh my God, Danny!"

Hannah tried to sit up, get out from under him, but he weighed too much and dead—

Please don't let him be dead!

—or not, she wasn't about to roll him off the seat to the floor. The sound of that, that thump, would be too much.

"Danny, baby, please wake up!"

"I'm afraid…he's not gonna do that."

The voice came from somewhere outside the car, a slight drawl to it, as if whoever spoke considered each word and was careful to enunciate every syllable before allowing them past his lips.

With Danny's weight pressing down on her, Hannah twisted her head around, tried to see outside the car, but she spotted nothing through the missing window where the shot had originated, and the others were covered in a thin sheen of steam. Ed Sheeran was still droning on, and Hannah wished to God she could turn it off, but she couldn't reach the radio or her phone. She forced her voice to work. "Who the hell are you?! What do you want?"

"I want you, Hannah. I have for a very long time. I'm thrilled you found your way to me, today of all days."

Hannah knew that voice but couldn't quite place it. Familiar, yet not.

A dark shadow drifted over the rear window, gone as quickly as it appeared.

A thick black fly crawled in through the open window and perched upside down on the headliner, looked down at her while rubbing its wiry legs together. It was rare to see them in the fall. They usually died off by July. This one was so fat it might have broken the odds and lived far longer than it should. It jumped from the headliner to Danny's head, and Hannah shooed it away.

"I used to see you, Hannah, out running after school. Nearly every day, you were always so disciplined about it. I'd see you and think, *Man, if God created women on the sixth day, he invented yoga pants on the seventh*. You running along in those tight black pants and skimpy sports bra kept me going through the rough days. Like a shot in the arm, directly from heaven. No matter how bad it got, I knew you'd be out on that sidewalk around four-thirty to make things all better. You even waved at me once, about six months ago, but I don't think you recognized me. Not then. I'm curious if you remember me at all."

The shadow rolled across the car again, and he appeared in the missing window. Gray overalls, covered in grease stains both old and new. She didn't see his face until he crouched down, took off a faded Red Sox cap, and scratched his head.

Malcolm Mitchell.

The name just came to her. He dropped out of high school last fall at the start of his senior year. She didn't know why, they hadn't talked, weren't friends or anything. He was just some guy who was in the halls at school, until the day he wasn't. He vanished from her thoughts as quickly as he'd vanished from Hollow High.

Several more black flies appeared. Two landed on his shoulder; another was in his hair. Malcolm didn't seem to notice them. He grinned in at her, a smile made of crooked yellow teeth. "You do remember me! I can see it in your eyes. Imagine that, Hannah Hernandez actually knows who I am." He reached through the open window, unlocked the door, and pulled it open. "I need you to get out of the car."

Hannah didn't move. Not only because Danny was still lying on top of her, but because nothing about her body wanted to work. It was like she was frozen, watching this in some bad dream, but unable to react.

Malcolm grabbed both of Danny's legs, gave him a hard twist, and rolled him to the floor. The smile never left Malcolm's face. It broadened when he spotted the corner of Hannah's discarded bra on the floor under Danny. "Sorry I interrupted. I bet you're all worked up, huh?"

Hannah didn't answer that. She couldn't.

One of the black flies skittered across Malcolm's cheek, crawled over his ear, and vanished inside. He didn't seem to notice that, either.

She swallowed the scream before it could get out.

Malcolm's slow gaze traveled from her bare feet up every inch of her body, came to rest on her eyes. "I originally planned to snatch you off the sidewalk, 'bout four months ago. Had duct tape in my car, parked along your usual route, even unlocked my door when I saw you coming up the street. I chickened out, though. I actually pissed myself, and I think the courage went out right along with it. Time just wasn't right, not for either of us." He smiled that yellow grin. "I'm glad I waited a beat. You got four months of dedicated foreplay in my head. We're gonna have ourselves a party."

Malcolm gripped her ankles and pulled her toward him, pulled her out of the car with impossible strength. On the way out, Hannah's head cracked against the seat, the bottom of the metal door frame, then the asphalt, and her world went black.

28

RILEY

RILEY SANCHEZ STARED DOWN at the drain in the kitchen sink.

She knew she heard it, some weird scratching noise deep in the pipe, but it only did it once.

She ran the water till the basin started to fill, even flicked the garbage disposal switch—let it grind away at nothing for a few seconds—then turned it back off and waited.

But the sound didn't come back.

A few hollow drips, then nothing.

Maybe she imagined it.

Who knows.

The internet had gone down about ten minutes ago, and the second that happened, the house got crazy quiet. Like some big monster sucked all the air out of the place through an open window. Riley had been watching *Umbrella Academy*, and Vanya froze midsentence. Unmoving, she was still up on the screen, but half her face was missing; the image had gone to a pixilated mess of tiny squares.

Riley unplugged the router just like her mom had shown her, counted to ten, and plugged it back in. The little light had gone from solid red to flashing yellow when she heard the scratching.

Imagined the scratching, she told herself. *Duh.*

Because things don't live in the pipes.

Alligators in the sewers, snakes in the toilet. Those things only happened in the movies or on the internet, not in real life.

But what if something was in there? Maybe crawled in last night and couldn't get out. Worse yet, what if it could?

She picked up her phone to text her mom, then dropped it back on the counter.

No.

She was acting stupid.

Acting like a baby.

There was nothing in the sink, and it's not like the power went out, only the internet. What could her mom do, anyway?

Riley knew exactly what her mom would do. She'd stop letting Riley stay home alone when she was working at the diner. That's what she'd do. She'd have her abuela drive in from Barton and stay with her like last year, or worse—pay Patty Norhouse to babysit again. Patty was fourteen, only four years older than Riley. It's not like she watched her. She didn't even play with her. Whenever Patty came over, she spent the whole time on the couch texting her boyfriend. She only—

Scritch, scritch, scratch.

Riley's heart thumped.

Okay, that time she heard it for sure, and it came from the drain.

Came from the drain *for sure*.

Riley leaned forward and looked in the sink, saw nothing but her cereal bowl from this morning filled with milky water, the handle of her spoon sticking out, and the dark maw of the drain beside it. The black rubber, still glistening from the water she'd

113

run and slightly gummy with mac and cheese from last night's dinner. Her mom dumped everything down the disposal.

Maybe whatever's scratching is still hungry.

The second *that* thought popped into her head, Riley wanted it to go away.

Her mom was always telling her she had a good imagination—her teachers, too. Sometimes that was good, other times it was bad, and right now, it was decidedly bad. Whatever this was, there was a reason for it, something silly, and if she let it scare her, it would be her own fault.

Riley reached for her phone, ignored the fact that she was shaking, and switched on the flashlight.

Held it over the drain.

Played the light around the hole.

She couldn't see much.

Couldn't really see anything.

Because there's nothing to see, she told herself.

Scratch, scritch.

She fumbled the phone, nearly dropped it.

Okay, that was real, and it was loud. It was right near the top.

Whether she could see it or not, it was right there.

Without taking her eyes off the drain, Riley reached over and hit the garbage disposal switch.

Nothing happened.

Of course not, because that's how these things worked. She'd seen enough horror movies to know the garbage disposal didn't work when it was supposed to, then someone would stick their hand down the drain, and it would roar to life. Chew them up. She wasn't an idiot.

That particular realization made her feel good, made her feel strong. Real or not, she wasn't going to let this scare her. She was going to deal with it. And when her mom came home, she'd tell her how she handled it. Handled it like a grown-up, not some spooked kid.

Riley switched off the garbage disposal, then reached under the cabinet and unplugged it for good measure. Then, with her flashlight above the drain, she took her spoon from her cereal bowl and stabbed it down into the hole. Wiggled it around, beat it against the sides. When it caught on the blades, she yanked it out and shoved the handle down in there—if something was down inside, she'd either kill it or run it off, send it scurrying down the pipe to wherever all the gunk in the sink went. It could find someone else's sink to call home.

"Screw you!" she yelled, and that felt good, too.

Felt good to let it out, so she yelled again.

When she finally stopped, she was out of breath.

She dropped the spoon on the counter, leaned over the sink, and listened.

Silence.

That brought a grin.

Her mom couldn't have handled that any better. Her abuela or Patty Norhouse, either.

A minute passed with nothing.

Riley switched off the flashlight and was ready to go and tackle the internet problem when she saw it.

Something was swimming in her cereal bowl.

29

MATT

MATT SHOVED THROUGH THE door of the sheriff's station with Eisa Heaton under his left arm and tugged Josh Tatum by the handcuffs on his right. All three froze as they stepped inside.

The small space was packed with people.

The chairs under the front windows were full; other people were standing. Voices shouted to be heard over each other. Ed McDougal was holding a package of frozen peas over his right eye as he argued with his neighbor, Ben Molton, jabbing his finger into the man's chest. Stacy and Tracy Bergman, identical twin sisters married to twin brothers, both clutched pairs of screaming infants in their arms as they shouted at each other, red-faced. Conner Evans had one arm snaked up through the flimsy plastic door of the snack vending machine and was beating on the side with his other hard enough to rock it on its feet.

When the crowd spotted Matt, the voices went quiet for a quick moment, then they all started shouting at once, coming at him. Across the room, he spotted Sally standing behind her desk, phone pressed to her ear. She raised an empty palm in some kind of surrender and shook her head in disbelief before turning back to her desktop and scribbling feverishly in her call log.

"I'll be with you all in a second!" Matt shouted over the voices. "I need everybody to be patient!"

That only made things worse. The yelling grew louder. Everyone was on their feet, angrily shoving toward him.

"I've been waitin' the better part of an hour!"

"Someone stole my car!"

"This asshole killed my dog!" Ed McDougal yelled.

Ben Molton shook a bloody arm at Matt. "His damn dog tried to take my arm off!"

"Enough!" Matt shouted over all of them. "I'm not helping anyone unless they've got their butt planted firmly in a seat and their mouth shut. You want to act like a toddler, take it outside. This isn't the place for it!"

Matt didn't mean for the words to come out as harsh as they did. His voice barely sounded like his own. For a quick second, he was reminded of his father, the angry drunken shouts that came before the hitting started. And when he snapped from that reverie, he realized he'd squeezed his eyes shut against a fist that hadn't found him in more than twenty years—his father had driven into a tree on his way home from the Black Moose Tavern—no seat belt, died on impact.

The room had gone quiet again, all eyes still on him.

"Where's Ellie?" McDougal barked before someone else could speak. "Why isn't she here?"

Matt shook off the memory and looked over at Sally; her back was turned, and she was shouting into her phone. He turned back to the older man and lowered his voice. "Take a seat, Ed. I'll be with you right after I deal with this." He lifted Josh's cuffed hands. Ed McDougal seemed to notice Josh Tatum and Eisa Heaton for the first time. His eyes fixed on the blood droplets on the side of Eisa's face, then glared at Josh.

Before he could start asking questions, Matt steered Eisa and Josh through the crowd toward the cell at the back of the room.

When Josh saw where Matt was leading him, he dug his heels in the ground. "No way, I'm not going in there!"

Matt gave him a gentle push forward through the door. "It's only until we figure things out."

Eisa Heaton didn't protest. He led her to the back of the cell and helped her sit on the bunk. He leaned forward and whispered, "This is for your own safety, Ms. Heaton. Just sit tight for me, okay?"

Her head bobbed softly in what might have been a nod, but she said nothing.

He gave her forearm a reassuring squeeze and turned back to Josh. "Let me see those cuffs." As Matt worked the key into the lock and removed them, he said, "Ellie told me to call Harvey Cooper for you. It's best you don't talk to anyone until he gets here, understand?"

The sullen look returned to Josh's face. "I would never hurt Lynn or the kids. Never."

"I know," Matt told him, even though he knew no such thing. "There's one other thing I need to do, and you won't like it, but it's to protect us both."

Josh frowned. "What?"

Matt Mirandized him.

Tears were streaming down the side of Josh's face by the time he finished. He couldn't look at him anymore as he stepped out of the cell and locked the door.

At the very least, that settled the crowd into a nervous silence. All eyes were on Josh and Eisa as Matt made his way over to Sally's desk.

"I'll get someone out," she said to whoever she was talking

to before hanging up and glaring at Matt. "What the fuck is going on?"

Matt could only shake his head. "Where is Ellie?"

"We got no radios or cell service, so I've been tracking her car on GPS." She looked at him accusingly. "*Yours* isn't working." There was a map on one of her computer monitors, and she pointed at a red dot. "Ellie's stopped out on 112 near Lower Falls."

"What's she doing back out there? Isn't that where she found the abandoned car this morning?"

"I don't know why she stopped. She's supposed to be taking Mr. Newton to the hospital in North Hollow."

Matt frowned. "Stork? What happened to him?"

Sally told him.

Matt's body tensed with each word. When she finished, he made sure nobody could hear them and said, "I've got Norman Heaton's body in the trunk of my car."

Sally's phone was ringing, and every line flashed with calls on hold, but she ignored all of that. Her face went white as she looked from him to Eisa Heaton sitting in the back of the cell, then to Josh standing at the bars looking out. "Did one of them…"

"Eisa killed Norman, right in front of me and Josh…" Matt said quietly before telling her the rest.

By the time he finished, her eyes were glassy with tears and her hand was pressed to her mouth.

"Listen," he said quietly, "I can't leave Norman's body in my car. I'm going to take him over to the coroner's office, then come right back and help you deal with all these people, okay?"

She nodded, although she didn't look okay. She looked like she was on the verge of a nervous breakdown.

He gripped one of her trembling hands and pressed it between both of his. "I need you to do something else. Free up a phone line and try to reach the sheriff's office in Jackson. If you can't get them, try the feds. Get us help. I don't care who. National guard, if you have to." He didn't turn around. It felt like if he did and he made eye contact with just one of them, he'd be applying a spark to a powder keg. "If these people turn on us, we're seriously outnumbered."

"They're our friends," she breathed.

"Not today." Matt had been thinking that for the better part of an hour, and it somehow felt good to say it out loud. "I'm not sure what's gotten into everybody, but it's getting worse fast."

Sally let that sink in, then nodded toward Ellie's office. "What about her?"

Matt followed her eyes through the open blinds.

Wearing an oversize sweatshirt and jeans from the lost and found, the girl from the diner was sitting across from Ellie's desk, looking out at all the people. Her dark hair covered half her face and left the other half in shadows, yet he felt her gaze shift to him when she realized he was watching her.

"Has she said anything?"

"Not a word."

"Just keep her in there until I get back."

Sally's voice cracked as she said, "What if this is happening everywhere? What if that's why I can't get anyone on the phone?"

"Try," he told her. "I'll be right back."

30

RILEY

IT HAD GRAY SKIN.

Riley only caught a glimpse of what might have been its back before whatever was in her cereal bowl vanished again in the milky water. She watched for bubbles, signs of something breathing, but there were none. Whatever it was didn't come up for air.

"Okay, that didn't happen."

It did, though. Even as she said the words, the tiny ripples in the milky water worked their way out to the edge of the bowl, bounced back, and slowly faded to nothing. Riley stared until the water went still, unwilling to blink or breathe, forcing every ounce of her being to not move and betray the fact that she was there because her gut told her if she did, that tiny gray thing would leap up and attack. It would go for her mouth or her eye and burrow deep. That's what things like that did. The same horror movies that taught her about garbage disposals taught her that, too. It would get inside her, eat its way to her brain, and take over like in that book by Jack Finney; she'd read that one last summer.

No way she'd become an alien zombie—she'd kill it.

Riley tightened her grip on the spoon, eased it toward the bowl, and tapped the side.

Nothing.

She swallowed and tapped again, hit the bowl hard; jostled it. Nothing moved.

It's all in your head, Riley.

Then she saw it again, just a glimpse, but there it was—maybe an inch long, gray, just below the water's surface. It quickly circled the outer rim of the bowl and vanished again in the murk. Whatever *that* was, it wasn't alone—the scratching from the drain returned, frantic and fast, like something desperately wanted out, took a running start, and didn't make it all the way up.

Riley was trying to wrap her head around all that when her phone dinged with an incoming text—she yelped, honest-to-God yelped. Her stomach jumped and she fell to the floor, twisting away from the sink and counter when her body decided it was time to go without clearing the motion with the rest of her. On her way down, her fingers caught the edge of her phone, not enough to grip it, but enough to send it spinning over the side of the counter to the tile floor. It hit facedown with a nasty crunching noise Riley had heard before, and when she managed to scoop it up, the message appeared behind a web of cracks:

ARE YOU ALONE?

All caps from a number she didn't recognize.

Riley barely had time to process that when her bowl clattered in the sink above her, like it jumped. Like something hit it from below.

She'd left the cabinet door beneath the sink open when she unplugged the garbage disposal, and her eyes landed on a tiny red nub at the base of the machine. Riley knew *exactly* what that was, because her mom complained about it all the time—some kind of safety circuit breaker or something. It tripped whenever her mom tried to put too much down the drain. It was sticking out now, and that was the reason the disposal hadn't worked the second time she hit the switch.

Riley moved fast, because she knew if she didn't, she'd think about what she was about to do and whatever courage she managed to muster would vanish as quickly as it appeared.

Reaching under the sink, she fumbled the plug back into the outlet, then she pressed the reset button on the bottom of the disposal. She expected it to pop back out (sometimes it did that), but when it didn't, she got back to her feet and leaned over the sink.

The milky water in the bowl was a wild frenzy, the gray—monster, fish, alien, whatever-the-hell—swimming in quick circles, following the outer rim.

Riley reached in and flipped the bowl—spun it hard enough to crack it in half on the side of the sink—milk, water, and that *thing* splashed out, circled the drain, and vanished, but not before she got a quick look at it—its skin glistened, like it was covered in oil. Worm-like. It was gone fast, but she didn't see any eyes, feet, flippers, nothing like that. It did look like it had gills on the sides and this ugly little mouth she knew was probably full of sharp teeth, although she saw nothing like that.

Riley slammed the back of her fist into the garbage disposal switch hard enough to crack the plastic plate.

The motor ground to life with a sickening chew, the crunch of small bones, and Riley didn't know if that was the gray thing, whatever was scratching in the pipes, or something else, and she didn't much care. She turned the water on full, as hot as it would go, watched the steam rise. She let it all run for nearly a minute before finally turning everything back off.

She couldn't bring herself to look in the sink.

No way.

Her back against the cabinet, Riley dropped to the floor again and waited for the tears to come, but she didn't even get a chance to do that—her busted phone dinged with another message.

WE KNOW YOU'RE IN THERE—ARE YOU ALONE?!?

31

MATT

EVEN THOUGH IT WOULD have been a straight shot down Main, Matt took side streets to the coroner's office at the rear of Furber's Funeral Home and backed his cruiser in the space between two hearses near the narrow loading dock at the rear of the building. The last thing he needed was someone spotting him as he unloaded the lifeless body of Norman Heaton from the trunk of his car.

At the top of the ramp, he went to the double doors and pressed the buzzer.

When there was no answer, he pressed it again.

Matt glanced around nervously. "Come on, Ger."

Gerald Furber lived alone in the three-bedroom apartment above the funeral home, same place he grew up. Forty-seven now, he'd never married. He'd inherited the family business when his parents passed and tended to keep to himself. He'd once told Matt he preferred the company of the dead over the stupidity of the living. Unsure how to respond to that, Matt hadn't said anything at all, but he was fairly certain he understood why the man was still single.

When nearly a minute went by, Matt tried the door and found it unlocked.

He stuck his head inside and called out, "Ger? You in there? It's Matt."

Wired to motion sensors, overhead fluorescents ticked on down the length of the hallway, filling the space with harsh bright light and a low buzz. Several steel gurneys lined the wall on the left; Matt grabbed one and wheeled it back to his car.

After another look around, he opened the trunk.

Still wrapped in the blue tarp, Norman Heaton had shifted slightly and his legs had caught under the tire jack fastened to the side wall. It took a moment for Matt to wrestle him free, longer still to lift him from the trunk to the gurney, and by the time Matt finished, he was sweating.

He wheeled the gurney up the ramp and back through the doors, half expecting to find Gerald Furber waiting for him inside. The hallway was still empty, though.

Matt reached around to the buzzer and pressed it three more times. He knew it rang in the coroner's office, the funeral parlor, and the residence upstairs. Unless Gerald was in the shower or something, he would have heard it. He didn't own a car, only the two hearses, and with both in the lot out back, he couldn't have gone far.

Still nothing.

He couldn't wait on him—not with all the craziness happening around town. He'd get Norman tucked away in the freezer and track down Gerald later.

Following the hallway, Matt maneuvered the gurney to the exam room on the far end.

As in the hall, the lights came on automatically.

Large and with white tile covering the floor and extending up the walls, the room was bright. The light glistened off the various metal surfaces. There was an exam table in the center, designed to drain down into the floor. The counter to Matt's right was filled with neatly arranged tools and trays. There was a video camera and several scales, a box of latex gloves, and matching gowns. The cabinets were filled with bottles and gallons of various chemicals ranging from bleach to fluids with names Matt couldn't pronounce any more than he wanted to understand their purpose. Although meticulously clean, the space smelled harsh, and Gerald kept it so cold Matt wouldn't be surprised if he saw his breath. As cold as the room was, Matt knew from bringing in past bodies it wasn't cold enough to preserve a corpse. He couldn't leave Norman Heatón out here; he had to put him in one of the lockers at the back.

There were fifteen in total, three rows of five. Several had names written on tape in Gerald's neat script; the rest were empty. Matt positioned the gurney next to one of the doors on the second row and tugged it open with the heavy handle. Cold air rushed out in an icy cloud. Matt shivered, vaguely remembering Gerald told him once bodies were stored at fourteen degrees Fahrenheit.

He pulled out the large tray, positioned the wheeled gurney next to it, adjusted the height, and slid Norman over with a grunt. He debated whether he should remove the tarp, then decided he'd leave that to Gerald on the off chance it was preserving some kind of evidence.

Matt couldn't imagine this going to some kind of trial—Eisa had killed her husband in full view of at least half a dozen people, including himself. When the time came, she'd either plead guilty or claim some kind of temporary insanity, most definitely self-defense. Whatever happened, this would never go to trial.

He pushed the tray holding Norman back inside the drawer, closed the door, and went over to the counter to write a note for Gerald. He was about halfway down the page when he heard moaning coming from behind him.

32

RILEY

RILEY STARED DOWN AT the cracked screen of her phone, the message—

WE KNOW YOU'RE IN THERE—ARE YOU ALONE?!?

Not only did she have no idea who sent it, but the meaning of the word *WE* wasn't lost on her. From the sink above her, a soft gurgle rolled from the pipes, and Riley let out a breath she hadn't known she was holding. With two shaky thumbs, she typed out a reply. Only five words, but she had to backspace and fix typos three times before she got it right:

No, my mom is here.

Riley clicked over to the home screen and opened a browser window, typed in some random letters, and hit search. If text messages were coming in, maybe the internet was back, but the window only hung there for about ten seconds with the progress bar creeping across the screen and freezing at about the midway point before returning a **page cannot be displayed** message. Riley hit refresh and got the same thing. She was about to dial her mom when the phone dinged with another text:

LIAR. WE SAW HER AT THE DINER.

We again. Riley's heart thumped, and she felt the hairs on the back of her neck stand up.

Highlighting the phone number with her thumb, Riley copied and pasted it into Google, hoping to find out who it belonged to, but she only received another internet error.

That made no sense. If the internet was down, how was she getting text messages? Maybe those things came from a different part of the internet?

From her spot on the kitchen floor, she could see the corner of the television in the other room. Most of Vanya's pixelated face was gone now. Internet still down for sure. She quickly typed:

She came home early. She's right here.

Riley barely hit Send when the reply came back—

LIAR!!!

A second later—

YOU NEED TO COME OUTSIDE OR WE'RE COMING IN

Riley barely processed the words when something struck the kitchen window above her head.

33

MATT

MATT HADN'T IMAGINED THAT—someone moaned.

He thumbed the leather strap on his holster and noiselessly withdrew his service weapon. With his finger resting on the trigger guard, he held the gun at his side and listened.

The room had gone quiet.

The harsh chemicals lofting through the air were giving him a headache, making him dizzy. The cold air didn't help. Only a few minutes ago, it was a dull throb behind his temples, but it was quickly growing worse. He'd gotten migraines in the past, and this was well on its way. Today of all days, exactly what he needed.

He tried to will it away, and heard another groan.

Faint.

Eyes open.

The bright lights felt like a smack in the face.

Matt cleared his throat. "Ger? That you?"

No reply.

This is an old building, his mind muttered. *Probably just the pipes.*

Then he heard it again.

Deep, guttural. Louder this time.

Not the pipes.

Without raising his weapon, Matt turned toward the sound and found himself facing the wall of lockers.

34

RILEY

RILEY'S HEAD SWIVELED UP and she glared at the window. There was a smudge in the top right corner of the glass, dark red, looked like blood, and a small crack a few inches long. She hadn't seen whatever struck, but it didn't sound like something hard. Instead, it sounded muffled, heavy, like a bag filled with something wet.

Riley's legs didn't want to work, but she forced them to. She slowly climbed to her feet and peered out the corner of the glass, careful not to expose any more of herself than she had to.

Three small figures were standing on the sidewalk in front of her house, deep in the shadows of the Millers' red maple. Kids, no taller than her. She couldn't see their faces, but she could make out that much. One was holding a baseball bat, resting on it like a cane. Looked like a boy, but Riley couldn't be sure. The middle one wore a blue-and-white sundress, one she recognized. Riley couldn't see the girl's face, but she was certain that was Evelyn Harper. She was a year older than Riley, should have been a sixth grader, but got held back in kindergarten for missing too many days. She picked on Riley and half the other girls at Hollows Bend Elementary; she wore that same dress at least once each week, sometimes twice. The third was short, probably Evelyn's eight-year-old little brother, Robby. He got in trouble last year for bringing a dead cat to school in his backpack. He told everyone it got hit by a car, but Evelyn let it slip he beat it with a hammer in the vacant yard behind their house. Nobody believed her; Robby wasn't like that. Either way, he got suspended for a week. He had the same backpack with him, resting against his leg, his hand twisted around the strap.

Evelyn stepped forward, peeled from the shadows of the large maple, and glared back at Riley, her head at an odd angle.

35

MATT

SEVERAL OF THE LOCKERS were labeled, names written on masking tape in Gerald's neat script. The moan had come from the locker on the bottom left—untagged—supposed to be empty.

This time, Matt *did* raise his gun. He eased his finger over the trigger guard as he stepped to the locker and knelt.

When he pressed his ear to the cold stainless steel he heard it again.

Faint this time, but definitely coming from inside.

With his free hand, Matt reached for the heavy latch and tugged. The lock disengaged, and the door swung open with a belch of frigid air. The drawer slid out as effortlessly as the one on which he'd placed Norman, only this one wasn't empty—

Fully dressed, his impossibly pale skin covered in a layer of white frost, his teeth chattering, was Gerald Furber.

The tips of his fingers were bloody, and three of his nails were gone. Red streaks lined the sides of the stainless-steel drawer. There were droplets on his shirt, too, and Matt knew if he were to look inside, the ceiling of that drawer would be red. He had no idea for how long, but Gerald had tried to claw his way out and failed.

Several seconds slipped by, and Matt only stared because what he was looking at didn't seem real, couldn't possibly be real. Then his grip tightened on his gun and he looked back toward the hallway, at the stairs leading up to the residence beyond that. "Ger, is somebody else here? Who put you in there?"

The coroner looked up at Matt with unblinking eyes, unnaturally wide. A sound escaped his lips, barely a whisper, and Matt had to lean down to hear him.

"...hiding. Got locked...in..."

"Hiding from who?"

Gerald's tongue slithered out between his clicking teeth and licked his chapped lips, this dead-looking gray thing that had no business in the body of the living, as if it had already crossed over and had been waiting for the rest of Gerald's body to join it.

"They don't like...what I do to them after...they pass. They're angry...with me. They're..."

He turned his head to the side and coughed. Mucus bubbled at his nose. When he turned back to face Matt, his eyes rolled up toward the locker directly above him, labeled MILLER. "I only wanted to be close to her. Didn't...didn't want to say good-bye... yet, but that made the others mad. Always...quiet. Quiet...until today..."

Miller was Aubrey Miller. Thirty-one. She'd died from a brain aneurysm two days ago. Her husband had found her dead on the kitchen floor. Ellie had taken that call and waited with Aubrey's husband until Gerald arrived with the hearse and brought her back here.

Matt slipped his gun back in the holster and tried to understand. "What others? What did you do?"

Gerald Furber licked his lips again. "She was so..."

Pretty.

The word popped into Matt's head only because Ellie had mentioned it. She said Gerald had taken a look at the dead woman's eyes with a penlight and immediately knew the COD, he'd seen it before—burst vessels in the left, no longer facing the same direction as her right eye, but instead pointed off to the side. He'd still perform an autopsy to confirm his theory, but he seemed absolutely certain. *She was so pretty*, Gerald had told Ellie. *It was a shame to cut her up.* It wasn't the words that bothered Ellie as much as the way he stroked Aubrey Miller's hair as he said them, the way he spoke, as if Ellie weren't in the room. As if she were a voyeur looking in on some private moment.

The revulsion flooded through every inch of Matt's body. He leaned closer to the shivering man. "Did you do something with...to...Aubrey's body?"

Gerald didn't answer.

He didn't have to.

Matt could see it in the coroner's face.

They don't like...what I do to them after...they pass, Gerald had said. *They're angry with me.*

Gerald sat up, jerked upright so quickly his head smacked against Matt's jaw with a painful crack. "They're coming for me... every last one of them...it's not safe here! Don't you hear them? *DON'T YOU HEAR THEM?!*"

Pain shot up through Matt's jawbone, where his teeth had cracked together, stunned him. If not for that, he might have gotten a better grip on the man before Gerald rolled off the side of the metal tray and dropped to the tile floor.

"Gerald, don't—"

Matt grabbed for him, but the coroner shuffled out of reach, his bloody fingers leaving dark smears on the otherwise pristine white tile floor.

"They want to take me!" Gerald shouted. "Bring me back with

them! Make me answer for what I—" His voice cut off abruptly. His beady eyes locked on the door behind Matt. Still trembling, either from cold or fright, he raised his hand and pointed over Matt's shoulder with a bony finger. "Tell her she can't have me! I didn't mean to hurt her! Stop her, Matt! *STOP HER!*"

Matt spun around, his hand back on his gun, and found no one.

They were alone.

"Ger, you need to calm down!" Matt told him. "I think the cold is making you—"

"Delusional? Crazy?" He shook his bloody finger. "She's right there!" On wobbly legs he rose, stumbled, then steadied himself against the gurney Matt had used to bring in Norman Heaton. "Get back, Aubrey! I'm sorry! I'm so sorry!"

With whatever strength he could muster, Gerald Furber pushed the gurney forward. It shot across the exam room, bounced off the edge of the door frame, and rocketed back toward Matt. Matt caught it, but not before it blocked his path as the coroner ran from the room. By the time Matt reached the hallway, Gerald was at the front door of the funeral parlor, fumbling the locks with bloody hands. "She's right behind you!"

There was nobody behind Matt. He bolted down the hallway, but by the time he reached the door, it was open and Gerald was thirty feet down the sidewalk, his body jerking and stuttering like a car that didn't want to start.

Matt would have chased after him if he had not seen Gabby standing kitty-corner across the street, in front of the now deserted Stairway Diner. Someone had managed to get plywood up over the broken windows. Gabby had her phone pressed to her ear, her face lined with concern.

When she spotted Matt, she waved him over. "Riley's not answering!"

36

LOG 10/16/2023 21:18 GMT-4
TRANSCRIPT: AUDIO/VIDEO RECORDING

Sordello: Was he hallucinating, or do you believe he actually saw a dead person?

Maro: Seriously? What kind of question is that?

Analysis Note: A 16.9 fl oz bottle of water was provided to the subject. He drank approximately two-thirds before setting it aside. No change in his vitals either before or after.

Sordello: I'm simply asking for your opinion.

Maro: I think he *believed* he saw a dead person, but there was nobody there. He was clearly traumatized, possibly on something. I didn't get much of a chance to investigate. If I had to guess, it was probably from the cold of being in that locker, the start of hypothermia. Hallucinations are common when overexposed to extreme cold.

Sordello: That wouldn't explain what caused him to climb into the locker in the first place.

[*Silence*]

Maro: I'm sorry, was that a question?

Sordello: You appear to be getting agitated, Deputy. Are you okay to continue, or would you prefer to take a break?

Maro: [*Waves hand in air*] I want this over. Let's keep going.

Analysis Note: Sordello removes the stack of folders from the pass-through and replaces them with the file on the coroner, Gerald Furber. She slides the carrier forward, allows Maro to retrieve the folder.

Sordello: Prior to relocating to Hollows Bend, the man you know as Gerald Furber lived in Aurora, Illinois, under the name Benjamin Kramer. He worked in the coroner's office for the better part of two years and was released from duty when it was discovered he was having sex fairly regularly with the bodies that came in. Two or three times per week. Young females...mostly.

Maro: [*Retrieves file*] That's not possible. Furber grew up in the

Bend. He lived in that house his entire life. Inherited the business when his father passed.

Sordello: I have no reason to lie to you. There's video. That's how he was caught. And his prints are on file. Staff at the coroner's office are required to be registered with the state. There's no mistake. It was him.

Maro: [*Removes a page from the folder and presses it against the glass, his finger indicating the top left corner*] Then how do you explain this? It can't be him.

Sordello: We'll get to that. When Ms. Sanchez told you she was having trouble reaching her daughter, how did that make you feel?

Maro: Are you psychoanalyzing me now?

Sordello: You were on duty, Deputy. The proper course of action upon exiting the coroner's building would be to return to the sheriff's office and regroup with your superior, but you didn't do that, did you? Instead, you went with your girlfriend. *One* of your girlfriends.

Maro: Gabby *is* my girlfriend, not one of them. There is nobody else. Let's be clear on that. And Ellie would have done the same thing.

Sordello: That doesn't make it right.

[*Silence*]

37

RILEY

WHEN EVELYN HARPER'S EYES landed on her through the window, Riley dropped to the floor. Which was stupid—she knew Evelyn saw her, the others, too—but every bone in her body told her to hide anyway.

She blindly reached for her phone on the counter, managed to find it, and dialed her mom.

It rang twice, then connected. Riley didn't give her mom a chance to speak. "Mama, I need you to come home! Somebody's outside! A mean girl from school. Remember the one I told you about? It's her. Her, her brother, and someone else. I don't know what they want, but they're right outside, Mama!"

Riley sucked in a breath and waited for her mom to reply, but there was nothing.

"Mama?"

The display said **disconnected**.

She dialed again, and the call didn't go through at all.

Someone knocked on the window.

Knocked hard enough to rattle the glass.

"Let us in, Riley! We need to talk to you."

It was her, Evelyn.

The kitchen door shook a moment later, someone yanking at the knob.

"I called the police!" Riley shouted out.

"Phones don't work right."

This came from outside the kitchen door, a boy's voice.

Evelyn hit the window again. "We just want to talk. Let us in!"

From outside the kitchen door: "I found the key. *Who actually leaves a key under their doormat? That's just stupid.*"

Riley heard the key jiggle in the lock and scrambled to her feet. She was about to run when the door opened. The boy with the baseball bat was standing there—Mason Ridler. A seventh grader who lived two houses down from Evelyn and Robby. He played second base for the Hollows Bend Bobcats. Big for twelve. He'd probably grown a foot since the last time Riley had seen him.

Mason tapped his shoe with the tip of his bat, then raised it up and pointed it toward Riley as if it were an extension of his index finger. "World's going to shit, and you're hiding in your kitchen?"

Robby appeared behind him holding something in his hand.

A dead crow.

Its head hung all wrong, neck broken.

"You got about a dozen of these outside your house," Robby said. "You know that? The only other place we found them was out on Main."

He dropped the bird into his red backpack and closed the flap, as if that were the most normal thing in the world. When he hefted the bag back over his shoulder, it looked heavy. She didn't want to know what else was in there.

Evelyn pushed by both boys and walked right into the kitchen as if it were her house, her eyes fixed angrily on Riley.

"Her mom works at the diner right where all the other birds hit. Got more here. You ask me, that's no coincidence." She stepped closer and pointed at Riley. "You and your mom into some kind of witchcraft? That it? Some hocus-pocus mumbo-jumbo old-world Mexican shit? That's what I think."

Riley tried to back up but had no place to go; the counter was right behind her. Tears bubbled up, but she choked them back. She wasn't about to cry in front of these three, no way. "I don't know what—"

"I don't know what you're talking 'bout," Mason mocked. "Ev, she don't know shit. Look at her; she's a kid. We're wasting our time."

Evelyn took a step closer. "That true, Riley? You didn't do it? Don't know nothing?" She stretched her hand out behind her back toward her brother. "Give me that backpack. Maybe she just needs a closer look."

Robby seemed to like that idea. This ugly grin bent his lip as he started to wiggle the pack off his shoulders.

Riley tried to ignore him and kept her eyes on Evelyn. "If phones are down, how did you text me?"

"Not all things are down. Landlines are still working as long as you don't try to dial outside the Bend. I don't know why texts are going. Some do, some don't." Evelyn gave her an accusing look. "You sure you and your mom didn't start this? My dad says it's got Mexican juju written all over it."

That just made Riley angry. "We're not Mexican. My abuela is from Honduras. My mom grew up in the States, and I was born in Exeter. I don't even speak Spanish."

"Whatever." Evelyn waved a dismissive hand.

Riley eyed the block of kitchen knives on the far side of the counter. She could make it if—

"Oh, give me a break." Evelyn rolled her eyes and took a step closer, blocked her.

The two boys closed on her from the right and left, boxing her in.

Riley tried to keep her voice from cracking. "I don't know anything about birds, but I saw…something."

Evelyn eyed her impatiently. "Oh yeah, what?"

Riley told her.

She knew how crazy it sounded, and talking about it aloud only made it worse, but she told them all about the scratching in the pipes and the thing she saw in the sink.

By the time she finished, both Mason and Robby had flashlights out and were peering down the drain. Evelyn hadn't taken her eyes off her.

"Are you sure?" she said. "People are seeing all sorts of things. How do you know it was real?"

Riley had no proof. She should have taken a picture or something, but she hadn't thought of that.

Mason crouched down, was looking in the cabinet under the sink. "We could take the pipes out. Maybe it's caught in the trap."

"Not if she ran the water that long," Evelyn told him. "It's long gone."

"All chopped up, anyway," Robby pointed out.

Evelyn got right in her face. Her breath smelled like old hot dogs. "Did you get dizzy? A couple hours ago?"

Riley's mouth fell open, then she quickly clamped it shut. She hadn't told anyone about that and didn't plan to. If she told her mom she got dizzy on the stairs and nearly fell, she'd never let her stay home alone again. She shook her head.

"Yeah, she did," Mason said. "Look at her. She's a shitty liar."

Evelyn tilted her head slightly, like a dog studying a new bone. "The whole world went sideways for a second, real fast like, then slowly fixed itself, right? Like standing on a teeter-totter? And things got all quiet, like you were underwater?"

Riley had no idea how the girl knew that, but it was as good a description as any. All three of them were staring at her. Then she understood—it happened to them, too. "What…was it?"

Evelyn's eyes grew narrow. "You're saying it wasn't you or your mom who did it?"

Before Riley could answer, Mason said, "We should search her house. There'd be dead chickens or something. Hoodoo, I think that's what they call it. I bet it's all in the basement. That's where they always do that sort of thing."

"We got plenty of dead birds," Robby pointed out, shaking the pack on his back.

"We don't have a basement," Riley told them, unable to hide the irritation in her voice even if she was scared. "My mom's a waitress. She's been working all morning. And you three are crazy."

Mason pointed the bat back at her. "Hey, watch it."

Evelyn let out another hot dog breath and sighed. "I think she's telling the truth. Look at her. She look like some kind of witch's kid? She's shaking, like she's gonna cry. We're wasting our time here."

"I'm not gonna cry."

"Baby's gonna cry, for sure," Mason chimed in.

"I killed one," Riley threw back at him. "I bet none of you can say that."

"For all we know, you imagined all that."

"Or she's making it up," Robby added.

Riley pointed at the sink. "Or I'm not, and there are more of those things out there. Maybe I'm the only person who's seen one."

Tires squealed loudly outside, and all four of them looked to the window.

"Oh shit, five-oh," Mason muttered, starting for the door. "Let's go, Ev!"

Evelyn didn't move. She remained fixed on Riley. "We should take her with us."

A wave of anxiety rolled over Riley. She didn't like any of them. Evelyn and her brother gave her the creeps. Mason was no better.

Robby shuffled to the door behind Mason, looking like he might buckle under the weight of his backpack. "Mason's right, Ev. Come on!"

The jingle of a key in the front door.

Evelyn gripped Riley by the chin. "You tell them anything, I'll kill you. Understand? What you saw isn't for them. They might be part of it. *Don't trust them*."

Riley forced a nod.

Evelyn ran. She bolted out the kitchen door behind Mason and Robby a moment before Matt and Riley's mom came in from the front.

The tears finally came, and Riley slammed into her mother with enough force to nearly knock her over.

Her mom hugged her so tight she could barely breathe. "It's okay, baby. Mama's got you. We're going to stay with Matt for a little while."

Riley pressed her face into her mother's side, nodded, and let her lead her back to Matt's patrol car at the curb. She helped her climb into the front seat.

None of them saw Mrs. Nguyen.

She surprised all of them.

38

MATT

"YOU PLANNING TO BE that child's new daddy, Deputy Maro? Rather than your own baby?" Mrs. Nguyen called out from across the street.

Asian, in her sixties, she'd grown up somewhere in California and moved to the Bend when her husband was struck by a drunk driver crossing Mulholland outside Santa Monica and confined to a wheelchair. He'd passed away two years ago, some complication related to his spine. She was wearing a wrinkled pink evening gown, barefoot on her lawn. Black eyeliner stained her cheeks. She looked like she'd just returned from a night on the town that had gone horribly wrong.

Matt stared at her, dumbfounded. "Everything okay, Mrs. Nguyen?"

She was holding something in her hand, but Matt couldn't make it out.

"You need to do the right thing by Addie Gallagher. That's what you need to do if you want to make things okay."

"I think you should get back in your house."

Mrs. Nguyen shrugged. "You should stop playing with the help and take responsibility for your mistakes. Addie's child is going to need a father. Its *real* father."

From the corner of his eye, Matt caught a glimpse of Gabby, realized she hadn't gotten in the car. She'd loaded Riley inside and was standing next to the open door. Her eyes were red, rimmed with tears, and her right hand was balled in front of her mouth. It was one thing for her and Matt to talk about the rumors surrounding him and Addie in private; it was another thing entirely to hear one of her neighbors spout it out as fact. There were no secrets in small towns; rumors and gossip spread faster than wildfire. True or not, they still stung.

When Gabby's eyes shifted from Mrs. Nguyen to him, when he saw the hurt there, he wanted to tell her it wasn't true, just like he had every other time it had come up. He wanted to assure her he had been and would continue to be faithful—just like he had every other time it had come up. He wanted to hear her say, *I know*, as she had *every other time it had come up*. But something about the way she looked at him told him she wasn't quite so sure anymore.

Matt turned from her, even though he knew that was a mistake. Guilt pulsed behind his temples, not because the rumor was true, but because his actions subjected Gabby to this. Her life had been hell. She'd been through so much, aside from his mistakes, and she deserved better.

Gabby gasped, and when Matt looked back at Mrs. Nguyen, she was holding a knife.

She raised it to her neck.

Matt started toward her, but she stopped him with a glare. "Not another step, Deputy."

She slipped the blade of the knife under the single shoulder strap of her dress and sliced. The thin fabric gave with little effort, the strap snapped, and the dress fell, pooled at her feet. Mrs. Nguyen stood there, naked.

Matt opened his mouth to say something, but nothing came out.

Mrs. Nguyen gripped a handful of her black and silver hair, pulled it tight, and sawed through it with the blade. She dropped the clump at her feet and went to work on more. "Children who grow up without a father in their life are scarred, broken. Unwanted. Unloved. Life is hard enough when you don't begin the journey with some sort of handicap. Don't ruin that child's life before it starts, Deputy. You owe it more than that. My father left when I was two. I should know."

"You should go inside, Mrs. Nguyen," Matt told her. "Just set the knife down and go inside."

Another chunk of her hair fluttered from her fingers, caught the breeze, and spread out over the lawn. She quickly sliced away more until her pale scalp was visible in several places, until her hair was no longer long enough to grip, then she closed her eyes and raised her face toward the sun. "No, today's not the day to be cooped up inside. I think I'll go for a walk. It's beautiful out, don't you think?"

The knife slipped from her fingers and embedded itself in the ground less than an inch from her foot with a soft *thunk*. The naked woman turned and started down the sidewalk, whistling some song Matt didn't recognize.

A long, silent minute went by before Matt managed to say, "Get in the car, Gabby."

Gabby watched Mrs. Nguyen vanish over the hill about a hundred feet down the road. "Shouldn't we stop her?"

Matt wasn't sure of many things at that moment, but he did understand stopping that woman was the least of their problems. He shook his head. "We need to get back to the station."

39

MATT

THEY DROVE IN SILENCE, Riley sandwiched between them, trembling.

Matt didn't slow until a block before Main Street, and he only slowed because he didn't have a choice. People were jumping in front of his cruiser, trying to stop him. Yelling and beating on the vehicle when he didn't. Even Artie Johnson, all 350 pounds of him; he thundered out from the sidewalk and smacked both meaty palms against the driver-side door. He had a black eye and his nose was bloody, resting at a weird angle, certainly broken. He shouted something about Henry Wilburt, the man who owned the local drugstore, then flipped Matt off and wobbled back to the sidewalk when Matt only shook his head and pressed the button that chirped his cruiser's siren.

"What the hell is happening, Matt?" Gabby said in a voice that might have come from a child. "It's like they're all…"

She didn't finish the sentence, probably for the same reason Matt couldn't complete the thought in his head, not for lack of trying, but he couldn't find a word that fit—

Sick? Infected? Crazy? Angry? Paranoid?

Maybe all of the above. Maybe this couldn't be described with one word.

He was only certain of one thing—it started this morning with the birds. It started when that girl appeared from nowhere.

Hitting the siren one more time to clear the space in front of the sheriff's office, he parked at the curb and killed the motor. From outside, the sounds of all the chaos rolled in—alarms, shouting, a scream in the distance. He could only imagine what was going on inside. Matt turned to Gabby. "When we get in there, I want you and Riley to head straight for my office and lock the door. You don't open for anyone but me, Sally, or Ellie, understand?"

Gabby's eyes were still rimmed with red, but she had moved on to anger. It only grew worse when Addie Gallagher appeared at the front door of the sheriff's office, motioning for Matt to get inside with a frantic wave of her hand.

Gabby looked like she could tear the woman's throat out with her teeth. "No. I don't think I'll do that."

Grabbing Riley by the arm, she started to get out of the car.

Matt stopped her. "Promise me you won't start anything in there."

She snorted out a breath. "Yeah, because *I'm* the problem."

Her daughter held close, Gabby was out the door and inside the building before Matt could respond. He swore under his breath and chased after them.

Addie caught him at the entrance. "Thank God you're back!"

She tried to hug him, and he shrugged her off. "Don't, Addie."

"Don't what?"

"Just don't."

He pushed her out of his way with a little more force than he probably should have used, and that wasn't lost on the people watching him from inside. Those numbers had doubled since he left earlier. Standing room only now. Everyone watching him.

Judging him. Making up their mind about things they couldn't possibly know. Things that were none of their business.

Conner Evans must have lost the battle with the vending machine, because it was lying on its side, the glass shattered. Matt spotted Gabby and Riley hovering over it, Riley picking a Snickers bar from the rubble. He started toward them, but Gabby shook her head and pointed at Ellie's office. At the strange girl sitting calmly in front of Ellie's desk, her back to them.

He realized she was right—he'd smooth things over with Gabby later. Right now, he needed to talk to that girl.

"Matt!" Sally's shrill voice cut through all the others. She shoved her way through the crowd and grabbed him by arm, pulled him toward her desk. "I need to show you something."

"I need to talk to that girl, Sally. I think she knows what's going on."

Sally huffed. "Half the people in here have tried to talk to her. She still hasn't said a word. Got so bad, I had to lock the door. Got worried someone might try to hurt her. She can wait. This is more important."

Matt gave the back of the girl's head another look before following Sally to her desk. A map of the area was loaded on her monitor. "Remember how I said I was tracking Ellie with GPS?"

"Yeah, sure."

She tapped at a pulsing red dot in the top left corner of the screen. "Well, her cruiser hasn't moved since I showed it to you earlier. She's still parked up on 112 near Lower Falls."

Matt frowned. "She didn't take Mr. Newton to the hospital?"

"You listening to me? She hasn't moved, period. Can't get her on the radio. Can't get her on her cell. Her car's been sitting there in the exact same spot for the better part of an hour. She's either broke down, or something worse."

Matt bit his lip. "Have you had any luck getting us some kind of help?"

She shook her head and ticked off two of her fingers. "No cell service. No radios. And get this—best I can tell, landlines only work in town. I can dial someone local and get right through. I dial anything else, I get two rings, the call sounds like it connects, then it drops. Same thing every time."

"What can cause that?"

"This ain't no line down or system outage. Something's got us cut off on purpose," Sally told him. "Watch this—"

She minimized the tracking software and opened a Google search, typed in *best food near me*. That hung for a second, then filled with results.

Matt didn't understand. "So the internet is back up? Just slow?"

Sally didn't answer him. Instead, she opened another search and typed *Barton Police Department*. This time when she hit Enter, nothing happened, the screen froze. "I can pull up random bullshit—restaurants, movie times, mating patterns of aardvarks, but the second I try to search for law enforcement, government agencies, hospitals, the screen hangs. Same thing seems to be going on with email. I'm receiving just fine, but can't send outside the Bend, and watch this—"

She composed a quick email to herself with *test* in the subject and hit Send. It took about thirty seconds before it appeared in her inbox. She folded both arms across her chest. "See?"

Matt looked at the message sitting in her inbox but had no idea what she was getting at. "No. I don't see."

She tapped the screen with her index finger again. "See how the subject line *isn't* bold?"

Matt nodded.

"Normally, when email comes in, the subject stays bold until I read it. As of this morning, none of my subject lines on new messages are bold. *Somebody* is reading these *before* they come in. Screening them. I think the same is happening with internet searches. That's why there is a delay. Someone, or some *thing*, is reviewing the search first, then deciding whether or not to show the results. It's happening fast, but it's happening, I'm sure of it."

"I think you're getting a little paranoid."

The moment Matt said that, he thought of the coroner, Gerald Furber. He'd been paranoid, too. Was Sally infected by whatever was impacting the rest of the town? Could he trust her? For that matter, could he trust himself? If everyone else was infected, why not him? Why not Gabby? Sally? Riley? He didn't feel any different. He thought about how he'd just pushed Addie out of his way at the door. Had he simply overreacted, or was that something else?

"Paranoid, my ass." Sally went back to ticking off her fingers. "No radios. No cell service. Local calls only. Internet partially blocked, like searches are being filtered before they're allowed to go through. Same with email. That ain't paranoid. Those are facts."

She clicked back through her screens and brought the GPS map back up. "Tell you what. You bring Ellie back here safe and sound, show me I'm wrong."

Matt stared at that blinking red dot for a long moment, then said, "I need a minute."

He spotted Gabby in the far corner of the office, near the copy machine. She was crouching down, talking to Riley, her hands on either side of her daughter's head. He started toward them.

"Ellie could be hurt, Matt!" Sally called out behind him.

He held up a finger. He'd go, but he had to talk to Gabby first.

Matt pushed through the people, nodding and attempting to calm those who cornered him with questions, concerns, or angry shouts. When he reached Gabby, she didn't look up at him. Her gaze was locked with Riley.

"Is she okay?"

They'd both checked Riley for signs of physical injury in the car and hadn't found any, but the girl hadn't spoken.

Gabby ran her fingers through her daughter's hair and stood. She spoke in a low, concerned voice, "She's not trembling anymore, but she's still not talking, not really. She muttered something about Evelyn Harper, then went quiet again." Gabby chewed her lower lip. "About a month ago, that Harper girl took a picture of Riley in her underwear when she was changing for gym, then she sent it to a bunch of boys at school. Riley was devastated. So was I. The school wouldn't do anything—Harper used some kind of app, so there wasn't proof it originated with her, but a few other kids told Riley it was her. That wasn't enough."

"Why didn't you tell me? That's technically a felony. At the very least, me or Ellie could have put the fear of God in her or her parents."

"Her parents." Gabby huffed. "They're worse than their kid. I went over there, and her dad just laughed at me. Said, 'Might as well get used to it. Girl like her's bound to end up in porn. All she'll be good for.'"

"He said that?"

"Oh, that wasn't the half of it. He came in the diner every day for lunch for the next week and left these flyers on the counter for Marshall's Farm up in Barton."

Matt knew where this was going. Marshall's had gotten hit with a substantial fine about a year ago for hiring undocumented immigrants to pick apples at less than a dollar an hour. They housed them in these old barns that weren't fit for animals. Made them sleep on the dirt floor.

"Matt," Gabby said, "my mother worked there when she first got to the US. I don't know how he knew that, but he did, he must have."

"He was just trying to get under your skin."

"Yeah, well, it worked," she said flatly. Then her voice dropped so low he could barely hear her. "Just now, when she said that girl's name, you know what popped into my head? I wanted to grab your gun right off your belt, track her down, and drop her like some wild dog, put her down. I wanted to see the look on her asshole father's face when you told him. Like that would somehow make everything okay." Her eyes welled up with tears again. "I'm not that person, Matt."

"You're a mother. They threatened your daughter."

"I wanted the girl dead. I wanted her father to suffer. Her mother, too. All of them." She hesitated, then added, "If I had had the gun, I would have shot her. All of them." She glanced down at his belt. "Hell, I still want to."

Addie Gallagher crossed the room and stopped about ten feet away, and Gabby caught her from the corner of her eye. "And that one…" The tears were gone, and her face darkened. "You don't want to know what I'd like to do to that one…" She rattled off a few choice words in Spanish.

Addie walked away.

Matt brushed her cheek. "I need to run back out and get Ellie. I won't be gone long. I'd really like you and Riley to wait in my office."

"I'm not hiding."

"I'm not asking you to. I just want to know you're safe."

"Then take us with you."

"I can't do that. I won't be long, I promise."

On the opposite side of the room, Addie had her back against the wall and was watching them. When Matt's eyes caught hers, she didn't look away.

Matt shook his head and focused on Gabby. "Maybe when this is over, we should go somewhere, just the two of us."

She forced a smile. "I'd like that."

He kissed her forehead. "I'll get back as fast as I can, I promise."

40

HANNAH

HANNAH WOKE IN A dark place.

Nothing but buzzing around her. There was a vibration, too, a rumble, and she realized she was moving. She was in the trunk of a car. Her hands and feet were bound and there was something oily in her mouth, some type of cloth or rag, sealed there with a piece of tape. She could feel the tape pull against her skin when she twisted her head.

I originally planned to snatch you off the sidewalk, 'bout four months ago. Had duct tape in my car...

Malcolm Mitchell's car, had to be.

Hannah had no idea what he drove, but it had to be something old—she smelled exhaust and caught glimpses of daylight through rusty cracks in the walls of the trunk.

Something landed on Hannah's cheek, skittered across her face, then took off when she shook her head. The buzzing increased, like a frenzy.

She thought of the flies in Danny's car. The one that had crawled into Malcolm's ear.

When another landed on her forehead, she screamed and nearly choked on the oily rag in her mouth.

Hannah shook her head again, but this time the fly didn't leave, it only crossed from her forehead to the side of her temple where the insect paused only long enough for another fly to land, this one so close to her ear the buzz sounded like a freight train for a brief second before it went silent and there was nothing but the tickle of its tiny feet on her earlobe.

Hannah shook her head again, rolled over in the tight space, and smashed the side of her head against the floor of the trunk as hard as she dared, hoping to crush one or both flies, but she felt them leap off in the last second only to land on her head again when she went still. More were in her hair, on her arms and legs. The car rolled over a bump or through a pothole, and while the jar of that surprised them and caused them to take flight, they seemed to land again in larger numbers, their buzz so loud it drowned out nearly all else.

Hannah shuddered, an involuntary ripple through her entire body.

They might have driven for ten minutes or ten hours. The concept of time was lost on her. There was nothing but that buzz, the flies. She only noticed that the car stopped moving because the flies seemed to notice they'd stopped, too—all at once, they ceased angrily bouncing around. And in the blackness, Hannah could only imagine them perching around the interior of the trunk, their tiny legs gripping metal and filthy carpet, silencing themselves in wait, ready to pounce.

The car stuttered as the motor choked and died. Then there was silence.

Hannah heard the soft click as the lock disengaged. The trunk opened slowly, and a slice of harsh light blinded her, spilling in from around Malcolm's silhouette. He was holding a flathead screwdriver, the sharp blade pointed at her.

"You make a sound, you try to scream or get away, and I'll have to hurt you. Do you understand?"

Oh, she wanted to scream.

As her eyes adjusted to the light, she saw several of the flies rise from the trunk and land on his head. One crawled up and into his nose, vanished inside. Malcolm gave a soft snort, but otherwise didn't seem to notice or care. The grin on his face was unbearable. The tight skin around his left eye was moving, writhing with whatever lived beneath.

How could he not feel that?

The panic raced up her throat, and she gagged on the oily rag again before pinching her eyes shut.

There's nothing in his head.

There's nothing in his head.

Because there couldn't be.

Had he drugged her?

Maybe that was it. But she hadn't eaten or had anything to drink since breakfast. Maybe when she was unconscious. Or maybe something on the rag; every swallow was tinged with something oily.

Hannah started to whimper, didn't mean to, it just slipped out; some self-defense mechanism running on autopilot, and Malcolm moved fast—he slapped her. Not hard, but hard enough to stun her back into silence.

He brought the tip of the screwdriver close to her eye. "Things will go much smoother for you if you cooperate, but I'm okay if you don't. Sometimes that's fun, too. Think you can behave?"

The words came at her in slow motion, as if they traveled through molasses. Something was very wrong

with her, with him, with both

Hannah managed to bob her head and winced with pain,

feeling for the first time the blow to the back of her skull that had knocked her unconscious.

Malcolm rolled his eyes, as if her discomfort were some kind of nuisance. "Lean forward. Let me see your head."

Hannah hesitated for a second, then did as he asked.

Malcolm moved some of her hair aside, touched the spot where it was tender, then straightened back up. "You've got a nasty bump, but the bleeding stopped. There's not much blood at all, really." He held the screwdriver back up to her face and let out a soft sigh. "I need you to get out of the trunk, Hannah. Slowly."

Hannah tried not to look at his face, couldn't. She knew his skin was nothing but a bag of flies. Small, large, larva, maggots, eating him from the inside out. She didn't know what happened to all the flies that had been in the trunk. Surely there had been more. Some voice told her that if she moved they'd pounce, they'd dart out from wherever they were hiding and swarm her mouth, her nose, her ears, her—

Malcolm grabbed her shoulder and yanked her forward, wrestled her into a sitting position. "Will you move already?!"

With a yelp, Hannah waited for the buzz, waited for tiny feet to squirm across her skin, but nothing happened. She wanted to believe they were gone, but she knew that wasn't true, they were just patient.

Malcolm grabbed her ankles and swung her legs over the lip of the trunk. When she finally got a good look around, she realized where they were—he'd taken her to the old Pickerton place. The decrepit old house up on Mount Washington where that family died years back. The place where Danny and some of the other guys on the basketball team sometimes went to party.

A lump formed in her throat at the thought of Danny. Had Malcolm just left him there? Dead in the car? Oh, God, was Danny really dead?!

Malcolm cut the tape from her ankles with the blade of the

screwdriver, got her feet on the ground, and tugged her toward the house. "Come on."

When they reached the porch, she tried to dig her heels in, but that barely slowed him down. He was wiry, but all muscle. He kicked the front door open, yanked her forward, and pulled her inside.

The windows were all boarded up, and the gloom struck her with nearly the same force as the bright light had when he opened the trunk. Her eyes were still adjusting when he dragged her across the dusty floor and forced her to sit at the mouth of a hallway between an old grandfather clock and a heavy oak side table. He crouched down next to her, tore a length of duct tape from the roll, and secured her hands to the table.

She couldn't look at him. His head was crawling with flies. His shoulders, chest, his filthy clothing. When he spoke, she pictured them rattling around in his lungs, crawling up his windpipe, and—

Malcolm smacked her cheek again. "I don't know where you keep going, Hannah, but you need to focus. What I'm about to tell you is important." He twisted the screwdriver between his fingers, the light seeping around the boarded windows glistening across the blade. "You know where we are, right? The old Pickerton place. There's nobody around for miles. Nobody saw us come up here."

Hannah swallowed.

Malcolm took her phone from his pocket, held it up, and inserted what looked like a small USB drive in the port. A red light came on and began to flash. "You're going to like this." A second later, the red light turned to green and the lock screen on her phone vanished, replaced by her home screen. Malcolm licked his yellow teeth. "Best thirty-nine bucks I ever spent. It takes longer if the phone's operating system is current, but it looks like you're a few versions behind. You really should stay on that."

He brought up Hannah's messaging app, clicked on the conversation with her mother, and turned the screen so she could read it. Not that it mattered. She knew what it said. Her heart sank.

"You told your mom you were going over to Sandra Horner's house to study. No mention of Danny or whatever you really had planned today." Her mother's reply was right below—

K sweetie. Have fun.

Malcolm thumbed through a few more messages and found the thread with Sandra. Hannah knew what those said, too. She told Sandra she was going to Boston with Danny for the day and needed her to run interference with her mom. There were a few after that, but Malcolm didn't need to read them all, the last was enough—

Got you covered!

His toothy grin widened when he got to it. A large fly hopped from the corner of his mouth to his chin and circled around to the back of his neck. Hannah barely saw him. Her gaze was locked on her phone, what Malcolm did next. He opened a new message to Hannah's mom and typed—

Hey mom, when you suck cock do you think it's better to spit or swallow?

His thumb hovered over the Send button but he didn't press it. Instead, he pressed the Back button and deleted the text one character at a time. "If I have to, I can send messages to your mom, to Sandra, whoever. I already turned off your location services, did that before we started driving, so nobody can track you. You need to listen to me very carefully. What happens next is completely up to you." He set her phone aside and reached for the tape on her mouth. "If I take this off, you promise not to scream?"

Hannah nodded.

"Nobody knows you're here," Malcolm repeated, slower this time, as he peeled away the tape.

"I won't tell anyone!" Hannah managed when he pulled the rag out. "I'll tell them I didn't see who shot Danny. Drop me out on Route 112 somewhere. I'll tell them I woke up out there and I don't remember anything after banging my head. We can still fix this. We can—"

"Shhhh." Malcolm pressed a grimy finger to her lips. "There's no easy way to say this, so I'm just going to put it out there. You're number seven, Hannah. You're the seventh girl I've brought out here. You haven't heard of any of them for the same reason you haven't read about me or seen me on TV...I'm very good at what I do. Each of those girls—"

A floorboard squeaked somewhere behind him, and Malcolm spun around, squeezing the handle of the screwdriver.

His movement stirred the dust, but there was nobody.

"Who's there?" Malcolm called out.

There was no response.

Had he checked the house? Probably not. He'd opened the trunk right after they stopped moving. There were no other cars outside. The place was far too remote for someone to walk.

Several flies had perched on the wall behind Malcolm's head, watching them.

Hannah let out a soft whimper.

"Shhh." Malcolm growled. "Shut the hell up."

At least a minute slipped by without another sound.

With all the windows boarded up, Hannah couldn't see much. Thin streams of light shone through between the cracks, sliced up the dark. She caught glimpses of old rotten furniture, discarded cans and bottles, snippets of graffiti on the walls. No movement, though. That didn't mean they were alone.

Still holding Hannah's phone, Malcolm switched on the flashlight. He teased the light over the dilapidated interior, rolling over the walls and floor. When he played the light over the floor of the hallway leading deeper into the house, a breath caught in his throat.

41

MATT

WHEN MATT PASSED THE sign that said LOWER FALLS, 1/2 MILE, he slowed his cruiser. A few moments later, he came upon the abandoned red Honda. Nose down in the ditch, ass up, doors open, tags stripped just as Ellie had said. He slowed further as he drove by the car, tried to get a glimpse inside, but the windows were smeared with mud. He took a few pictures with his phone. About fifty feet beyond the Honda, he came upon a dark blue Buick stripped of its tags, one he recognized as belonging to Lonnie Floyd. Lonnie owned the Gas 'n' Go on the far side of town, near the high school, and usually manned the register on Sundays so his wife could attend church.

Matt passed three more abandoned cars on the left before they began appearing on the right side of the street, too. He photographed all of them. Most had flat tires—not just one flat, but all four—and that kind of thing didn't happen by chance or accident. He slowed his cruiser to a crawl, carefully scanning the pavement ahead for boards with nails or some other kind of hazard. By the time he came upon Ellie's cruiser, he'd passed twelve other cars and had yet to see a single person.

Like most of the others, both front doors were open, and her tires were flat. The cruiser was angled in the breakdown lane, the tail end partially blocking the road. None of her lights were on, not even her flashers, and that was strange because if Ellie was a stickler for anything, it was protocol.

Matt parked behind her, switched off his motor, and took out his gun for the third time today, and that wasn't lost on him, either. Until today, he'd only removed it from its holster twice in the line of duty over all his years in uniform, and now three times in a single day.

Stepping from the car, the air felt oddly still, like stepping out into a void. There was no breeze. He didn't hear any birds or animals scurrying around in the woods on either side of him. All he heard was the gentle hum of Lower Falls about a quarter mile up the mountain to the east and the tick of his cooling engine. Considering all the abandoned cars, none of that made sense.

Where did the people go?

As he neared, Matt realized Ellie's tires weren't just flat, they'd been shredded. Nails hadn't done this. He'd seen this kind of damage before. This was caused by a spike strip or something similar. He had one in his trunk. When deployed, it covered a distance of twenty-five feet and a width of ten inches. It had hundreds of triangular spikes designed to penetrate and tear rubber. He'd never had to use it, but he'd been trained on it in the academy. He had little doubt that's what caused this, and probably the others, too.

Looking back out over the stretch of road, he saw no sign of a spike strip, but he did see fresh skid marks zigzagging the asphalt. They started about a quarter mile back and ended with the abandoned cars.

Matt kept the gun at his side as he came around Ellie's car on the driver's side and bent to get a better look at the interior. Ellie's bundle of keys with the white rabbit's foot dangled from the ignition and the car was in neutral. Her radio was smashed and there was blood on the passenger seat. He didn't think it was Ellie's; most likely it came from the librarian, Edgar Newton, but the sight of any blood in an abandoned car was unnerving. Knowing it was Ellie's car only made things worse.

Blood from Newton was one thing. A smashed radio was another thing entirely.

This was no accident. Someone had done this.

Matt tried to piece it together.

Someone deployed a spike strip, disabled the car, and what? Forced Ellie and Newton out? Took them away? Then put the car in neutral and pushed it off the side of the road and smashed the radio? Nothing else made sense. But who? Why?

Matt stood up and looked back out at the other abandoned cars.

Nearly twenty of them.

At least twenty people, maybe more, all missing.

All of them were at Matt's back. Ellie had made it the farthest. There were no cars beyond Ellie's.

Matt could only see about a hundred feet in that direction. Route 112 crested at a hill, and he had no line of sight beyond the break.

Still holding his gun, he started walking in that direction. He'd only gone about ten yards when the asphalt at his feet burst in a puff of black dust followed a millisecond later by the crack of a rifle.

42

HANNAH

THERE WERE FRESH FOOTPRINTS in the thick dust covering the hallway floor.

Not shoe prints, but bare feet.

Small, about the same size as Hannah's.

Probably female.

Malcolm trained the flashlight beam on them, traced them with the light. They seemed to start somewhere deep in the house, cross the very spot where she and Malcolm were in the hallway, then continue through the living room and out the front door. A single set of tracks left by someone leaving, no indication of them entering the house unless they'd come through a window or something in the back.

Malcolm worked the light in the opposite direction, traced the prints back from the front door, and lost them in the gloom at the far end of the hall. The same direction the sound had come from. In his other hand, he rolled the screwdriver in his grip, anxiously twisted it, faster and faster. Behind his eyes, the gears were turning.

Whatever this was, he hadn't expected it.

"Somebody help me!" Hannah shrieked. "Somebody!" She yelled so loud the words seemed to tear her vocal cords, like a speaker blowing out.

Malcolm punched her.

Not a slap like before, but he tightened his grip around the screwdriver and drove his fist hard into the side of her chin. Her jaw cracked shut and caught the corner of her tongue between her teeth, and when she opened her mouth to cry out from the pain, he shoved the rag in, nearly choked her, and quickly replaced the tape.

Warm blood filled her mouth, and she had no choice but to swallow it as he glared at her, his face bright red, his skin writhing even worse than before, as if she'd angered the flies right along with him. "You dumb bitch. It's like you want to get hurt. Why'd you make me do that?"

His voice was low, barely a whisper, and he only looked at her for a second before turning his attention back down the hall. "There's nobody here. We don't even know these tracks are from today."

When he said that last part, Hannah wasn't sure if he was talking to her or trying to convince himself. She barely had time to process that when he added, "She didn't go down there, did she?"

Those words slipped from him so quietly, Hannah wasn't sure he'd actually meant to say them aloud. Like they were simply a thought that escaped.

You're number seven, Hannah. You're the seventh girl I've brought out here.

She saw the marks on the table leg then, hadn't noticed them before. Dried adhesive, probably from more duct tape. Scratches in the wood finish, maybe from zip ties.

At one point, he'd secured all his victims to the same spot where he had her now.

Hannah twisted her face back to Malcolm. The movement beneath his skin had stopped. His blank stare might have been carved in stone as he slowly rose and peered down the hallway. He rolled the screwdriver in his palm several times, switching between an overhand and underhand grip, before settling on overhand. "Wait here," he told her, as if she could get up and leave whenever she wanted. Then he started down the hall, following the tracks deep into the dark.

43

MATT

THE BULLET JUST MISSED him.

Matt dove to his right and landed hard on the pavement. He rolled off the side of the road and down into the ditch, coming to a stop when he hit the mud. Two more shots followed, the last one disappearing in the earth no more than six inches from his left hand. Then the world went quiet; nothing but echoes.

With all three shots, the bullet struck before Matt actually heard it. That meant whoever was firing wasn't close, but shooting at a distance, most likely with some kind of high-powered rifle. There were plenty of those in town—this was New Hampshire, after all—but most were meant for deer, and locals tended to opt for using the sights rather than a scope. There was more sport in it. Whoever had just fired on Matt had struck too close to be a missed shot at a deer. Those shots had followed his path and hit within inches of him—rapid-fire, only seconds apart. That kind of marksmanship came from a skilled sharpshooter able to fix his target while reloading, someone with a scope. He had no idea where the shots had come from; the trees and mountains distorted the sound, bounced it.

Matt reached for the radio clipped to his shoulder. "Ellie? Sally? Either of you hear me? Got shots fired out on 112. I'm pinned down. Over."

He didn't expect an answer, but he had to try. Even if one of them did respond, he wasn't sure what they could do.

At a slow crawl, Matt edged up the side of the ditch until he could see over the pavement. The ditch offered little cover, and he was sure whoever was shooting could have killed him if they wanted to. They'd only fired warning shots, drove him back, but back from what? He needed to see over the hill where 112 crested, but it was still a good fifty feet off.

He scrambled a little farther up the muddy incline, got to his knees, and raised both hands above his head. "I'm a sheriff's deputy!" Matt shouted. "Hold your fire! I'm coming out!"

Every muscle in his body tensed, and he tried to squash the thought of a small red laser dot on his forehead as he slowly got to his feet. He stood on the edge of the road, waited for a bullet to tear into him, but none came.

"I'm putting my weapon away!"

His service pistol was still in his hand, now covered in mud. He slowly lowered it and slipped it back into its holster.

He felt eyes on him, and he tried not to think about that as he took a step forward toward the crest in the hill. He got about three feet before another bullet struck the ground close enough to cover his shoes with chipped blacktop.

Matt froze.

It had come from in front of him for sure, seemed like his left side, but he couldn't be 100 percent sure.

If they wanted you dead, you'd be dead.

That thought wasn't very reassuring, but it was all he had.

He took another step.

Two shots this time, quick succession. One clipped the edge of his shoe, the other struck the ground to his left. Matt's heart was pounding so hard he imagined whoever was shooting could see it throbbing in their scope. Some vein on the side of his head was beating like a snare drum. That second shot, the one that hit on his left, at least gave him a general direction. If they'd been shooting from his right, the bullet would have to have gone through him to hit there. It came from the left for sure. He looked up toward the mountains, through the trees, searched for some flash or glare giving away their position, but saw nothing.

He had two choices. He could take another step, watch for the muzzle flash, or he could step backward, retreat. Do what they wanted him to do. If he took another step forward, there was a very good chance they'd shoot him. If he ran, he wouldn't learn anything new.

Matt knew what he had to do, but that didn't make it any easier.

He drew in a deep breath and took another step forward.

His foot hadn't touched the ground when two quick shots rang out.

Two muzzle flashes—one from the northeast on his right, the other from the northwest. At least a thousand yards out, maybe as much as two.

Both struck the ground on either side of him.

Multiple shooters.

The gunner on his left fired again and came within an inch of Matt's shoe.

These weren't some hunters clowning around. These were pros with military precision.

"All right!" Matt shouted, raising both hands higher. "I'm backing up! Don't shoot!"

He counted silently to ten, then took a slow step back. When nobody fired, he took another. Matt was halfway back to his car when he finally turned and ran. He dove inside the cruiser, started the engine, and hit the accelerator before he even had his door closed. He skidded the car through a sloppy three-point reverse turn and raced back toward town.

At least a minute passed before he remembered to breathe.

44

HANNAH

HANNAH TWISTED HER HEAD and tried not to lose sight of Malcolm as he worked his way down the hall, but with little light and the heavy table partially blocking her view, that was tough. He reached a closed door at the end of the hall, hesitated, bent, and studied the floor. Then he switched off the flashlight, tried to peer under the door, grunted, and got back to his feet, switching the light back on.

"They came from in here," he said in a muted whisper. Hannah wasn't sure if the words were meant for her or if he was talking to himself again, but if someone was waiting on the other side of that door, they'd surely heard him. The house seemed oddly quiet, as if it were listening, too.

Malcolm pressed his palm against the door, then quickly pulled it away, startled. He brought the light up and looked at the spot he'd touched.

Even at this distance, Hannah could see his handprint there. It glistened, as if the door were a cold pane of glass, a window covered in frost.

She grunted behind her gag, and he answered as if he could read her mind.

"The door is freezing cold." He tentatively touched the brass knob and jerked his hand away. "Like ice."

That made no more sense to Hannah than everything else that had happened today. It was only October. It would be another month or two before they had their first real cold snap. The temperature outside was probably somewhere in the sixties.

Raising the screwdriver, ready to strike, Malcolm reached for the knob again, gave it a cautious twist, and eased the door open with the toe of his shoe.

A rush of icy air lofted out, a frigid breath Hannah felt roll down the hallway and wash over her. Malcolm blinked it away. He scissored his arm back against his chest with the blade of the screwdriver pointing out, phone flashlight held high in his other hand. He seemed ready to charge the room, tackle whoever might be inside, but even from her obstructed view, Hannah could tell nobody was in there.

Motionless at the threshold, Malcolm shut off the flashlight—he didn't need it.

There was a large four-poster bed against the far wall, a dresser beside it with an antique lamp, the yellowed shade sitting at an angle on top. The bed was all wrong, too; the frame had partially collapsed at the foot, the side closest to the door. A large tree limb, as thick as Hannah's waist, rested on top. It had come through the ceiling and sliced through the old wood like butter, leaving a hole in the roof and a jagged gash in one of the walls. Another branch, an offshoot from the first, had punched through the mattress and impaled the floor. Knotty and thick, like a broken bone that had healed all wrong. All of it was stained white, glistening with frost and ice. Branches and leaves filled the far side of the room like some giant houseplant forgotten and grown out of control, and the sun streamed in from above. Several crows were perched about, tiny black eyes watching Malcolm intently when he muttered, "Stop. Just stop, already."

Hannah thought he was talking to the birds, or maybe the flies buzzing around his head, but he didn't swat at any of them, made no effort to drive them away. Instead, he peered into the room, as if he were talking to the room.

When Hannah grunted again behind her gag, Malcolm seemed to remember she was there. His head twisted partially around, caught her from the corner of his eye, then went back to the footprints.

"These make no sense," he muttered. He slipped the screwdriver into his back pocket and snapped several photographs of the prints with Hannah's phone. "They start at the bed. Like whoever made them started there too, then..."

Malcolm shook his head, and several of the flies rose and hovered above him, buzzing about.

Hannah watched as he stepped into the room, following the trail, moving in slow starts and stops across the room until he reached the edge of the mattress. Still staring down at the floor, he turned and sat.

"They start right here," he said. "Makes no sense. There are no tracks leading into the room. They start right here like the person who made them swung her legs over the side, stood, and walked from the room, down that hall, and out the front door."

The fact that he said *her* wasn't lost on Hannah. The footprints were nearly identical to her own. Either from a girl or a small boy, but Hannah somehow knew it was the former.

Malcolm turned slowly on the bed, raised his feet to the mattress, and lay down next to the large branch. With the crows watching him and flies clouding the air, he looked up at the ceiling.

And that was when he screamed loud enough to put Hannah's pitiful cries to shame.

45

RILEY

MAYBE IT WAS THE adrenaline from earlier or, more likely, the fact that the adrenaline had faded, but the moment Riley lay down on the couch in Matt's office with her head resting on her mom's lap, she fell asleep. Thankfully, it was a dreamless sleep. The monster she'd spotted in the kitchen sink, whatever had been clawing its way up the pipes, those things didn't return to finish what they started. In the car on the way over to the police station, she told herself she'd killed it, whatever *it* was, but some voice in the back of her head was quick to point out that she'd only killed one of them, maybe two, and where there were two...

Riley's eyes snapped open with that thought lingering like a bad taste in her mouth.

Her mom was no longer in the office with her. She'd taken off Riley's shoes and draped an old quilt over her. Even found a pillow. Riley knew Matt sometimes slept here; the quilt smelled like him. Not in a bad sweaty kind of way, but in a warm, comforting kind of way. Riley pulled the quilt tight up around her neck, nuzzled into the pillow, and tried to find sleep again. She told herself everything that happened back at the house *didn't happen*, it'd all been in her head, because that was way easier than accepting that it had been real.

In the other room, the adults were shouting.

Loud.

First, she tried to tune them out, ignore all the angry voices, and when that didn't work, she tried to listen, figure out what they were all yelling about. That didn't work, either, because it seemed like they were *all* yelling and they were all so mad, their voices all tripped over each other. By the time she realized *that*, she wasn't tired anymore.

Still draped in the quilt, Riley got to her knees and peered between the blinds out into the main room of the police station.

There were a lot of people in the small station. Even more than when they'd first arrived. She knew her mom was out there somewhere, but she didn't see her, not at first, then she spotted her on the far end of the room with Sally Davie. Riley liked Sally; she'd come to career day at Riley's school last year to tell them what it was like to be a cop. Bobby Klitz had said she wasn't a real cop, she just handled the radio, and Sally was quick to tell him, "Behind every *real cop* was a solid dispatch officer, and it took both of them to arrest Bobby's daddy for something called D&D the summer before last." Riley's teacher had rushed her out after that.

Hey.

The single word came from her left like a whisper at her ear, but when Riley turned, there was nobody there. Matt's office was a cluttered mess, but otherwise empty.

Riley shivered, and when she exhaled, her breath lingered in the air, a tiny cloud of white.

That made no sense. It wasn't winter, and she was inside. The room was cold, but not *that* cold.

What's your name?

Riley jumped with that one. Honest-to-God jumped, because she heard the voice clear as anything, yet there was nobody there.

A girl's voice.

She gripped the thick material of the quilt and pulled it up around her neck, as if it were some protective cape, and slowly eased off the couch. The only place anyone could hide in Matt's office was under his desk, but there was nothing under there but a pair of Matt's old hiking boots covered in dried mud and a couple of paper clips caught up in the carpet.

You're like me. You don't want to be like me. You should leave.

Riley shivered, and not from the cold.

The voice had come from her right that time, and when she turned in that direction, she found herself facing the wall that separated Matt's office from Sheriff Ellie's. There was a map of the town hanging there along with a collection of bulletins and reports, and Matt's college and high school diplomas. There were also a few old newspaper clippings from back when he played football.

None of those things explained why the wall looked wet.

Riley reached out and tentatively touched it, then quickly pulled her hand away and buried it in the folds of the quilt.

Not wet, but cold. Covered in a thin layer of frost.

When Riley's phone vibrated in her back pocket, she jumped and nearly screamed.

She fumbled it out and read the text message:

Where r u?

Evelyn again.

She replied with

I'm at the police station with my mom.

A second later—

Look outside.

Riley went over to the window behind Matt's desk and wiped away the condensation so she could see out. Evelyn, Robby, and Mason were all out there, staring up at her from the small parking lot where the sheriff kept the county truck with the plow on the front and a couple of extra patrol cars that probably hadn't moved since Riley was born. One of them was up on blocks.

Evelyn attempted an *open the window* motion with her hands, pretending to lift the sash from ten feet away, and it took a second for Riley to understand what she meant. She flipped the latches and forced it up.

Evelyn said, "You need to come with us."

Riley glanced over her shoulders in the direction her mom had been, but with the blinds closed, she couldn't see her. "I can't. I need to stay with my mom."

Mason groaned and frowned at Evelyn. "I told you she was chickenshit."

Evelyn ignored him. "We think we figured out where that thing in your sink came from."

"*I* figured out where the thing in your sink came from," Robby corrected her.

Evelyn rolled her eyes. "Whatever." She took a step closer. "Climb out and jump. You can come back after. It's not that far. Your mom will never know you left."

Matt's office was on the ground floor, only a few feet up. Riley looked back over her shoulder.

"Do you need to ask Mommy for everything?"

Mason again.

He was right: she was being stupid. Robby was younger than

her, and he was out there. On any normal day, her mom wouldn't have a problem with her hanging out with friends.

Are they your friends, though?

Not the girl's voice that time—that one was all Riley herself—and she didn't know the answer. Not really.

"Thirty minutes, tops," Evelyn said. "It's right down the street."

Riley almost turned around again and caught herself. Evelyn was right; her mom probably wouldn't even notice she was gone, and text messages were working, so if she did notice, she could just send her a message and she could come right back. *If* she even noticed she was gone.

Before she could change her mind, Riley shed the quilt, sat on the edge of the windowsill, and dropped to the ground. The sun felt good on her skin, as if she'd just stepped out of a freezer.

"There might be hope for you yet," Mason told her when she reached them.

Evelyn frowned. "What's that?"

Riley didn't know what she was talking about. "What's what?"

Evelyn grabbed her arm and pointed. "That."

Written on Riley's arm in what looked like blue ballpoint was a name:

Mason Ridler

She didn't remember writing it there.

46

MATT

MATT JUMPED THE CURB parking his cruiser and didn't much care. His hand slipped off the gearshift three times before he managed to get it in park, and he scraped his knuckles on the steering column when he went to retrieve the keys.

Every inch of his body trembled and wouldn't stop.

He'd never been shot at before.

Hollows Bend just wasn't that kind of place.

He had friends in other jurisdictions where gunfire was an everyday part of the job, particularly in some of the more rural portions of New Hampshire where the opioid crisis was running rampant, but not here, not in the Bend.

The Bend was different.

Matt gripped both sides of the wheel and drew in a deep breath through his nose, held it for a moment, then let it out from his mouth.

Get it together, he told himself. *You need to get it together.*

A palm smacked against his window, and Matt jerked.

Stu Peterson.

He had a 9mm on his left hip in an open-carry holster and was holding Jimmy Newcomb by the back of the neck. The man's hands were bound behind his back with what looked like a length of clothesline.

When Matt got out of the car, Peterson thrust Newcomb toward him. The man was like a rag doll in Stu Peterson's meaty grasp. "Caught him trying to get into my house through the storm cellar. Clipped the lock with a pair of bolt cutters."

Newcomb's eyes were bloodshot, his clothing stained with sweat. He twisted his face toward Matt. "I needed a gun, and I knew this asshole wouldn't give me one."

"Damn right, I wouldn't," Peterson said. "You voted for Prop 84. Why the hell would I give you anything?"

Prop 84 was a hot topic during the last election. If passed, assault rifles would have been banned throughout Monroe County. Jimmy Newcomb and his wife had spent Voting Tuesday in front of the courthouse holding up homemade signs in support of the bill, while Peterson made it a point to circle the block and yell at him. Neither man had escalated—Matt had been thankful for that—but it put an end to the weekly poker game down at the VFW.

"Why do you need a gun?" Matt asked Newcomb.

The man stared at him as if that were the craziest question he'd ever heard. "Why do I need a gun? For the bears. Why else?"

"What bears?"

"I seen at least five grizzlies come down off Mount Washington today alone, and if I saw five, you know there's more. Fuckers tore apart my trash cans and nearly killed my dog."

"We don't have grizzlies around here," Matt told him. "There's a few black bears out there, but that's it. They don't come down this time of year."

Newcomb's face grew red. "You think I don't know the difference? These bears were brown, not black. Way bigger. And the claws on them were at least four or five inches long. That ain't no black bear. They were grizzlies!"

Still gripping the man by his neck, Peterson gave Newcomb a solid shake. "Don't matter if you saw the Viet Cong marching down off that hill, you don't get a free pass for trying to break into my house." He glared at Matt. "I want to press charges. Write him up for whatever you can." He reached into his pocket and took out a USB drive, pressed it into Matt's hand. "Got it all on video, right here. He's such a fan of the law, let him experience it firsthand."

Matt twisted the USB drive between his fingers, then dropped it in his pocket. He took out his pocket knife and sliced the rope from Newcomb's wrists.

"What the hell you doing?" Peterson barked.

"I'll write it up," Matt told him. "Ellie will decide if she wants to press charges."

"But it's on video!"

"I'm sure she'll take that into consideration. In the meantime, I want both of you to go home and stay there."

"What about the bears?" Newcomb said, rubbing his wrists.

"Just stay inside. You see them again, call me."

"Think I didn't do that first?" Newcomb told him as he started down the street back toward his house. "Maybe you should tell Sally to pick up the phone."

When he was gone, Peterson growled. "That was stupid, Matt. We don't need folks like him around here, and you're throwing away your chance to rid us of him."

"Go home, Stu. If Ellie wants to pursue charges, we know where to find him."

"Where is Ellie?"

Matt couldn't tell him the truth, no way. "She's cleaning up a mess out on 112."

"You know I got a police radio back at the house, right? I haven't heard her on there all morning."

"Radios are down."

Peterson's eyes narrowed, and he poked Matt in the chest. "Seems lots of things aren't working the way they should today. Got a meeting at my house in an hour to talk about that very thing with a few of the guys from the VFW. Maybe you should stop by, explain yourself." His voice dropped to a conspiratorial whisper. "Wanna tell me about that naked girl who strutted into the diner? This shitstorm started with her."

Matt knew better than to take the bait. He stepped past Peterson and started for the entrance to the sheriff's station. "Go home, Stu."

A wall of noise hit him the moment he stepped inside.

"Things get hairy, you'll want me as a friend, Matt," Peterson said as the door swung shut between them.

47

MATT

MATT IGNORED EVERYONE AND went straight for Sally's desk. She looked up, her face frazzled. "Did you find her?"

He didn't answer. Instead, he pulled the framed county map off the wall behind Sally's head and set it on an empty desk. His index finger landed on the center of Hollows Bend; he circled the small town, leaving a smudge on the glass.

Mount Washington was directly behind them, with the Saco River bordering the east and the Swift River on the west; all of it protected federal land known as the White Mountain National Forest. The rivers could be crossed, he'd done that plenty of times, but the woods surrounding them were another story—dense, impenetrable, nearly a million acres of wilderness. There was only one way in or out—Main Street became Route 112 at the edge of town, and 112 became nothing for nearly fifteen miles before running through Barton, and Barton wasn't much to look at. Jackson might be the closest real town, and you'd have to drive for more than an hour to find anything bigger, nearly two for the closest airport or the feds in Portsmouth. Growing up, he'd loved the isolation of the Bend. It was like being tucked into a warm blanket and peering out from the folds—safe, secure—someplace he could retreat to away from the rest of the world. Now he realized that was a two-edged sword.

They were completely alone.

"She wasn't there, was she?"

Matt didn't take his eyes off the map. "I found her cruiser," he told Sally low enough so nobody else could hear. "Abandoned. There were signs of a struggle. Someone smashed her radio. Some blood, too, but that was probably from Newton." He *hoped* it was from Newton. His voice dropped lower. "Her car wasn't the only one out there. I found at least a dozen more. Someone disabled them with spike strips and forced them off the road."

"Forced how?"

"There's at least two snipers out there, positioned on either side of 112. When I tried to walk toward the crest at Lower Falls, they fired warning shots to hold me back."

"Someone shot at you?"

"Whoever they are, they're not letting anyone leave town. I think they took whoever tried."

Matt's index finger was still on the map. He didn't realize how hard he was pushing until he noticed the tip of his finger had gone white.

Sally said, "You found abandoned cars, but what about the drivers? Passengers? Any other people?"

Matt shook his head. "I'm guessing they took them somewhere. Everyone who's tried to leave town. I think most of the tourists got out, or there'd be more cars. It started right after that...with the birds."

It took a lot to silence Sally, but that did it. She didn't speak for a long time, and when she did, her voice was shaky. "So I was right about our communications, the internet. Someone cut us off."

"Matt?"

Gabby had sidled up beside him. Matt wrapped his arm around her shoulders and pulled her close. He didn't want to let go. He felt Addie's eyes on him from across the room but refused to look. He kissed the side of Gabby's head. "How's Riley doing?"

"Sleeping. She passed out the second her head hit the pillow."

Matt looked around the room. If Riley was sleeping, she was the only one. While a few people had left since he was here earlier, others had come in. The chairs near the door were all full; others sat around the various desks and tables. A couple on the floor. And more still were just wandering about, circling the room, slow and listless. Someone had righted the vending machine and cleaned up the broken glass, tried to restore some kind of normalcy, but the tension was thick in the air. People were either watching him (and quick to look away when he met their eyes) or lost in their own worried thoughts. A couple were huddled outside the door to Ellie's office, including Ben Molton and Ed McDougal, whose right eye was swollen shut and black. He didn't like the way they were looking inside, looking at the girl.

"Matt," Sally said, following his gaze. "You know this didn't start with the birds. It started when *she* showed up. You don't get in there and get the truth out of her soon, someone else is bound to take a run at her. The only thing that has kept that from happening so far is a flimsy lock and a bit of civility. Neither of those things will hold up if what you just told me gets out."

"What did he just tell you?" Gabby asked, rolling out from under his arm.

Careful to ensure nobody else heard, Matt quickly told her.

The color left Gabby's face. "It's some kind of sickness, isn't it? We've all been exposed to something, and someone is keeping it from getting out."

"You've seen too many movies," Matt told her. "It took the government four days to figure out how to get bottled water to

New Orleans after Katrina. No way they could pull something like this off."

"If it's not that, what is it?"

Matt knew Sally was right. He needed to talk to the girl. If he were being honest with himself, he should have already done that, but he hadn't. It was like he didn't want to. At every opportunity, something steered him away. Even now, glimpsing her through the window of Ellie's office, some instinct was telling him not to go in there, something primal, lizard brain. He felt the headache coming back on at just the thought of it, the one that first hit him in the coroner's office, this throbbing behind his eyes.

"Matt, are you okay? You look like you're going to pass out," Gabby said.

"I'm fine," he said, although he wasn't. "It's a lot to take in, that's all."

"I can go in there with you, if you want. She might be scared. Might open up if there's a woman with you."

Somehow, Matt knew that girl was anything but scared.

"I'm fine," he said again. "I mean, I'll be fine." He started for Ellie's door, then stopped halfway and faced the crowd. "Listen up. If you're here to report a crime, work with Sally to fill out the necessary paperwork, get it on record, then go home. There's no reason for anyone to linger around here. The safest place for each of you is your own house with your loved ones. Lock the doors. Stay inside until this blows over, *and it will blow over*. Everyone's on edge, and you don't want to get caught up in something that makes things worse. Go home."

He didn't give anyone a chance to respond. Before they could, he unlocked Ellie's door, slipped inside, and locked it again behind him. He closed the blinds on the windows looking out toward the main room of the station and did his best to ignore the growing headache as he turned and faced the girl.

48

RILEY

RILEY STARED AT THE name written on her arm just above her left wrist:

Mason Ridler

"I didn't write that."

Mason glared down at her arm. "Great, not only is she chicken-shit, but she's a mental case with a crush on me." He frowned at Evelyn. "Tell me again why you want to bring her along? I didn't sign on to be a babysitter for some little psycho 'tard."

"I'm not a—"

"Why did you write his name?" Evelyn interrupted.

"I didn't write it." Maybe her mom wrote it there for some reason, or someone else at the police station while she was sleeping. She certainly didn't write it on her arm, she would have remembered that. "It's not even my handwriting."

That was the truth, too. Did her mom even know who Mason was, though?

Robby tapped his foot impatiently. "Ev, come on. We don't have time for this. Let's go."

He hoisted his red backpack over his shoulder. His entire body shifted with the weight of it. The bottom was stained dark, looked wet, and after seeing him stick a dead bird in there, Riley didn't want to know what else he kept in that bag.

Evelyn gave Riley's arm one last look, let out a soft *tsk, tsk*, and started across the parking lot. "Come on," she said, "it's not far."

Mason rolled his baseball bat through the air, rested it on his shoulder, and went after her, with Robby trudging along behind them.

Riley gave the open window of Matt's office one last look before going after them.

Evelyn was right; it wasn't far.

Rather than take the sidewalks on Main Street, they took the access road that ran behind the businesses, crossed the parking lot at the rear of the pharmacy, and cut through an open field near the middle school until they reached the chain-link fence surrounding the town's water tower.

"You think those things came from here." Riley craned her head and looked up. The tower was so much bigger up close. From school, the base looked like it could barely support the big, round part up at the top, but standing right there next to it, it was ginormous.

Robby set his backpack down in the tall grass. "It's one hundred and twenty feet tall and holds seven hundred and twenty thousand gallons of water." He pointed to a shed off to the right of the tower, just inside the fence. "The pumping station over there can move up to two thousand gallons per minute at peak hours, but averages five hundred gallons per minute over the course of a full day. Every drop of water for Hollows Bend comes from here."

Riley gawked at him. "How, exactly, do you know all that?"

"Robby's 'on the spectrum.'" Evelyn made air quotes as she said this. "That's what we're supposed to tell people, but it seems like they call it something different every time he sees a new doctor. He's got something called Asperger's. It's a type of autism."

"Ass-burger," Mason muttered under his breath with a laugh.

Evelyn punched him in the arm. "*Asperger's*. What's your excuse? Oh, I forgot, you're just a dick."

Mason rubbed his arm. "Whatever."

Evelyn went on. "It means Robby is smart with some things and dumb with others, but mostly smart. He remembers all sorts of stuff. Reads it one time and can spout it back out a year later, word for word. He's really good at solving puzzles, and you *don't* want to play cards with him."

Mason shrugged. "Yeah, well, he also picks his nose, so it's not all sunshine and rainbows."

Evelyn tightened her fist again, but Mason got out of the way before she could throw the punch.

Riley knew what autism was but had never heard of Asperger's. She didn't think Evelyn was making all that up, though.

Robby didn't seem to care they were talking about him. He was at the gate in the chain-link fence, studying the padlock, oblivious. He looked at both the front and back, then unzipped a pocket on his backpack and took out a faded black leather case. He set it on the ground, unzipped it, and spread out the contents. Riley stepped up to get a better look—some kind of tool set— long, thin pieces of metal that looked like something a dentist would use to scrape your teeth. He carefully selected two of them and slipped them into the keyhole on the lock. Robby closed his eyes, wiggled the pieces of metal around, then gave one a yank. The lock popped open.

Riley's chest tightened. "I don't think you should have done that."

Robby carefully replaced the tools in the leather case, sealed it back up, and put it back in his bag. Then he removed the lock, hung it from the fence, and opened the gate.

"That's breaking and entering," Riley pointed out. "We could get in a lot of trouble."

Evelyn stepped through the gate and started up the sidewalk to the water tower. "It's public property. If my parents actually paid their taxes, it would mean we owned part of it. I'm guessing your mom pays her taxes, so that makes it okay by proxy. Besides, to get in trouble, we'd have to get caught, and your mom's boyfriend has his hands full today."

Mason held out his bat. "If you don't want to go in, you can stay out here and be lookout. Cry out real loud if you see someone. I bet you excel at crying."

Riley looked back the way they'd come. The school was deserted, the field, too. They hadn't run into anyone since they'd left Main Street. The wind wasn't even blowing, it was so quiet.

Evelyn grabbed Mason by the hair and pulled him through the fence. "Get in here where nobody can see you, close the gate, and stop worrying about stupid shit." She looked back at Riley. "You gonna make me hurt you? Either way, you're coming in. I learned a long time ago if you're gonna break the rules, *everyone has to break the rules*. That's the easiest way to keep anyone from talking. I haven't decided if I can trust you yet."

Scared or not, Riley wasn't about to let this girl push her around. Mason, either. She shoved past both of them, spotted Robby over by the pump station, and made her way over. He was crouching next to a rusty water spigot built into the side of the small building. He'd removed another padlock and opened a metal lockbox fastened to the wall. Inside, there were plastic collection containers about the size of a pill bottle, test strips, and several small bottles of chemicals lined up neatly on shelves above those. Robby was busy reading the labels. "Mr. Buxton's supposed to test the water at least once every day, but I've never seen him come out here. I'd be surprised if anyone does it on any kind of schedule."

Evelyn came up behind them. "Our dad says Buxton's a drunk, and he should know, 'cause he's one, too. He knows the secret handshake."

"Mr. Buxton?" Riley frowned for a second. "Oh, you mean Buck."

"No luck, Buck," Mason said in a singsong voice. "Down on his luck and useless as—"

Evelyn smacked his shoulder.

"How 'bout you stop hitting me?"

"You're blocking the light," Robby told them both. He'd filled one of the clear collection bottles and was holding it up toward the sun with one hand. In the other, he had a test strip.

Evelyn dropped down next to him and peered at the bottle. "Do you see anything in there?"

Robby gave Riley a quick look but turned away when their eyes met. "Nothing like she described, no. Iron and alkalinity are a little higher than normal, but not enough to be dangerous."

"So, no little monsters swimming around?" Mason asked.

"Nothing visible with the naked eye, no."

"What I saw would barely fit in that bottle." Riley held up her hand. "It was about the size of my thumb."

"This is stupid," Mason said. "If we had little sea monsters floating around in our water, don't you think someone else would have noticed them? Someone who's maybe been out of diapers for a year or two?"

This time, it was Riley who hit him. She curled a fist and punched him hard in the thigh.

Mason hopped back a step. "Okay, everyone stop hitting me!"

"Then stop being an asshat." Evelyn looked back at her

brother. "Is it possible there's something in there and you just can't see it?"

"Sure. Remember the pond water from Ms. Teshner's class? Didn't see nothing in that until we got it under a microscope and it was full of arthropods, copepods, water fleas, and ostracods..."

"Fleas in the water?" Riley felt like she might throw up.

Mason stood and looked across the field at the middle school. "Teshner's classroom is on the first floor, right?" He swung the bat. "We get in and find a microscope, how much time do you need?"

"We're not breaking into the school," Riley told them. "No way."

"Bawk, bawk, bawk, bawk..." Mason clucked, this time from a safe distance, where nobody could hit him.

"We don't have to break in," Evelyn said. "I stole one of the microscopes last month." She gave Robby a half grin. "It was supposed to be your birthday present."

"You did?" Robby smiled.

"I hid it out at the Hawk."

"Well, we can't take *her* there," Mason said, eyeing Riley again. "No way."

Riley had no idea what they were talking about. "What's the Hawk?"

49

LOG 10/16/2023 21:26 GMT-4
TRANSCRIPT: AUDIO/VIDEO RECORDING

Analysis Note: The subject has been staring at the water bottle for nearly two minutes without a sound. Sordello has made no attempt to break him from this reverie. Although his vitals have not changed in any way, I would like to point out the stillness of him; it's like he's catatonic or sleeping with his eyes open. When this moment appeared in the video, I had to consult the time stamp to confirm the image hadn't frozen—he is that still. When she finally spoke, he blinked. Seemed to snap out of it.

Sordello: What do you think she saw back at her house?

Maro: She's just a kid. Could be anything.

Sordello: At some point, you must have suspected the water.

Maro: Hollows Bend has some of the purest water in the world.

Sordello: Did you test it? Like those kids?

Maro: Hollows Bend has some of the purest water in the world.

Analysis Note: He repeated this three more times, like some kind of mantra. Like he was trying to convince himself.

Sordello: *Sick. Infected. Crazy. Angry. Paranoid.* Those are the words you used to describe it. If not the water, what did you believe was the cause? At this point, you still hadn't talked to the girl. Did you believe she was connected or just another victim? What do you think was behind it all?

[*Silence. Subject scribbles something on the back of the coroner's folder.*]

Sordello: Deputy? What did you just write?

[*Subject holds up the folder so she can make it out. He wrote: We suffer the Malcolms of the world.*]

50

HANNAH

MALCOLM'S LOUD CRY HAD ceased nearly as abruptly as it started, and the silence that followed frightened Hannah more than his terror-filled shriek had. Malcolm went completely quiet, his body was still. The only sounds in the old house were Hannah's breathing, the buzz of flies, and the rustle of crows as they shifted around that far room from one perch to another, as if trying to get a better view of the boy below.

Had something hurt him?

Did he pass out?

Was he…

She hoped to God he was. Hannah had never wished death on anyone, but after what he did to Danny…*six other girls*…he deserved the worst. He deserved to die as painfully as possible.

Hannah tried to pull free of the tape, but her hands didn't budge. Malcolm had not only secured her to the table leg but wrapped the tape around a thick support brace on the underside of the table near the top. Between both, there was no play. She tried to twist around, use her legs as leverage, but she couldn't loosen it.

In the other room, flies buzzed, crows shuffled, and Malcolm didn't move.

With the bed frame broken, the mattress was resting at an odd angle. The foot of the bed was touching the ground while the back side near the headboard was at least two feet off the ground. With Malcolm sprawled out on top, it almost appeared like the bed was displaying him. Holding him with the icy tree limb at his side, the fingers of his left hand within inches of that. For some reason, Hannah was grateful he wasn't actually touching that branch. She knew that was silly—it was a branch—but it shouldn't be covered in ice and frost, and from where she sat on the floor, those things looked more like some slowly spreading infection than something simply cold. And it was spreading, right? That wasn't her imagination. More of the branch was covered in that ice than only a few minutes ago, the temperature in the hallway had dropped as cold seeped from that room, and—

Malcolm's foot twitched.

Hannah jerked her wrists with enough force to drag the heavy table nearly an inch across the floor.

She screamed behind her gag, choked, swallowed more of the oil and grime, then screamed again. She screamed with so much force the back of her throat felt like it tore open.

Malcolm moved again. This time, it wasn't just his foot, but his entire left leg that moved, then his other leg. He let out a soft moan, slowly rocked back and forth, and glanced around as if seeing that room for the first time.

When Malcolm reached for the branch, no doubt hoping to use it as leverage to hoist himself into a sitting position, Hannah screamed again.

She didn't know why—couldn't begin to explain it—but she knew he shouldn't touch that branch. Nobody should. Not the birds. Not the flies. Not anything, and certainly not Malcolm, because that would lead to something far worse than the monster that had killed Danny and brought her here. If he heard her, he gave no indication. His fingers wrapped around bark just above the place where it punctured the mattress, and he pulled himself up.

Malcolm jerked his hand away as if he'd been burned, studied his palm for a second, then climbed off the bed and stood on wobbly legs for a long moment before turning toward her and coming back down the hallway.

Backlit by the room, the sun streaming in from the hole in the ceiling, Hannah had trouble making him out as he shuffled toward her. He was nothing but a dark shadow surrounded by blotches of light as her eyes fought to adjust to the gloom after staring into that bright room. It wasn't until he was nearly on top of her that he came into focus, and the moment he did, Hannah knew something was terribly wrong. His pupils were both dilated, the left more so than the right, like black stains on the irises. His skin was covered in a sheen of glistening sweat, and just below his left temple was a small patch of frost.

When Hannah saw that, her gaze immediately jumped to the hand that had touched the branch, and that was even worse. Malcolm's fingers, his palm, were white. Not just pale, but *white*. Not because the blood was gone, but because his hand was layered in frost, too. He wore it like a glove, and Hannah could clearly see the spot on his wrist where it stopped, just below the base of his palm.

Malcolm knelt down next to her, close enough for her to smell what could only be described as rot on his breath, like something had died inside him. He licked his lips, then reached for the table leg where her wrists were taped. He ran his fingers over several deep gouges and scratches, no doubt left by the girls who preceded her. "I never meant to bring *you* here," he said in a voice that held a little more gravel than his own. "I wanted something different for you. You're not like the others. I had—*have*—feelings for you. They meant nothing. But you, you're special. I always thought so. That's what makes this so hard."

Hannah jerked at her bindings, little good that did.

Malcolm reached into his back pocket and retrieved the screwdriver. Rolled it between icy fingers. "I'm going to kill you. I'm going to fuck you first, use you in ways you couldn't possibly imagine in your worst nightmares. You'll beg me to kill you. But I won't at first. I'll keep you alive for a few days, maybe a week, then I'll bash your pretty skull in with a rock and toss whatever is left of you down into the gully on the back side of this house. Maybe in one of the streams or rivers, I haven't decided yet. Those are facts; they just haven't happened yet. I know you think you can talk your way out of it or maybe get away—girls like you always do—but none ever has. Well, that's not exactly true. I did let one live…she was special, too. Different from you, but special in her own way." He shook his head. "Too different, I think. That's why I was able to trust her. You're special, but not like her. You're not someone I can trust."

Hannah jerked her head up and down, muttered his name from behind the gag. She tried to tell him he could trust her, but nothing came out but a garbled mess.

"How special are you, Hannah?" There was a calmness to his voice that had no business being there. He didn't see her as a person, only an obstacle. A threat to be erased. The frost on the side of his head glistened in the dim light. Malcolm scratched it with the tip of his finger, and that fingertip came away moist. He added softly, "Do you want to hear the single scenario where you get to live?"

51

MATT

THE CLOTHING SALLY HAD given the girl was far too large; it hung off
her frame so loosely that it gave the impression she was shrink-
ing. She watched Matt as he rounded Ellie's cluttered desk and
dropped into the chair on the side opposite her.

"Sorry you had to wait so long. It's been a busy morning."
Matt forced his tone to remain calm and even; he didn't want to
rattle her. He rummaged through Ellie's top drawer, found a bottle of Advil she always kept handy, swallowed two without water,
then set the bottle aside. "Why don't we start with your name?"

The girl only stared at him, as if reading him in some way that
didn't require words.

The thought he'd had when he first saw her at the diner popped
back into his head—she looked ethereal, angelic. He couldn't
quite place her age, maybe around sixteen. Best Matt could tell,
she wore no makeup, yet her skin was as flawless as a newborn
aside from a small birthmark on her neck, under her chin—

brown, crescent-shaped. She might be the most beautiful person he'd ever seen.

Prettier than Gabby? Prettier than Addie?

Matt shook that thought away before he allowed himself to answer it, because just having such a thought felt like a betrayal, and there'd been enough of that lately.

Taking out his phone, Matt located the pictures he'd taken of the red Honda out on 112 and slid the phone across the desk to her. "Is that your car?"

She leaned forward, studied the photograph for a moment, then eased back without a word.

Matt didn't need this right now. "Look, I know you can understand me. It's obvious you went through something upsetting this morning, but until you start talking, I don't know how to help you. Do you need to see a doctor? Did someone hurt you?"

The girl shook her head.

"Good. That's good. At least I know you're okay and you speak English. Are you able to talk?"

She scratched her arm, but said nothing, only watched him.

Matt had never encountered a mute before, but he knew they were out there—people who couldn't speak. His gut told him that wasn't what this was. He was fairly certain this girl could talk, but she was choosing not to. He'd play along, for now.

He grabbed a pen and took a sheet of blank paper from the stack next to Ellie's printer, slid both over to her. "Can you write your name for me?"

She shook her head.

"Do you remember your name?"

Hesitation this time, then she shook her head again.

"Do you remember walking into the diner this morning?"

She nodded and scratched at her other arm.

"Good. Okay. Let's start there. Where did you come from?

Where were you right before the diner?" He tapped the edge of the paper. "Write it down."

The girl looked down at the pen, concentrated, then let out another sigh before melting back in her chair.

"You don't remember?"

She shook her head.

Matt shivered.

Why was Ellie's office so cold?

The thermostat was out in the main bullpen. Someone must have kicked the air conditioning all the way down. He twisted around and opened a window—it was warmer outside than in the office.

If the temperature bothered the girl, she gave no indication. She only scratched her arms again, this time more vigorously.

"Is that sweatshirt irritating your skin? I can try to find something else."

Both her hands dropped to her side, as if he'd caught her doing something she shouldn't. She shook her head again.

He let it go, tried to focus. "So you don't remember where you were prior to walking into the diner. Let's try something else. What's the earliest thing you do remember?" He tapped the paper again. "Can you write that down or draw a picture or something?"

She rolled the tip of the pen around on the paper, dotting the page with ink. He got the impression she wanted to, was trying, but couldn't remember.

"Do you know why there are people preventing us from leaving town?"

She appeared genuinely confused by that, then resolutely shook her head *no*.

"You don't know who those people are?"

Again, she shook her head, and Matt saw nothing to indicate she was lying.

"Look, you showed up right when all this started," Matt told her. "I'm willing to chalk that up to bad luck. Came in for the weekend with some friends and didn't get out in time. Wrong place, wrong time. I'm willing to consider that, but there are a bunch of folks in the next room who don't see things that way. They think you're part of whatever is going on. Maybe the cause of it all. While that may be some superstitious nonsense, people are spooked. I don't get the luxury of being spooked. I have to deal in facts. You wandered into the diner in your birthday suit. That means one of two things—either someone did something bad to you and you got away, or you've got something loose upstairs. Now, I'd love nothing more than to put you in my cruiser and take you up to the hospital in North Hollow and let them examine you, but the gunmen out on 112 aren't letting anyone out of town. If you're not with them, that means you're stuck here with the rest of us until help comes. Considering I don't know when that will be, I don't know how long I can protect you, because pretty soon those people in the other room are going to realize the only thing keeping them from you is me, and there are a lot more of them. They're spooked. They're upset. They're getting desperate, and desperate people do desperate things. *Stupid* things. Do you understand what I'm saying?"

Matt couldn't help but think of Stu Peterson and his friends at the VFW. He could picture them lining up every weapon they could find on a table. Cleaning them, prepping…Guys like that waited for a day like today to come around.

Maybe it was the bright sunlight streaming through the window, or maybe it was the fact that he was staring at her, doing his best to hold eye contact, intimidate her a little, but that pain behind his eye beat back the Advil and came at him with a vengeance. Matt's headache grew worse, and he found it difficult to look at her. When he finally did glance back, she had dropped the pen and was scratching both her arms again.

Matt reached for her wrists. "Let me see what's going on there. We've got cortisone in the med box, if you need it."

She held out her arms and tugged up the sweatshirt sleeves.

Matt let out a soft gasp.

Her arms were covered in writing.

Not just writing, but names. The names of people in town. So many, possibly everyone in town. Several had lines drawn through them—Lynn Tatum, Norman Heaton—others were inflamed, irritated; the source of the itch. It looked like blue ink, but the pen he'd given her wrote only in black.

Matt reached for her wrists. "What the hell is this?"

She tried to pull away, but not before he grabbed her. Electricity shot up his fingertips, through his arms and torso. Matt's body went stiff, and his vision burst in a bloom of white.

52

MATT

THE PAIN BEHIND MATT'S eyes exploded, expanded out from his pupil, then blinked back out as quickly as it came. The world rolled sideways, and when it righted itself he was standing in the living room of his small apartment, facing the kitchen.

Addie Gallagher was there, so was he. Somehow, Matt was watching himself with her from across the room.

Addie was holding a bottle of Jim Beam, this mischievous look on her face. "Does that uniform of yours come with hand-cuffs, Deputy?"

Her words were slurred, obviously drunk. She brought the half-empty bottle to her lips anyway and gulped down two large swallows.

"You shouldn't be here," both Matts said—the one standing in the living room and one standing next to Addie in this, what? Dream? Vision?

Memory.

Living Room Matt knew exactly what this was, because this

wasn't the first time he'd relived it. He wanted nothing more than to forget it, take it back, undo what came next, but he knew he couldn't do that any more than he could erase words carved in stone.

"If you didn't want me here, why did you call?" Addie stepped closer to the Matt in the kitchen and held the bottle toward him. "It's okay, nobody will ever have to know. This can be our little secret. I'll give you the things she's not and not a single soul has to know."

Kitchen Matt snatched the bottle from Addie's hand, ripped it from her grip, went to throw it across the room at the wall in some drunken rage, but Living Room Matt knew he wouldn't. On some level, they all knew that, even Addie, because she only smiled. Her fingers fumbled through the buttons on her blouse until it was hanging loosely from her shoulders. She wore a black silk bra beneath. "Hey, remember that party at Brian Lowman's house in tenth grade? His parents were gone and he invited everyone over, then kept us down in the basement, thinking his folks would never know as long as nobody went upstairs?"

"We went upstairs," both Matts said softly, his words as slurred as hers.

"We went upstairs," she purred. "Went up to the kitchen and had a party of our own."

"That was a long time ago," both Matts replied, both stepping closer to Addie.

Still facing him, Addie backed up to the kitchen counter and hoisted herself up. "You put me on the counter, just like this, told me to lie back"—and she did—"just like this. Then you did a shot off my belly...my breasts..." She drew her finger down from the center of her breasts, over her torso, slipped it under the waist-band of her jeans.

"That was a long time ago," both Matts muttered for a second time, the words bumping together in a single drunken breath.

Kitchen Matt raised the bottle to his lips and took a long, hard drink—both Matts felt the smooth burn in their throats, their bellies.

Addie unsnapped the button of her jeans and pulled the zipper halfway down, revealing a hint of pink underwear. "I'll do things to you Gabby would never consider, let you do things to me...whatever you want. I know what you like, Matt, I always have. And it will be our little secret."

Both Matts stood in silence for several long moments, then Kitchen Matt raised the bottle of bourbon back to his lips even as Living Room Matt muttered, "No, don't..." because he understood that was the moment he went over the edge, with that drink.

Kitchen Matt shuffled closer, got within inches of her, set the bottle down on the counter.

"I'm glad I came back," Addie breathed, her fingers playing across the buckle of Matt's belt. "All these years, nobody's ever fucked me like you."

Neither Matt heard what she said next, because Kitchen Matt grabbed her by the band of her jeans and pulled her toward him as if she weighed nothing. Living Room Matt shouted for him to stop, lunged toward them both—

Matt cracked against the desk, his knees and thighs hitting the center drawer with enough force to nearly tip the desk over. Both legs on his side smacked back down against the tile with a loud crack and Matt fell back into his chair. The bottle of Advil rolled across the top of the desk and fell to the floor, then the office went silent.

When Matt managed to look back up again, the girl was no longer in the chair opposite him but standing in the far corner of Ellie's office, her back pressed against the wall, vigorously scratching at one of the names on her arm—Arwa Gilmore—there was a line drawn through it that hadn't been there a moment earlier.

Words slammed into his head. Unspoken, yet as loud as a shout—

Hope not ever to see Heaven. I have come to lead you to the other shore; into eternal darkness; into fire and into ice.

From the other room, someone called out—

"THE LIBRARY'S ON FIRE!"

53

HANNAH

"**DO YOU WANT TO** hear my idea?" Malcolm asked again, licking his lip. Just the thought of it seemed to excite him. He was growing hard; she could see it through his jeans. Every instinct in her body told her she should tell him no, let him do his worst, because somehow she understood even if he killed her, it would be better than what he was about to propose.

Malcolm tugged out his own phone from his back pocket and tapped through several screens. "Maybe it's better I show you." He found the image he was looking for, studied it intently for a few seconds, then held it out to her. It was a picture of that cheerleader, Marcie Holden. She was sitting in the same spot where Hannah was now. Both her wrists were red. The pieces of two zip ties were on the floor under the table.

Malcolm swiped left and brought up another picture. In this one, Marcie was naked, cowering against the side of the grandfather clock. One arm stretched across her breasts, her other hand covering her crotch. Her face was streaked with tears. A smile spread across Malcolm's face as he brought up the next image; he stared at it for a long moment before showing it to Hannah— Marcie trying not to look at the camera, crying for sure. She was on her back on the dusty hallway floor, touching herself even though she clearly didn't want to.

Hannah tried to turn away, but Malcolm grabbed her by the chin and twisted her head back toward the small screen.

"If you want to live, you'll let me do things to you," Malcolm said in that horrible gravelly voice. "Unspeakable things. I'm going to film it, take pictures. Whatever I want. We don't finish until I say we're finished. When we're done. *When I'm done*, I'll let you go, just like I did with Marcie Holden. But...and here's the important part, the part you need to completely understand... if you tell a single person about today, if you even hint about it, all the pictures and videos will go online. I'll post them publicly, every social media platform. I'll send copies to your friends, your parents, your teachers—and make sure everyone sees them." He brought the tip of the screwdriver to her face, less than an inch from her eye, and slid it down her cheek. "Aside from me, you're the only person to see those photos of Marcie. I promised her I wouldn't share them, and I kept that promise. You've seen her around school—*after she came back*—so you know I let her go. You do as I ask, and I'll let you go, too. We'll move forward and pretend today never happened."

It had happened last fall. Marcie Holden vanished for three days. When she appeared again, she told everyone she'd run off with a boy she met online, she'd been in New York. She refused to give anyone his name, not even her parents or the police. When they asked to examine her phone, she handed it over, but not before telling them she had wiped it of all data. The police had dropped it after that, and although Marcie's parents had probably pressed the issue at home, Hannah hadn't heard much else about it. Marcie was back and safe, and that was all anyone really cared about. She'd gotten quiet, though, dropped out of cheerleading and her other after-school activities.

Several of the flies found the icy spot on Malcolm's cheek and appeared to be hungrily lapping at it. The spot had grown larger. Not much, but it had. Malcolm did nothing to drive the flies away. Instead, he raised the screwdriver back to Hannah's eye. "If I have to kill you, I will, but I don't want to. What happens next depends entirely on you. If you're willing to do as I ask, *everything I tell you to do*, nod your head one time."

Hannah knew she had no choice; she nodded.

"Good." The yellow smile returned to Malcolm's face. "That's my girl. I told you we wouldn't have to kill her."

At first, Hannah wasn't sure she heard that last part correctly. The *we* again, but then he said—

"I always do...You think I'm some sort of idiot?"

—and Hannah was certain: He was talking to someone else.

Someone who wasn't there.

Malcolm slipped the screwdriver back into his pocket and reached for a drawer in the table at Hannah's side. He took out a small burlap sack and tugged it down over his head. Two eye holes had been cut out, another near his mouth. He twisted the mask around, positioned it so he could see out. "This will all be over soon."

54

MATT

MATT FOUND HIMSELF UNABLE to move.

The girl had done that. Spoke to him without words—

Hope not ever to see Heaven. I have come to lead you to the other shore; into eternal darkness; into fire and into ice.

She put a thought in his head. Not only that, but the thing with him and Addie, she—

Someone banged on the door, tried the knob, and shouted when they found it locked.

"Matt! The library!"

Gabby.

He snapped back and rounded the desk, fumbled with the lock, and opened the door.

Gabby grabbed him by the arm and pulled him to the large window facing Main. "Look!"

The library was on the opposite side of the street about a block down. Thick black smoke was pouring from an open window on the second floor. Ed McDougal and Ben Molton crowded up next to him. Conner Evans was at another window. Matt craned his neck and shouted, "Sally, did you call—"

"Nobody picking up at the fire station!" she replied before he could finish.

The fire station was only two doors down, across the street from the library.

"Oh my God!" Gabby gasped, covering her mouth. "Is that Arwa Gilmore?"

Tied to a chair, the old woman stumbled out the double doors of the library and rolled down the granite steps to the sidewalk below. She was on fire.

An image of her name scrawled on the girl's arm flashed through his head—her name with a line drawn through it. He pushed it away. "Ed! Ben! You're on the volunteer squad, right? Come with me!" Matt shouted on his way out the door.

He bolted down the sidewalk. When he passed the fire station, he waved an arm and yelled over his shoulder, "Find out what the hell is going on in there!"

Both Ed and Ben were overweight, huffing as they tried to keep up, but they heard him.

Matt tore off his jacket as he crossed the street. When he reached Gilmore, she was under the chair, still alive, her body jerking and thrashing, covered in flames. What might have been a scream moments earlier was now nothing more than a guttural moan coming from the place her mouth had been. Matt kicked at the chair, rolled it over, and smothered her with his jacket. Little good that did—she'd been doused in some kind of accelerant; he could smell it.

The woman stopped moving.

She was gone.

Matt dropped back on his hands, out of breath.

The sky was filled with black smoke. It wasn't just coming out the open windows now, it was coming from the roof. The clock tower was completely engulfed.

Across the street, Ed McDougal was pounding on one of the fire station's large garage bay doors. He glanced back at Matt. "I can see people inside, but they won't open up!"

"What do you mean, they won't open up?!"

Matt barely got the words out before one of the doors started to rise.

Engine number 7, the older of the two, roared to life. The engine revved and someone let out two loud blasts from the air horn.

Still standing in front of the door, Ed McDougal gave Matt a thumbs-up.

The door was only open a third of the way when the throaty engine revved again and came crashing through, sending aluminum cascading down both sides of the truck. Ed managed to swivel his large frame about halfway before the truck struck him. It didn't even slow as he vanished under the chrome bumper and thumped under the tires as the heavy vehicle rolled over him. Matt couldn't make out who was driving, only a silhouette, but they flicked on the lights and siren, gave the air horn another blast, and turned left on Main, picking up speed as they headed out of town.

Clearly in shock, Ben Molton stood motionless off to the side of the station house, staring at the large stain that had been Ed McDougal only moments earlier. Thankfully, the truck had left him facedown.

If not for the heat of the fire, Matt might have remained on the ground next to the dead woman in the chair, as catatonic as Ben appeared to be, because his brain wanted to stop—wanted *everything* to stop—but he felt the flames hungrily eating away at the library like a cancer working from the inside out and managed to snap back, knowing that if he didn't move, those same flames would find him. The wind gave a hardy gust, and Matt realized the heavy smoke above the library was alive with glowing embers. They left the rooftop and floated lazily above, some landing harmlessly in the grass and on the pavement, others vanishing from sight as they drifted over the various buildings on Main Street. Most of those buildings were over a hundred years old, and at least half were constructed of wood. They'd go up like a tinderbox.

Matt forced himself to his feet and darted across the street. "Ben, we need to get that fire out!"

"Yeah, the fire," Ben replied flatly, trance-like. He glanced down Main, in the direction of his house, and muttered in a voice that sounded half asleep, "I'll be right back, buddy." Then he was gone, shuffling down the road as if he were on some Sunday stroll, all else forgotten.

Matt let him go; he didn't have time to chase him.

The Bend's second fire truck was still in the other bay, but when Matt stepped through the mangled door and got a good look at that second truck, he realized all its tires had been slashed. The fire ax was still embedded in the left rear. Not only had someone destroyed the tires but they cut up all the hoses and pounded the various connectors and valves to the point of useless. Fire extinguishers littered the floor, their contents sprayed out, depleted, coating everything in white.

55

RILEY

THEY MADE RILEY WEAR a blindfold. Well, sort of. Even though it was only October, Robby had a scarf in the side pocket of his backpack. Before Riley could ask why he carried a scarf when it wasn't cold, Mason had told her, "Don't ask," and wrapped it around her head twice before tying it in the back. Riley was less concerned with *why* he had a scarf than she was with *where* it had come from, because Robby had at least one dead bird in that bag, and who knew what else, but she didn't say anything because she didn't want to give Mason another opportunity for a baby joke. She was ten—hardly a baby—and he was an idiot.

"She's slowing us down," Mason muttered from somewhere up ahead.

Evelyn was holding Riley's arm, guiding her, little good that did. It was one thing when they were on pavement, it was another entirely when they'd stepped into the woods and the ground became uneven, covered with who-knew-what she might trip over. She moved as quickly as she could, but she wasn't about to fall.

"I'm taking the blindfold off," Evelyn said. "We're deep enough into the woods, she won't know where we are."

"She does figure it out, and I guess we'll have to kill her," Mason replied, unable to keep from laughing at his stupid joke.

They'd talked like that since the blindfold went on—like she couldn't hear them. Like the wool over her eyes blocked her hearing as well as her sight. It was a little muffled, but she heard them just fine. She also had a pretty good handle on where they were. They'd entered the woods at Bolson Pass; that was the closest path to the water tower, and they hadn't walked on the pavement long enough to reach another. They were moving uphill, too. She could feel that easily enough. There'd been one left turn and one right, and she'd briefly heard the sound of the waterfalls near Diana's Baths before they left the well-worn trail for some secondary path far less traveled.

"Hold up a second." Evelyn untied the knot at the back of Riley's head and unwrapped the scarf. Riley squinted as the sun came into view, high and to her right. She knew that meant they were heading north. Matt had taught her how to figure out her direction pretty much any time of the day using the sun. He even showed her how to figure it out at night with the stars. And he told her if she ever got lost in the woods, she should try to find water and follow it downhill. Downhill and south would always bring her back to Hollows Bend.

Looking down at her feet, she realized the trail they were on wasn't much of a trail at all. Unlike the ones she normally took with Matt and her mom, this one looked like even the deer ignored it. They were sandwiched between a wall of rock on the right and a dense forest on the left. Both Mason and Robby were busy moving the branches of a deadfall aside. Several of them were tied together, and she realized they'd been placed there to hide the path.

"Robby's idea," Evelyn told her. "In case some tourist gets too close."

"Too close to what?"

Then she saw it, just beyond the deadfall. The mouth of a small cave.

"Come on." Even though she was no longer blindfolded, Evelyn took her by the arm as before and guided her to the opening. "Watch your head. It opens up inside."

Riley followed Evelyn through the narrow opening and found herself standing in complete darkness, like the sunlight wasn't allowed in. The air was cool and damp.

A match flickered to life, and Evelyn lit an old oil lantern. "Robby figured out how to get this going with some magic formula of vegetable oil and who-knows-what, but it burns a lot longer than the battery-operated one we first brought up here." She twisted a small knob, and the flame grew brighter.

Riley gasped.

The cave was much bigger than she expected—at least twenty feet tall at the center and as deep as the light could reach. For the most part, the ground was flat; someone had taken the time to rake it. They'd also brought in some old plastic lawn chairs, a folding card table. There was a cooler and a radio...

"We've been bringing stuff up with us whenever we can," Evelyn explained. "Things from the dump, mostly. Or the curb. You'd be surprised what some people throw out."

Riley stepped up to a rope hanging from a stalactite above. The bottom end vanished inside a red five-gallon gas can with a garden hose spigot rigged into the side. "What's that?"

"Oh, that's more of Robby's doing." Evelyn plucked a paper Dixie cup from atop a plastic milk crate and filled it from the spigot. "Water comes down off the ceiling, follows the rope, and fills the can. Robby tested it when we first found this place and said it's more pure than the water from our tap at home. Really cold, too. Want some? We got more cups around here somewhere."

Riley shook her head.

"Suit yourself." Evelyn drank the water in one gulp, then placed the cup back where she found it. She walked off toward the back of the cave, vanished in the dark for a moment, then returned with a black duffel bag. Inside was a microscope with PROPERTY OF HOLLOWS BEND MIDDLE SCHOOL stenciled across the top.

"Don't you worry about getting in trouble?"

"With school?"

"With anyone," Riley replied. "You guys broke into my house. Into the water tower. Stole that. What happens if you get caught?"

"You gonna tell your mama's boyfriend so he can throw us in kiddie jail? Maybe foster care or juvie?" She opened her mouth as if to say something else, then promptly clamped it shut.

"What?"

She looked at Riley, and for one quick second, the ice left her eyes. Then she quickly blinked it back. "It's nothing...You just crack me up. I bet you think your life is hard with no daddy around. You probably never considered it could be worse if he was."

Before Riley could respond to that, Mason and Robby came in.

Evelyn took the microscope from the bag and smiled a real smile for the first time today. She held it out to her brother. "Happy birthday!"

Robby waved toward the card table without looking at her. "Set it up over there."

The smile vanished and her shoulders slumped, as if the microscope doubled in weight.

"Ass-burger," Mason said in a voice so low, nobody but Riley probably heard him.

Robby set his backpack down on a piece of old cardboard near the cave wall and began removing the contents one by one. There were three dead birds; at least one being the crow he'd picked up outside Riley's house, a ziplock bag filled with dirt, another filled with leaves, and several other things Riley couldn't quite make out in the dim light. He took one of the birds, laid it on its back, and spread its wings. Using pins from a small plastic box, he fastened the bird to the cardboard.

Riley swallowed. "What's he doing?"

"Oh, you're gonna love this, he's gonna dissect it," Mason told her.

He was only eight, and that was something they didn't teach in school until eighth grade. First worms, then frogs, then pigs. Everyone knew about it because the entire school smelled like a jar of bad pickles for nearly a month. "Does he know how?"

"Ass-*burger*," Mason said again, this time emphasizing the second word like he was making some kind of statement. "Little man knows how to do all kinds of crazy shit."

"But he still picks his nose."

Mason nodded slowly. "But he *still* picks his nose. I don't get it, either."

"You'll wanna see," Evelyn said, stepping closer to her brother to get a better look.

"I think I'm okay right here."

"Naw, she's right," Mason told her. "If it's like the other one, you'll want to watch. Breathe through your mouth. It's not so bad."

"What other ones?"

"From the diner. Hurry up, before we miss it!"

Mason pulled her by the arm until they were hovering over Robby.

"Flashlight, Ev," Robby said. "Maybe record it this time?"

"Good idea."

Robby produced a scalpel, no doubt pilfered from the middle school, too. He waited for his sister to shine the beam of her phone's light down on the bird and brought the blade to its belly. Riley wasn't sure she could watch.

"Recording?"

"Yeah."

Mason whispered, "I know it's gross, but don't look away. It happens fast."

Riley was about to ask him *what* happens fast when Robby pressed down on the blade and drew it down the bird's belly in one quick motion, like a doctor on TV, only this wasn't TV, and the camera didn't cut away. There was a soft crunching noise, like potato chips breaking, and a thin, dark line appeared in the feathers. Riley thought it was blood, at least until it started to smoke.

56

HANNAH

THE MASK WAS SO Malcolm couldn't be recognized in the pictures; Hannah was able to figure that much out. She also understood that meant he planned to show the pictures to someone, or he wouldn't care. Maybe a lot of someones. Maybe he'd post them anyway. Maybe he planned to sell them. That explanation was horrible, but none of that mattered unless she got out alive.

"You scream, and you're dead," Malcolm said in that low, gravelly voice. He removed the tape from Hannah's mouth and pulled out the rag. She sucked in a breath but said nothing. He brought the blade of the screwdriver to the tape on her wrists and forced it to cut through. "I'm freeing your hands so you can undress yourself. You try anything, and I mean anything, and—"

"You'll kill me."

"Now you're getting it."

Malcolm shuffled away from her, until his back was against the opposite wall of the hall. Between the mask and his long limbs, he looked more like a spider than a person skittering across the floor. He moved the screwdriver to his left hand, scooped up his phone with his right, and watched her through the small screen as he snapped a few pictures, then switched to video. "Okay, stand up. Slow."

Both Hannah's legs were asleep, and she had to use the table on one side and the grandfather clock on the other to leverage herself up. The feeling quickly returned to her limbs, but that didn't stop the shaking.

"Now take off your jeans, slow."

Hannah fumbled with the snap, got it open, and pulled down the zipper.

"Wait. Stop," Malcolm ordered. "First, the sweatshirt, then the rest. That'll be better. You're not wearing a bra, right?"

The memory of Danny fumbling with the clasp and finally getting it came back to her, the warmth of his gentle touch. It all felt so long ago. The tears wanted to come, but Hannah wasn't about to give Malcolm the satisfaction. She reached for the hem of her baggy sweatshirt, started to pull it up.

"You can at least try to look sexy. Marcie did."

And that made her angry.

The blood boiled within her.

People always talked down to her, disrespected her. Danny had been one of the few who didn't, and now he was gone. Everyone treated her like they were better than her, and now she was letting this guy…yes, she was letting him do this to her. She could either stop it or let it happen; *that* was totally in her control.

Hannah had no idea where these thoughts came from, but she welcomed them, because they beat back the fear, made her feel strong. She placed one hand on the edge of the grandfather clock, and ran the other down the side of her breast with a mischievous grin growing on her face. "Better?"

Malcolm bobbed his head. "Yeah."

"Good."

Hannah eased her hand around the back of the grandfather clock and yanked it forward with every ounce of strength she could muster. The large clock tipped and came down on Malcolm with a satisfying crunch before he could scuttle out of the way. She snatched her phone and the screwdriver from his hands and ran.

57

RILEY

"WHA…WHAT JUST HAPPENED?" RILEY stuttered as a cloud of black smoke drifted toward the ceiling of the cave.

When Robby cut the crow, its blood smoked, but it didn't end there. He pulled his hand away just as the feathers started to smolder, then crumbled. There was no other way to describe it. It was like the bird was actually some kind of delicate sculpture and it collapsed under its own weight. The pins were still in the cardboard, but there was nothing left of the bird but a pile of black ash.

For the first time, Riley noticed the other black stains on the cardboard. "Are those spots from other birds?"

Mason nodded. "The ones from the diner."

Riley watched in stunned silence as Robby repeated the process with the remaining two birds from his backpack. When they were gone, he carefully collected the black dust in three ziplock bags and labeled each with a black marker.

"They smoke, but they don't actually get hot," Robby explained.

"They melt, but they're not damp. Just the opposite. The dust that's left over is so dry it's like all the water vanished from their bodies in a second or two."

"When you cut into them," Riley said softly.

Robby removed the pins from the cardboard and placed them back in the plastic container he'd gotten them from. "Did you ever eat astronaut ice cream?"

"Sure."

"When they freeze-dry it and remove the water, they compress it into those square bricks. The overall size is reduced by a factor of seven. If they didn't compress it, it would turn into powder. I think the smoke that appears when I cut the birds is the water leaving their bodies, but since they don't get compressed, they dist...dist..."

"Disintegrate," Evelyn chimed in.

"Yeah, disintegrate."

"Why would the water leave their bodies when you cut them?" Riley asked.

"Because there's something wrong with it," Evelyn said. "Duh."

Robby's gaze drifted to the small bottle of water they'd collected at the town's tower. "Seventy-three percent of the human brain is made up of water. If the brain gets dehydrated, cells don't work right. It can cause anything from headaches to poor judgment."

"Hallucinations," Evelyn added.

Mason grunted. "Like slime monsters swimming in your cereal bowl."

Riley looked back at the stained cardboard. That didn't make any sense. "Birds don't drink the same water as us."

Mason pressed down on his baseball bat and twisted the tip around in the dirt at his feet. "The birds drink from the lakes and streams. Rainwater, sometimes. The water in that tower comes from underground. Streams below us feeding down off the mountain. It all comes from the same place."

Riley thought of her water glass next to the bathroom sink. The other one she kept in the kitchen. She always drank from the tap, her mom, too. "But don't they...I don't know...clean it somehow?"

"Between pumping it from the ground and going in the tower, the water runs through a filtration system," Robby said. "It's out near the Saco River. Other parts are underground, but it's not like in a city where it runs through some treatment plant. It's mostly just sand. Water from the mountains and the underground streams is some of the purest in the world. It's the kind of thing they bottle and sell. It doesn't have to be cleaned much before you can drink it. It really doesn't need to be cleaned at all."

"Sand takes out the solids," Mason muttered. "Chemicals are supposed to kill the rest."

Evelyn let out a sigh. "Guess who's in charge of adding the chemicals..."

"No luck, Buck," Mason told her before Riley could answer.

Riley felt a lump grow in her throat.

"Who knows if he's been doing it."

Riley swallowed and eyed the microscope. "Test the water with that."

Robby was already working on it. He'd opened the bottle he'd collected at the tower and carefully tipped it until a drop fell onto a glass slide. He pressed another piece of glass on top, sandwiched the water in between, and put it on the microscope. When he looked down through the scope, he went quiet for a long time, slowly adjusting the various knobs.

Evelyn was getting impatient. "What do you see, Robby?"

Mason leaned toward Riley and whispered, "Imagine a million tiny versions of the thing you saw in your sink swimming around in there, *in the water you've been drinking*. Gross, huh?"

Riley's stomach lurched, but she managed not to get sick.

"Robby..." Evelyn said again.

Nearly another minute went by before he leaned back from the microscope. "I don't see anything."

Evelyn nudged her brother aside and looked for herself. "There's got to be something in there."

"Not something visible," Robby said. "That doesn't mean there's nothing wrong."

"Bugs so small you can't see them swimming," Mason said quietly.

Riley wrapped her arms around herself and squeezed, like a self-hug. She didn't realize she was scratching herself until she caught Mason staring.

"What the hell is that?" He pointed at her wrist, near the spot where his name was written.

Riley felt the blood leave her face.

Roy Buxton had appeared there in the same blueish ink.

She rubbed it with her thumb but it didn't smear.

Evelyn's eyes narrowed. "Give me the pen."

"I didn't write it."

"Bullshit. Where are you hiding it?" Before Riley could stop her, Evelyn was patting her down, turning her pockets inside out. When she found nothing, she let out a frustrated grunt.

"I told you."

"You want us to believe those names magically appeared on your arms. Just like that."

"They did."

Robby smeared something across her skin, wet and cold. It was an alcohol wipe. She had no idea where he'd gotten it. He looked at the pad, then her arm, and said matter-of-factly, "It's not ink. It's below her skin. Like a tattoo." He went back to the water samples as if a tattoo appearing all on its own was the most normal thing ever.

Riley, Mason, and Evelyn all stared at each other.

Robby went over to the makeshift water collection system

he'd rigged under the stalactite. Rummaging through his pockets, he found one of the test strips he'd pilfered from the water tower, held it under the spigot, twisted the knob, and soaked it. He shook off the excess and held the strip up to the light.

"We'll figure out your Harry Potter ink in a minute. I don't like where this is going," Evelyn said. "I just drank that water."

Robby stared at the strip, and for the first time since Riley had met him, he looked confused.

Evelyn drew closer. "Well?"

He removed the strip he'd used at the water tower from his back pocket and held it up to the other one. Now Evelyn looked confused, too. "What the hell is that supposed to mean?"

"Roy Buxton doesn't live very far from here," Robby said. "We need to show him this."

58

MATT

MATT TOSSED THE EMPTY bucket back across the street to Conner Evans, who heaved it over his shoulder to Sally at the door of the fire station. Sally handed it off to Gabby, took the full one from her other hand, and glared back at Conner, who was standing on the yellow line of Main Street. Her face red and sweaty, Sally said, "Christ, Conner, I can't toss a full bucket, you lazy shit, get over here!"

Conner didn't move. Instead, he bent over with his hands on his knees, out of breath. "This is stupid! We're not even making a dent in it!"

Gabby shielded her eyes from the sun and pointed toward the roof of the library. "Matt, he's right! It's spreading!"

Matt followed her finger.

Visible between the black smoke spewing from the library's windows, glowing hot embers circled the air around the clock tower, caught the wind, and drifted lazily through the sky. Some dropped to the street and grass; others vanished on the rooftops of the surrounding buildings. Tendrils of smoke were already drifting up from the roof of the pharmacy two doors down. Same with the bank. Left unchecked, the fire would take all of downtown, and without working fire trucks or additional help, there was nothing he could do to stop it.

Matt had picked up another empty bucket and felt it slip from his hand and thump to the ground at his feet.

Where the hell did everyone go?

An hour ago, half the town seemed to be out in the streets. Now nobody was around. Even the people who had been in the sheriff's office had run off.

A window on the second floor of the library blew out with a deep grunt. Matt shielded his face and eyes. The heat of it smacked into him, and he took a few stumbling steps in the opposite direction before finally calling out to whoever was listening, "We need to evacuate all these buildings! Get everyone out!"

It was Sunday, so most were closed, but he couldn't risk someone getting trapped inside.

A block down the road, Sally shouted something back, but he couldn't make it out. She grabbed Gabby by the hand, and the two of them started going door to door. When they found one locked, they beat on the windows before moving on.

Matt turned back around. "Conner, I need you to—"

Conner Evans was gone. No doubt took off to save his own skin, like Ben Molton and the others had.

Matt swore under his breath and was about to head back into the fire station to salvage whatever he could when he spotted the strange girl standing in the street, her long, dark hair fluttering in the wind. She was vigorously scratching at her left arm.

A pang of fear tweaked Matt's chest as he thought of all the names written on her arms, how she'd been scratching at Arwa

Gilmore's name moments before the woman stumbled out of the library and died. The line through her name.

The heat of the fire on his back, Matt ran to her, grabbed her wrist, and yanked up the sweatshirt sleeve.

The name *Eisa Heaton* was bright red, inflamed, a fresh line down the middle.

59

HANNAH

HANNAH BOLTED FROM THE Pickerton house, nearly tripped on the last step as she came down off the porch, then stumbled again as her foot slipped in the mud and pine needles, but she managed to stay on her feet.

Rather than follow the road back down to town, where Malcolm would surely catch her long before she reached help, she went for the trees. She knew that wasn't much better—fifteen years of watching television and movies told her the girl never got out of the woods alive when some psycho was chasing after her—but she had no choice. There was no place else to go.

She could no longer see the house, had put at least a hundred yards between her and Malcolm, when he shouted from somewhere behind her. "I'm glad you did that, Hannah! This will be much more fun! I'll even give you a head start! Wait until you see what I found—way better than my screwdriver! You can keep that if it makes you feel better!"

Hannah's grip tightened around the handle. She knew it wasn't much, but it was better than nothing.

"You'll have to kill me!" he shouted. "Think you have that in you? Think you can stick a blade in another person, give it a good twist, and watch the life leave them? You won't be the first to try, so you better hope you get it right!"

Hannah quickly looked around, tried to get her bearings.

She knew these woods; she'd played in them when she was a kid. If she kept moving, she could outrun him. She'd get to the Saco River, follow the water down the mountain to Route 112. From there, she could flag someone down. It wasn't that far, maybe a mile. Two at the most. She just had to keep moving. Had to be careful. Watch her footing. A twisted ankle, broken foot—it only took one wrong fall. She'd heard enough of those stories over the years. Half the people who died on the mountain were found with some kind of injury—the kind of injury that happened when you rushed.

Hannah rounded a large granite boulder sitting atop a five-foot drop, reached for a tree trunk, and used it to carefully work down the hill, moving as fast as she dared. When she reached somewhat level ground again, she checked her phone. She had a signal, three bars. Quickly keyed in 911. The call rang twice, connected, then dropped.

"I think you busted one of my ribs with the grandfather clock, Hannah! Hurts like a mother!"

He sounded close.

Much closer than Hannah hoped.

His voice echoed off the trees and granite, making it difficult to pinpoint. "Do you remember London Dobson? She was the first girl I brought out here—wow, three years ago already! Crazy how time flies. I slipped her a roofie at the victory party after we creamed Exeter in the state football finals, then brought her out here. Kept her in that house for eight days tied to the bed in back. Had her there for so long, I actually got bored with her, figured I'd try something different, so I cut her ropes and told her to run. I think she thought I was kidding at first, 'cause she just sat there. Then she bolted. She got as far as the waterfalls at Diana's Baths before I caught up with her. She was hysterical at that point, screaming her head off. I guess that added to the fun, seeing the fear in her eyes. I can't tell you how exhilarating it was when I finally ended her!"

Easing further downhill, Hannah kept moving. She thumbed Redial on the phone.

Same thing—two rings, the call connected, then dropped.

"You know the best part?" Malcolm went on. "I didn't have a shovel with me, you know, to bury her body, so I dragged her off into the trees and covered her with some leaves and branches. Figured I'd come back and get her in the ground later. So that's what I did. Got back out there the next morning with a shovel, a pickax, some plastic...everything I needed to do it right. You know what I found? Not much of anything. The animals had gone to town on her overnight. Took her down to her bones, even hauled some of those away. I had my dick in that girl not twenty-four hours earlier, and I couldn't recognize her anymore. You believe that? That's when I realized I didn't have to bury her; it was better if I didn't. The wildlife would make her disappear far faster if I let her be. I kept going back to see what was left. It only took *six days* for every trace of her to vanish. Mother Nature's awesome. Gotta respect her."

Hannah tried to ignore him, focused on her movement. She dialed 911 again, but the call dropped like before. She flicked through the various screens, loaded the navigation app, and keyed in Gas 'n' Go. The station was at the base of the mountain on 112. The app hung for a moment, the small hourglass spinning, then said **unable to connect**. She still had three bars, so the signal was strong enough, but it wasn't working.

Her right foot caught the corner of a rock. She nearly fell but managed to grab the trunk of an old oak tree and right herself.

"I'm gonna try something a little different with you, Hannah!" Malcolm shouted. "I'm gonna slice you wide open, scoop your insides out onto your belly. See if that speeds up the process. I bet I can cut that six days down to three if I do that. What do you think?"

Hannah always forgot how much thinner the air was up on the mountain. Each breath she sucked in felt wrong, like taking a drink through a straw that had a hole in it. She didn't realize she was panting until she paused for a second to try to find the compass app on the phone. She got the app open, but it wasn't working, either. The screen was frozen, no matter what direction she pointed the phone.

Doesn't matter. She didn't need it.

She'd been in these woods a million times. She'd find the river, follow it to 112, get help.

Hannah repeated that as she went—river, 112, help—like some kind of mantra, as Malcolm called out her name again, dragging out both syllables, "Hannnnnaaaah…"

60

MATT

MATT BURST THROUGH THE doors of the sheriff's office, quickly looked around. Everyone was gone. Even Addie Gallagher. The space was silent save for a soft whimper coming from the cell in the back.

Although sun streamed in through all the windows, the cell was dark, as if the shadows had all gone there to wait out the day.

Josh was nothing more than a silhouette pressed so tight against the brick of the wall on the left he might have been part of the original design. He sucked in a breath. "I tried to stop her, but I was too slow. I just…she hadn't moved the entire time we've been in here. I didn't expect her to…"

When Matt drew closer, he saw her on the floor, kneeling awkwardly behind the bars, lifeless. Held in an upright position by some freakish act of gravity. Her face was slick with blood, the flesh swollen, pulpy. The whites of her eyes were blinding against the dark red, and her mouth hung open like a black maw.

Josh sunk deeper into the shadows. "I didn't touch her. She was on the bench. She'd been there, so quiet for so long I nearly forgot she was even in here with me. Then she jumped up and ran headfirst into the bars. Didn't even try to slow down, like she meant to run through them or something, then she dropped. Landed on her knees, like she is now, and started banging her face into the metal. I...I grabbed her hair, tried to stop her, but..." His arm peeled away from the dark, he held out his hand. There was a clump of gray hair twisted in his fingers. He let it go, and it floated to the floor.

An image of Josh's wife kneeling next to the bathtub popped into Matt's head, his dead children floating beneath the water.

Matt cleared his throat. "Josh, I need you to step to the back of the cell, face the wall, and put your hands above your head."

"I didn't do this, Matt. I didn't hurt her. You're not pinning this on me."

"Move to the back. Do as I said."

Matt took out his handcuffs and keys and waited for Josh to move away before unlocking the cell door. He carefully stepped around Eisa Heaton's body and got the cuffs on him, cinching them tight enough for Josh to let out a groan.

"This is on you, Matt. She clearly needed help, and you locked her in a cell. You let this happen. Who's next? Me? You gonna get me killed?"

Behind him, Gabby screamed. She was at the door with Sally, her hand over her mouth.

Sally stepped closer. Her angry gaze jumped from Eisa Heaton to Josh Tatum. "You mother—"

"Sally, get that girl," Matt interrupted. "Don't let her out of your sight."

Sally nodded and went back outside.

"Riley..." Gabby muttered softly before running to Matt's office.

"Come on." Matt gripped Josh's arm and turned him toward the door.

"I want that lawyer you promised me. I'm supposed to get one, right? Where is he? Or is that a sham, too? You just buying time until you find a way to put a bullet in me? You sure look like you want to."

"I'm keeping you safe."

"The fuck you are."

When Gabby returned from Matt's office, her face was white. "She's gone."

"Where would she go? Why?"

"Your window is open. I don't know. Maybe home?"

Sally came through the door with the girl. One hand on her shoulder, the other holding the hood of her sweatshirt. "We need to go. The fire crossed the street. We got maybe a few minutes."

The girl took it all in fast, then wrapped her arms around herself.

Matt shuffled Josh toward the door. "Everyone in my cruiser. Now."

Gabby didn't move. "I'm not going anywhere without Riley."

"We'll find her, I promise," Matt assured her. "Right now, we need to get someplace safe."

"Ellie's house is our backup," Sally said. "She's got a generator, radio, landline. If she can't find us here, that's where she'll go."

"Send Riley a text, tell her to meet us there," Matt told Gabby.

"I thought texts aren't working?"

"Some are. You never know. She couldn't have gone far."

"What about her?" Sally said, pointing at the body of Eisa Heaton.

Matt just shook his head.

Outside, the air was acidic, thick with smoke. Matt loaded Josh in the back seat, and Sally got in beside him. "Somebody has to ride back here." She shrugged. "We can't all fit up front."

"Don't hurt him."

"I ain't making no promises."

Gabby rounded the car while frantically pecking away at her phone, Matt and the girl beside her.

Matt didn't see Stu Peterson or the others until he twisted the key and started the motor.

61

HANNAH

HANNAH COULDN'T BE LOST.

Couldn't be.

She knew every inch of these woods, or thought she did, but as she huddled behind what was left of a fallen oak, trying to get her bearings, she didn't recognize anything. She'd avoided the familiar paths the moment she ran from the Pickerton house and cut through the trees, knew that if she just headed down the mountain and found the river, she'd eventually get to the highway and find help. But she hadn't found the river, and it felt like she'd gone too far. She was still heading down, that much was certain, but if she ventured too far from the river, she'd miss the highway altogether and end up somewhere down in the valley.

"You're making my job easy, Hannah. Nobody'll find your body way out here!"

Hannah's breath caught in her throat. She spun around and pressed her palm against the bark of the fallen tree. Although Malcolm had shouted that, he sounded far closer than he had the last time she heard him. When she craned her neck, she heard the snap of twigs and branches under his feet. He was making no effort to hide. She caught sight of him a moment later, no more than fifty feet away coming toward her at a slight angle. He paused, faced the sun, then turned in a slow circle. She couldn't see his face. He still had that burlap mask on his head, but somehow she knew he was smiling. She thought of the flies under his skin, her mind's eye conjuring up hundreds of them crawling around his head, his ears, his nose. Frenzied in the trapped, humid air of that mask. Their buzz somehow fueling him.

He clutched something in his hand, and when he completed his circle she realized it was an ax. The *something much better than the screwdriver* he found back at the house.

She had to move, couldn't stay here. He'd surely find her, and if he managed to get close, hovered over her in that mask holding an ax, she'd lose it. She wanted to believe she was stronger than that, that she'd fight him off; she wanted to be the girl who pushed a grandfather clock on top of him, but her heart was beating like a wild drum, tears were streaming from the corners of her eyes, and every inch of her body was trembling. Strength and reason had fled. That was the truth. If he managed to corner her, she was dead.

Hannah drew in a deep breath and ran.

She pushed up from behind the tree and bolted as quickly as she could. She knew he'd hear her, but it didn't matter. He was too close to hide; all she could do was run.

"There you are, baby doll!" Malcolm swiveled in her direction, but didn't come after her, not at first. Instead, he rolled the ax in his hand. "Thought I'd have to chase you all the way to Barton, but this is as good a spot as any. Hold still, and I'll make it quick. Promise."

Hannah got maybe thirty feet when she heard a car. No, a truck. Something big. It had to be the highway, she'd found it after all! She'd—

Hannah didn't see the small patch of mud until her foot slipped out from under her. She tumbled over some loose rocks, fell, and rolled down the hill. She slipped over an embankment, went airborne, and cracked against a copse of trees at the bottom, finally coming to a stop. When she managed to roll to her back and look up, she realized she'd fallen much further than she thought. Malcolm appeared on the hill above her, nearly thirty feet up. He first looked down at her, then beyond her, and froze.

Hannah twisted around, every inch of her body hurting, and realized what he was looking at.

She was at the base of the mountain, maybe a hundred feet from Route 112. Between her and the highway was a chain-link fence. Hannah wasn't exactly sure where she was, but she didn't remember ever seeing a fence along the highway before, especially one like this. It was at least twelve feet tall, topped with razor wire. About every twenty feet there were signs that read:

DANGER
ELECTRIFIED FENCE
FATAL

Below that, the message was repeated in Spanish.

The fence posts were cemented down into the ground, and she could see fresh tire tracks in the mud on the other side. The fence itself went as far as she could see in both directions.

Hannah scrambled to her feet.

Both her palms were scraped and bleeding. She had a nasty cut on her left forearm. Her right leg hurt like hell, but nothing was broken.

Behind her, Malcolm was carefully scrambling down the hill, using the ax for leverage.

Hannah heard the truck again, that was followed by several voices barking orders at one another somewhere down the fence line to her left. Hannah ran toward them as Malcolm dropped to the ground behind her.

62

MATT

STU PETERSON WASN'T ALONE.

He stood in the center of Main Street, a rifle cradled in his hands. Four people to his left, another five on his right. All people Matt knew and respected. With a couple of feet between each of them, they'd effectively blocked the road. Matt couldn't get through unless someone moved.

Peterson wore a Boston Red Sox cap, and he inched the brim up with the tip of his finger before breaking rank, walking over to Matt's side of the car, and motioning for him to roll down his window. Matt pressed the button.

"Abandoning ship?" Peterson leaned down and studied the faces of those in Matt's car, his gaze lingering on the girl between him and Gabby. "Maybe you should leave her with me."

Something in the man had changed, Matt couldn't quite put his finger on it. Stu Peterson had never frightened him. For the most part, he liked the guy, but the edges of his face somehow seemed harder, and the warmth had left his eyes. There was a calculating flatness to his voice Matt had never noticed before. This wasn't the Stu Peterson he'd grown up with; this was the Stu Peterson who'd spent far too much time in the streets of Kabul questioning locals about IEDs. This was the Stu Peterson who'd once told him in confidence he couldn't bring himself to stand next to a stranger wearing a bulky winter coat for fear of what might be underneath. "PTSD never goes away," he'd told Matt. "If you're lucky, it sometimes sleeps. Never soundly, but it can sleep. You make do when it does."

The wind kicked up, swirled the thick smoke. Glowing embers fluttered around like manic fireflies.

"This fire is out of control," Matt told him. "You and your people need to get someplace safe."

"And where would that be? This *someplace safe*?" Peterson scratched the side of his nose. "Maybe we should all come with you to your *someplace safe*. You can deputize my little posse, make us official. Help you keep an eye on things." As he said this, his gaze never left the girl. He took in every inch of her. "You watch that video yet?"

"Not yet."

"You'll want to watch the video."

"I will. When I get to—"

"—when you get someplace safe." He nodded. "I understand, Deputy. Busy day."

Another window blew out on the second floor of the library, followed by a cloud of black smoke.

"The fire will take everything on Main Street," Matt told him. "Probably jump over to Hampton next. That's what, two blocks from your house? You want to help? Get these people to rig up some hoses. Do what you can to slow it down until we can get trucks from North Hollow or Barton in here."

"Ain't nobody coming. I think you know that. If you haven't figured that out yet, maybe you shouldn't be wearing that uniform."

Gabby leaned across the seat, partially blocked his view of the girl. "Have you seen my daughter?"

Peterson's gaze lingered on the girl a moment longer. Then he looked over at Gabby. "She run off on you? When?"

Gabby told him about the open window.

"Stu!"

The shout came from John Hicks. He was standing at the door of the sheriff's office.

"He's got Eisa Heaton in the holding cell," Hicks told him. "She's dead—fucking mess—head bashed in against the bars or something!"

Peterson's face grew red, and he leaned deeper through the window, looking first at the girl again, then at Josh in the back seat, the cuffs on his hands. "Did you hurt Eisa?"

Josh shrunk away from him, shaking his head.

"I'm not so sure I believe you."

"He's in custody, Stu. He's not going anywhere," Matt nodded out the windshield. "I need you to tell everyone to clear out of my way."

"I think you already know I can't do that."

"I don't want to arrest you."

"I'm not so sure you have the authority to do that anymore."

Matt's hand inched toward the gun on his hip, barely moved, when Peterson said, "That's the wrong move, Deputy."

"What would you consider *the right move*?"

"Leave the girl with me and my friends. I think I'd like you to leave Josh here, too, so I can get a handle on what exactly happened to Eisa. Then you take Sally and your girlfriend to your someplace safe and wait this out." He looked over at Gabby. "We'll comb every inch of this town. When we find your daughter, we'll bring her to you. You got my word on that."

While they were talking, Peterson's men had spread out. Several of them rounded Matt's cruiser and flanked them from both sides. Their weapons were all pointing at the ground, but Matt caught Rodney Campos flick off the safety on his 9mm as he edged over toward the sidewalk.

Matt eased his hand away from his own gun. "Okay. But if you hurt Josh, make sure it looks like some kind of accident. Eisa Heaton's not the only one he hurt today. He's got it coming."

Peterson's eyes narrowed. "Who else did he—"

Matt brought up his elbow and caught Stu Peterson under his chin with enough force to send the top of his head into the door frame with a hard *thunk!* Then he yanked the gearshift down into drive and stomped the gas. "Hold on!"

The engine screamed and the car shot forward, straight for the men in the street. Still in the window, Peterson twisted, cracked against the side of the car, and vanished behind them as the other men dove out of their way. They were still picking up speed when the gunfire started. Matt yanked the wheel hard to the left, and they skidded off Main to Thornily, but not before their back window blew out as the shots tore into the car.

63

HANNAH

MALCOLM YELLED OUT SOMETHING behind her, but Hannah ignored him. She ran as fast as she could, following the fence line toward the voices, the sound of heavy machinery. She'd gone at least two hundred feet before they came into view around the thick trees— at least a half dozen trucks, a flatbed weighed down with rolls of chain link and tall metal poles. Some kind of tractor with a corkscrew drill as tall as her and as wide as her waist was busy chewing into the ground as at least twenty or thirty men busily worked extending the fence. Those men wore white overalls, orange vests, and hard hats. Scattered between them were soldiers—dressed in black and gray fatigues, holding large rifles.

"Help!" she screamed out. "He's trying to kill me! Help!"

The soldiers were busy watching the workers installing the fence and seemed surprised at the sound of her voice. The one nearest her looked to be no more than early twenties. His gun hung loosely from his neck, and he was holding a bottle of water in one hand and a rugged-looking tablet in the other.

Behind him, someone shouted, "Stop her! Somebody stop her!"

Hannah followed the voice and froze.

A priest.

Dressed in a full-length black cassock, standing near a bulldozer, he raised his arm and pointed. Rosary beads dangled from his fingers. "Do not allow her any further!"

The soldier dropped the water bottle and tablet and fumbled for his rifle. He brought the barrel up, pointed it directly at Hannah's head.

Another shot rang out, followed quickly by two more. Those came from a soldier twenty feet down the line. Hannah turned fast enough to see two red blooms in Malcolm's chest and a black hole in the center of his burlap mask, directly above his eyes. His body jerked and dropped. The ax clattered down next to him.

Hannah screamed and shuffled back toward the trees.

The first bullet caught her in the left temple, passed through her brain, and came out the center of her right cheek. She never heard the other three shots.

64

RILEY

"THOSE WERE GUNSHOTS." RILEY froze and looked deep into the trees. Rather than go down the mountain and have to come all the way back up to get to Roy Buxton's cabin, they'd cut through the woods. It was tough to say, but it sounded like the shots came from somewhere below them.

"Probably hunters," Mason suggested before continuing down the path, although he didn't look like he believed that any more than the rest of them.

"Someone screamed, too. I heard a scream."

"That wasn't a scream." Mason pointed the tip of his bat in the direction the shots had come. "That was a buck dropping. Maybe a wild turkey or something. You plug them wrong, and they make all kinds of noises."

Evelyn had stopped a few paces between them both. She reached out and tugged the hood of her brother's sweatshirt and held him still. "Everybody stop moving for a second. Just listen."

"It's just hunters." Mason groaned but did as she asked. "Black bear and buck season started two weeks ago."

Robby twitched next to Evelyn. "That wasn't a hunting rifle. That was an assault weapon."

"That what your Rain Man Spidey-sense is telling you?" Mason asked.

"An M4 carbine, gas-powered, magazine-fed assault rifle. Developed in the United States during the 1980s. It's a short version of an M16, first used in—"

Evelyn yanked her brother's hoodie. "Zip it, Robby. Everyone just listen for a second."

"Listen to what?" Mason muttered. "I don't hear jack."

"Jesus, Mason, shut the hell up."

When he did, when they all stopped talking, Riley understood what Evelyn meant. "I can't hear anything. No birds, no bugs, no animal sounds at all. The wind isn't even blowing. There's nothing."

Evelyn twisted around and stared up into the trees. "Weird, right?"

Riley scratched her arm. "Yeah, weird."

Mason was growing impatient. "We should keep going. Buxton's little shithole is right over the next ridge."

Evelyn ignored him. She'd turned her attention back to Riley. "You're scratching again."

"So?"

"So, let me see. Pull up your sleeve."

Riley didn't want to. She had no idea how Mason's and Roy Buxton's names had gotten there, and that scared her, but the idea that another name might be there frightened her even more. And none of that was as bad as what Evelyn and the others would probably think of her if there was something else there. They'd tell everyone she was some kind of freak or monster or worse. "It's nothing, just a mosquito bite."

Evelyn rolled her eyes, stomped over, grabbed Riley's wrist, and pulled up her sleeve. "Mosquito bite, my ass."

"Let me guess," Mason said. "She drew a big heart around my name?"

"I didn't write anything."

Evelyn frowned at her. "Empty your pockets. Turn them inside out."

"Why?"

"Because when I figure out where you're hiding the pen, I'm going to beat the living hell out of you."

Riley tried to pull away, but Evelyn held her still and told Mason, "Pat her down."

"You pat her down. I'm not touching her. That's how you end up on a list on the internet."

"Turn your pockets inside out," Evelyn insisted.

Riley did, and when Evelyn saw they were empty, she started touching Riley all over, real fast—the front and back of her shirt, the waistband of her jeans, her shoes, and socks. "Where are you hiding the pen?"

"I don't have a pen. I didn't write it. I didn't write any of it!"

"You make her strip down, and I'm out of here."

"I'm not gonna make her..." Evelyn fell back on her heels, stared at Riley, then stood. "You're telling me that stuff is just magically appearing on your arms?"

Riley wasn't about to say magic. "*I* didn't write it."

"Well, we didn't, either, and there's nobody else out here."

"If it's not a heart, what is it?" Mason came over and looked at Riley's arm. "Who the hell is Hannah Hernandez?"

"I don't know anyone named Hannah," Evelyn said.

"I don't, either," Riley told them. "I swear."

Robby said, "Hannah Hernandez. Fifteen years old. Lives on Birch Street. Mother is Martha, father is Luis."

Mason glared at Robby. "You're seriously getting on my nerves with that. You're like an internet that walks and farts."

The name was written a little smaller than the others, and at a slight angle, but it was easy enough to read.

Evelyn licked her thumb and tried to smear it off, but that didn't work. "It's like a tattoo. I think it's under your skin, like Robby said."

Riley looked back at Evelyn, her eyes wide. "It won't come off?"

In a low voice, Robby said, "It was Hannah Hernandez who screamed."

This only angered Mason. "Okay, no way you can be sure of that."

Robby didn't reply to that, but he didn't have to. They all knew he was right.

Mason stomped off down the path. "Let's just get to Buck's house."

Evelyn was still holding Riley's arm when another name appeared.

65

TRANSCRIPT: AUDIO/VIDEO RECORDING

Analysis Note: The subject's vitals stopped reporting for thirty-seven seconds. All are back now and appear normal, but the subject has gone oddly quiet.

Sordello: Deputy? What's going through your head right now?

Maro: Can we take a break?

Sordello: I don't think that's a good idea.

Analysis Note: Sordello retrieved the files for Hannah Hernandez and Malcolm Mitchell and placed them in the carrier but did not send them over to the subject. Instead, she removed them and set them on top of the others at her side.

Sordello: Did you know Hannah Hernandez?

Maro: It's a small town. I knew her enough to wave or say hello. I couldn't tell you any personal details. That's probably a good thing. It means she never crossed my radar.

Sordello: Never got in trouble, you mean?

Maro: Yeah.

Sordello: Was that true of Malcolm Mitchell?

Maro: I knew he dropped out of school. Ellie had him on her radar as a potential problem, but nothing much came of it. Caught him shooting once, about six months back. Out near Misty Pass. Just some Coke cans with a .22. Said he'd gotten the gun from his father. His dad backed him on that, but I had the impression his father was just covering for him. No crime, though, nothing I could prove. This thing with Hannah…that was…that was horrible, but I'm not aware of any prior incidents. Marcie Holden never mentioned him. If she had, we'd have looked into it. There's no way he took six other girls. Town this size, that just doesn't happen. A girl disappears, we…

Sordello: You what?

Maro: We mobilize. We work together. Always have.

Maro: What's that?

Sordello: His six other victims.

Maro: I don't know any of those names. If that's true, they're not locals.

Sordello: Did Malcolm Mitchell ever mention living in Columbus, Ohio, to you?

Maro: Columbus? No.

Sordello: Same mask. Same MO. Six dead girls attributed to the same killer, four of whom were connected by DNA. One girl escaped, claimed her abductor kept talking to himself. Probably schizophrenic. If I were to take a sample from Malcolm Mitchell, do you think it would match?

Maro: Unless he was traveling back and forth, I don't see how. When were the Ohio girls taken?

Sordello: Did you expect Stuart Peterson and his group to fire on you? Has he ever exhibited violent tendencies in your presence?

Maro: Peterson is one of those people who always feels the need to be in charge. He's the first to report potential poachers when he spots them up on the mountain, and he's not shy about speaking up at town meetings when something doesn't go the way he'd prefer. But take out a gun and fire on someone? No way.

Sordello: Do you think that was him showing his true self, and the time you'd known him had always been some kind of charade? Or do you think the stress of the current situation caused something in him to snap?

Maro: That's probably a question better left to a shrink.

Sordello: I'm asking you.

Analysis Note: The subject's vitals dropped again. No readings for twelve seconds. Although Sordello was told through her earpiece, she did not authorize someone to go into the subject's chamber and check the leads. She didn't want to interrupt. When his vitals returned, the subject opened the water bottle and took a long swig. He grimaced and spit it out.

Maro: This tastes terrible. Did you do something to it?

Sordello: It hasn't left your chamber. Nobody touched it.

Analysis Note: The subject clearly knew this. He spent the next thirty seconds staring at that bottle. If he had further thoughts, he didn't communicate them. Nor did he drink more. He set the bottle down and continued.

66

MATT

"ANYONE HIT!?" MATT SHOUTED as they skidded across Thornily, nearly taking out two mailboxes on the corner before Matt jerked the wheel in the opposite direction and managed to regain control of the car. *"Is anyone hit!?"*

Gabby had dropped low in her seat. She quickly checked herself, then the girl. "No…we're good. We're okay."

"Matt…"

Josh's voice was thin, barely audible from the back seat. Matt found him in the rearview mirror. "What? Did you get—"

It wasn't Josh, though. When the man twisted, Matt saw the red stain on the back of the seat where Sally had been sitting. She was slumped to the side now, her head resting on the door. Blood bubbled from between her lips and dripped down her chin in a thin stream. She tried to talk, but only a soft cough came out.

Gabby twisted around and gasped. "Oh no, Sally!"

Matt wasn't ready to slow the car just yet; he wanted more distance between them and Peterson's people, or this could get worse fast. Keeping one eye on the road, he craned his neck, tried to get a better look. "I don't see an exit wound. Put pressure on her back—wherever it went in!"

Josh held up his cuffed hands. "Take these off and let me the hell out of here before they get me, too!"

"Cuffs stay on; you can still move. Help her, you selfish prick!"

Josh held his gaze in the mirror a moment longer, then carefully took Sally by the shoulder and turned her body. She was conscious, but barely holding on. Her eyes twisted toward him on a delay, as if she'd only then realized someone was touching her. She tried to speak, but instead coughed up dark blood. Matt knew that meant the bullet hit her gut, maybe her stomach, who knew what else.

The color left Josh's face as he got a better look. He glanced back at Matt and gently shook his head.

"Where'd it go in?"

Josh swallowed. "About halfway down, left side, looking at her back."

Liver, stomach, pancreas…Matt tried to picture her vital organs.

Gabby was still wearing her apron from the diner. She peeled it off and handed it back to Josh. "Here, use this to try and stop the bleeding."

Josh took it from her and slipped it behind Sally's back. "There's a second bullet down lower, center of her back. I can see where it went in, but there's hardly any blood."

"Did it hit her spine?"

Josh nodded. "Yeah, I think so."

They were coming up on the turn for Ellie's street. Matt faced forward, didn't want to miss it.

"Matt…" Josh muttered.

"Keep pressure on it. We're almost there."

"Matt, she's…"

"Ellie will have some kind of first aid kit. We'll stop the bleeding, get her stable, then find some way to get her up to North Hollow."

Gabby was still twisted around in her seat, watching Josh. She turned back to Matt, reached over the silent girl, and gently squeezed his arm. "I'm sorry, Matt. She's gone."

When Matt looked back at Josh in the mirror, the man turned away, wouldn't face him.

Matt hit the brakes, brought them to a sliding stop in Ellie's driveway behind her old Ford pickup, and beat both his fists into the steering wheel. "Fuuuuuck!"

67

RILEY

"DOESN'T SALLY DAVIE WORK at the sheriff's office with your mom's boy-friend?" Evelyn tried to rub away the new name on Riley's arm, but like the others, the ink didn't smear. It appeared to be under her skin. They'd all watched the name appear, first faint, barely visible, then it darkened.

Riley started scratching it without realizing she was even doing it. It itched as bad as the others. No, worse.

Evelyn pulled her hand away. "Stop. You're going hurt yourself."

"I want it to go away!"

"I know," the girl told her. "I think I would, too."

Robby gave Riley's arm a quick glance, then started down the path again. "It's called dermatographia. Come on, we should keep moving."

He didn't offer any kind of explanation or definition, just threw the word out there like they should already know what it meant. As if it were as common as pizza.

Mason shrugged and chased after him.

Evelyn pursed her lips, looked like she wanted to say something else, and changed her mind. Still holding Riley by the arm, she pulled her along behind the others.

They reached the small clearing and Roy Buxton's cabin ten minutes later.

His truck was in the gravel driveway, and although it was warm for October, there was a thin line of white smoke drifting up from his chimney.

The four of them crouched down in the bushes at the tree line.

"What exactly do we tell him?" Mason whispered to Evelyn. "Hey there, your name appeared on this girl's arm, so we figured we'd walk all the way out here and let you know. Oh, and we busted into the water tower and messed with your stuff. Figured we'd confess to that, too, while we're here."

"We could tell him we were hiking in the woods, heard gunshots, got scared, and came here when we spotted his cabin," Evelyn offered. "Please protect us, grown-up, sir. We're helpless children alone in the woods."

"Yeah, that will work...if he's sober."

"Oh, I'm sober," a gruff voice said from behind them. "And you all are trespassing."

They turned together and found Roy Buxton standing there with a shotgun, the barrel pointed at Mason. "How 'bout you roll that baseball bat over to me before you do something stupid."

68

MATT

"I'M SO SORRY, MATT," Gabby whispered again.

Matt glanced up at the rearview mirror, caught sight of Sally's lifeless eyes, and had to turn away. He couldn't bear to look at her. This was his fault, all of it. He loaded them in the car. He raced out of there. He should have confronted Peterson there in the street, set him straight. Took the guns and sent them all home. Ellie certainly would have, but instead, he ran, and now Sally was dead.

Not just Sally—
Norman Heaton
Eisa Heaton
Lynn Tatum
Gracie and Oscar
Probably Ellie, too
—all dead on his watch.

And those were the ones he knew about. He'd heard the sporadic gunfire, the shouting, same as the others.

Gabby squeezed his arm. "We shouldn't stay out here. It's not safe."

"Won't he see the car, you stupid fuck?" Josh craned his head and looked out what was left of the back window at the street. "Maybe we should move it before you get the rest of us killed."

Matt felt his skin grow hot. He fought the urge to get out, yank Josh from the back, and beat the shit out of him. Most likely, he killed his family *and* Eisa Heaton. It was her death that triggered Peterson. Maybe he should have left Josh to them. Maybe it wasn't too late to do exactly that. Was street justice really such a bad thing? *For someone like him?*

"Matt?"

Gabby was staring at him.

He was gripping the steering wheel with enough force to turn his knuckles white, some part of him wanting it to be Josh's neck. Every inch of him was trembling.

"We can't stay in the car, baby," she said softly, stroking the fine hairs on the back of his wrist.

Matt released the wheel, drew in a deep breath.

He needed to focus, stay on point. It wasn't his place to pass judgment on Josh any more than it was Stu Peterson's. He needed to see this through, get them all to safety, then let the system do what it was designed to do.

Matt looked up and down the street. There was no sign of Peterson or the others, but that didn't mean they were far. Gabby was right; they couldn't stay out here. Frankly, Josh was right, too. He needed to do something with the car. "Give me a second."

Before Gabby could respond, Matt got out, slammed the door behind him, and ran up the porch.

Ellie kept a spare key hidden in the base of a potted plant that looked like it died around the same time Ronald Reagan left office. Matt's hand was still shaking as he fished it out. When he went to put it in the lock, he realized the door was already open.

Not much, only an inch or so, but Ellie would have never left it like that.

He took out his gun and nudged the door open further with the tip of his shoe. The light spilled in across the dark living room bright enough to illuminate the dust caught in the air. "Ellie? It's me, Matt. Are you here?"

As with all old houses, the bones of Ellie's house creaked and ticked, but he heard nothing else as he stepped inside.

There were muddy footprints leading across the living room toward the kitchen in back, small drops of blood, too. Matt crouched to get a better look; the blood was still wet.

"How do I know you're okay?" Ellie said in a low voice from somewhere to Matt's right. This was followed by the pump of a shotgun. A shadow moved, and as Matt turned slowly he saw her partially hidden in the gloom. She was standing in the far corner of the room behind a recliner, the shotgun pointed at him. The only light in the room came from Ellie's aquarium, a hazy, misty blue rolling over the side of her face, which was crusted with blood and darkening bruises. Her hair was a frizzled mess, half pulled out of her usual ponytail. Her eyes were wide, maniacal. She held the gun steady, though. "At least four people have tried to kill me in under an hour. How do I know you're not number five?"

"Ellie, it's me, Matt. I—"

"I know who the hell you are. That doesn't seem to matter much, not today," she fired back. "Not ten minutes ago, the sweet old lady who lives next door came at me with a butcher knife. Ten minutes before that, a green Prius tried to run me down; that was Ed Philips, the bastard was smiling when he came at me. Circled around twice before I ducked back in the trees and lost him. Ran into a hiker out in the woods. Whole bottom half of his face was covered in blood, his shirt, too, none of it his. He told me he had an argument with his girlfriend, they'd been camping out near the falls. Said she started screaming about him cheating and tried to cut his pecker off—he told me he had to defend himself. *He bit her to death*. Told me that right before he lunged at me like some damn zombie in a bad movie. I had to kill him, Matt. Didn't give me no choice. None of them compares to Edgar Newton. I'm not ready to talk about him just yet. I didn't get a chance to process what he did before someone blew out the tires on my cruiser and started taking shots at me. Soldiers, Matt. Goddamn soldiers out on Route 112. Everyone has gone crazy, so how do I know you're okay?"

Matt looked at his hands, thought about what he wanted to do to Josh just minutes earlier, what he *still* wanted to do to him. "I took a psychology class in college, and our professor asked a question once. He wanted to know if a crazy person knew they were crazy, then he told us about a man who checked himself into the ER with abdominal pain. The man told the attending nurse he was pregnant, and when she examined him, she found a large slice in his gut, from his belly button to his nipple. He'd stuffed a doll in there, the hair was sticking out. He looked her right in the eye and asked if she could save his baby."

"Holy fuck, Matt."

He licked his chapped lips. Nothing about Ellie seemed right. Matt wanted to believe that was the adrenaline, her body trying to process everything that had happened today, same as him, but everything about her seemed off. From the wild look in her eyes to the way she was rambling off thoughts so quickly. She was normally one of the calmest people Matt knew, even under stress. It was one of the things he admired most about her, but something had snapped. She was broken. Or was it him? "Have you lost it? Have I? I have no idea anymore. I'm not sure I'd recognize sane or crazy. Maybe we're all off the rails and just don't know it." He looked up at her. "They shot at me out on 112, too. I didn't see anyone, but it was probably those same soldiers. Happened when I went out there looking for you."

"When was that?"

Matt told her.

"So you haven't seen the fencing," she pondered. "That went up later."

"What fencing?"

"At least twelve feet high topped with razor wire and electrified. I don't know where it starts, or how the hell they got it up so fast, but I think it completely circles town, maybe the entire valley. Only way in or out is at the highway, and they've got a double gate there, guards posted everywhere. I walked maybe a mile of it before heading back here."

"Can you lower the gun, Ellie?"

She didn't. The barrel continued to twitch in his direction as she went on. "They're not normal soldiers, Matt. The uniforms are all wrong. No name tags or rank insignia. Strange colors. I think they're private contractors, but I don't see how anyone could mobilize that fast. All I know is they're containing this, whatever *this* is." Her eyes somehow managed to grow wider, and she looked toward the door. "Are you alone?"

"Ellie, please put the gun down."

"You didn't answer my question."

Matt almost lied to her, but that wouldn't do any good. She'd see the others soon enough. "I've got Gabby with me, and Josh Tatum." He paused for a second, but there was no easy way to say it, so he just spit it out. "Ellie, Sally's dead."

This time, the barrel of the shotgun dropped and her mouth fell open. "What? How?"

Matt told her.

Told her everything.

He rattled it off as quickly as he could.

When he finished, Ellie rounded the recliner and fell into the cushioned seat, resting the shotgun on her lap. Matt told her what Sally had said before she died—delayed internet searches, filtered results. How she thought someone was reading her emails before allowing them to go through. "I thought she was just being paranoid, but I think she was right. Whoever locked down the town is also monitoring all our communications."

A creak came from above, movement on the second floor.

Matt was still holding his gun. He raised it and pointed it toward the stairs. "Is someone else here?"

Before Ellie could respond, Addie Gallagher came down the steps wrapped in a towel. She was drying her hair with another. "Thanks for letting me use your shower, Ellie. I was a—" At the sight of Matt, she froze and blushed. "Hey."

"What are you doing here?"

Addie held up her right arm. It was wrapped in gauze just above her wrist. "I was walking home and Ellie's neighbor jumped out of the bushes screaming, came at me with a knife. If Ellie hadn't been there, I might be dead right now."

Matt recalled what Ellie had told him when he came in. "Butcher knife, next door?"

Ellie nodded. "It was like she was rabid, the way she charged."

Matt didn't have to ask how she stopped her. The look that passed between both women told him she was dead. The hows didn't much matter at this point.

Gabby appeared in the open doorway. "Josh keeps insisting we move your car before Stu Peterson sees it, and I think he's right. I'm gonna take it and go look for Riley. She must be…" Her voice trailed off at the sight of Addie half naked on the stairs.

Addie turned slowly on her heels and started back up. "I think I'd better get dressed."

69

CODY HILL

UP UNTIL THAT MORNING, Cody Hill had been an eighth grader at Hollows Bend Middle School.

Two hours earlier, he decided he no longer planned to return to that life.

He'd had an epiphany.

A realization.

A come-to-Jesus moment.

He wasn't particularly popular, never had been. Most kids didn't see him when he walked down the halls, and that was just fine by him. The assholes of the world, guys like Mason Ridler and Brett Murphy, the ones who *did* see him, he wouldn't miss at all. Hell, just two weeks ago they'd tied him to one of the metal beams under the bleachers after a school pep rally and left him there for the janitors to find three hours after school let out. A month ago, they'd dragged him into the showers fully clothed.

Cody went out of his way to ensure guys like that didn't see him, and after tonight, they never would.

After tonight, those worries would be gone.

Cody smiled, bent closer to the light, and held the soldering iron still long enough to fix the thin lead wire directly to the contact on the nine-volt battery. The instructions he'd pulled from the internet didn't include anything like that, but it couldn't hurt. No reason to risk the battery getting jostled and coming loose. It's not like he'd ever have to replace it.

The people of Hollows Bend had gone bat-fucking crazy. Cody wasn't exactly sure why. He'd managed to put a couple of theories together, but none of them really mattered. All that mattered was that it had happened, it had happened today, and it would give him perfect cover for what he had planned. Nobody would suspect him, and even if they did, he could blame it on whatever crazy juju was in the air. *I did what? Oh, man, I didn't mean to! I'd never hurt anybody! You gotta believe me!* Yadda, yadda, yadda.

He was always so quiet.

Cody figured they'd say something like that. That's what they always said. He could be loud, though. They'd learn that soon enough. Originally he planned to write it all down, create a manifesto, a crowning fuck-you listing all the dead and why they deserved to be that way. He'd started that project about a month ago, but it didn't take him long to realize he wasn't much of a writer and couldn't properly communicate the assholeishness of his targets. Even when he listed them by name along with every crappy thing they'd ever done to him, they didn't come across as the villains of the story, at least not on a level that satisfied him. He tried drawing pictures, too, but he was a worse artist than he was a writer. The manifesto wasn't working, so he burned it. It was somewhere in those flames he found his plan B—why shoot them when he could use fire? He'd originally planned to use his dad's AK and chase everyone down in the halls at school, but he'd seen that story play out on television enough times to know how it ended. He'd be dead, and he wouldn't get them all. But fire? A bomb? There's no stopping a good bomb. With a bomb, it's over before anyone realizes it actually started.

Besides, his dad had gone hunting up in Maine and taken the AK. The gun was out, the bomb was in. He wasn't sure he could wait until school tomorrow, though. Not with all the craziness going on. Tonight would be better. He just needed to get everyone in one place. That was easy enough.

His computer printer went quiet, ran out of paper, and Cody loaded in another stack. When it got back to work, he picked up one of the flyers:

EMERGENCY MEETING!
9:00 P.M.
HOLLOWS BEND MIDDLE SCHOOL AUDITORIUM

The timer on Cody's phone went off.

Setting down the soldering iron, he silenced the phone and leaned over the mixture on the hot plate at the corner of his workbench. He'd added the oil, gelatin, petroleum jelly, putty, and starch when the water started to boil. He stirred it again and lowered the heat.

It was thickening up nicely, just like in the YouTube video.

Cody tested the mixture with his hydrometer and got a reading of 14. When it hit 17, he was supposed to take it off the heat. At that point, it was supposed to have the consistency of ice cream, and he could shape it. Originally he planned to turn the makeshift C-4 into a series of square bricks—that's how it always appeared in the movies—but all the websites he had studied said shaping it into balls was better. Spheres guaranteed the highest detonation velocity. That meant he'd have to pack the explosives in the pockets of his vest rather than affix them to the exterior. It wouldn't look as cool, but if it worked better...

The explosive vest was his plan C. He'd wear it, but he'd only set it off if he got in a jam. The bomb on the corner of his desk, that was his crowning jewel. His masterpiece. Timer *and* remote. Not only was it packed full of explosives, but he'd added nails and ball bearings. Bye-bye, Hollows Bend Middle School. Bye-bye, assholes. If all went well, he'd get to watch them die and nobody would ever know about the vest. If it didn't go well, he'd still get to watch them die; he just wouldn't be able to revel in it as long before detonating the vest. He wasn't about to go to jail.

The microwave timer went off upstairs.

Cody's stomach rumbled.

Food, then finish.

He took the steps up from the basement two at a time and nearly tripped over the body of his mother on the kitchen floor. She stared up at him blank-faced, the butcher knife still in her neck. Cody had forgotten all about her—he'd have to move her somewhere before heading out.

70

RILEY

ROY BUXTON LEVELED THE shotgun on Mason, "I said, give me the bat."

Mason smirked and tightened his grip. "This is a DeMarini Zoa, cost me five hundred bucks. No way I'm giving it to you. You'll just have to shoot me."

Evelyn snatched the baseball bat from Mason's hand and tossed it across the ground over toward Buck. "Don't be an ass, Mason."

Buck kicked the bat off to the side, and it disappeared in the bushes.

"Oh, you better hope you didn't scratch it," Mason muttered.

Buck ignored him. "The four of you got about thirty seconds to tell me what you're doing out here before I fast-track you down the side of the mountain."

Evelyn nudged her brother. "Show him, Robby."

Robby removed his red backpack and fished out the test strips from the front pocket. He held them out to Buck. "This one is from the water tower, and this one is from a cave about half a mile from here."

Buck's eyes narrowed. "The water tower is locked. Want to tell me how you got in there?"

"That's not important," Evelyn replied. "How do you explain that? And I hope you can, because I drank that water," she added, tapping the second strip.

"It's probably just a bad test."

Robby took four more from his backpack. "All of these came out the same."

Mason edged closer, studied the test strips, and frowned. "What's the difference?"

"The water from the tower shows slightly high iron, normal fluoride, lead, nitrates, and nitrites. All within the normal range. The water from the cave shows nothing at all."

"Because the strips are bad," Buck insisted.

"If the strips were bad, they wouldn't show a pH, but they do," Robby replied. "They just don't show anything else. Because there is nothing else. No elements, no chemicals, no minerals or impurities."

"Water can't be that pure, it just ain't possible. That would make it the purest on the planet. There are always some minerals. You got bad strips."

Robby wasn't about to back down. "Or this water is coming from someplace deep below ground, someplace it's been for a very long time. Before the industrial revolution. Before pollution. Before everything. If it got trapped someplace like that and recently got out, that would explain it."

Buck rolled his eyes. "Yep, maybe you tapped Bigfoot's personal well. Who gives a shit? Nobody complains about clean water."

"I didn't say it was clean. I only said nothing in it showed up on the test strips," Robby told him. "I'm not so sure it's even water. I think it's something...older...something *before* water. It just looks the same."

Buck bit his lower lip and huffed. "I'm guessing you're supposed to be on some kind of medication and your SpongeBob alarm didn't go off this morning to remind you to take it."

"In 1911 a scientific expedition in Antarctica dug out a core sample that contained nearly a gallon of hydrogen peroxide. That's H_2O_2. It shouldn't have existed there in the ice. They had no explanation for how it got there, it just was. Same elements as water, different combination. I think that's what this is," Robby said pointing at the test strip. "Almost water, but not. Something is slightly off in its chemical makeup, and that something is enough to prevent the normal elements from accumulating."

"You're not gonna out-Robby Robby," Mason quickly told Buck. "If he says it, it's true. Best to believe and move on."

Robby said, "H_2O is perfectly safe to drink. H_2O_2 will kill you. So if this water is something else, there's no telling what it might do to a person."

Buck went quiet; he had no response to that.

"How does the water get to the tower?" Evelyn asked Buck, even though Robby had explained that on the walk out.

Buck scratched the side of his nose, then studied the tip of his finger before answering her. "Comes down off the mountain, mostly underground, hits the Saco River, runs through the filtration system out near the falls, then gets pumped to the tower." He added smugly, "You know, the place you kids entered illegally."

Evelyn tapped the test strips. "Well, right now, this stuff that looks like water is getting in there somewhere along the way, and people are drinking it. That's causing everyone to go bonkers."

Buck stared at her a moment, then groaned. "Got it all figured out, huh? Are you supposed to be Velma or Daphne?"

"Who?"

He shook his head. "Never mind, it doesn't matter. The four of you need to go home to your folks and stay inside until this blows over. You shouldn't be running around out here. It ain't the water. You're chasing a ghost."

Mason kicked the dirt and frowned. "He smells like a distillery. I told you he'd be drunk. He won't help."

Buck turned on him. "Christ, kid, I bet you get the shit kicked out of you all the time. If not, maybe it's about time you did, 'cause that mouth of yours will be the end of you before you're old enough to drive a car." He looked back at Robby, Riley, and Evelyn. "Go home. All of you. Take Peckerwood here with you."

Evelyn planted her feet. "Show him your arm, Riley."

Riley didn't move. She just wanted to go home and be with her mom.

"You don't show him, you know I will." Evelyn glared. "Do it."

Riley bit her lower lip and edged closer to the man. Mason was right, he did smell. Not only did he smell like alcohol, but he smelled like he hadn't taken a bath in a week. His skin was covered in a thin layer of sweat flecked with dirt and grime, and his clothes were no better, stained and filthy. She turned her head away and breathed through her mouth as she tugged up her sleeve and showed him the writing. When he grabbed her arm and pulled her closer, she tried to pull away, but he held her too tight.

"What the hell is that?"

"Your name just showed up on her arm," Evelyn told him. "I know it looks like it's written there, but it's not. The ink, or whatever that is, is below the skin. If you're not meant to help us, why would your name appear on her like that?"

The color drained from Buck's face, and his grip loosened on the shotgun. He nearly dropped it. "I don't give two shits about my name, how the hell do you kids know Emily Pridham?"

71

MATT

AT THE SIGHT OF Addie on the stairs dressed in only a towel, Gabby's face darkened. She spun on her heels and started back toward the car. "I'm going to look for my daughter. Unless you want me to take Josh, too, I suggest you get his ass out of the car."

She made it halfway down the front steps when her phone dinged with an incoming text. "It's from Riley..." Her voice trailed off as she read it. "She says she's safe, with friends. Not to worry about her."

"What friends?"

Even as Matt said that, Gabby was frantically typing back with both thumbs. He stepped over and read over her shoulder. Gabby had barely gotten the word *who?* off before Riley's next message came in:

> Evelyn Harper and her brother. I'm fine. We're at the
> rec center in Barton. A bunch of people from town are
> here.

"What the fuck? Evelyn Harper?" Gabby muttered as she typed.

Matt was confused. "I thought she didn't get along with the Harper girl?" He thought of the roadblock, the shooters. "How did they get to Barton?"

"I...I don't know..." She was frantically typing back.

From her spot on the recliner, Ellie cleared her throat. "This the same Harper who lives out on TR-138 in one of those shotgun houses?"

Matt nodded. "Yeah. The one with the sagging porch and blue tarp up on the roof. Neighbors call us at least twice a week with noise complaints."

Mother is permanently parked in front of the television, and the father closes down the Black Moose Tavern whenever he's not changing oil at the Smart Lube. I picked up the daughter about a year ago for shoplifting. She tried to steal some bread and mayonnaise from the QuikMart. The owner didn't press charges. I paid for the food so she could take it home."

"Sounds like a lovely family," Addie chimed in from the stairs. She'd been listening in. Gabby's glare was enough to get her moving. "All right. Going to get dressed."

Another message came in:

> They closed the roads right after we got out. I'm safe.
> Don't worry about me. Stay where U R. I want U 2 B
> safe 2.

This didn't make Gabby appear any less worried. In fact, she looked worse. She clicked on her daughter's name, then the small map that appeared on the screen. An hourglass appeared, spun, then said, **Location not available**. She quickly typed back:

> Are you with her parents? Who drove?

No response came. After about half a minute, she got **Message cannot be delivered**.

Gabby swore, and Matt caught her arm before she could throw her phone out into the street. "She's okay, that's what matters."

From the back seat of his cruiser, Josh Tatum stared at him. Beside him, Sally's body slumped against the window. The front seat was empty. Matt's heart thumped. "Where's the girl?"

He saw her a moment later. She was standing off to the side, her back turned, looking up at Mount Washington.

"Is that her?" Ellie said from behind him. "The girl from the diner?"

"Yeah."

"We should get her inside."

"What about Josh and Sally?"

Ellie drew in a deep breath as she considered that, blew it out slowly. "I have a freezer in the garage. We can put Sally in there until it's okay to move her to the morgue. With Josh…" Her voice trailed off as she looked around the room and settled on the radiator. "We'll cuff him to that until outside help gets here and can haul him off to county or maybe the pen up in Barton."

The smoke from the fire in town had turned the sky to the west black. Matt could smell it, thick with timber and God only knew what else.

"How bad is it?"

Matt told Ellie about the fire station. "Without help, we'll lose all of Main Street. If the wind kicks up, there's a good chance it will spread to some of the houses. From there…"

"It will spread to the mountain," Ellie finished. "Nobody wants a wildfire, but that could help us. That might be how help finds us."

Knowing Riley was safe didn't seem to make Gabby feel any better. She turned away from them and thumbed in another text, swore when it didn't go through, and tried again.

Matt got a better look at Ellie's face. Although most of the blood had dried, she had a nasty cut on her cheek, another above her left eye. "We need to get you cleaned up. You might need stitches."

She shook her head. "First we get Sally out of that car. She deserves that much. I've got a nice quilt upstairs we can wrap her in until we find something better. We'll get your cruiser off the street, there's room in my garage. Then we'll deal with Josh and—"

The silent girl turned around and started toward them. It was the first time Ellie had seen the girl's face, and the sight of her took the woman's breath away. "Did her prints come back?"

"No. Sally got them in the system, but we lost communication before she received the results."

"So we still have no idea who she is."

"She hasn't spoken yet."

But that wasn't true, was it? Matt thought of the words she'd planted in his head, somehow told him without speaking aloud.

"Does 'Hope not ever to see Heaven. I have come to lead you to the other shore; into eternal darkness; into fire and into ice' mean anything to you?"

The wild look Matt thought had left Ellie's eyes returned, if only for an instant, then vanished again. Because she recognized those words. She was staring at the girl, and he was pretty sure she recognized her, too.

72

MATT

MATT AND ELLIE MADE quick work of it all. Josh struggled as they dragged him inside, pleading his case with Ellie, who heard none of it. Together, they wrestled him down to the floor next to the radiator and fastened his handcuffs around the thick iron pipe. Ellie threatened to tape a sock in his mouth if he didn't shut up. He finally did. Once Josh was secure, they drove Matt's cruiser into the garage and closed the door before gently removing Sally from the back and resting her in the freezer. The quilt Ellie had mentioned was sitting on top of the workbench at the back of the garage, neatly folded and smelling of fabric softener. She placed the quilt over Sally's body and tucked her in like a small child before closing the lid and resting her palm on top in what Matt thought was some sort of prayer or silent reflection. When she was done, she said, "You trust me, don't you, Matt?"

"Of course."

"Even with all this going on? I know I'm a little jumpy right now, not exactly myself, but you still trust me, right?"

Matt nodded, but he couldn't hide the doubt in his eyes.

"You can't bullshit a bullshitter, Matt. I know you don't, and I don't blame you for it. The truth is, you shouldn't trust me any more than I should trust you. We don't know what's causing whatever is happening here. We don't know if we've been affected by it, and considering how many people seem to be, it would be naïve of us to believe we haven't been, too. Josh, Gabby, Addie—everyone in there. Everyone in town. We don't know who we can trust, and until we figure that out, we can't trust anyone, including each other. That makes what I'm about to tell you that much harder, because you need to trust me in order to believe it."

Although she didn't say it, Matt understood what she was struggling to tell him. It was written all over her face; he saw it upstairs. "You know who she is, don't you?"

Ellie bit her lower lip. "I can't possibly be right. And thinking I am makes me believe I'm just another piece of all the crazy."

He followed her down the concrete steps to the basement. She reached for a string and tugged, and a bare bulb came to life. Dust stirred and circled their heads, tiny flecks riding still air. Matt had been down there several times over the years. Every November, they cleared old case files from the cluttered storage room at the office and brought them here—overflow for their overflow. The state of New Hampshire allowed them to destroy files older than seven years, but Ellie preferred to hold on to them. Her basement wouldn't exactly fly when it came to chain of custody rules, but aside from Ellie, nobody really cared about old speeding tickets or noise complaints, and that was what most of this stuff amounted to.

What Ellie said next wasn't what he expected. "How well do you know Buck?"

Matt rolled his fingers through his hair and leaned back against an old exercise bike. "Nice enough guy, fairly dependable. Aside from the drinking, and a few lapses of judgment caused by it, I've never had a problem with him. I suppose he's been the town drunk for as long as I remember, and he doesn't seem to have any interest in changing that. He seems harmless enough, so we let him be."

Ellie studied his face before turning back toward the gloom. "Do you know why he's like that? Where it started?"

Matt shook his head.

Ellie chewed the inside of her cheek for a second and picked her words carefully before she continued, "Back in eighty-seven, my daddy was sheriff and I was a deputy going on my third year. Twenty-five years old. Believe it or not, I was actually young once, too. I've got seven years on Buck; he was only eighteen at the time, about to graduate. I was working the front desk when he stumbled into the sheriff's office with dried blood all over his hands, more blood smeared on his shirt. His face was covered in dirt, streaked with tears. He said he'd been hiking with his girlfriend up on Mount Washington near the old Pickerton place and said she vanished. She went off into the bushes for a bathroom break and never came out. He told my dad that when he went looking for her, he found a rock covered in blood where Buck thought she'd been, but nothing else. Buck said he knew he shouldn't have touched it but wasn't thinking straight. I suppose that was the first red flag. He had a lot of blood on him for someone who just touched a rock. I get maybe one finger"—she held out her index—"just a tap to confirm what you were looking at really was blood, but it was all over his hands and his clothes. Didn't make sense to me, and certainly didn't make sense to my daddy. He wanted to lock Buck up then and there, but we needed him to take us up the mountain, find this rock. We might have found it on our own, but with a missing girl, we couldn't risk the extra time. My daddy took a bunch of photographs of Buck, caught him from every possible angle, then swabbed his hands for the lab, took his shirt…got him a spare from the lost and found.

287

Probably the same box you pulled the sweatshirt and pants you gave the girl from."

Sally had gotten the clothing for the girl, but Matt didn't see the point in mentioning that. He let Ellie continue.

"All that went fast, maybe ten, fifteen minutes at most. Daddy made a call to the State Police, told them to send someone out, then the three of us went up the mountain. We found the rock, Buck took us right to it. It was just like he said—soaked in blood—mostly baked in from the sun, but still dripping down the sides, puddled around it in the dirt. My daddy gave me this look that confirmed what I was thinking—nothing loses that much blood and walks away. There was no sign of the girl, though. No evidence of a struggle. We checked the Pickerton place ourselves, but when that turned up nothing, we got a volunteer search team together. Started with ten, but that grew to more than fifty as the day grew long and word got out. Nearly seventy-five turned out the next day. We found nothing. Days turned into weeks. No sign of her. Through all that, Buck stuck to his story. Daddy and I interviewed his friends, family. Nobody knew of any problems between Buck and his girlfriend. Nobody saw them fight. Home-life for both was good. People were split on their opinions—half thought Buck hurt her and hid the body, the other half figured she slipped and fell out there somewhere. Plenty of cliffs around there. We searched down below as best we could, but at that point, we knew it was a lost cause. It rained twice that first week, and there were always the animals to consider. Mother Nature has a way of cleaning up after herself. We'd lost our share of tourists and amateur hikers in those mountains over the years, but she was our first local." Ellie paused for a second. "The blood came back from the lab as avian, not human at all. *Corvus brachyrhynchos*, the American crow." She waved a dismissive hand and went on before Matt could say anything. "Buck was never charged. Nothing to really charge him with. And over time, people forgot. Not Buck, though. When the drinking first started, we used to find him out there, wandering. A bottle in one hand as he called out her name at all hours."

"What was her name?"

"Emily. Emily Pridham."

Ellie shuffled around several of the boxes and found the one she wanted. EMILY PRIDHAM / MISSING / 16 YO was written in faded black Sharpie across the front. She peeled the lid off, dug around inside, and found an old copy of the *Hollows Bend Gazette*. Emily Pridham's photo was on the front page, and she was a dead ringer for the girl upstairs.

73

RILEY

"OW, YOU'RE HURTING ME!" Riley yanked her arm from Buck's grip and shuffled back several steps.

He stared at her, dumbfounded.

Evelyn just seemed confused. "Who the hell is Emily Pridham?"

She stomped over and looked at the name on Riley's arm. "When did that one show up?"

"I…I don't know."

"You don't know," she repeated, a mocking tone to her voice.

Riley tugged her sleeve back down and scratched her arm, her nails digging in. She wanted that writing gone. She didn't want any part of this. She considered running away from all of them, running down the mountain back to town, when her phone vibrated with an incoming text. It was from her mother but made no sense.

Mason snatched the phone away, held it above Riley's head, and read the message aloud: "So bitter is it, death is little more;

But of the good to treat, which there I found, Speak will I of the other things I saw there." He frowned at Riley. "What the hell is *that* supposed to mean?"

Buck stepped closer. "Read that again."

Mason did, this time with a terrible British accent. "Sounds like Shakespeare from school, or some crap."

Riley smacked him in the chest. "Give me my phone!"

"Christ, baby. Here you go." He dropped the iPhone back into her hand.

Riley typed back,

> Where are you? Still at the sheriff's station?

Her reply was as weird as the other message:

> Do not be afraid; our fate cannot be taken from us; it
> is a gift.

Riley quickly keyed in a question mark and hit Send, but the message failed to deliver. Worse, both messages from her mom vanished, same with her question. In a blink they were gone, leaving only the messages that failed to send back at their house, like the recent ones never happened.

"Hey guys, something's burning," Evelyn said, pointing at the sky above town.

Still shaken up, Buck's gaze was locked on Riley. Several beats slipped by before he seemed willing to turn away. He studied the black smoke, then waved the shotgun toward his run-down cabin. "Get inside, the whole lot of you."

Riley, Evelyn, and Mason all looked at each other, but none of them moved. Only Robby followed when Buck stomped off toward the cabin, as if following a strange man holding a gun into his lair was the most natural thing in the world.

"Robby!" Evelyn whispered loudly between clenched teeth. "Get back here!"

Robby ignored her and vanished through the door.

"That little shit." She went after him.

Mason started shuffling around in the bushes, looking for his bat. By the time he found it, Riley had gone into the house, too.

74

MATT

"THAT CAN'T BE HER," Matt told Ellie as he held the newspaper toward the single bulb in the basement and studied the photograph in the light.

"I know that. It's impossible," she replied, fishing out an old high school yearbook from the box and turning to a marked page. "I keep telling myself that every time I look at her. But I can't explain this." Her thumb landed on the girl; smiling at the camera, her head angled slightly. "You can't tell me you didn't notice that."

Matt first saw the birthmark when he sat down with the girl in Ellie's office. Brown, crescent-shaped, like a small moon on her neck. Identical to the girl in the yearbook, Emily Pridham. "That's not possible." He looked up at her. "Can birthmarks be hereditary?"

"Most, no. There are some. I'm no doctor, but the way I understand it, to be hereditary they need to pass down through genes. The only kind I know of like that are port-wine stains, something called Klippel-Trenaunay syndrome. I had a cousin growing up with one of those. Has something to do with too many capillaries near the surface of the skin. They're red, though. This one is brown. And they usually appear on the face, not the neck." She tapped the photograph. "The size and shape are all wrong, too. This is something else. This looks *the same*."

Matt didn't believe for a second the girl who died thirty-five years ago was somehow standing upstairs. This was some crazy coincidence. Most likely, Emily Pridham slipped while going to the bathroom and went over a cliff, just like Ellie said. There were a few near the Pickerton place. She slipped, maybe rolled, maybe dropped—none of those things made as much noise as people thought. It could easily happen with Buck standing twenty feet away and he wouldn't hear it. She probably vanished somewhere below, and the animals finished her off before her body could be found. That was the hard truth of it. None of that explained who the girl upstairs really was or why she had no memory before this morning.

Matt cleared his throat. "So what do we do? Show her this stuff and see how she reacts? Figure it out from there?"

Ellie quickly shook her head and went to the large gun safe on the back wall. She began twisting the combination dial. "We don't show her anything, don't tell her anything, not until we talk to Buck. I know him. I don't know her."

She tugged up on the handle and swung open the heavy metal door. Reaching inside, she took out a KelTec KSG tactical shotgun along with two boxes of shells and handed it all to Matt. She loaded an identical shotgun for herself. "I'm taking her up the mountain to his place. I want you to stay here and keep these people safe. I've got extra blankets and pillows in the hall closet. There's plenty of food in the pantry. Help yourself. Get everyone comfortable. They all need rest, and after everything that happened, they're bound to crash. Keep trying the phone. Try to get help in here. This is going to get worse long before it gets better."

"What about you? You need to rest, too." He pointed at the cut on her cheek. "We still need to clean that up."

She pumped the shotgun and chambered a round. "Never do today what can be put off until tomorrow."

"I don't think that's how the saying goes."

"No? I'm pretty sure that's how my grams had it embroidered on her favorite pillow." She reached back into the cabinet, retrieved several shells from an open box, and filled her pocket. "That reminds me, the other saying you asked me about—*Hope not ever to see Heaven. I have come to lead you to the other shore; into eternal darkness; into fire and into ice*—that's from Dante's *Inferno*. I've got a copy upstairs somewhere. I'm guessing you never read it?"

Matt's face flushed. "I'm more of a comic book guy."

Ellie groaned. "I suppose if they had comics in the fourteenth century, Dante might have fit the bill. *Inferno* is part of an epic poem called *The Divine Comedy*. There were three parts— *Inferno*, *Purgatory*, and *Paradise*. *Inferno* describes Dante's journey through Hell, guided by a Roman poet. He was sorta like the ghosts in Dickens's *A Christmas Carol*. You've read that, right?"

"I saw the movie with Bill Murray."

"Christ, your generation is hopeless. Educated by video games and the backs of cereal boxes," Ellie muttered. "Dante describes Hell as nine circles. They get progressively worse as you near the middle—Limbo, Lust, Gluttony, Greed, Wrath, Heresy, Violence, Fraud, and Treachery." As she ticked these off on her fingers, she looked up at him. "Before you bring up that movie with Morgan Freeman and Brad Pitt, yes, this is where the seven deadly sins came from. Religious folk lifted them from Dante. Contrary to what most people think, they're not listed in the Bible, at least not in this kind of detail. Dante described the ninth circle as a lake. The worse your crime, the deeper you got to spend eternity."

"A lake of fire," Matt said, matter-of-factly.

Ellie shook her head. "No. In Dante, Hell's not all fire and brimstone. The lake is frozen." Her eyes narrowed. "Where exactly did you hear that phrase again?"

"The girl."

Ellie's battered face twisted in confusion. "I thought you said she hasn't spoken?"

"She hasn't. Don't ask me to explain it. You'll think I'm—"

"Crazy? Aren't we all just a little today?" Ellie threw the newspaper and other material back in the box. "You tell me when you're ready. In the meantime, I'm taking her to Buck's. I wanna see his face when he sees her. You lock this place down and try to get us some help in here. I don't care if you have to send smoke signals to the folks in Boston."

She was halfway up the steps when Matt called out, "Hey, watch out for Stu Peterson."

Ellie paused, cradling the shotgun. "Do I want to know why?"

Matt told her about his run-in with Jimmy Newcomb and what happened when they had to evacuate the sheriff's office.

Ellie considered all this for a long moment, then continued up the stairs shaking her head. "Fucking Peterson."

75

CODY HILL

WITH ALL THE NAILS and ball bearings, the bomb was much heavier than Cody expected, and he was glad when he finally got it under the bleachers at the middle school. He spied the oversize Hollows Bend Bearcat mascot costume sticking out of its storage box. The bomb would fit nicely in the large head.

What the hell was a bearcat, anyway? Damn thing looked like a giant discard from the wrong side of Sesame Street. The inside was even worse: wire mesh held together by glue, tape, and the sweat of generations of losers tasked with wearing it. It stunk like an old gym sock dipped in raw eggs and left in the sun.

Cody tucked the bomb inside, stuffed the costume back into its giant plastic storage coffin, and got out of the middle school without running into a single person. He set the timer for 9:00 p.m. Cell phones weren't working right, so he'd used an old set of Motorola two-way radios for the backup remote trigger. When he was safely across the street, he checked the signal and was happy to see four out of five bars. The signal didn't drop completely until he was on the far end of Main Street watching the fire. He'd gotten lost in that—watching the hungry flames chewing away at the old buildings. A few were unrecognizable; others appeared untouched. Like the flames were a kid who didn't want to eat something on his plate and pushed it aside.

Nobody was out on Main Street, either.

No cars.

No people.

Nothing.

He'd gone to the diner that morning to grab a bagel, scope things out, and the street had been bustling, packed with yahoos coming and going, but now, nothing. Nobody watching the fire, nobody attempting to put it out.

Like he was the last person on Earth, like in that old Isaac Asimov story. Or was it Ray Bradbury?

He worked his way down the street, hanging flyers anyway. He'd printed five hundred of them and wasn't about to let them go to waste. Someone would come along; word would spread. Those cowards would need to crawl out of their houses at some point, and they'd want answers. Where better to find those answers than an emergency town meeting?

COME YE, COME ALL!

Small towns loved to come together.

Cody held a flyer against the tree near the entrance to Lou's Laundry and stapled it in place, then stepped back to admire his handiwork. Earlier, he'd considered wearing the bomb vest as he hung the flyers, sort of a trial run, but with the heat of the fire at his back, he was glad he didn't. Aside from the handful of YouTube videos he'd watched, he didn't know much about C-4. He was pretty sure heat couldn't set it off, but today wasn't the day to confirm that particular theory.

He was debating whether to hit Thornily Street or head down Lincoln when he spotted the car at the back end of the parking lot behind the laundry.

A Ford Fusion. Puke-green stained with rust. The back door was open, and what was left of the window glistened on the asphalt, nothing but a pile of safety glass.

Cody didn't hear the buzzing until he got close.

At first, it looked like something was moving inside, a blob of black darker than the shadows, throbbing and inching back and forth on the seat, wall, and remaining windows. As Cody drew closer, he realized this wasn't a single thing but a million little things—black flies, crawling over the interior. He'd never seen so many in one place before, like a black beehive. He was standing at the open door before he realized there was a person beneath them on the floor, barely visible under the living blanket.

"Don't touch that, kid. He's dead."

"No shit," Cody replied.

The voice had come from behind him, but Cody didn't turn. He couldn't take his eyes off the beautiful mess before him. The buzz of the flies was like music. They were feasting on the body, life born of death. Cody wanted to roll in it, be part of it.

A heavy hand landed on Cody's shoulder and gently squeezed. "You shouldn't be out here. It's not safe."

This time, Cody did turn. Angry. Who the hell thought it was okay to interrupt him?

The man was older, fifties, or sixties, or seventies, Cody had no clue. They all looked the same when they went gray. He'd seen him around town before, always wearing that same ratty Boston Red Sox cap and flannel shirt, like the man had homed in on his signature style years back and committed for his remaining days above the dirt. He wasn't alone. Cody hadn't heard them pull up, but there was a Chevy pickup parked at the entrance to the lot with two other men in the front seat and four or five others in the back of the truck. The angle made it hard to see. A couple of them had guns.

The old man pushed the ball cap farther back on his head and eyed the flyers in Cody's hand. "What you got there?"

Cody handed him one.

He studied the text and was either slow or putting some serious thought into the eight words on the page, because nearly half a minute ticked by before he looked back at Cody and spoke again. "This your idea, or you hanging them for someone else?"

"Sheriff Ellie asked me to do it," Cody lied. "Gave me twenty bucks and said she'll give me a free pass on my first parking ticket when I learn to drive."

"Did she now." The man considered this. "When'd you see her?"

"This morning, right after the shit hit the fan."

One of the men jumped off the back of the truck and wandered over. He had a 9mm strapped to his hip, right out in plain sight. The old guy held the flyer out to him. "Get a load of this, Rodney. Kid said the sheriff asked him to hang them up."

The man with the 9mm read the text and nodded slowly. "Half the town will come out for something like this. All in one place. We could vet them at the door, only let out the ones who aren't sick, keep the others back…"

"I'm thinking the same thing," the old man replied before turning back to Cody. "We've got numbers. Want us to give you a hand getting those out?"

Cody glanced at his watch. It was coming up on seven. He'd wanted to do this himself, but with only two hours left, he'd be lucky if he covered a quarter of the town. With a little help from Old Guy and Friends, he might just get the whole stack of flyers out. He might have time to print more. He tried not to sound too excited when he said, "I got my twenty bucks. You want to help, I'm not gonna say no." He handed the man the bulk of the remaining flyers.

The man with the 9mm, the one he'd called Rodney, walked the stack of flyers back to the truck and told the others. The old man ruffled Cody's hair. "My name's Stu Peterson. What's yours?"

"Dylan Klebold," Cody lied again.

Klebold had been on Cody's mind a lot lately. Back in 1999, he and another senior named Eric Harris shot up some school out in Columbine, Colorado. Cody had studied everything they did right. More importantly, he'd also studied everything they did *wrong*. He was no idiot. No reason to repeat mistakes. Perfection was all about weeding out the errors.

76

MATT

FROM A WINDOW IN the living room, Matt watched Ellie load the strange girl into the passenger seat of her Ford and drive off down the street toward the mountains. Gabby was in the kitchen, making a pot of coffee. Josh had given up struggling and settled into the corner next to the radiator and gone quiet.

Even though he made it clear he didn't want her there, Addie sidled up beside Matt smelling like fresh lavender. Her damp hair darkened the collar of an FBI T-shirt she no doubt pilfered from Ellie's closet. When she spoke, she kept her voice low. "Let's just get in your cruiser and leave, Matt. You and me. Drive until we find an ocean somewhere and start over." She pressed against him and ran her fingers down the length of his arm until she reached his hand.

He shrugged her away. "Will you back off? Stop flirting with me around Gabby."

She gave a sideways glance back toward the kitchen before

focusing back on him with a sly smile. "Just so I'm clear, it's okay when Gabby *isn't* around?"

"It's *never* okay," he shot back in a hushed whisper. "*This* is not going to happen. You and me will never happen. I love Gabby."

"No you don't. I think you love the idea of Gabby. She's safe. You can picture yourself living in a little house behind a white picket fence with her and her daughter. The three of you might look like a Norman Rockwell wet dream, but that doesn't make it real." She touched the tip of her finger to the back of his hand again. "That there, the electric feeling you get when I touch you, when you touch me, *that's right*, that's *real*. You can try to deny it, but your body won't let you. That kind of attraction doesn't happen by accident. We were meant to be together. I know you don't feel that when she touches you. You want to, but you don't. You tell yourself those feelings will come with time, but they won't. She can't give you what I can." Her hand moved to her belly, and for the first time, Matt realized she was showing a little bit. "You'd be a father to this child from the start. Gabby's kid will never see you that way. To her, you'll always be the guy sleeping with her mother. A stand-in. A substitute."

Matt felt an angry twist in the pit of his stomach. "I'm not that baby's father."

"You keep telling yourself that."

"I swear, Addie, if you don't stop I'll—"

"Coffee's brewing, and I found a pack of cinnamon rolls that expired two months ago in Ellie's fridge, I don't know about you, but I'm—"

Gabby's voice cut off when she saw Addie next to Matt at the window, so close the light didn't pass between them.

Matt fought the urge to move away quickly and instead turned as if he had nothing to hide.

Because he had nothing to hide, he told himself.

When Addie shifted around, she kept her hand on her swollen belly, drawing Gabby's eye on purpose. "Have you heard anything else from your daughter?"

Gabby didn't take the bait. She kept her gaze fixed on Matt. "Ellie has a landline in the kitchen, but calls aren't getting out. When I dial the rec center in Barton, I get the same thing as everywhere else: two rings and it disconnects. Nothing at all when I dial Riley's phone." She nodded at the window. "Any sign of Stu Peterson?"

Matt was about to say no when Peterson's pickup truck rounded the corner one block to the west and coasted slowly down Ellie's street. "Shit! Get away from the windows!" He shoved Addie with a little more force than he should have; she stumbled but caught herself on the corner of the couch.

"Down! Get down!" Matt told them.

The location of Ellie's house was no secret. Half the town showed up on her doorstep when they had a problem and couldn't find her at the sheriff's office. At one point about four years back, Peterson had been a regular at Ellie's Thursday night penny poker game. She'd put an end to that when he kept picking her brain about police procedural stuff and cases around town. Not because it wasn't any of his business (it wasn't), but because the purpose of the weekly game was to distract from the toils of local law enforcement, not dredge it all up as some weekly recap.

Crouched beneath the windowsill, Matt couldn't see the truck, but he heard the rumble of the engine as it neared, tensed when it seemed to pause outside, then only felt slightly relieved when it drove off. He only looked back out when the sound faded and he caught a glimpse of the truck as it vanished around the far bend.

Addie was beside him again. "Did those come from his truck, or were they already out there?" she said, pointing at the street. At least a dozen sheets of paper were fluttering around on the breeze.

"Stay inside. I'll be right back," Matt told them all.

He opened the front door slowly, carefully checked the street, then retrieved one of the pages. He locked the door when he got back inside the house. "Looks like some kind of flyer for a town meeting tonight at the middle school. Nine o'clock." He looked at his watch. It was ten after seven. "Less than two hours."

"We should go," Gabby said. "Maybe someone found a way out."

"That's risky. It doesn't say who organized it," Matt replied. "What if it's the same people putting up fences and shooting cars when we try to leave? Maybe they're just trying to round us up? Ellie was right. We should stay here and find some way to get outside help. I know she has a shortwave radio around here some-where, we should—"

"You're a pussy," Josh muttered from his place next to the radiator. "Admit it. You'd rather hide than risk your own skin." He nodded at Gabby and Addie in turn. "Same reason you won't marry this one, and same reason you won't admit to fathering the kid growing in that one. You're a coward looking out for numero uno and nobody else. If you had half a ball, you'd put Peterson and the others in their place. You'd walk into the middle of that meeting and act like a leader, not some loser who couldn't hack it in the real world and had to come running home. Someone who disappears when life throws real responsibility at them."

"Fuck you, Josh," Matt fired back. "You want me to gag you, just keep talking."

"Go ahead. When I get in front of a judge, I can't wait to tell him about the police brutality I've suffered today. How you tossed procedure out the window and let your emotions get the better of you." Josh looked up at Gabby, a grin slipping across his face. "He ever call you Addie when he's slipping his dick in? I bet he has."

Gabby nearly kicked him, but Matt managed to grab her foot before she could connect. She struggled in his arms as she glared down at Josh. "You're a piece of shit. Every time you step into the diner, half the town starts talking about you and Nancy Buckley. How you're off screwing her while your wife was at home coming apart. How you fed Lynn pills like some kind of Band-Aid. You know, even if she killed your kids, then killed herself, that's on you. You put her in that state of mind. And that's a big *if*, because I think you killed all of them, you crazy shit!"

Both his arms around her, Matt lifted Gabby from the ground and spun her around so she was facing the opposite direction. He pressed his mouth against her ear. "Don't let him get under your skin. That's what he wants. Take a breath, ignore him. He's going to spend the rest of his life behind bars, just like he deserves."

"Let go of me," she hissed back between clenched teeth. Her eyes shot toward Addie. "I'm not so sure he's wrong about you."

She pulled away from him and stomped back into the kitchen.

Matt let her go. He knew better than to try to reason with her when she was upset.

"Lovely girl," Addie mocked. "It's so obvious what you see in her."

Josh chuffed. "I think he just likes Mexican."

Matt held both his hands up. "Enough! Both of you. This isn't high school." He crossed over to the kitchen doorway, grabbed the phone off the wall, and tossed it down to Josh. He caught it in his free hand.

"What am I supposed to do with this? You heard your girlfriend; it's useless."

Matt took out his cell, loaded his emergency contact list, and tossed that down to him, too. "I want you to call everyone on that list. When you reach the bottom, you start over. You stop, and I'm locking you in a closet until this is over." He turned to Addie. "And you..." He bit his lip, choked his anger back. "Ellie has a shortwave radio around here somewhere. I need you to find it."

"Sir, yes, sir." She held his gaze for a moment, offered a mock salute, then went upstairs.

"Peterson's gonna come back," Josh said. "He'll put a bullet in your head, then mine, then both your girls, and that will be on you, just like all this other bullshit, because you're a shitty cop."

Matt wasn't about to take the bait. "Dial."

At the mention of Peterson's name, he remembered the USB drive Peterson had given him and took it from his pocket. He glanced around the living room and spotted Ellie's old Dell laptop on the coffee table under some various pieces of mail.

He powered on the machine, located the sole video file on the drive, and clicked Play.

Matt watched the video in complete silence, somehow managing to tune out the others. There was nothing but the thumping of his heart. When it finished, he hit Play again, dumbfounded.

77

Analysis Note: The subject's vitals dropped again for nearly a minute before restoring. Sordello has made it clear she doesn't want anyone going in there to check the equipment.

Sordello: Tell me about the video.

Maro: I don't want to talk about the video.

Sordello: I'm curious. Is that because you know it's real, or because you know it's not?

Maro: You've clearly got a copy. Why don't you tell me?

Sordello: That's not how this works.

Maro: [*Frustrated; rubs both temples*] I can't explain it any more than half the other things that happened.

Sordello: We don't need to discuss it yet, but we *will* talk about it.

Maro: [*No response*]

Sordello: Do you believe hiding in the sheriff's house was the correct course of action for you to take? You were still an active deputy at that point.

Maro: I was following orders. Staying put. Trying to get outside help. That was the right thing to do.

Sordello: Yet you gave that particular task to a suspect in your custody rather than try yourself. You sent one of your girlfriends off to try to work the shortwave radio rather than do it yourself.

Maro: I'm one person. I had to delegate. I needed to think. Part of me wanted to get out in the streets, but if I'd left the house and tried to defuse one situation after another, there was a good chance I would have gotten myself killed and Ellie would have been alone. The only law left. Something happens to her, and there's no one. We needed a better plan. We needed options, and we had none.

Sordello: Because the inmates were running the asylum? Is that how you see it?

Maro: We were completely outnumbered.

Sordello: Why do you think you were spared?

Maro: Spared? We weren't spared. Things were just as crazy in that house as they were everywhere else. Maybe worse. Nobody was spared. We were all one wrong comment away from killing each other, same as the rest of the town. [*Grows visibly agitated*] How about you explain why you cut us off? One phone call—that's all we needed—one call to bring in help, but you let nothing out.

Sordello: That wasn't us.

Maro: That's bullshit.

Sordello: What if I told you we made attempts to contact you and couldn't get through? The few times we did, we did everything we could to try to keep you safe?

Maro: I'd know you were lying.

Analysis Note: Via the private comm channel, Sordello's supervisor told her not to overstep. She no doubt heard him but didn't acknowledge. Nonetheless, she changed the subject.

Sordello: You've since learned the meeting at the middle school was orchestrated by a boy named Cody Hill. Looking back, what would you have done differently? To stop him.

Maro: [*No response*]

78

SHERIFF ELLIE

THE TOWN LOOKED LIKE a war zone. Ellie could think of no other way to describe it. With the sun setting, the sky was a mix of reds and yellows and deep black from the rising smoke. She could taste it in the air, acidic and dry. They needed rain, but the few clouds dotting the darkening sky didn't look like they intended to provide much of anything, and the forecast had no rain listed for two days. Main Street, possibly the entire town, would be cinder by then.

The girl who looked entirely too much like Emily Pridham sat silently in Ellie's passenger seat, her head turned to the side, staring out the window. Her hands rested in her lap and she barely moved. Ellie couldn't tell if she was so horribly traumatized she was unable to speak, or if the sight of all this hadn't fazed her at all, like it was commonplace. Ellie was leaning toward the latter because the girl looked calm, and that frightened Ellie, because all the crazy bullshit *should* scare the bejesus out of her.

"What do you make of all this?" Ellie finally asked.

The girl didn't respond.

"I'm not buying the silent treatment, young lady. You best find your tongue. *Vee got wayz of making you talk*," she added in her worst East European accent as a joke, hoping to draw out some kind of reaction, but got nothing. The girl's eyes never left the window.

Ellie shook her head and turned back to the street.

The few people who were out were a mixed breed. Some walked the sidewalks in a daze, staring off at the darkening sky with mouths agape and few words passing between them. Others were running, although Ellie couldn't figure out exactly where they were running; there was no place to go. She didn't need to visit the town lines to know the fencing she spotted out on Route 112 encircled them.

They were rats in a cage.

She'd driven about a half mile before she realized nearly everyone was heading in the same direction. That's when she noticed most seemed to be holding some kind of paper in their hands. Several read whatever it was as they walked.

Ellie spotted the local pharmacist shuffling along with the others. No longer wearing his pharmacist's jacket, the sleeve of his white shirt was torn, revealing pasty skin. He had a black eye; looked like he'd been on the wrong end of a fight. Slamming the brakes, Ellie rolled down her window and leaned out. "Henry!"

He turned toward her, the same worn look on his face as so many others. Then he squinted and recognized her. "Ellie?"

"What is that?" she pointed at the crumpled paper in his hand. "What does it say?"

This seemed to confuse him. "You mean the meeting? I was told you called it."

When he walked up to her truck, she snatched the paper from his hand and read it, her frown growing with each word. "This wasn't me."

The last thing she needed was townfolk getting together and getting riled up beyond the current state of fucked-upness.

"If not you, then who?" Henry Wilburt touched a crusty cut on the corner of his mouth and winced. "Figured you were rolling out some kind of martial law, and with phones down this was the easiest way to tell everyone."

"Curfew isn't a bad idea, but if I wanted to do that wouldn't it make more sense just to put out flyers with that stamped across the top? Safest place for everyone right now is in their own home with the door locked."

Maybe this was Stu Peterson, Ellie thought. If not him, then maybe it was the same people behind the fence. Whoever the hell *that* was. No good could come out of corralling everyone in some confined space.

Ellie crumpled the flyer and tossed it into the Rutledges' hedges. "Henry, I need you to tell whoever shows up at this thing to just go home. It's not safe." She glanced at the clock on her dashboard. It was quarter past seven. "I need to run up to Buck's place. I'll be there right after. Clear as many people out as you can."

For the first time, he looked past Ellie at the girl in the passenger seat, and his face hardened. "I don't know who organized the meeting, but I'm glad somebody did. I want to hear what they have to say. I'm not going to tell people to leave. They have a right to be there, same as me. You want to help, show up with some answers. Show up with *her*." He nodded roughly at the girl. "A lot of people want to talk to her."

Henry Wilburt took several steps back from the truck and raised his voice. "I bet you just about everyone wants to talk to the girl from the diner this morning, Ellie! This shit show started with her!"

When he pointed at Ellie's truck, half the people on the sidewalk stopped and faced her.

He raised his voice even louder. "Why are you protecting her, Ellie? You're supposed to be protecting us!" He rolled his chubby fingers around the air above his head. "Or maybe you're in on all this? That would explain the bang-up job you've done today! Someone paying you to look the other way?"

There were several angry shouts, and at least a dozen people had started coming toward her, from the surrounding houses and sidewalks, stepping out into the street. They'd surround her if she let them. No telling what else they would do, to her, to the girl.

"All of you need to go home! Get someplace safe!" Ellie shouted from her window before stomping her foot down on the gas.

Her pickup might be old, but it had pep. The rear tires let out a chirp, and they shot forward with enough force to throw both her and the girl back against the seat. She quickly weaved around the people in the street and made a quick turn on Marston, heading up toward the mountain.

Frazzled, she said, "You don't give me something, I might just hand you off to those people. They're not exactly wrong."

When Ellie glanced at her, she realized the girl was no longer looking out the window, she was staring back at Ellie. Before Ellie could say another word, the girl grabbed her wrist and the world vanished in a sea of black.

79

SHERIFF ELLIE

ELLIE FOUND HERSELF STANDING at the back of the Gas 'n' Go at the base of the mountains out on Route 112.

She knew that wasn't possible. She knew she was driving her truck—or at least had been driving her truck—not a moment earlier. She was so certain of that her hands ached from gripping the steering wheel so tight, and that meant she couldn't be here.

But…

When she drew in a breath, her lungs filled with the sour scent of hot dogs left to char all day on the metal rack, the faint scent of gasoline and motor oil carried in by customers at the pumps. She was standing next to the end display on the third aisle, the one with all the Hostess snacks, and she'd be damned if she wasn't holding a pack of HoHos, her favorite, but something she'd given up years ago under doctor's orders.

That wasn't the strangest part.

At the far end of the large cooler lining the back wall, holding the third door open and retrieving a bottle of water, was her.

Not her current self, but a younger version of herself, mid-thirties at most, wearing not a sheriff's uniform but a deputy's uniform with the exception of the hat. As always, her hair was pulled back in a tight ponytail, and this version of her was also holding a package of HoHos.

Ellie was still staring at this doppelgänger, this other version of herself, when the bell above the door chimed. She probably wouldn't have turned away to look if not for the gruff voice, low and urgent.

"Empty the register in a bag, and hand it over!"

He was wearing a black ski mask, filthy camouflage jacket, and jeans. A large revolver gripped tight in his shaky hand, pointed over the counter at the kid Ellie somehow knew worked the night shift every Wednesday through Saturday.

The much-younger Ellie at the cooler had turned, too, her eyes growing wide as the cashier responded, his voice nearly an octave higher than normal.

"I just emptied the register into the safe. There's only a hundred dollars in the till."

"Put it in a fucking bag, then empty the safe, too. Hurry the hell up!"

"The safe is time-locked. I can't open it for another fifty-three min—"

"Put the money in the fucking bag!"

The young Ellie at the cooler slowly set her package of HoHos on a rack of car batteries to her side along with the bottle of water and carefully unsnapped the leather strap on her service weapon, quietly removing the gun. This wasn't the weapon Ellie usually carried, but instead was the old Colt her father had given her when she graduated from the academy. An L-frame double-action .357. Big and bulky, compared to the semiautomatic she favored today.

Ellie knew this younger Ellie was making a mistake. She had

a better view of the gunman, could see how bad he was shaking, but more important, she'd caught a glimpse of his teeth when he barked out that last command. Many were missing, others were black—a telltale sign of a meth head. He was high right now, that was in his eyes. Probably smoked right before coming in. That meant unpredictable. Dangerous. The better plan was to let this play out. Let him take the cash and go. Get him outside where no one else would get hurt. She tried to signal Younger Ellie and realized she couldn't move.

Younger Ellie crouched low, slowly began making her way up the aisle toward the front of the store as Older Ellie watched helplessly.

"I ain't gonna tell you again!" the man shouted. He swept his arm across the counter and knocked down a display of lighters and bottle openers with a loud crash.

The cashier jumped. He beat on the register until it popped open and began filling a plastic bag with money.

"Whatever you got under the till, too! I know you hide the big bills there! Move!"

Ellie could see the cashier hadn't been lying. There were only two twenties and a handful of smaller bills.

Younger Ellie had closed the distance by half and was raising her gun. Her stance was all wrong; too much weight on her back foot, and her finger was on the trigger rather than the guard. Although not as bad as the man at the counter, she was shaking, too, and Ellie knew this was about to go bad in the moments before it did.

The gunman spotted the safe. Under the counter, behind the cashier, the cabinet door left open just enough for the safe to be visible. Ellie had no idea how she knew this, because she couldn't see it from the place where she was frozen watching everything play out, but she was as absolutely certain of those facts as she was in knowing Younger Ellie was about to make a terrible mistake.

Younger Ellie yelled out, "Police, don't move!" as the gunman leaned over to try to read a sticker on the cabinet housing the safe—the sticker Ellie somehow also knew read TIMED OPEN—CASHIER DOES NOT HAVE A KEY. He leaned over as Ellie yelled, and that bit of movement was enough to cause Younger Ellie to jerk back on the trigger.

The Colt went off with a loud explosion. With Young Ellie's weight on her back foot instead of the front, the force of the blast jerked her arms up. The shot sailed over the leaning gunman and caught the cashier just above his right eye and exited the back of his head, destroying the corner of the cigarette rack on the back wall.

The cashier fell.

The gunman twisted around.

From her spot, frozen near the back of the store, Ellie wanted to yell at Young Ellie, scream for her to jump to the side, but no sound came out. Even as the gunman's arm jerked out, as his gun came around and pointed at Young Ellie, she couldn't make a sound.

Ellie didn't hear his shot.

Her eyes snapped open when the girl in the passenger seat of the Ford released her wrist.

Somehow, Ellie was still driving, and although she had no memory of it, they'd followed the switchback up the mountain and were slowing as Buck's cabin came into view. She managed to get them into his short driveway and throw the truck in park before the shaking began. Every inch of her was quivering when she forced herself to look at the girl beside her. *"What the actual fuck was that?"*

80

MATT

MATT HAD WATCHED THE video twice and was nearing the end for the third time, his heart knocking against his rib cage. The first two times, he'd watched it straight through without stopping. This time he'd slowed the video down, paused it in several key places, and attempted to find anything to prove it was a fake.

Ellie's laptop was older than dirt. The resolution was terrible, and the hard drive whirred so loudly that it would have drowned out the audio from the file if it had any. There was no sound, though, only video, and if it was a fake, it was a damn good one.

Had to be a fake.

Matt clicked back to the beginning of the video and hit Play.

The footage was grainy. Probably not shot digitally but on some old film like 8mm transferred to digital at some later point. When Matt was a kid his dad had one of those 8mm cameras, and it didn't have any audio. The lighting was terrible, too. Too bright on the left side of the screen and nothing but shadows on the right, most likely from a single bulb just off camera. Matt knew filmmakers on a budget used some of these tricks to conceal shams and falsities, things that couldn't be hidden when filming in high def.

The camera was stationary, most likely on a tripod. It faced the front of an old wooden desk in what looked like a basement, but not a basement Matt recognized. The walls were paneled in dark brown. What little was visible of the drop ceiling was covered in dark water stains. Matt couldn't see the floor, but his mind's eye put shag carpet there, orange or green. The entire space was a time capsule caught back in the 1960s or '70s. The walls themselves were disturbing. They were covered in photos, newspaper articles, what looked like military medals, and a single poster near the center with words that struck Matt in his gut:

JOIN THE KKK AND FIGHT FOR RACE AND NATION!

For the first twenty seconds of the video, there was no movement. Then a man dressed in a white gown and pointed hat entered the frame, leaned in close to the camera lens, then settled in a chair opposite the camera behind the desk. His face was concealed behind a mask, eyes nothing more than dark pinpricks visible through holes. There was a red cross in a circle on his left breast.

The man sat there, unmoving for nearly a minute, those blank eyes looking into the camera, before reaching to his side and holding up a Birmingham, Alabama, newspaper dated September 16, 1963. The headline read:

FOUR CHILDREN DEAD IN 16TH STREET BAPTIST CHURCH
BOMBING: KKK SUSPECTED

Matt knew of the bombing; he'd studied it in school. The KKK had placed several bombs under the church and detonated them moments before Sunday school was meant to let out. Four girls died, all Black, between the ages of eleven and fourteen. Four men were suspected of carrying out the bombing, but the first wasn't tried until the late seventies. Two others finally were sentenced in 2001 and 2002. The last man died before facing prosecution. Although their various attorneys insisted the four men acted alone, most believed others were involved. What happened next in the video backed that theory.

The man in the video set the newspaper down and stared at the camera again from behind his mask, as if unsure of what he planned to do next. Then he drew in a deep breath and held up a sheet of paper with I'M SORRY scrawled across it in big, blocky letters. By the time he set that paper back down on the desk, his hand was shaking so bad it was nearly unreadable.

The man tugged off his mask.

Stu Peterson stared directly into the camera lens.

Even though the footage was poor quality, Matt could make out the red puffiness around Peterson's eyes, either from lack of sleep or tears or maybe both, there was no way to know for sure. Peterson looked no older than he did today, which meant this was filmed recently and the newspaper was some kind of relic or reprint. The video itself was made to look as old as that story, and that's why it was all wrong.

Matt knew from Peterson's gun permits the man was sixty-seven. That meant he was only seven years old when the church was bombed in 1963. Was it possible a seven-year-old Peterson was somehow involved in that bombing? Sure. Matt had heard far worse stories about the KKK.

But then there was the calendar.

It was hanging on the wall behind Peterson, partially blocked by his left shoulder.

January first through the eighth were crossed out. The year at the top of the page was 1964. That could easily be a prop, too, but something about it made it feel authentic.

Matt shook his head. The calendar couldn't be real, nor could the footage. None of it could be real because of what happened next.

Nearly a minute slipped by with Peterson staring at the camera before he picked up the gun. A silver-plated Magnum, one Matt recognized from those registered by Peterson.

Stu Peterson placed the tip of the barrel under his chin, thumbed the hammer back, and pulled the trigger.

No flash.

No bang.

No sound.

The camera continued to roll as Peterson's hand dropped away and his body slumped. The top of his head was missing, and the KKK poster behind him dripped with gore.

The camera rolled for about twenty more seconds after the shot, then stopped. The footage ended. There was nothing else on the USB drive.

Matt was mentally preparing himself to watch the video again when Addie came down the stairs slowly, her face a mix of confusion. "I got someone on the radio, but what they said didn't make any sense."

In the corner of the room, Josh tossed the phone aside. "Well, I haven't gotten shit. I'm done with it."

Matt ignored him and asked Addie, "What did they say?"

"It was a young girl, she barely spoke English." Addie lowered her gaze and put some thought into what she said next. "She told me she lived just outside Warsaw, in Poland, and she needed me to send help because the Nazis were coming. She just kept repeating that. Said her father told her to."

Gabby came in from the other room, busily tapping away at her phone. Without looking up, she said, "Riley reached my mother. She's driving in to pick her up from the rec center in Barton. She's going to stay with her until this is over." Gabby finished typing, looked up, and let out a relief-filled sigh. "At least she's safe."

Matt had been so busy with the video, he hadn't realized the sun had gone down. He reached to a lamp at his side and flicked the switch. The bulb flashed and blew, went dark.

"I saw a box of bulbs in the pantry." Gabby started back toward the kitchen.

She said something else from the other room, but Matt didn't hear her. He'd removed the lampshade and was staring at something he found clipped to the underside.

A bug.

Some kind of listening device.

81

SHERIFF ELLIE

WHATEVER ELLIE EXPERIENCED HAD been as vivid as any dream, but unlike a dream, it didn't vanish. The images remained in her head with the sharpest of clarity. When she blinked they replayed in the momentary darkness, each time more vivid than the last.

From her place in the passenger seat, the girl watched Ellie in silence, but unlike before, her eyes told a story. She'd not only seen the same vision Ellie had, but she understood what it meant, and now there was pity there. Pity and sorrow.

Ellie watched as the girl tugged up her sleeve and pointed at a place just below her elbow. Written there, among a hundred others, was Ellie's name, and as she saw it, the words Matt had told her back at the house came rushing back with the force of a Mack truck.

Hope not ever to see Heaven. I have come to lead you to the other shore; into eternal darkness; into fire and into ice.

It was all too much. The breath left Ellie, and she had to force herself to inhale, like her body no longer wanted to perform the simple task on its own. Her stomach heaved, and Ellie jerked the door open. She managed to stumble over to the tall grass alongside the driveway before vomiting.

When it was over, when her body finally righted itself, she fished a tissue from her pocket, wiped her mouth, and drew in a deep breath of the cool mountain air. Even though the air was tinged with the acidic smoke from the town, it was enough to help clear her thoughts.

Ellie turned back to her truck and stared down the girl. She had a job to do. "Get out."

At first, the girl didn't move. Then she opened her door and climbed out. She'd pulled her sleeve back down, and Ellie was grateful for that.

Leery of touching her, Ellie guided the girl to the door of Buck's cabin and knocked. When he didn't answer, she pounded on the door with the back of her fist. "I know you're in there, Buck! Open up!"

There was the rattle of locks.

The door opened.

Buck was standing there, holding a shotgun.

He took one look at both of them, then leveled the barrel at the center of the girl's chest and fired.

82

MATT

THE DEVICE WAS SMALL, secured with double-sided foam tape. Just a black box about an inch in diameter with a rubber nub on the side, most likely some kind of antenna. No lights or anything else to indicate it was on, but clearly a microphone, and that meant somebody was listening.

He didn't realize both Gabby and Addie were staring at him until he looked up.

Matt showed them both what he found and held a finger over his lips.

Gabby silently mouthed, *Stu Peterson*?

Matt shook his head.

He couldn't be sure, but he doubted it was Peterson.

Then a terrible thought popped into his head, one he didn't want to be true. He motioned for Gabby to hand him her phone and set it on the table between them with the texts from Riley still on the screen. He gave Gabby a solemn look and raised his voice.

"We can't stay here. I think we should load everyone in my car and make a run at the fence. Hit it as hard and fast as we can and try to get through."

He'd barely finished the sentence when three dots appeared on the phone screen indicating someone was typing. The dots remained there for nearly half a minute, then vanished.

Whoever was listening was also on the other end of Gabby's phone.

The realization that she hadn't been texting with her daughter hit Gabby a moment later, and her eyes welled up with tears. When she reached for the phone, Matt shook his head and held up a single finger, then he typed—

Who is this?

The three dots appeared again, then disappeared. When nothing happened for nearly a minute, Matt leaned close to the bug and spoke loudly. "Quit the bullshit. I know you're listening. Who is this?"

On the floor, Josh craned his neck. "Who the hell are you yelling at? What's going on?"

Matt held up the lampshade and pointed at the small device.

The three dots appeared on Gabby's phone again and hung on the screen for an impossibly long moment, disappeared, then came back again. When the next message appeared, Addie let out a soft gasp.

Stay in the house, or we cannot help you. You're already dead.

Gabby glared down at the phone as the words sunk in, then managed, "Where's my daughter? How'd you get her phone? Do you have her?"

Three dots, then—

Dead.

"You're lying," Gabby spat back.

...all dead. Soon you

No dots. Nothing.

The three of them stared at the small screen, waiting for the rest of that sentence, but nothing came. When more than a minute ticked by, Matt typed **WHO ARE YOU?!?** again, but only received **Message cannot be delivered** when he hit Send.

"Fuckers," Addie muttered.

Matt reached for Gabby's arm, but she shrugged him off. His heart was pounding a mile a minute, but he did his best to keep his voice calm. "They lied. What reason would they have to hurt a little girl?"

A loud bang came from behind him. Matt swiveled around in time to see Josh smash the phone receiver against the radiator for a second time. The plastic broke into several pieces, and he fished through them, found the round microphone, and held it up to the light. There was another bug attached to the two wire leads, clinging to the back.

Matt quickly glanced around the room.

How many more were in Ellie's house?

How long had they been there?

Gabby didn't care who was listening. "They got a fence up around town in under a day, and they're shooting anyone who tries to leave. *That's who has my daughter!* For all we know, they snatched her right out of your office." She glared at the small microphone. "You hurt her, and I'll fucking kill you. I'll kill every last one of you!"

From upstairs, music blared impossibly loud. All four of them jumped. The volume somehow increased, and that was followed by a louder *pop!*, then silence. Matt didn't know the song but recognized the language—German.

"That was 'Die Fahne Hoch,'" Josh said in a low voice. When nobody responded, he added, "It means 'raise the flag.' It was the Nazi anthem during World War II. My dad was a history buff, used to drill that crap into my head."

"It must have come from the shortwave radio," Addie said. "That girl I was talking to. Sounded like it blew the speaker."

Matt's head was spinning, trying to make sense of all this. "Go check," Matt told her.

"You go check. I'm not going up there."

Outside, the faint sound of an engine quickly grew louder. Matt returned to the window just in time to see Stu Peterson park and climb out of his truck. Several others jumped out the back and quickly ran around the sides of Ellie's house, all of them armed.

Peterson came about halfway down Ellie's driveway, then cupped his hands around his mouth. "Matt. I don't want to hurt anyone. Send out the girl, and we'll be on our way!"

83

SHERIFF ELLIE

THE WORLD MOVED IN slow motion.

Ellie reached for her sidearm and managed to unsnap the leather guard on her gun the moment before Buck jerked the slide on his shotgun, chambered another round, and fired again.

The second shot blew through the girl's shoulder, causing her body to twist and pivot.

Ellie yanked her gun out and leveled it at Buck as he chambered another shell. "Drop it!"

Buck fired.

Point blank, directly at the girl's face.

What happened next would remain ingrained in Ellie's mind for the remainder of her life.

There was no blood, no gore, no brain matter or bits of flesh, none of the things she expected. Instead, there was a flutter of black—small bodies, wings—this explosion of harsh movement from where the girl stood beside her in all directions at once, and when Ellie's brain managed to make some sense of what she saw, she realized the girl had burst into hundreds of crows, all of them shooting out from center mass with the force of an explosion. They twisted through the air, found the wind, the trees, the sky, and then they were gone with nothing but their angry cries left to echo in Ellie's ears behind the thundering blast and ring of the shotgun.

Ellie wasn't sure how long she just stood there. It might have been a lifetime, or it might have been half a second. Her mind had reached some kind of breaking point and flipped a switch. It wasn't until Buck spoke over the ringing in her ears that she found the string attached to reality again and managed to tug herself back. His deep voice resonated through every inch of her being as he held out his hand, grazing the tip of her gun with his fingers. "No, Ellie."

Her finger was already moving toward the trigger, though. She couldn't stop that involuntary motion any more than she was able to stop the younger version of herself from firing at the meth head in that store.

84

MATT

"GET DOWN!" MATT HAD left the shotgun leaning against the wall near the front door.

Dropping to a crouch, he scrambled over and scooped it up. With his back against the wall, he checked the chamber, then tugged his service weapon from his holster and slid it across the floor to Gabby. "Take that and go down to the basement. Anyone but me comes down those stairs, you shoot them."

There was much about Gabby's past Matt didn't know; entire years she refused to discuss, and he never pressed. She eyed the Glock for only a moment before scooping it up, checking the magazine, and pulling the slide slightly back to ensure the weapon was fully loaded and ready to fire. "I'm not going anywhere. We kill that fucker, then we go and get Riley."

Matt knew better than to tell her no; he also knew he couldn't do this alone. "Okay, take the back door. Nobody gets in."

Gabby nodded and darted back into the kitchen.

Addie remained still. Her eyes wide, filled with fear. Her hand was clutching her belly, her fingers nervously twisting the fabric of her shirt.

"Go back upstairs, find someplace to hide."

She quickly glanced back toward the kitchen and shook her head. "No, give me a gun. I want to help, too."

"You need to think about the baby."

"I am."

"You don't have to prove anything."

"I want a gun."

Matt had no time to argue. "Ellie told me she keeps an old Colt in the top drawer of her nightstand. Go find it and see what you can see from the upstairs windows. Just be careful, don't let anyone spot you. I don't think these guys will hesitate to shoot."

Addie started to go, then hesitated. "Would you even care if they did?"

"Addie, we can't do this right now."

"No matter what I do, I'll always be second best. Your consolation prize. If I died, would you be sad or relieved?"

"Matt!" Peterson shouted from outside. "Don't make me ask again."

"You don't have to answer," Addie said. "I already know."

Before Matt could say anything else, she was halfway up the stairs. She turned the corner at the landing and vanished from sight.

At the radiator, Josh yanked at his handcuffs, tried to pull free, but that thing was older than both of them and made of cast iron. It didn't budge. He glared at Matt. "Uncuff me and give me a gun!"

"Not a chance."

"How many are there? You seriously think you can hold them off without me?"

"You know I can't cut you loose."

Josh licked his lips nervously. "I didn't kill my wife, and I didn't kill my kids. I would never do that. It doesn't matter how bad things might have been between me and Lynn, I could *never* do that. You and I may not see eye to eye, but you have seen me at the range, you know I can shoot. Give me a fucking gun."

"Matt!" Peterson barked again. "I got people all around. I'm gonna give you a ten count to send the girl out. You don't do it, and this will get sloppy."

"She's not here, Stu!" Matt shouted back. "Ellie took her. I don't know where they went."

Several seconds slipped by, then Peterson broke the silence. "Well, that's unfortunate."

Josh rattled the handcuffs again. "Let me go, Matt!"

"Shut the hell up!"

Josh gave the cuffs another yank, then craned his neck. "Ellie took the girl up to Buck's place, Stu! They left maybe half an hour ago!"

When Peterson replied, he sounded like he was right outside the front door. "Is that so?"

"Matt has a shotgun! He's in the front room with me! Gabby is in the kitchen watching the back, and he sent the pregnant one upstairs! They're both armed, too! You don't need to come in here—head up to Buck's, you'll get what you want!"

Matt's grip tightened on the shotgun. It took everything he had to *not* put a hole in Josh.

Peterson said, "If the girl's gone, you won't mind if me and the boys come in and have a quick look-see, will you? Not that I don't believe you, but I'd prefer to confirm that with my own eyes."

Matt did his best to keep the fear from his voice. "Get back in your truck and go home, Stu! You do that, and I'll give you a pass on all this. You don't, and you'll find yourself in a cell come tomorrow!"

Three quick shots rang out with a metallic clang as they struck the outside of the door near the lock and ricocheted. Sounded like they came from a .45, but Matt couldn't be sure.

"The door is steel core with two dead bolts," Matt told him. "Same with the back. You're not getting through. Get the hell out of here!"

"There are many ways into a house, Matt. You know that. Many ways to make someone come out, too."

The large picture window above the couch shattered with a rain of glass. A rock the size of Matt's fist bounced off the coffee table, rolled across the floor, and came to rest near the far wall. Matt heard glass break upstairs and near the back of the house, too; that was followed by a scream from Gabby in the kitchen.

Clutching the shotgun against his chest, Matt started toward her when a Molotov cocktail sailed through the opening where the picture window had been and shattered on the floor, setting the hardwood aflame.

Outside, Stu Peterson yelled, "Come out when you're ready, Matt! I'm a patient man—I'll wait for you!"

85

SHERIFF ELLIE

BUCK SLAPPED ELLIE'S GUN to the side and didn't so much as flinch as the bullet tore through the wood decking at his feet and vanished in the earth below with a thunderclap. His eyes never left hers. She might have fired again if he hadn't twisted the gun from her hand and taken it from her, even as her index finger twitched.

She was in some kind of shock.

On some level, Ellie understood that, but understanding it and using it to override her body's natural instinct to withdraw into itself were two very different things. She managed to twist her head to the side and face the spot the girl had been standing only moments earlier, but what she found clarified nothing, only created more questions.

There was no sign of the girl.

No body.

No blood.

No nothing.

Even the birds had vanished from sight, but Ellie got the

impression they hadn't gone far, because Buck was staring past her into the trees, the lines of his face deepening.

He slipped Ellie's gun into the waistband of his jeans at the small of his back and took her by the wrist. "You need to get in here."

His touch was rough. He had the hands of a working man, gritty, made of sandpaper, but Ellie didn't pull away. She let him lead her over the threshold into his cabin and close the door behind her. There was a fire burning in the hearth, crackling softly.

Ellie had never seen where Roy "Buck" Buxton lived, and in all the years she'd known him her mind had constructed an image of what such a place might look like based on her encounters with him, none of which were particularly good. She realized she thought of him simply as the town drunk and completely forgot there was a person behind there. As tragic as it may have been, Buck had a lifetime behind him she knew little about. The air inside was warm and dry. Welcoming, not what she expected. While the furniture was outdated, it was well kept. A few of the pieces looked handmade, possibly by Buck.

Sitting atop the fireplace mantel was a single framed photograph—a teenage version of Buck with his arm wrapped around Emily Pridham, standing near the bleachers of the high school, a big grin across his face and a radiant smile on hers. As Ellie took several steps closer, all doubt fell from her mind—as impossible as it seemed, this was the same girl Ellie had brought here, the same girl Buck had just shot, the same...

Ellie's voice cracked as she brushed the wood frame. "Tell me that wasn't her."

Buck's lungs rattled as he drew in a breath and came up behind her, stepped by, and leaned the shotgun against the side of the fireplace. He answered her in a grave whisper. "That ain't the first time she come back. I seen her four times today. First when I went to clean up them birds down in the commons. Again about an hour later at the town dump. Once right here in my fucking house standing right there where you are now, and one other time just standing out there in the woods, watching me. I don't know what that is…was…but it ain't my Emily, that's for damn sure."

"How…"

"How is that possible? Damned if I know. How is any of what is going on today possible?"

Ellie caught movement from the corner of her eye, and when she turned she found a young girl watching her from the open doorway of a room at the rear of the cabin. It took her a second to make the connection, because the girl had no business being here.

"Riley?"

Mason Ridler appeared behind her and froze at the sight of Ellie and told someone, "Oh boy, po-po in the house."

That someone turned out to be two someones—Evelyn and Robby Harper.

"I don't understand." Ellie eyed Riley. "You told your mother you were at the rec center out in Barton. You said you were all out there. You and a bunch of other people from town."

Confusion washed over the little girl's face. "No, I didn't."

"Yes, you…" Ellie tried to force her brain to work. No easy task, considering what had just happened on Buck's doorstep, what he just told her. She held her hand out. "Let me see your phone."

Riley Sanchez took the iPhone from her pocket and handed it over. She didn't have a lock code installed. It took Ellie a moment to find the messaging app and locate the thread with her mother, Gabby. There were many messages today, but like Gabby's phone, most had failed and gone unsent. The message Gabby had received from Riley back at her house, the one that said these kids were in Barton, was not there. It hadn't come from Riley's phone.

Stranger still, there were messages from Gabby, messages Ellie was fairly certain Gabby hadn't sent. All of them told Riley to stay at Buck's cabin until she could find a way to come and get her.

Only one thing made sense—whoever was intercepting and blocking their communication today was also using the tech to send false messages.

The little boy, Robby Harper, looked up at Buck with big, worried eyes. "Did you have to kill her again?"

"I did."

"Do you think she's done coming back?"

"I wish I knew the answer to that."

Evelyn Harper placed a hand on her brother's shoulder and gave him a reassuring squeeze, then told Buck, "You need to show Sheriff Pritchet what you showed us."

"Buck's got a theory, and it's crazy as fuck." Mason Ridler snickered.

Evelyn elbowed the boy in the gut. "I told you not to talk like that around my brother, Asshat."

Riley ignored them both. "Is my mama okay? Is she with you?"

Ellie went down on one knee and stroked the girl's hair. "She's fine, and she's safe. I left her back at my house with Matt."

"Can you take me to her?"

Ellie was about to tell the girl yes when she caught a glimpse of the room behind her. She gave Buck an unsettling glance. "In a minute, honey. I think Evelyn might be right. I think Mr. Buxton needs to show me whatever he showed you."

86

MATT

JOSH CRIED OUT.

A high-pitched, animal-like shriek, and Matt realized a tendril of flames from the Molotov cocktail that came through the window had reached him and the man's leg was on fire.

Matt shot up from his position at the door, jumped the growing fire in the center of the room, and grabbed the corner of Ellie's large fish tank. With a grunt, he yanked it forward, toppling the tank from the table—water, sand, fish, and a tiny castle splashed out, soaked his pants, and rolled across the floor like a mini tidal wave, quickly snuffing out most of the fire but missing Josh—he screamed even louder, batting at his leg, twisting and jerking, only making it worse.

From a nearby chair, Matt grabbed a throw pillow, dropped down next to Josh, and systematically began smothering the flames. He worked up and down the man's leg until they were all out, then used his weight to hold Josh still. "It's out, it's out," he assured him. "Stop moving; I need to see how bad…" His voice trailed off as he got a better look.

Some of the gasoline must have splashed on Josh's right leg. From his knee to just above his ankle, his khaki pants were black, smoldering. Some of the material had melted into the charred flesh below. Easily second- and third-degree burns. He needed a doctor.

Josh was breathing in short, quick gasps, sucking the air between clenched teeth.

"You'll be okay," Matt told him, knowing that was a lie. "Just stay still."

Matt had dropped the shotgun when he went for the fish tank, and he caught Josh's eyes flash to it a moment before the man lunged.

Matt brought his knee up and caught Josh under his chin. His teeth cracked together, and he let out another cry as Matt retrieved the weapon and rolled away from him.

Two shots came from the kitchen.

He remembered Gabby, then.

She'd screamed right before the firebomb came through the picture window.

He bolted through the kitchen doorway and found Gabby crouching behind the sink, the window above her gone, and smoke rising from the barrel of her gun.

"There's at least three of them out there," she quickly told him. "Same creeps Stu had with him earlier. They took cover somewhere, but I'm not sure for how long. We need to get out of here."

Matt's cruiser was in the detached garage.

"We can't get to my car without going outside. It's too dangerous. Josh is hurt. There's no way to move him fast." He quickly told her what happened.

"Fuck Josh. You shoulda let him burn."

"Matt!"

That came from Addie upstairs.

Gabby shook her head and turned back toward the missing window above her. "Just go."

"You know I love you, right?"

She chewed at her lower lip and refused to look at him. "I know you want to, but that doesn't always make it so."

"That's not fair."

"No," she replied softly. "It's not." She craned her neck to get a better look at the backyard. "Go. Make sure Addie is okay. I can take care of myself. I always have."

Matt didn't want to—this felt like the end of them—but he had no choice. For better or worse, he had a job to do. Against every fiber of his being, he rose, darted from the kitchen, and headed for the staircase.

87

SHERIFF ELLIE

ELLIE WAS HALFWAY TO the room at the back of the house when Buck gripped her shoulder and held her still. "Before you go in there, I need to know you can keep an open mind, because everything I'm about to show you is going to make you question some things, *a lot of things*. You're not gonna believe it at first, rightfully so—I sure as hell didn't—but I need you to stow that part of your head, the part that tells you what's real and what ain't. The part that tells you certain things can't possibly be real under no circumstance. When you do doubt me, I want you to think about that girl who looked like Emily Pridham and what you just witnessed on my front stoop."

"I don't know what I saw, Buck."

"You know what you didn't see, and that was a girl dying like she should from multiple shotgun blasts. That's the part you gotta grab on to and hold tight."

Mason Ridler tapped the side of his forehead. "Prepare to have your mind blown."

Buck released Ellie's shoulder and gestured toward the room.

She stepped inside.

The space wasn't very large, only about twelve by ten, but the lack of furniture made it appear bigger. There was no bed, no dressers. There was nothing but a card table in the center with a single folding chair on one side. Aside from an overflowing ashtray and hundreds of water stains from cans or bottles on the brown Formica top, the table was empty. It was clear to Ellie that Buck spent a significant amount of time at that table, in that chair, and when she saw the walls, she understood why.

Every inch was covered—maps, printouts, newspaper clippings—all of it tied together behind an intricate pattern of multicolored strings fastened with thumbtacks.

"Jesus, Buck. Do I want to know how long you've been at this?"

"How long you think?"

"Since Emily."

"Since Emily," he agreed.

Riley and the other kids returned to the room but stood silently in the corner. While Mason, Riley, and Evelyn watched Ellie, the younger Harper child was looking at the walls. Ellie got the impression that he not only understood what it all meant, but he somehow was building on it. Connecting dots beyond whatever theory had taken Buck years to construct. The boy's eyes were darting back and forth, following the strings, studying the text and pictures. She could only imagine what was going on in his head, but she was fairly certain she wouldn't be able to keep up.

Buck stepped over to the first of several maps, this one of Hollows Bend. "What do you think of our crime rate here in the Bend?"

While Ellie knew it was no laughing matter, she couldn't help but let out a soft chuckle at that one. "Damn near perfect, up until today. I'm fairly certain our select board will be pushing to replace me if there's anything left of this place come tomorrow."

"This ain't your fault, Ellie. Get that thought out of your head; the guilt will eat at you. I know that better than anyone." He gestured at the map. There was a single thumbtack marking a place near where they stood. "Best I can tell, we got one major crime on the books, what you would consider *felony level*, and it wasn't a crime, because I didn't kill my Emily, regardless of what everyone thinks. That means not a single major crime in the Bend over the past fifty years. Not one."

Ellie opened her mouth, ready to argue that point, then promptly clamped it shut. He was right. They've had their share of D&Ds, but aside from Buck, those were mostly tourists who let the fun get a little ahead of them. A few marital spats that amounted to nothing more than loud arguments. She had several missing persons over the years, her father had, too, but those always turned out to be slip and falls up here on the mountain— horrific, to be sure, but accidents. She had a few runaways on her docket, but angsty teenagers running from home was hardly a crime, certainly not felony level. Until today, the Bend had been a quiet place.

He walked her over to another map. This one covered all of New England, from the uppermost point of Maine down to the bottom of Connecticut. Unlike the first map, this one was covered in thumbtacks. So many points had been marked, Buck had switched to straight pins in some places just to fit them all in.

"That's every felony in New England over the same period, fifty years."

Studying the map, Ellie expected Boston to be bad—large city, concentration of people—she imagined if you did the math and divided the crimes by the general population, it wasn't as bad as it looked, but it looked bad. It was some of the other states that surprised her—Vermont, Maine, Rhode Island—the mountainous regions just outside Hollows Bend and rural New Hampshire were hotbeds of crime.

·"A lot of this is opioids, right? Drug related?"

Buck nodded. "A good portion, sure. But you've also got plenty of murders, rapes, theft. We're standing in the oldest part of the country, and people have been treating each other like shit from the moment we hopped off the boats. Go back further, and the Native Americans weren't much better. Some of the nastiest wars between tribes took place right here in these mountains. New England's soil is rich with their blood. Originally I tried marking them all, went back to the beginning of written records, but there was too much. Figured I'd need a bigger map to go down that rabbit hole."

With that, he took her to a third map. This one covered all of North America. It, too, was covered in pins. As Ellie studied it, one thing was very clear—with the exception of California, the bulk of the crime was concentrated on the East Coast, the north- ern East Coast. New England. There was a logical explanation for that. "Like you said, this is the oldest part of our country. Settled first with the largest population. It makes sense for it to be heavier here, then lessen as you branch out to more remote places. Crime follows people."

Buck nodded at that but remained facing the map. "That's very true, but you ain't seeing it yet. Look closer."

Behind her, Evelyn shuffled her feet. "Don't feel bad. We stared at that map for about five minutes, and only Robby figured it out."

"That's not true, I got it," Mason shot back. "Got it before you."

"Both of you pipe down, let her concentrate," Buck ordered.

Riley said, "Take a few steps back, Sheriff. It's easier to see if you don't stand so close."

Ellie was about to tell them all she didn't have time for any of this but shuffled back instead. She was nearly against the opposite wall when she understood.

Mason whistled. "Oh, there it is. She got it."

Ellie narrowed her eyes, squinted slightly. "That can't be right."

"It's right," Buck insisted. He pointed at the wall on his right. There were dozens of file boxes stacked nearly floor to ceiling. "All the records are right there. Every one of those pins ties out to a real crime."

Ellie stared at the map for nearly a minute, then shifted back to the one of New England. It was easier to see on that one now that she knew what she was looking for. From the outer edges of the map to the center, the concentration of pins grew thicker, became solid lines when she squinted, with a blank spot at the very center where Hollows Bend was located marked by the single red thumbtack representing Emily Pridham. When Ellie squinted further, the illusion thickened—she was looking at concentric circles radiating out from the center. She was looking at some sort of bull's-eye, with her town in the middle.

"I got a cousin who lives down in Florida. Calls me whenever they got a hurricane coming their way. Sends me pictures. That's what this reminds me of—a hurricane with an eye at the middle, a calm spot."

"Calm, up until today," Ellie heard herself mutter.

"Someone shoved a stick in the eye, and it's bleeding."

Ellie didn't want to buy into this, but it was hard to argue with the data, and she had no reason to doubt what Buck was telling her. He'd done his homework. Something was off, though. She took a closer look at the map of New England, then returned to the one of the Bend and surrounding area. "Town isn't the exact center, is it."

"No. The exact center is about a hundred yards from where I lost Emily. Near the old Pickerton place."

"You need to tell me what happened that day. Every bit of it."

88

MATT

MATT WANTED ADDIE TO scream again, because that would mean she was okay, but instead, she'd gone quiet. Not so much as a squeaky floorboard came from upstairs. Matt did feel a light breeze, though, and that meant the shattering glass he'd heard had been another window, like the one downstairs. Unlike the broken window downstairs, he doubted they'd tossed a firebomb through— he didn't smell smoke. That meant either a rock or someone got in. As he crept up the steps, Matt tried to visualize the outside of Ellie's house, wondering if it was possible to get up to the second floor without a ladder.

His palms were sweating by the time he reached the second-floor landing. Matt wiped them on his pants and clutched the shotgun tight against his chest. He gave himself a silent three-count, leveled the barrel, and swept around the corner to the upstairs hallway, finding it empty.

He froze and listened.

Nothing.

No sound. No smoke. No nothing.

The second floor of Ellie's house wasn't very large. The ceilings were low, only seven feet, which was common for many older homes in New England. The hallway was narrow, more so than it should be. Ellie had once told him her father rebuilt the upstairs walls when she was little to add a couple of extra feet to the two bedrooms, both on Matt's left as he looked down the hallway with a small bathroom at the far end.

The doors to all three rooms were open.

Ellie used the smaller of the two bedrooms, once her childhood bedroom, for storage. She'd moved into the master about a year after her father passed away. Her original bed was still in the old space, still covered with a pink bedspread, but the top was covered in boxes. Most of the floor was taken up with furniture she'd moved out of her father's room and had never brought herself to part with. Although the room was cluttered, Matt could see enough to know nobody was in there. The window was closed, the curtains were drawn. There was no place to hide.

Matt continued toward the master bedroom while keeping one eye on the bathroom at the far end of the hall. Although that door was open, the shower curtain was closed. He couldn't get to the bathroom without stepping past the open door of the master. If he wanted to ambush someone, he'd hide behind that curtain, draw them to the master, then come at them from behind. Or he'd stand in wait at the bedroom door and take out his adversary when they passed the opening. Either plan was solid. If one of Stu's men had gotten up here, which would they choose?

A sound from the bedroom.

A soft sniff.

Addie.

Possibly in trouble.

Possibly bait.

Matt crouched low, firmly gripped the shotgun, and drew in

a silent breath. Kicking off from his back foot, Matt closed the distance, got an angle on the bathroom, and fired once—dead center on the curtain. He yanked back the slide and chambered another shell as he brought the barrel around and pointed it into the bedroom.

Standing at what remained of the bedroom window, Addie let out a soft gasp.

In the bathroom, a heavy weight fell against the curtain, grabbed it from the inside, and fell over the side of the tub to the bathroom floor, bringing the curtain down with him.

John Hicks.

One of Stu Peterson's buddies.

Dead.

Addie whimpered but didn't move.

Both her hands were at her side, and Ellie's Colt was on the floor about three feet in front of her. Her eyes darted toward the wall to the left of the doorway, then back to Matt.

Matt trained the shotgun on the back side of that wall and silently mouthed the words *how many?*

Before she could answer, Rodney Campos's deep voice rolled from the bedroom. "I'm wearing a vest, Matt. You can try and shoot me through that wall, but you're unlikely to hurt me. You might even hit your girlfriend with some stray buckshot or whatever the hell you got in there. This is the important part, so you'll want to pay attention. I got my 9mm pointing at her belly. You can guarantee I'll get at least one shot off before you can put me down—*if* you can put me down. I don't like to brag, but I'm pretty quick on the draw."

Downstairs, more glass broke and Gabby fired two shots, screamed, and went quiet. Matt heard the stomping of boots across the wood floors, what sounded like the couch under one of the windows toppling over.

"That's Stu and a few more of the guys," Rodney went on. "We can do this without anyone getting hurt, or we can do it with a lot of people getting hurt, that's entirely up to you. You ask me, it's already over. Best not to make things hard on yourself."

Matt stared in at Addie.

He motioned with his hand, tried to get her to dive to the side, give him a chance to take a shot, but she was either too panicked or didn't understand. She didn't move.

"You know me, Matt. I ain't got much in the way of patience."

From downstairs, Stu Peterson shouted up. "We got no reason to hurt Gabby, Matt. Don't give us one! I need you to put down your hardware. Surrender yourself to John and Rodney."

"I think John's dead!" Rodney Campos shouted back. "Matt shot him!"

There was a momentary silence, then, "That's fine, Matt. I won't hold it over you. I never much liked that kid."

"You're not the law, Stu! You're setting yourself up for a lot of time behind bars! Whoever you got with you, too!"

"All I'm doing is safely escorting all of you to a town meeting, like any good citizen. Anyone asks, that's why we're here. Would have helped the sheriff and that girl get there, too, but looks like Josh told the truth about them leaving. We came here to help you, keep you safe, and you started shooting. You killed a man. You're acting irrational. That's how I'll tell it to the staties if they eventually show. Let's see who they believe." Peterson paused a beat. "We don't have to turn this into a pissing match. Just put down your gun, come with us peacefully, and nobody else will get hurt. You got my word on that."

Framed by the light of the window, Addie shook her head.

Matt's heart was pounding so hard, he could hear the blood rushing through his ears. "We all go to the meeting. Talk this out with the rest of the town. Nobody else gets hurt!"

"You got my word," Peterson repeated.

Matt edged the barrel of the shotgun closer to the spot where he believed Rodney was standing and tightened his finger on the trigger.

"You really gonna make me kill your kid, Matt? Your kid *and* your girlfriend?"

Matt saw it then: Rodney's reflection in the mirror at the corner of Ellie's room. Rodney was watching him, able to see his every move.

He couldn't risk it.

Matt had no choice.

He gently placed the shotgun on the floor and raised both his hands over his head. "Okay! Nobody else gets hurt!"

89

SHERIFF ELLIE

BUCK'S GAZE FELL TO the floor, and there was a quiver in his lips. Even after all these years, it was clear he still loved Emily Pridham. His voice cracked when he finally spoke. "I suppose you heard the same story everyone else did—Emily went off into the bushes to go to the bathroom, stepped too close to a cliff, and vanished. Probably fell."

Ellie nodded. "That's what's in the report."

"Emily grew up on this mountain, same as me. She knew every inch. Could probably walk it with her eyes closed. Hell, sometimes I think she knew it better than me. We were hiking and came across the damnedest thing not far from Legion's Gully, back behind the Pickerton house. Crows. A lot of them. At first, there were only two or three. They were up in the trees. We heard 'em but didn't see them. The numbers grew and the sound of 'em became deafening. I figured a flock had settled up there for a spell, resting on their way to who-knows-where."

"A murder," Robby said quietly. "A group of crows isn't a flock. It's a murder."

"A murder," Buck corrected, with a nod to the boy. "We kept moving along the path. I made some joke about it raining bird shit if we didn't get out of there quick enough, and we picked up the pace. That's when they started showing themselves, and they weren't shy about it. First in the branches up ahead, then standing in the path. A dozen. Then fifty. Then maybe a hundred or more. They were everywhere. So many we couldn't see the ground. It was like this breathing blanket of black at our feet. And loud. So damn loud. Got to the point where I wanted to turn around, but not Emily, no ma'am, she wanted to figure out what was going on. We were holding hands and she pulled me forward, into the thick of 'em. The birds let us through, reluctantly. They closed the space behind us. Some pecked at our shoes. Got more aggressive with each step, but Emily wouldn't stop. She had to know. It felt like we walked an hour before we came up on the tree, but in reality, it couldn't have been more than a few minutes. Time didn't seem to be moving right. It was moving like it does in dreams, and I remember thinking I'd nodded off and found myself in the middle of some crazy dream."

Ellie's brow furrowed. "What tree?"

"Just an oak tree. Nothing special about it. Old enough to tower over us, thick with gnarled, arthritic-lookin' branches." Buck licked his lips. "Every inch of that tree was covered by the birds. Being late in the year, most of the leaves were gone, but I'm pretty sure even if it had been in full leaf, I wouldn't have seen them under all those damn birds. I'm not gonna lie, I froze. My legs just stopped working, refused to move. Not Emily, though. She had to see. Had to get close."

Buck's voice fell away, and his eyes grew glossy. "She was wearing this sundress and moved with such grace. It was one of the most beautiful things I'd ever witnessed, watching her slip through the birds to that tree. She *glided* more than walked, and I had the strangest thought—the birds *wanted* her to get closer, wanted her but not me. They'd pecked at my ankles to the point of drawing blood, yet hers were bare and without a scratch. When she reached the tree, her back was to me. She stood there for the longest moment. I said her name, called it out, but between all the noise and whatever held her, she didn't hear me. *I barely heard me.* She reached out and touched the bark. The birds moved, let her do that. *Wanted her to do that.* I got no doubt 'bout that. When she touched the tree, everything went silent. I got no doubt about that, either. The birds, the wind, everything. I heard nothing but my own breathing. Time froze, then my Emily said my name— *Buck*—this hushed whisper, akin to a gasp, and…"

Ellie wasn't sure if the children had heard this story from him before she arrived, but they were riveted, all eyes locked on him. All but Robby, who was still studying the maps, lost in his own head.

Buck's voice dropped low. "The ground…opened up beneath her. Swallowed her. One second she was standing there, then she was falling, then she was gone. I tried…I tried to get to that tree, but the birds wouldn't let me, they swarmed, attacked, drove me back. I took shelter in the Pickerton place, and when I came out they were gone. Not a trace of them. My Emily was gone, too. I ran for that tree. Combed the ground. There was no hole, no place for her to go. There was blood, though. I found a rock at the base of the tree covered in it. Bunch of dead birds around it."

"Did you tell my dad?"

"Hell yeah, I told him. But you think he believed me? I drug him out there, to that very spot. Showed him the tree right where she vanished. He gave it one look, then went about thirty more feet into the woods to the edge of the cliff, that nasty one out behind the Pickerton house. He stood there for the longest time, looking down. When he turned back to me, something had changed. I realized he thought I'd done something to her or figured I was covering up what really happened. I started digging at the base of the tree with my bare hands. The dirt was packed hard. I hit granite not very far down. I wasn't exactly sure what I'd seen at that point. Maybe it had been some kind of dream. I told myself that. Convinced myself. When your dad suggested Emily had just gone off into the bushes on her own, maybe slipped on that cliff and fell, I wasn't so sure he was wrong. I just didn't know what was real and what wasn't. I kept my mouth shut. I searched with everyone else. But deep down, I had the truth, even if I didn't want to believe it. I'm certain now, have been my whole life since." He nodded up toward the map of Hollows Bend, at the single red thumbtack marking the spot where Emily vanished. "Something took her. Took her right there. Something bad." He gestured at the other maps. "Whatever it is, it's been here long before us, and today it decided it ain't hiding no more."

Ellie didn't know what to make of all this. Maybe Buck was telling the truth, at least his version of it. Or maybe the decades of drinking had rotted his brain. She didn't have time to humor wild theories. She needed to get back to town before that meeting started, because her gut told her if she didn't, everything would become far worse. She drew in a deep breath and let it out slowly. "I know you're hurting, Buck. I get it. But I need to get these kids back to my house and get in front of this mess before it gets worse. I promise, when it blows over, you and I can dig into this deeper. I have all my dad's old files. The photos, videos, statements, we can go through—"

As she spoke, Robby Harper reached into the red backpack at his feet and pulled out a dead bird. The largest crow Ellie had ever seen. The bird's neck swiveled loosely, most likely broken. Its black eyes held the same dead stare they had in life. He set the bird on the card table, picked up a pen, and stabbed it in the chest.

Ellie knew she'd never be able to articulate what happened next, but the image of the bird crumbling into dust would be etched into her mind until the day she died.

Robby blew the black powder from his hand and pointed up at the single red tack. "That's ground zero. If you want to stop what's happening, we need to go there. You won't solve anything going back to town."

90

MATT

"THEY WERE TELLING THE truth," Rodney Campos said. "No sign of the sheriff or the girl. Her old truck is missing; she's probably driving that. No telling how long ago they left."

Rodney was standing on Ellie's front stoop. Eli McCormick was inside making a mess of the place. From where Matt had been forced to kneel on the sidewalk, he caught glimpses of Eli through the missing windows—turning furniture, knocking books off the shelves, searching for God knows what. Addie and Gabby were on the sidewalk to his left, both quiet. Josh was lying on the grass behind them. Even with the burns on his leg, Peterson had tried to force him to kneel twice and finally gave up. He stepped closer to Josh and nudged him with the barrel of his rifle. "Where did you say they went again?"

Josh rolled his head toward him. His skin was pasty, covered in a thin sheen of sweat. "Oh, so you do remember *I'm* the one who told you where they went?"

Rodney kicked Josh's injured leg, then pulled back and got

him again in the gut. "You think that earns you some kind of prize, shit bag?"

Peterson raised a hand. "Easy, Rodney. Josh here is right. How 'bout you get the first aid kit from my truck and patch him up. It's behind the passenger seat."

Rodney glared at him. "You heard what he did to his family, right? Both kids and his wife. He's got no right to be breathing."

"I didn't…" Josh managed before a coughing fit took hold. He curled up like an injured animal.

Peterson knelt next to him in the grass. "Grab a bottle of water, too, Rodney." When Rodney stormed off, Peterson's face morphed into a smile that wanted to be warm but couldn't mask the ice beneath. "I take care of those who take care of me, Josh, always have. I've got a big ol' bottle of prescription painkillers in my kit. You're welcome to as many as you need until we can get you proper medical attention. Now, you said Ellie took the girl up to Buck's place. Do you know why?"

Josh swallowed and twisted his face toward Matt. "She didn't tell me, but he knows."

"That right," Peterson mulled slowly, turning toward Matt. "Care to explain how that old drunk fits in to all this?"

"Don't we have a town meeting to get to?"

Peterson glanced at his watch. "We've got a little time. Traffic's light today, too. I'll get you there in time, don't you worry about that. Why Buck?"

Before Matt could answer, Eli came through the front door holding the file box from the basement with several guns and boxes of ammo perched precariously on top. "Found this downstairs with a bunch of other old cases. It was the only one open. There's a gun safe down there, too; lots more where these came from."

Ellie hadn't locked the safe back up after handing Matt the shotgun.

Peterson glanced at the file box. "Emily Pridham? Wasn't that…" He gave Matt another quick look, then removed the lid and looked around inside. He removed one of the photographs and studied it closely. "Well, I'll be damned." Again, he glanced at Matt. "That's why she brought her up there?"

There was no point in lying. Matt nodded.

Peterson looked to the photograph again. "It is uncanny, I'll give you that. She ain't Emily any more than I am, though."

There were people in the street, hustling in the direction of the middle school. People Matt knew. The few who glanced in their direction quickly turned away, unwilling to get involved. None stopped. Some actually picked up their pace. Even Maggie White, the woman who ran the local food bank every Christmas, only gave Matt and the other a quick look before quickening, one of those flyers clutched in her arthritic hand.

"Matt," Gabby said in a hushed breath, looking down the opposite side of the street. "It's her."

When Matt spotted her—the girl who looked like Emily Pridham—his first thought was she was some kind of mirage. She stepped from the gloom of the setting sun about a block away, the shadow of Mount Washington at her back. She looked different than she had only an hour ago. She had changed clothes. Gone were the sweatshirt and baggy pants. She now wore a yellow sundress dotted with the images of flowers. Her hair was alive, filled with body and curls that weren't there before. And as she neared, Matt realized there was a glow to her skin—she radiated—reminiscent of when she first walked into the diner what seemed like a lifetime ago, but in reality had been less than a day.

Stu Peterson followed Matt's gaze and spotted her, too, about the same time Rodney Campos returned with the first aid kit and a bottle of water. "About time," Peterson muttered.

Although he said it to Rodney, Matt got the impression he was talking about the girl.

Peterson took the items from Rodney and set them to the side, just out of Josh's reach. He opened the first aid kit, removed an old prescription bottle of Oxy, and set it next to the bottle of water.

"I really need some of those," Josh begged.

"In a minute. There's something we need to get out of the way first."

The girl who looked like Emily Pridham reached them, and although she took it all in, she didn't seem the least surprised to see Matt and the others being held at gunpoint.

Matt glared at her. "Where's Ellie? Why isn't she with you?"

She said nothing, only approached Peterson and stood before him. His face filled with impatience. "'Bout damn time. I've been chasing you down all day. We got work to do." He grabbed Josh under his shoulder and yanked him back into a sitting position, ignoring the pain-filled yelp that slipped from his lips. "This is Josh Tatum. Let me see your arms."

The girl studied Josh for a moment, then held her arms out. Unlike the sweatshirt she'd worn earlier, the sundress did nothing to conceal the writing that covered her skin. It started just below her shoulders and went nearly to both wrists. Names. Dozens of names. Peterson's eyes squinted as he read. He even reached for his shirt pocket, searching for the glasses he normally kept there. He swore softly when he realized they were gone. Then he drew in a breath and shook his head slowly when he found what he was looking for. "I fucking knew it. Right there—see it?"

Rodney leaned in but seemed hesitant to get too close to the girl. He saw the name about the same time Matt did—*Josh Tatum* was scrawled in blue ink just above her right elbow.

Rodney twisted back toward Josh, looked like he was about to kick him again, but Peterson stopped him. "That's not how we do things."

"Yeah, well maybe it should be how we do things."

Clutching his shotgun, Peterson knelt down in front of Josh

again and pushed both the first aid kit and bottled water out of reach. "You'll burn for what you did, do you understand that?"

Josh's face had gone horribly white. "I didn't do it! It was Lynn! You don't know the half of how bad she was—the depression, the medication—she'd been suicidal for months, I tried—"

Peterson slapped him across the face with the back of his hand. "Save it." He got back to his feet and pointed his shotgun at Josh's head.

"Stu, no!" Matt shouted. You can't—"

Peterson's face twisted back to Matt, burning with anger, then turned toward the girl. "Show him."

The girl who looked like Emily reached out and gripped the back of Matt's neck with icy fingers.

Matt's world flashed bright white, then quickly flooded with images—he saw Josh enter the second-floor bathroom in his house, both kids in the tub with Lynn crouched at the side, her back to him. She wasn't just sobbing, she was bawling. The children stared at her in shocked silence. They didn't even look up at their father when he came in, shoved Lynn's head beneath the surface of the water, held her there. She didn't fight back, didn't try to stop him. It wasn't until her body spasmed that she moved at all, then went still. When Josh reached for the heads of Oscar and Gracie, Matt was grateful when the vision abruptly cut off. He didn't need to see what came next for the image to haunt him for the rest of his life. When his eyes blinked open and he found himself back on the sidewalk, the girl was looking down on him, her expression unreadable. He forced the words to come out. "What are you?"

With the barrel of the shotgun still pressed to Josh's head, Peterson said, "She's Judgment."

The blast boomed, and Josh's head vanished in a spray of red and gray.

Gabby screamed.

Addie remained frozen in stunned silence.

Rodney twisted the 9mm around in his hand and gripped it by the barrel over Matt. "You should have killed me when you had the chance."

He brought the gun down on the back of Matt's neck, and all went dark.

91

LOG 10/16/2023 22:03 GMT-4
TRANSCRIPT: AUDIO/VIDEO RECORDING

Sordello: Judgment? That's what he called her?

> Analysis Note: Sordello's supervisor came over the private channel, told her to be careful with what she said next. Reminded her of the lines she was not permitted to cross. But I have to admit, I personally do not think she cared at this point. If she did care, she wouldn't have veered off script.

Maro: Yeah. That's what he called her.

Sordello: And she somehow showed you Josh killing his family?

Maro: Yeah.

Sordello: Tell me about the names on her arms.

Maro: I don't know what to make of those.

Sordello: Who were they? Did you recognize all of them?

Maro: The ones I saw, yeah. There were so many. I only caught glimpses.

Sordello: All residents of Hollows Bend, though, right?

Maro: [*Nods, then remembers to speak*] Yeah. Damn near everybody.

Analysis Note: Sordello retrieved a photograph from her briefcase. I want to take this opportunity to state for the record that Sordello's supervisor should have shut things down at this point. She had no business showing that photograph to the deputy; it could have compromised everything. Her supervisor didn't stop her, though. So, for the formal record, I opposed this. If I had been in a position to stop her, I would have. I can't be held accountable. The fault is on Beatrice Sordello and her supervisor. You want to write me up for saying that, go ahead, but you certainly can't write me up for not ending something I had zero control over.

Sordello: [*Presses photograph to the glass*] Is this what you saw?

Maro: [*Studies image. Appears confused. Looks back at Sordello*] No. Those names…are different.

Sordello: They don't match the ones you saw on that girl?

Maro: No. There are only a handful here. That girl's arms were covered. This arm is wrong, too. It's too thin. Younger. Who is this?

Sordello: Do you recognize any pattern? Or maybe the opposite. Do you see anything different about these names versus the ones you saw on the girl Stuart Peterson called "Judgment"?

Analysis Note: The subject's vitals dropped off again. He became so still staring at that photograph, he might have been a statue.

92

CODY HILL

CODY HILL WAS PLEASED.

He stood outside Hollows Bend Middle School near the entrance to the quad in total awe of himself.

Not only were people actually showing up, but they were coming in droves. Many looked relieved at the sight of so many other bodies all moving together, finally doing something with purpose. Others seemed downright giddy about the whole damn thing. Brenda Trendle's mom had set up a table at the entrance to the gym, and together with a handful of cheerleaders (two of whom had even put on their uniforms) was passing out bottles of water and sandwiches. Principal Martinez was standing at the door, shaking hands and ushering people inside with that fake understanding look smeared across her face, the same one she'd worn when Brett Murphy stole Cody's underwear from his gym locker and ran them up the flagpole in front of the school. As if she had any clue what *that* felt like. As if she had any clue what people were feeling now. Oh man, Cody wished he'd thought to put up cameras so he could record this and watch it all on a loop if he somehow managed to come out alive on the flip slide.

At just the thought of that, the weight of the heavy vest bit into his neck and threatened to pull him to the ground. It didn't weigh as much as the bomb he'd stashed under the bleachers, but it still added at least thirty pounds to his wiry frame. Exercise had never been at the top of his priority list, and he was a little pissed that no one mentioned how much heavy lifting was involved when he combed the various bomb-making blogs. Even the jihad sites he'd read with Google Translate didn't cover that. He had no idea how some of those skinny fuckers managed to tote their cargo from their cave to the market or whatever the hell they did out there.

No matter.

Less than an hour.

He glanced at this watch.

Forty-seven minutes, to be exact.

Cody slipped his hand in the pocket of his hoodie and thumbed the corner of the Talk button on the Motorola radio. It would be so easy to just set off the other bomb from here, watch it go boom, and wander home when the last of the flames fizzled out. He'd hoped to have his endgame figured out by now but was seriously still on the fence. Part of him wanted to watch it all, be here tomorrow when some authority finally swept in and tried to piece it all together. He wanted to see how long he could string those people along, put a spin on it if any of them even managed to figure out he was behind it. He seriously doubted they ever would. But another part of him wanted to walk to the center of the gym, stand right in front of all those fuckers, and watch their faces when the bomb went off. Maybe even detonate his vest about thirty seconds before the big one blew, create a panic, let them trample each other trying to get to the doors. None of them would make it; the second bomb would get them all for sure, but damn… the fear he could create in those thirty seconds. The satisfaction of knowing it would happen was nearly enough for him to end it all. He had nothing to look forward to when this was over. If he managed to walk away, managed to talk his way out of who-ever came asking questions tomorrow, if he pulled all that off… then what? Where would he go? What would he do? He'd have a fun day or two, but the party would be over quick. Then what? Foster care? An orphanage? The streets? Maybe juvie. Adulthood. Some minimum-wage job doing some silly bullshit. None of those things sounded particularly worth sticking around for.

"You going in, Cody?"

Cody swung around so fast he nearly hit the button on the Motorola, and wouldn't that just sum up his entire life? He'd go down in the books as not even getting that right.

Marcie Holden was standing there—hot as hell, never said two words to him, high school student—Marcie Holden. She offered him a bottle of water. "Ms. Trendle told me to give you this and tell you it's best to stay hydrated. People forget that when they're under stress."

Cody took the bottle but didn't drink. "Do I look stressed?"

"I'd be concerned if you didn't."

Marcie was wearing jeans and a gray sweater that did a nice job of hugging her frame. Somewhere on his phone, Cody had a photograph of her naked and tied up. He'd bought it for a hundred bucks from some loser named Malcolm-something who dropped out of school a while back to follow his dream of changing oil and cleaning grungy bathrooms at the muffler shop down on Main.

Cody's eyes must have lingered a little longer than permitted on Marcie's breasts, because she crossed her arms over her chest and her cheeks flushed. "Crazy day, huh?"

"I prefer to think of it as lively."

"I suppose. My parents are freaking out."

"My mom, too," Cody told her. He'd dragged her body to the garage and loaded her into the large freezer they kept out there.

She was lying comfortably on top of two-year-old packages of ground beef and assorted TV dinners. "She went out this morning, said she was going to talk to a few of her friends to find out what was going on, and she didn't come back. I don't know where she is."

Marcie gave him an understanding look. She was much better at it than Principal Martinez. "I'm sure she's fine. She'll probably show up here when she realizes you're not home."

"Maybe."

"Ms. Trendle said Mr. Peterson is with the sheriff or something. Sounds like they know what's going on. They're all coming together."

Cody nodded toward the black smoke above Main Street. "I love the way they handled all that. Can't wait to hear what they have to say."

Although nobody was near them, Marcie's voice dropped to a whisper. "I heard there's a fence up around town, and whoever put it there isn't letting anyone out or in."

Cody hadn't heard that, but then again, he'd been busy. Even if it were true, it didn't change much.

He didn't expect Marcie to take his hand, so when she did, he flinched, jerked away.

Marcie's cheeks flushed a darker shade of red. "I'm sorry, it's just, you looked alone out here and I thought maybe you'd want to sit with me, at least until your mom gets here."

Cody's eyes darted around. He was only in eighth grade. Marcie was older—a *high school girl*. Way out of his league. Which meant this wasn't real. Couldn't be real. He looked for Mason Ridler or Brett Murphy; maybe one of them had put her up to this. They'd get him inside and do God-knows-what. But he didn't see them. He only saw people crowding into the gym.

Maybe that was it.

The sign.

A little nudge to help him decide his *stay outside, go inside* dilemma.

"Sure, I'll sit with you." Cody took Marcie's hand and started for the gym entrance. If he'd never get to see all these people burn, at the very least he could see the expression on their faces when he walked in with Marcie Holden.

93

SHERIFF ELLIE

WITH BUCK LEADING, THE four kids in the middle, and Ellie at the rear, they followed a narrow path from the side of Buck's house through the dense forest and undergrowth around the west side of the mountain toward the Pickerton place. It was clear the path hadn't been made by deer or other animals; some of the branches had been cut back by hand and tossed aside. When they crossed a narrow stream, they held a rope that had been fastened on both sides. Ellie couldn't help but wonder how many times Buck had walked this path over the previous three and a half decades. How often he'd gone looking for his lost love and come home alone.

"Hey, do you guys see those?" This came from Mason Ridler. He was carrying his baseball bat, swinging it in round arcs as he walked. He twisted it around and pointed the tip at a tree on his right. "More of those creepy birds. I can't tell if they're following us. They all look the same to me."

"It will get worse as we get closer, just like they did with Buck and Emily," Robby Harper said without looking up. "They might try to stop us, too. We need to be ready for that."

Mason swung the bat back down. "Bring it on. I could use the practice."

Ellie couldn't figure Robby Harper out. She knew he was autistic—she'd gathered that much with her numerous visits out to his house to break up arguments between his parents—but she had no idea how that played into all this. It was like he understood what was happening on some other level. Like it all made perfect sense to him. She remembered one particular call about three years ago. His dad had gotten drunk and decided to mow the lawn at eleven at night. At five years old, Robby had no business being up that late, but he was. He'd been sitting on the deck of their front porch, putting a puzzle together, and while that was odd, it wasn't the oddest part. He was completing the puzzle with the image facedown, only the blank cardboard side visible. More than half was done. She watched him for nearly a minute as he systematically scanned the remaining pieces and snapped them into place. It all seemed so effortless, like he already knew where each piece went. He had that same look in his eyes now, as if he'd completed this particular puzzle before and was only going through the motions.

Riley's phone dinged, and she looked at the screen and frowned.

Ellie caught up to her. "What is it?"

"A text from my mom. She wants us to go back to Buck's house and wait for her there. She and Matt are on their way. They found a way to get out of town."

Ellie frowned. "Can I see?"

The girl handed her the phone. The message was on the notification screen. "Mind if I reply?"

Riley shook her head. "Go ahead. I don't have a lock code."

Ellie quickly typed back:

This is Ellie. Riley is safe, with me. What is the way out?

Message failed to deliver appeared immediately when she hit Send. The phone had no signal. Ellie was about to hand it back to Riley when another message came in, also from her mother:

Where you're heading is nothing but death. Turn around.

The phone still showed that it had no signal.

A thought slammed into Ellie's head: *This isn't Riley's mother.* This was someone, something, else.

"I'm gonna hold on to your phone for a minute," Ellie told Riley. "In case she replies."

Riley just shrugged and followed after the others, scratching at her arm.

"It ain't much farther," Buck said. "Maybe it's best you all stay here and I scout it—" He paused and looked up at the sky. "You hear that?"

Ellie didn't hear anything. "What?"

"A buzzing sound."

"Is it the birds?"

"Mechanical. Not the birds."

The sun was nearly gone and the moon was out, but very little broke the canopy of trees. They all stopped and looked up, but Robby was first to point. "There."

Mason Ridley followed Robby's finger, then shouted, "Shit! Heads up!" And jumped to the side of the path a moment before something large and black fell from the sky and crashed into the earth with a resounding thud, missing him and the others by only a few feet.

"Eww, gross," Riley muttered, taking a few stumbling steps back from the object. "Is it dead?"

Ellie stepped by her and knelt. "It's not alive at all. It's a drone."

The mangled mess of plastic and metal was about three feet in diameter, or at least it had been. All four propellers were clogged with black feathers, bits of birds, and covered in the same dust the dead bird back at Buck's cabin had produced when Robby stabbed it. Ellie found two cameras—one on the nose, another beneath meant to record straight down. Both lenses were cracked.

"It looks old," Robby said quietly.

Buck grunted. "Not old but beat to hell for sure."

Robby quickly shook his head. "No, it *is* old. Look at the plastic. It's faded and cracked, like it's been in the sun a really long time. Plastic doesn't get brittle like that unless it's been outside a long time, exposed to changes in temperature, like toys left out during the winter. This has been through a bunch of winters."

Evelyn Harper, who had been uncharacteristically silent for most of the walk, finally spoke. "It must belong to whoever put the fence up around town."

Ellie didn't disagree. It looked military. No branding of any sort. Although there was no evidence of fire, parts looked melted. She looked up at the sky but saw nothing. From the trees, at least a dozen crows silently looked back at her, their beady eyes glistening with moonshine.

Still holding Riley's phone, she felt it vibrate in her hand with another message from whoever was pretending to be the girl's mother:

Turn back

Buck was standing over her when that one came in. "Maybe you should take the kids back to my place and let me go this one alone, Ellie."

"I think it's best we all stick together." She quickly told them what she suspected about the incoming texts. "I don't know if whoever this is is trying to help us or hurt us. Until I figure out that much, they don't get to give me orders."

"Well, it ain't much farther," Buck repeated as he turned away and started back down the path.

And it wasn't.

94

MATT

"GET YOUR ASS UP, Sleeping Beauty—"

Icy water splashed down over Matt's face, and his eyes snapped open. At first, he didn't understand where he was—why he was lying on his back, the dark sky rushing by above to the sound of a diesel engine. Then he realized he was in the back of Stu Peterson's pickup, with Eli McCormick and Rodney Campos hovering over him, holding him down. They'd zip-tied his hands, and his utility belt was gone, which meant he no longer had the box cutter he kept in there or his radio, little good that had provided. His gun was gone, and Rodney had Ellie's Colt tucked in the waistband of his jeans.

Matt twisted his head around but didn't see Gabby or Addie.

"Both your girlfriends are riding shotgun with Stu." Rodney nodded over Matt's right shoulder. "He wouldn't let that one in the truck, though. She's stuck back here with us."

The girl who looked like Emily Pridham was wedged near the front of the truck bed, sitting between the window and the wheel well, her legs stretched out, hair and dress fluttering in the wind. Her face was twisted up toward the dark sky, and while no stars were visible, she seemed fixated on something Matt could not see, her silent thoughts elsewhere.

"Stu called her Judgment. What did he mean by that?"

Rodney and Eli exchanged an uncomfortable glance. "Like you don't know," Rodney muttered.

Matt had no idea what to make of her. Every thought that came into his head was crazier than the last. How was she able to show him what Josh had done? How had she forced him to relive that memory with Addie when she touched him back at the station?

Judgment.

That's what Stu had called her.

The only thing that made sense made *no* sense, but he said it anyway. "She's not human, is she?"

Eli smirked. "Christ, Rod, how hard did you hit him?"

Matt tried to sit up, but Eli held him in place. He looked up at both of them. "It's not too late for either of you to make this right. Don't let Stu drag you down with him. Cut off the zip ties and help me disarm him when we stop."

"I love how you still think you're somehow in charge," Rodney said. "You're damn near hog-tied in the back of a pickup and still barking out orders. I'll let you in on a little secret—ain't nobody coming. Nobody ever was. We're alone in this fishbowl, just like it's always been. You best make peace with that, or you're gonna have a tough time with what comes next."

"What exactly comes next, Rodney?"

Again, Rodney and Eli exchanged a look mixed with both confusion and bewilderment.

"He really doesn't remember. I don't get how that's even possible," Eli said. "Isn't the whole point of this to remember?"

Rodney just shook his head. "Not our place to figure that out. Leave it to Stu"—he nodded at the girl—"Stu and that one."

The truck slowed and made a left turn.

Matt caught a glimpse of a street sign—they were nearing the middle school.

Rodney leaned down. "When it comes time to kill you, I'm hoping Stu lets me do it. I want to save you for last, though. Maybe Gabby first, then Addie, then you. That way you get to watch. I want to see the suffering in your eyes before putting a bullet in your skull. I've killed before, you know. Of course, we've never had the chance to talk about it, it's not really the kind of thing you bring up with the local law, but I've killed plenty. Back in the day, I used to comb Route 112 and pick up hitchhikers. Not often—I did what I could to keep it under control—but every once in a while I'd get the itch and set out on the road. Men, women, teens…it didn't matter much to me. There was just something about picking them up, watching that relief when someone finally stopped, then watching it slowly melt away when they realized they might have gotten into the car with the wrong person. There's not a whole lot you can do when you're moving at eighty miles per hour on an empty road at night. When I showed the knife or the gun or whatever I brought…man, the adrenaline… it just takes over, for both. Sometimes I'd slow, make them think they could jump. Other times I'd let them get the gun—it was unloaded for those, but they didn't know—then I'd gut them with a knife when they thought they had me."

Rodney let out a sigh, and Matt realized he was reliving the memory of whatever he'd done, relishing it. The thought sickened him.

Rodney smiled. "They're all buried out there along 112. So many, I got no need to do it so much anymore. When I get the bug, I just drive the highway and pick out the spots where I planted them. That usually keeps the urge in check. Usually.

Some days, I miss it, though." His mind meandered on that for a little bit. Then he nodded at the other man. "Eli here used to bugger children, didn't you, Eli? Why don't you tell Matt about your time driving the school bus back in Oklahoma. How you'd walk some of the young ones into their houses when their parents weren't home. You know, to make sure they got home safe. Help 'em with an after-school snack."

Eli's face went pale, and he looked away. "I don't want to talk about that. You shouldn't be saying nothing, either."

Rodney shrugged. "Matt here will be dead inside an hour. What's the harm?" He looked down at Matt again. "It's times like these that bring neighbors together, don't you think? I can't wait to hear your secrets." He looked over at the girl. "Eli, check her arms for Matt's name. See if he's written there."

Eli shook his head. "I ain't going anywhere near that bitch until I got to."

The truck slowed and made a right at the Hollows Bend Middle School sign, the one that said HOME OF THE BEARCATS. Lying in the truck bed, Matt couldn't see much, but he heard the voices. As the truck slowed and came to a stop near the building, he got the impression everyone from town had come out.

95

SHERIFF ELLIE

AS THEIR SMALL GROUP rounded a large outcropping of granite, the shake roof of the Pickerton house came into view. Faded and stained with age, parts were missing; other sections were covered in moss as the mountain slowly took back what had belonged to it long before people scarred the terrain. The Pickertons had still lived there when Ellie was a child; she'd been ten when their daughter had passed. She heard the rest from her father years later. The daughter had died after a long-lost fight with tuberculosis. On the day of her passing, the girl's mother had committed suicide, and Jeb Pickerton had come home to find them both. It's said he jumped from the cliff out behind their house, the same one her father believed had taken Emily Pridham, but like her body, his remains had never been found. In the years that followed, no one had come forward to claim the property, and as with all abandoned properties, it had gone to ruin. She knew the local teenagers sometimes partied there, same as her generation, and for the most part, she'd let that go. As her father had also told her, it's better to know where the kids are doing what kids will do than not.

Buck held up his arm and stopped them on the trail as he tried to get a better look.

"What is it?" Ellie whispered.

"It ain't right. Not at all."

Robby eased up beside them and pointed. "Is that the tree?"

Buck only stared for a long moment, then said, "That's it, all right."

"Whoa," Mason muttered, resting his weight on the bat like a thick walking stick.

The massive oak had fallen. Its large roots had ripped from the ground and were dripping with dirt, scraping at the night sky from a large hole in the earth where the tree once stood. The trunk of the tree and several branches had sliced through the Pickerton house as if it were made of warm rancid butter; the entire back corner was buried in gnarled branches. But it was the crows that caused death's finger to slip down Ellie's spine, all the birds. Thousands of black bodies writhed and squirmed along every inch of the exposed tree. They covered the back side of the house, too, as if the tree was somehow secreting them. It wasn't just the sight of the crows that made Ellie's skin crawl; it was also the silence. Unlike the story Buck had told them, these birds didn't caw. There was only the sound of their movement, this restless scratching of tiny feet on bark. Thousands of dark eyes facing them.

If Buck and the others had been under any illusion of stealth, it was gone. The birds knew they were there. But it was more than that; they all felt it.

"Why are they all looking at us that way?" Riley said, her voice barely a whisper.

Evelyn pushed closer. "Like what?"

But Ellie knew what she meant. The birds seemed to be moving together, moving as one, rather than the individual thousands that they were. Their heads turned in unison. They faced them together.

"It's not the birds watching us," Robby stated. "It's something watching us through the birds."

Ellie didn't want to believe that—it was crazy—but she did. The boy couldn't be more right.

Craning her neck to get a better view, Riley scratched her arm for the umpteenth time. Ellie had had enough of that. "Did you touch poison ivy or something? What's with the scratching?"

The girl shied away from her, but not before Ellie was able to take her by the arm and pull up her sleeve. She stared at the writing there, all the names, dumbfounded. "Did you do that to yourself?"

Riley shook her head.

Together, the kids quickly told her how the names began to appear earlier in the day. How they continued to appear as the day went on.

Mason Ridler

Roy Buxton

Hannah Hernandez

Sally Davies

Emily Pridham

As Ellie read them, Riley started to scratch again.

"They itch so bad. It won't stop!"

Buck had gone quiet.

Ellie swallowed. "Do you know what it means?"

Buck only shook his head. "I'm not so sure I want to know."

Ellie turned to ask Robby, because he seemed to have it all figured out, but he was no longer there. He had crossed the clearing, stepped around the birds, and was climbing the steps to the porch of the Pickerton house.

96

MATT

PETERSON DIDN'T BOTHER WITH the parking lot. He followed the blacktop right to the gym doors and parked in the yellow zone where the visiting school buses usually off-loaded. The truck jerked to a stop, and the engine stuttered out.

Eli jumped over the side, went to the back, and opened the tailgate. "Here's your stop, Loverboy. Time to go."

With one hand on the Colt, Rodney yanked Matt to a sitting position by his collar and forced him to the edge of the tailgate, then gave him another push.

Matt managed to keep his footing and was about to make a play for the Colt when Peterson came around the side, holding Gabby firmly by the arm. "Jesus, Matt, wipe that look off your face. You got no place to go. Stop making things harder on yourself. This is where you're supposed to be."

The crowd around them had gone quiet, their voices nothing but muffled whispers. Several people pointed at Matt; others were focused on the girl as she walked to the back of the truck and jumped down, her dress billowing out around her. She took in all the people for a moment, studying their faces in turn, then circled around the truck to the open doors of the gym and disappeared inside, walking with the confidence of someone who'd been there before and knew where they needed to go.

Against her protests, Eli pulled Addie from the cab of the truck. She tried to twist away from him, but he was far stronger. With one hand lodged on the small of her back, the other gripping her shoulder, he steered her into the building.

Peterson placed two fingers in his mouth and blew out a sharp whistle. "Everyone inside! Let's get this thing started!"

"Move," Rodney muttered, shoving Matt forward.

97

CODY HILL

CODY AND MARCIE WERE standing just inside the double gym doors when Mr. Peterson and his friends showed up, dragging Deputy Maro by his short-and-curlies like a stray dog on a leash. Hands all zip-tied. Head hung low. Wow, what a sight. Cody hadn't much liked Mr. Peterson until that moment, but the man clearly knew how to take charge of his shit. The local po-po had dropped the ball, and he wasn't about to let them wiggle out of their reckoning. Cody expected them to drag the sheriff in, too, but no such luck. Instead, they had the waitress from the diner and that woman who always dressed like she was ten years younger than she probably was, Addie something.

Marcie was still holding Cody's hand, and she gave him a gentle tug toward the bleachers. "We should go get a seat."

When Cody had entered the gym with Marcie, he'd wanted nothing more than to prance across the floor with Marcie at his side, make sure everyone got a good eyeful, but then he saw something he wanted even more—there was a chain hanging from the metal door's emergency push bar. Not just a chain, but a padlock, too, and holy hell was that fortunate, because Cody hadn't considered how he'd keep everyone inside when shit hit the fan, and now he had a plan.

As if to back up the ray of sunshine the universe was shining up Cody's ass, Mr. Peterson stopped at the door, eyed first the chain and lock, then turned to Cody. "Fasten that up when the last of them comes in, will you, kid? We don't want anyone wandering off."

Sir, yes, sir!

"Yeah, whatever," Cody muttered, trying to hold back the enthusiasm.

Peterson reached out and honest-to-God ruffled Cody's hair before heading toward the center of the gymnasium floor, where a microphone had been set up.

"You're sweating," Marcie said. "Maybe you should take your coat off."

Before Cody realized what she was doing, she reached over and tugged down the zipper on his jacket. He slapped her hand away and got the zipper back up, but not before she saw *something*. He couldn't be sure exactly what that something was, but it wasn't good. He could tell that much by the look on her face. Her hand in his seemed to go cold, and she tried to pull away. He gripped her tighter. "I think it's best you and I stay close. You try to run or tell someone, and I might panic, do something rash. You really don't want me to panic, do you?"

Marcie swallowed. "That's not real, right? It's some kind of joke?"

"It's no more a joke than what Malcolm Mitchell did to you."

Her face went white. "You know about that?"

"He's probably here right now. I bet you really want to get even with him. I bet you've thought about it every day. Well, today is your chance. You can get even with him and all those people who turned their back on you when you needed them most. They're all here. Every one of them."

"What are you going to do?"

"What God intended me to do when he put me on this planet. I'm here for a reason, and so are you." He squeezed her hand. "*This* isn't an accident. You're meant to help me."

They stood there in silence as the last of the people came in from outside and filled the bleachers. Marcie's grip on his hand loosened but didn't let go, and Cody knew he had her. Just like the chain, the lock, and everything else; it was all meant to be. He wasn't the least bit surprised when Marcie closed the metal door and clinked the lock in place all on her own. She'd died that day with Malcolm. This was her shot at being reborn.

98

SHERIFF ELLIE

"ROBBY! GET BACK HERE!" Ellie forced out between clenched teeth. If the boy heard her, he ignored her. He followed the steps to the porch and disappeared behind the partially open door into the house. "Well, damn it all," Ellie muttered, rising from the bushes to go after him. "You all stay here."

"The hell we are," Evelyn replied, ready to chase after her brother, but the moment she stepped into the clearing, the birds filled the space between her and the house.

"Sheriff..."

This came from Mason Ridler. He was facing the opposite direction, back the way they'd come. The narrow footpath was buried under the bodies of a thousand more crows, moving slowly toward them as one. They uttered not a single sound, there was only the slight ruffle of feathers and the crinkle of dry leaves beneath them. They were in the trees at their backs, too, and more were coming— black bodies raining down from the sky, filling every branch, somehow finding space among already impossible numbers.

Mason swung his bat, but the birds didn't flinch, only kept moving forward.

Buck pointed his shotgun at the sky and pulled the trigger.

Intensified by the night, the loud boom echoed off the mountain, rattled through the trees, but did nothing to discourage the birds from closing ranks around them.

Mason swung again, and this time he connected, catching one of the incoming birds. The blow sent it sailing off to the right, and it vanished somewhere in the underbrush. He hit another, and another, but they kept coming.

Evelyn screamed as two crows swooped down, clawed at her arm, and shot back into the sky, leaving two bloody streaks on the girl's skin.

Ellie pulled out her gun and yelped as another landed in her hair.

Buck swatted the bird away, but more were coming. Too many more. They were swarming around their feet, pecking at their ankles, attacking all but...

They weren't attacking Riley.

None of the birds were near Riley.

The ground at her feet was empty, the air; they didn't touch her.

Riley turned and started toward the house. The carpet of birds shuffled away from her, cleared a path, like they were allowing her to pass, like they *wanted* her to go inside. Her, but no one else.

"Everyone in the house!" Ellie shouted. "Now! Follow Riley!"

The birds left the trees, the branches, the bushes. They came at them all at once, like a thick black cloud of feathers frantically beating the air.

Ellie and the others broke into a run, arms flailing, charging through the birds in an attempt to catch up with Riley before the crows could close ranks behind her. Ellie felt her shoes crunching down on soft bodies, thin bones breaking underfoot, but she dared not look. Something told her if she paused, even for a second, she'd go down. And if they got her on the ground, she wouldn't get back up.

Riley reached the porch, quickly entered the house. Mason behind her.

Evelyn tripped on the first porch step, and Buck scooped her up with his free arm as if she weighed nothing. He carried her up and through the door; by the time Ellie reached them, there was no sky, there was no forest, there was no mountain. There was only the birds, a blanket of seething black choking them from all sides.

Inside the house, Ellie grabbed the edge of the old wooden door, felt it scrape against the floor, and managed to slam it shut.

The silence was deafening, broken a moment later as someone let out a sharp gasp.

99

MATT

"EVERYONE, LISTEN UP!" PETERSON tapped the microphone with the tip of his finger, and three loud thuds came from the speakers mounted on the ceiling above center court followed by a hint of sharp feedback. "Get yourselves situated. Take a seat!"

Although someone had set out several folding chairs, Rodney and Eli had forced Matt to kneel on the gym floor, a few feet to Peterson's right. Gabby and Addie were on the ground beside him. Pregnant or not, they'd made no concessions. The girl who looked like Emily Pridham stood beside Stu Peterson, her silent eyes gazing across the faces in the bleachers.

Peterson glanced up at the clock on the wall—it read ten till nine—and cleared his throat. "I know we're a few minutes early, but I think everyone who needs to be here is here, so there's not much point in waiting." He seemed to consider that, then looked over at Matt. "Well, everyone except this man's boss, our lovely sheriff. Best I can tell, Ellie's off hiding somewhere rather than facing all of us. After today, I say good riddance."

There was a mumbling from the crowd. Someone actually clapped a few times, then it abruptly went quiet.

Rodney Campos had Ellie's Colt out, the barrel pointed at Matt's head. Matt realized just how broken these people were, because nobody seemed to recognize the wrong in that. They had their own deputy on his knees with a gun pointed at his head in a general assembly in the middle school gymnasium, and nobody saw the wrong in that; they only sat there and watched.

"I understand how concerned you all are, rightfully so. This man here and his boss have let our town come apart, literally watched it crumble and burn—well, we're taking things back before their actions result in the death of all of us."

"Ellie's not here because she's busy trying to help all of you!" Matt shouted out. "We all need to take a breath. I know tensions are high, but we'll get through this. We'll all—"

Rodney cracked him on the back of the neck with the Colt. Not hard enough to knock him out, but enough to stun him into silence.

Peterson eyed this as if it were the most natural thing in the world, then said, "You'll get your chance to speak, Matt. Providing these people still want to hear from you when I'm through. Until then, I'd appreciate a little restraint. A little respect for the process."

"The process? What are you talking about?"

Confusion filled Peterson's face. He stood there for a moment, then stepped away from the microphone and knelt next to Matt. "You honestly don't know, do you? You don't remember?"

"Remember? Remember what?"

"Your station."

"My…"

Matt had no idea what he was talking about. Peterson had completely lost it. Snapped. Nothing else made sense.

Peterson pushed the brim of his ball cap up and leaned closer, as if the proximity allowed him to see deeper into Matt. "You've never forgotten before." He glanced over at the faces in the bleachers. "The rest of 'em, sure, but never you. That's new."

"I don't understand."

Peterson pursed his lips. "Well, you will soon enough."

"Stu!" Someone shouted from the crowd. "There's a fence up around the entire town, I walked it with my boy earlier today. Some kind of military presence. Religious folk, too. Who is it?"

Peterson rose and went back to the microphone. Shielding his eyes from the lights, he squinted up into the bleachers. "That you, Ben? I've had my boys walk that, too. We're still trying to figure out what to make of it, but best we can tell whoever it is isn't letting anyone in or out. They cut our communications. Effectively isolated us."

Someone else shouted, "What? Like we're caged in? What happens when we run out of food? Main Street's gone. We all gonna survive off the Gas 'n' Go out on 112? Screw that. We need to get out of here!"

This brought on another round of murmurs from the crowd. Peterson settled them with a wave of his hand. "Hush, all of you. This ain't nothing but a test. It's been that from the start." He swept his arm back and pointed at the girl who looked a lot like Emily Pridham. "Her arrival this morning was not a surprise. Not some kind of accident. It was expected. It was foretold. I admit, I was in the dark earlier, same as all you, but she showed me the truth. She brought me clarity. With one touch, all of it made perfect sense. I know why she's here. I know why those people have locked us down in our own town. I know what they all want from us. Yeah, that sounds crazy, I know that, too, and I don't expect any of you to believe me. I could tell you until I'm blue in the face, and you wouldn't believe me. It's easier to show you. Let her touch you. Let her *show you*. And we'll all understand. And once we understand, once we know our place, only then can we move forward."

This brought on more murmurs from the crowd.

Gabby leaned closer and whispered, "Matt, look."

He followed her gaze. Several of Peterson's men were moving around the outer edge of the gym, positioning near the doors. All of there were armed. A few of the doors were already chained shut.

Rodney Campos dug the barrel of the Colt into the back of Matt's neck. "You say a fucking word and I kill you, then her. Now's not the time to be a hero."

Peterson pulled the microphone from the stand and stepped to the side of the podium. "I'd like everyone to line up single file. Give her a chance to touch you, *a chance to show you*, and once we all understand our place, our station, we'll work out a plan. We'll take back the Bend. I won't force anyone. If you don't want to do this, just stay in your seat. But trust me on this, *you want to*. Does that sound fair enough?"

There were several more muffled conversations from the crowd, but when the first few stood and started making their way down the bleachers and across the gymnasium floor, others followed.

"Good. Good. Help them, Eli. Get a nice, straight line going. That's the way."

Peterson watched them for a moment, then went over to the girl. "We're in this together; always have been." He said into the mic, "While you all are getting organized, we need to do a little housekeeping. Because sometimes the easiest way to settle a beast is to feed it. Don't you all agree?"

He directed the words at nobody in particular, and the oddness of them brought on an uneasy quiet from the crowd. Peterson stepped closer to the girl and told her, "Hold out your arms."

Palms up, fingers splayed, she did as he asked.

Peterson leaned in, studied the writing, all the names, then seemed to settle on one. He turned back to the bleachers. "Keith Gayton, are you here?"

There was the rustle of shoes on the wood, then Keith stood. He was in the second row on the far right. His face twisted in a mix of fear and anxiety, partially lost in the shadows from a dead bulb above.

"Why don't you come down here, Keith. Join us."

Keith's eyes locked with Peterson's, then he offered a slight nod. The people around him parted, made a path. He slowly came down, stepped over the first row, and made his way over to Peterson and the girl.

"It's best you kneel, Keith. Kneel before her."

Keith Gayton clearly didn't want to, but he lowered himself to his knees anyway.

Peterson looked first at Keith, rolled his gaze slowly over the growing line and those still in the bleachers, then went back to the girl. In a low voice, he said, "Judgment."

Her hands, still outstretched, dropped on Keith's head.

The images smacked into Matt like a truck—Keith in an alley, his eyes red and wild, high on something. He had a knife in one hand and was holding a man by his hair with the other, screaming in his face. The other man held up a small plastic baggie filled with white crystals—meth. Keith snatched the baggie, took one look around the alley, and plunged the knife into the side of the man's neck. He gave it a twist and yanked it back out. He dropped the man and ran.

Matt snapped back.

Back to the gym.

He knew by the utter silence around him they'd all seen it.

Keith remained on the ground, his head low, the girl hovering over him.

"Judgment," Stu Peterson said again, then pressed the barrel of his shotgun into the small of Keith's back and fired.

Matt tried to jump up at him, but Rodney cracked him in the head again with the Colt.

Before the echo of the fatal blast died, Peterson was back at the girl's side, studying her arm. He looked back out over the crowd and shouted, "Cody Hill!"

100

LOG 10/16/2023 22:12 GMT-4
TRANSCRIPT: AUDIO/VIDEO RECORDING

Sordello: Stuart Peterson asked you if you remember. Do you, Deputy Maro? Do you remember?

Analysis Note: If the subject heard her, he gave no indication. He was still staring at that photograph. When he finally looked up, there was no life in his face. The color was gone. If I were forced to touch his skin (and thank God he was isolated in that chamber and I wasn't asked to do that) I know he'd be far too cold.

Maro: The arm, that's Riley, isn't it? Gabby's daughter.

Sordello: What makes you say that?

Maro: [*Agitated*] Just answer the damn question. I've answered all yours.

Sordello: Yes. That is Riley Sanchez.

Sordello: We don't have much time, Deputy Maro. *You* don't
have much time. I'm going to tell you what I can, and I need
you to listen to me very carefully.

101

SHERIFF ELLIE

ELLIE COULD SEE NOTHING.

With the door closed and the windows boarded up, not a sliver of moonlight found its way into the Pickerton house. The interior was freezing, like stepping into a walk-in refrigerator, like opening the door on a harsh winter night and stumbling out into the cold.

A light came to life and flooded the corner of the room.

Buck holding a flashlight.

What she saw made no sense.

The walls, the ceiling, the floor—all were covered in ice.

"It's like a goddamn ice cave in here," Buck muttered, swinging the beam around the room. "Where's it coming from?"

Mason and Evelyn were standing just inside the door. The boy pointed at a hallway leading toward the back of the house. "That way, I think."

"Where's your brother and Riley?"

Evelyn pointed down the same hallway.

Buck didn't wait for Ellie to ask. He stepped around what was left of an old grandfather clock on the floor and worked his way toward the back of the house, his heavy hiking boots leaving a trail on the frosty floor, his breath wisping through the air in white plumes.

They found both Riley and Robby standing at the door of a bedroom at the back of the old house.

The fallen tree they'd spotted outside had taken out a good chunk of the already failing structure, cut right through the ceiling and wall, and landed on what was left of an old bed. Several of the thick branches had punched right through the floor, and others filled the small space as if the tree had grown there; bastardized branches crawled around the air in a frantic search for daylight and nourishment. Not finding any, they'd withered and begun to die. It looked like it might have been that way for a hundred years, but Ellie knew that hadn't been the case. The house might have been abandoned, but between kids, tourists, and the random local, someone would have seen this, right? Told her? She sent Matt up here every few weeks to take a look around; surely he would have noticed.

No.

This was new.

This was fresh.

This had happened today.

Ellie couldn't prove it, but she was fairly certain that ugly old tree had fallen at the exact same moment that girl had appeared in the diner. It fell as those birds dropped from the sky. All of it together. All of it connected.

The branches were covered in crows, unmoving, and as Ellie stepped closer she realized they were slicked with frost and frozen in place. Yet she couldn't help but believe their eyes still watched them, followed them as they entered the room.

"Don't touch anything," Ellie whispered. "Not a damn thing."

"Maybe we should go back outside."

But even as Buck said that, Ellie knew it wasn't possible. They could all hear the birds out there, the air thick with them and more coming. They were thudding against the door and windows, the walls—some by flight, others pecking at the wood, all trying to get in. She glanced at the hole in the ceiling, the dark sky beyond. How long before the birds realized where they were and came down through there? Where would they go then?

Robby stepped closer to the tree, got within an inch of one of the frozen birds. "It's breathing."

"What's that on the bed?" Evelyn asked, pointing at the mattress.

Mason chuffed. "The high schoolers bang on there. It's probably—"

"It's black mold," Buck interrupted. "Don't touch it. It'll make you really sick."

"I wasn't planning on touching it either way. It's freakin' gross."

"It's on the ceiling, too," Evelyn pointed out.

Ellie looked up, realized she was right. There was a large black stain on the plaster directly over the large black stain in the mattress. And there was—

That couldn't be right.

Ellie stepped closer.

Buck had caught it, too, and positioned the flashlight at a slight angle to make it easier to see.

Black dust was rising from the bed, through the air, to the ceiling. Connecting both spots. Not dust, though, and while Ellie wanted to believe it was mold as Buck had said, she wasn't so sure about that, either. This was something else.

"Help me move the mattress."

Buck hesitated for a second, then handed his flashlight to Riley and set down his shotgun. He grabbed the far corner and nodded at one of the tree branches, the one that had gone through the mattress when the tree fell. "That one punched down into the floor. We'll need to twist the mattress. Go clockwise on three."

When the mattress didn't move, Mason grabbed a corner, Evelyn and Robby, too, as Riley kept the light trained. They heaved together.

The tree let out a rough groan, like it didn't want to let go, then relented.

The mattress turned like an old stone marking a tomb.

Buck had been right—that single thick branch had gone right through the mattress, down through the floor, and left a jagged tear in the hardwood.

Ellie knew the house didn't have a basement. There wasn't even a crawlspace. It had been built on a giant slab of granite ledge, and while it was physically impossible for a tree branch to punch a hole through something as substantial as solid stone, somehow this branch had. Beneath the splintered wood, there was a gaping maw, a crack in the rock so deep it only swallowed the beam of the flashlight when Evelyn drew closer.

"That smells disgusting."

The edges were thick with black mold. The spot on the floor was nearly twice the size of the ones on the mattress and ceiling. Frigid air rose through the hole, misty white tinted with flecks of black.

"Not so close," Ellie told the girl. "Probably shouldn't be breathing—"

Air burst up. A belch. An unearthly geyser from deep within the bowels below and Evelyn fell back. She instinctively grabbed the gnarled branch to keep from falling, and Ellie knew that was a mistake even as it was happening—she grabbed at the girl, tried to stop her. Mason did, too, but neither was fast enough. The instant Evelyn's fingers found the bark, they went white as icy frost glazed her skin, enveloped her—

My God, it's eating her!

Ellie's brain went to a childlike place at the sight of it, because her adult brain didn't understand. Didn't want to understand, as if not understanding could keep it from happening. But it did happen—the frost raced up Evelyn's arm, over her shoulder to her neck and head. The girl froze mid-scream, and while that should have silenced the shriek echoing through the room, it did not, and Ellie realized it was because she and Mason were both screaming, too, as the ice not only engulfed Evelyn but took them where they touched her.

102

CODY HILL

STU PETERSON JUST BLEW a hole in Keith Gayton. Did it like it was nothing. Even when bits of Keith sprayed Peterson's face, he didn't bother to wipe it away, didn't acknowledge it at all, he just smiled and kept talking. For that brief second, Stu Peterson was Cody Hill's hero. But then Peterson called out Cody's name.

Cody and Marcie were sitting in the fifth row. Half the crowd had gotten up to get in line, the other half jumped up with the shot, but the two of them had stayed down and were, for the moment, concealed. Marcie was making this godawful whimpering sound, and it was becoming increasingly clear she wasn't up for what would come next, not unless she grew a pair, but sometimes you had to improvise. You had to work under the gun. When Peterson called Cody's name a second time, Cody pulled the Motorola radio from his pocket and pressed it in Marcie's cold hands. "I need you to do me a favor. Think you can?"

Marcie whimpered again, and that would have to do.

"If I yell out your name, I need you to switch that radio to channel two and press the Talk button. That's it. You can do that, right? Easy-peasy?"

Cody had his vest.

The other bomb was set to go off at 9:05, but that was six minutes away, and six minutes was a very long time when it came to things like this. Six minutes was a lifetime. He couldn't risk something going wrong. He knew he wasn't leaving this gym—he was all good with that. As long as nobody else left, either, he was perfectly good with that.

"Marcie? Can you do that?" When she still didn't answer, he added, "I saw Malcolm Mitchell." Cody lied. "He's practically sitting on top of the bomb. You do this, and you're finally taking back what's yours. None of us are leaving, but you'll have peace. I need to know you can do it."

Marcie finally nodded, and her slender fingers wrapped around the radio.

"That's a good girl."

People were screaming. Shouting. Trying the doors, finding them locked. Finding Stu's men guarding the doors. Others were still in line, as if that were perfectly fine. Perfectly normal. Shock was a crazy thing. But this was all good. It was what Cody wanted.

Panic.

Panic was like chugging a Red Bull.

Someone grabbed Cody by the shoulders and lifted him to his feet. "He's up here, Stu! I got him!"

Cody twisted but couldn't see who it was. He became far less concerned with that when the man reached into Cody's pocket and yanked out the vest's detonator with enough force to tear the wires right out of Cody's damn near perfect welds, rendering it useless. He shoved the detonator in his own pocket, then shouted back down to Peterson, "Got the other thing, too!"

His face still speckled in blood, Peterson nodded up at them. "Bring 'em down here."

The man did.

He was twice Cody's size. No way he could break free. The

man shuffled him around like he was some kind of rag doll, got him to the gym floor, and forced him to his knees in the bloody puddle left behind by Keith Gayton. This insanely beautiful girl was looking down at him, and so was Stu Peterson.

Peterson bobbed his head toward the girl. "She showed me the vest. That's how we knew. We found the other bomb, too. I didn't want to fool with disarming it—that seemed a little risky—so we just reset the clock. It's set to go off at three in the morning now. Six hours should be plenty of time to figure it out. If not, we'll just bump it again. That was a ballsy move, kid. I don't need her to touch you; your judgment has come and gone."

Peterson raised the shotgun and pointed it at Cody's head.

"Wait!" Cody shouted. "I can help you!"

"Don't need your help."

"I know a way in and out of town. Someplace those people weren't able to block."

This was another lie, but Cody didn't want to go out like this. Not a gunshot. Not alone. He wanted everyone. And Marcie still had the remote. He didn't need the vest and the timer didn't matter, not as long as she had the remote.

"He's a kid, Stu, let him go."

The side of Deputy Matt's head was covered in blood; he'd been hit several times. His eye was swelling shut, but he still managed to look up at Mr. Peterson. "Christ, Stu, this isn't you. Stop."

"You still don't remember?" Peterson told Matt, sounding surprised. "I don't get it. Maybe you need something to jog your memory." He stepped over to Gabby and Addie, grabbed them both, and pushed them toward the girl. Gabby let out a yelp as he kneed her in the back to get her to face forward. "Judgment," he told the girl who looked like Emily Pridham. "You pick which."

Her face expressionless, the girl studied both women for a moment. Then her hand came down on Matt's head. Her fingers squeezed with inhuman strength.

103

BUCK

BUCK WENT TO GRAB Ellie, but the girl and that Robby kid stopped him, batted his hand away with the force of a 250-pound linebacker protecting his quarterback. Buck had no idea where that strength came from, but he was glad for it, because the boy might have saved his life.

It took less than ten seconds for the icy frost to crawl over Ellie, Evelyn, and Mason, completely cover their bodies. It was like they were flash-frozen, like something out of a movie, but this was no movie; it sure as shit happened right there in front of him. All three were screaming, then they were not. The room got so quiet Buck nearly choked on it.

"They're not dead," Robby said with an adult-like understanding. "Their pupils are moving. I think they're still breathing, and their hearts are pumping, but really slow."

He was right up on his sister, way too close, trying to get a better look at her neck. Like he could see her pulse if he looked hard enough. Maybe he could. The kid spooked him a little, but nowhere near as bad as what happened next.

Ellie and the two kids vanished.

There was no flash of light. No accompanying noise. The three of them were there, frozen to that godawful-looking fallen tree, and then they weren't.

No, that wasn't exactly right. They didn't just vanish; they fell. If the adrenaline hadn't been coursing through Buck's veins, he might have missed it, but adrenaline had a way of slowing things down just enough so you see more than you might want to, and Buck saw the three of them drop straight down into the hole in the ground.

And with that, Buck remembered Emily.

Remembered how the ground had swallowed her as she stood beside that tree all those years earlier. He didn't need to go outside and look for landmarks to know it was the same tree; he was certain of that the moment they came up on the house.

When Emily disappeared, there had been no hole in the ground; there was nothing.

As if to answer this, another burst of frigid air bellowed out from the dark hole and filled the room.

"They're down there," Robby said not as a question, but as a statement. As if he already knew. And Buck knew the boy was right.

Mason had dropped his baseball bat, and Buck retrieved it. He touched the rim of the hole with the tip of the bat, half expecting it to flash-freeze, but it did not.

"Touch the tree," Robby told him. "But be ready to pull away…"

Buck understood what would happen just like the boy did, but he tried it anyway, because on some level he wanted to be sure. The moment the bat touched the tree, icy frost raced down the length of it. Buck managed to let go as it found his fingertips. He shoved his index finger in his mouth and kept it there for a second. When he took it out, the tip was black.

"Frostbite," Robby told him.

Fucking frostbite, Buck thought.

"We need to go down there."

This came from Riley, who was still standing off to the side, following all of this with the beam of the flashlight.

Buck was already shaking his head. "*I* need to go down there. Both of you are gonna stay put right here."

"She's right," Robby said. "We all need to go. Don't ask me how I know that. I just do, and you gotta believe me." He looked over at Riley, at her arms. "Her in particular...it wants her more than anything."

It?

Buck didn't want to think of whatever this was as some kind of *it*. On some level, he was still trying to sell himself on the idea that none of this was even happening; he desperately wanted it all to just be some drunken stupor gone horribly wrong.

"Those maps you showed us," Robby went on. "This is the center. It's all coming from right here. More accurately, from right down there, below us. It's radiating out. Like when you throw a rock in the middle of a lake. It's starting down there and spreading. I think...I think it's been contained, until today, until this tree fell. The tree made a hole, this hole, and now it's getting out. This black stuff isn't mold. It's something else. Something ugly. Bad."

All of that sounded like a very solid reason not to let the kids go anywhere near that hole, force them to stay put, but Buck knew that was a loser's game; the second he went down there, they'd be right behind him. It was what the boy said next that convinced him.

"It took your Emily the same way it just took my sister, Mason, and the sheriff. You know it did. And if that's true, she's still down there somewhere, and I'd be willing to bet she's still alive. Just like them."

Riley moved to the edge of the hole and played the beam of the flashlight over the edge. It made as little sense as everything else did. While the fallen tree may have started it, somehow punched a hole not only through the floor but the granite below, it had only been a wedge. The branch was twice as thick as Buck's thigh, but the hole was bigger, had grown to nearly three feet across. He couldn't be sure, but he was fairly certain it had grown just in the few minutes they had been here, was still growing. The ragged edge of sharp rock going down the insides made it look like a mouth filled with rows of teeth. The flashlight tried to illuminate the length of it but failed miserably; he could only see down about seven or eight feet before the beam petered out.

Riley scratched at her arm again, and when she lifted her sleeve, Ellie and Evelyn's names had been added to the others.

Buck swallowed and repositioned his shotgun across his back in its sling, then took the flashlight from her.

If they were going to do this, they needed to do it now, because things were growing worse. He could feel it.

He clipped the flashlight to his belt so it was hanging down, then lowered himself into the hole. "There's plenty to hang on to; just be mindful of the tree branch. Don't touch it. Take your time. If you change your mind, you get scared, there's no shame in coming right back up."

As he said this, he studied both their faces and realized the fear rising in his gut was enough for all of them. He started down before some semblance of good sense got him to change his mind.

104

MATT

WHEN THE GIRL WHO looked a lot like Emily Pridham touched Matt's head, his vision flashed. He was back in his apartment, his body warm and drunk on the half-finished bottle of Jim Beam perched precariously on the kitchen counter next to Addie's half-naked body. He didn't remember her jeans coming off, but they were puddled there at his feet as she sat on the edge of the countertop, her bare legs wrapped around his waist, gripping him like a vise.

He was watching this scene as well as living it, no longer two separate Matts but one, both about to make the biggest mistake of his life.

"Fuck me right here, Matt. Right on the kitchen counter. Then tomorrow, or the day after, when you're cooking breakfast for Gabby, I want you to look at this spot and remember what we did. I want you to think about this…" Her hands found their way inside Matt's jeans; warm fingers wrapped around him and gently squeezed. "The next time you bed Gabby, when she's lying under you unmoving like some dead fish waiting for you to finish,

I want you to remember all the things I used to do to you back in high school, all the things the other girls wouldn't, and think about one simple truth: I've had ten years to learn more." She leaned in close and flicked her tongue across the side of Matt's neck, her words hot at his ear. "Some might say I've perfected my craft. I know a dozen ways to make you come…a dozen ways to remind you she'll never be more than a placeholder. Her only purpose is to keep you warm for me. I'm okay being your girl on the side, your dirty little secret. You can fuck us both—just promise me one thing: when you're inside her, I want you to think of me. I want my name in your head."

Addie tugged his jeans and underwear down over his hips, and although Matt knew everything about this moment was wrong, he let her. He stepped out of his clothing and kicked it all aside as she brought the bottle of Jim Beam to his lips and held it as he took a long swig. She drank, too, and when she did, Matt's hands moved with a mind of their own. His fingers brushed down the buttons of her blouse and found their way inside the folds of the thin fabric to her flesh beneath. She was still drinking when he tore the blouse open, sending those buttons skittering across the hardwood floor. He didn't remember removing her bra—one moment it was there, then it wasn't, and his palms were cupping her breasts, tentatively brushing her nipples, and Addie moaned softly. "Make it hurt, Matt. You know I love it when you make it hurt."

She tugged the back of his hair, then ran her fingers down his spine, her sharp nails digging into the skin of his back with enough force to draw blood. He didn't care. He wanted more. Matt pulled her so close, so tight, it was like both their bodies became one, folded over and into each other until there was only a single being, and he pulled her tighter still. She guided him inside her even as he thrust, raising her hips to meet his, gripping him with her thighs. The gasp that escaped her lips was filled with a hunger, an animal-like sound that only fueled the heat between them, and they both began to rock, pressing into each other with a ferocity that grew with each moment until Matt felt himself spill out inside her, unable to hold back anymore.

When it was over, they remained there, holding each other in a stillness that was only matched by the intense movement only moments earlier. The guilt crashed into Matt like a thick wave, and although he knew he should let go, get dressed, get her out of his apartment, his life, another part of him was unwilling to do all that. He wanted to love Gabby, he did, he told himself that over and over again, but that didn't make it true, and while he equally wanted to hate Addie, wanted to push her away, he couldn't. Every inch of his being wanted her to stay no matter how wrong it might be.

Addie's face was nestled in the crook of his neck when she whispered, "I think you just put a baby in me, Mr. Maro."

It had all happened so fast, so intensely, the idea of protection hadn't entered Matt's mind. A slight ting of panic rolled through him, but quickly vanished, melted away. If he got her pregnant, so be it. Maybe that was what he needed. *Maybe that was what he wanted.*

Yes. That was—

The door to his apartment slammed behind him.

He hadn't heard it open, and he certainly hadn't heard Gabby come in but there she was, standing in the gloom, her face masked in shadows. She was holding her overnight bag, clutching it far too tight. And although she didn't speak, her breathing told him all he needed to know.

There was no surprise.

No shock.

There was only anger.

This seething that only grew more intense as she stood there, her gaze boring into them both.

Addie's limbs were still twisted around him when Gabby lunged. He was still caught up in Addie, and while he tried to pull away, he simply wasn't fast enough. Gabby crossed the small room and pulled a knife from the butcher block on the counter as she came toward them, did it with a movement that was fast, purposeful, and fueled by pure rage. The blade glistened in the thin light as she raised it high and whistled as it came down in a harsh arc.

Matt blinked.

Matt blinked and found himself back in the middle school gym, crouching on the floor with both Gabby and Addie kneeling beside him as the girl who looked like Emily Pridham released his head.

It only took one look around the room to realize the vision the girl had shared hadn't been with Matt alone but with everyone in the room, same as Keith Gayton moments earlier, same as Josh Tatum back out on the street—they'd all seen it. The look Stu Peterson gave the three of them said as much. What he told them next was like a nail: "Judgment claims you all. There are no innocents here."

105

BUCK

IF SOMEONE WERE TO ask him, Buck couldn't tell them exactly how long the climb down took. Time didn't seem to work right in the hole, and it only got worse as they went deeper. He noticed something else, and this was far more disturbing—he had no trouble climbing down. Handholds seemed to find him, not the other way around, same with his feet. As if the hole wanted to get him to the bottom. The two kids climbed silently behind him, and he didn't have to ask to know they were experiencing the same thing. Robby probably had a theory on that, too, but Buck wasn't about to ask him. He didn't want to hear about whatever was at the bottom and what plans it might have. All he wanted to do was find Emily.

Rescue Ellie, Mason, and Evelyn.

But yes, find his Emily.

Robby said she was somehow still alive, and out of all the craziness that had come from that boy's mouth, that was the one thing he wanted to believe. *Had to believe.* Because, on some level, he knew it, too. He always had.

His breath hung all around him, this icy mist with no place to go. The air grew colder with each inch.

When Buck's foot found solid ground, it surprised him, and he looked down for the first time since they started descending. The flashlight beam pooled beneath him, a perfect circle in what could only be ice. But unlike ice found on the surface, this ice had a rough texture to it and when Buck lowered himself from the opening of the hole to it, he didn't slide.

"Careful now," he told Riley anyway, grabbing her by the waist and helping her down. He went to help Robby, but the boy gave him a look that quickly reminded him he didn't like to be touched. He backed up and let him drop from the hole himself. He was wearing his red backpack; how he managed to get that all the way down, Buck had no idea, but at the sight of it, he remembered his shotgun slung over his back. He retrieved that and handed the flashlight back to Riley, who quickly rolled the beam over their surroundings.

They were in a narrow cave.

The icy air smelled of sulfur, heady with minerals.

The beam only caught her for a second, but that was enough for the heart in Buck's chest to level a hard thump.

Emily stood at the far end of the cave, maybe thirty feet away. She wore the same sundress she'd been wearing the day she disappeared. She turned quickly and vanished down another passage, but not before a near-silent whisper left her lips—

This way.

106

MATT

THOSE WHO WEREN'T TRYING to flee the gym were staring at Matt, Gabby, and Addie.

Still holding the Colt on them, Rodney Campos had this shit-eating grin on his face. "I gotta admit, if you're going to step in it and end things the hard way, there are worse places to be than between these two."

Gabby spit up at him. "Fuck you."

She went for his face but came up short; it smacked across the knee of his jeans. That only drew a bigger smile from him. "Spicy till the end, like any good Mexican."

When Gabby lunged, Eli McCormick held her back. He shoved her back down to her knees and kept her there until she stopped squirming. Long enough for Stu Peterson to point his shotgun at her. "I gotta envy your spunk, but judgment is judgment. You made your bed. Don't matter how ruffled the sheets are, you gotta lie in it." He pulled back on the slide and chambered a fresh shell. "Time to pay the piper."

Matt turned to him. "You killed four children. Four *innocent* children. You said you were sorry for that. Was that bullshit, or did you mean it?"

At first, Peterson didn't move, then he edged the shotgun slightly to the side so he could get a better look at Matt. "So you did watch it? The video?"

"Birmingham, Alabama," Matt told him. "September 15, 1963. Four children dead in the Sixteenth Street Baptist Church bombing. KKK suspected. That *was* you. Don't ask me how, but it was you."

Peterson swallowed; guilt washed across his face. "Herman told us the bombs wouldn't go off until that night, when the church was empty. He swore it. Nobody was supposed to get hurt. We only wanted to scare 'em a little, that was all."

"Sunday school was in session. You killed four children between the ages of eleven and fourteen."

"Herman said—"

"Stu, you knew exactly when those bombs would go off. You can lie to yourself all you want, but you knew then just like you know it now. You did it anyway."

"I didn't set 'em off. I just placed 'em. I—"

"You knew."

Matt jerked his head toward the girl who looked a lot like Emily Pridham. "Go ahead, touch *him*. If you think you got some right to pass judgment on all of us, give him what he's got coming, too. Why should he get a pass?"

She processed all of this without any hesitation, as if her brain were working on a level far beyond the rest of them. She stepped toward Stu Peterson, but he jerked away.

"That's not the deal! That ain't how this works!"

"Maybe he's right, Stu," Rodney said. "Maybe it's time you get yours. Don't you worry, I'll take care of things from here."

He'd shifted the barrel of the Colt; although it wasn't pointing directly at Peterson, he'd edged it closer. He smirked at the girl who looked like Emily Pridham. "What do you say? Maybe you and I finish this? I think you'll find I'm a little easier to work with. Maybe we can come to some kind of understanding, and you give me a pass this round?"

Stu Peterson's face grew bright red. "We've all got our station, Rodney. There ain't no changing. There's only the same. Over and over, the same."

Rodney shrugged. "Maybe we make up some new rules. Feel it out as we go."

Eli McCormick rolled his eyes. "Jesus, Rodney, just once can you play by the rules? Why you always got to muck things up?"

Rodney rolled the Colt toward him, but not before McCormick managed to fire, putting two in Rodney's chest.

Confusion washed over Rodney's face as he looked down at growing red spots in his shirt, then his legs buckled and he collapsed.

Dead.

Peterson glared at McCormick. "That's not—"

Matt jumped up.

He gripped the barrel of Peterson's shotgun and shoved it to the side as Eli McCormick twisted his weapon toward him, thumbing back the hammer.

107

BUCK

EMILY WAS ALONE, THEN she wasn't.

Rodney Campos was standing next to her.

That didn't make a lick of sense, none of this did, and when Buck blinked, he half expected Rodney to vanish as quickly as he appeared, but he didn't.

Twenty paces ahead of them, Emily and Rodney rounded a corner and Buck found himself moving faster, trying to catch up, Riley and the boy on his heels.

When they rounded that same corner, the three of them found themselves in an enormous underground cavern. The frigid air was so cold it seemed thick enough to touch. Every inch of Buck's body ached with it—joints, muscles, tendons—all slowing, becoming less responsive, and he realized this was hypothermia setting in, ice stealing the life from his limbs. The walls of the cavern were covered in that same black mold they had found in the Pickerton place, but here it was alive, crawling over the stone and ice, moving with purpose, excited. Stalactites and stalagmites, every inch of the cavern walls was alive with it, and Buck had an unsettling thought—it looked like they were wandering the belly of some beast.

"We can't stay here."

The words left his mouth between chattering teeth in a voice he barely recognized, and when he risked a look back, he caught a glimpse of Robby with his arms around himself, trying to keep warm, and failing.

Riley seemed oblivious to the cold. Her eyes were wide, filled with bewilderment, and the oddest thing was happening with her skin—the names were glowing. All of them clearly visible in the dim light.

He needed to get them out of here. If they died, it would be on him.

When Buck turned back around, Emily and Rodney had stopped moving. They were standing at the edge of what could only be described as an underground lake. The waters were frozen, a mix of that black over ice, but they inched up the rocky shore, as if attempting to crawl out, and Buck realized that might just be what that black stuff was doing—it was crawling out of the lake, up the walls, and out the cavern. It was escaping this place through the hole punched out by that tree. This insane and horrible world was somehow leaking out into their own.

The three of them reached the edge of the lake, and Riley let out a sharp gasp, pointing below the surface. It took Buck a moment to understand what she had found because it simply couldn't be true, but as he stared, it remained—Ellie was several feet below the ice, one hand grasping up, her mouth open, caught in a silent scream. Buck thought she was frozen there, until she blinked.

Behind him, Robby softly said, "The lowest, blackest, and farthest from Heaven. Well do I know the way."

Buck had no idea what the boy meant by that. He barely heard it, because he realized Ellie wasn't alone in the icy waters of that lake. He saw Evelyn Harper next to her. Josh Tatum. His wife, Lynn, both their children. The old man from the library. One of the women, too. What was her name? Gilmore, something. Edna? No, Arwa. That was it. Keith Gayton was there. Eisa Heaton. Her husband, Norman. People from town. Some he'd seen just in the past hours; others he hadn't seen for years. They were all in that frozen lake, and somehow they were all still alive.

He turned back to Emily, his heart beating like a sledgehammer in his chest. "What the hell is this place?"

She eyed him with a sorrow so deep it pained him to look at her. "This is the end."

"The end of what?"

"The end of all things."

She gently stroked Rodney Campos's arm and pointed out toward the center of the frozen lake. He followed her gaze, then nodded solemnly and stepped out on the ice. Began walking toward the middle.

For the first time, Buck noticed the deep red stains on Rodney's shirt. Smaller in the front, much larger in the back.

Exit wounds.

He'd been shot.

He's—

The realization struck him, and he knew he had to be dreaming. Dreaming. Having a nightmare. Caught on the back end of some bottle-induced hallucination. Anything but this.

But when he looked back at Emily, he realized it was none of those things.

This was happening.

This was real.

Out on the frozen water, Rodney stopped. He was about thirty feet from them when he turned and faced back in their direction. When he started to sink, he didn't fight it. His body dropped slowly, like a man caught in quicksand. He stopped falling when it crossed his upper chest. His face twisted, and the most horrible of screams escaped his lips. It might have made Buck go mad if it didn't abruptly cut off when it did. Icy frost and black inched over him, froze him there, and while Buck wanted to believe the man no longer felt any of this, he knew the opposite was true—he felt all of it, and he would continue to feel it for all of eternity.

Emily had edged closer. "You shouldn't be here. Not like this. This isn't how you arrive. This isn't your station."

"My station?"

"Your place. Your purpose. Your end. Not yet. You need to leave." She looked at Robby. "You, too. You both must leave, now."

She stepped closer to Riley and examined the girl's arms. As her fingers rolled over the names, they glowed brighter. "You represent the innocents. Those caught unintended, but here nonetheless. It is for those I grieve most. You will stay as I have stayed. A shepherd to those innocent. That is your station, Riley Sanchez."

Buck shook his head and pulled Riley away from her. "The hell she will! None of us are staying." He jerked a thumb down at Ellie and Evelyn in the water. "We're taking them back, and we're all going."

"I didn't say it was a choice. It is what's meant to be. We can all only do what is meant to be."

She looked back down at the frozen water, and a tear trickled from her eye as she focused on another body beneath the water.

Inches from her feet, just below the surface, was Emily Pridham. *His* Emily Pridham. Exactly as she was the moment she disappeared all those years ago.

Her mouth twitched.

Frozen in the unholy lake, she managed a single word.

Buck.

108

MATT

GABBY WENT FOR THE Colt. Matt had never seen her move so fast. She rolled to her right, grabbed the gun, and came up with it as McCormick squeezed off two rounds in Matt's direction. The first struck the gym floor about a foot from his left hand, the second went wild, up toward the bleachers. Several people screamed, and Matt saw someone drop from above, roll down the wooden bleachers, and come to a stop at the base inches from the girl who looked a lot like Emily Pridham—Henry Wilburt—the town's pharmacist. She reached down and grazed Wilburt's cheeks with her fingertips, almost like an afterthought—

Judgment—

A quick image of Henry Wilburt's fat, naked body hovering over a prostitute jerked into Matt's mind. The girl's eyes bulged out, her face blue. His hands were still around her throat.

Then Matt was back in the gym.

He was still gripping the barrel of Peterson's shotgun when he pulled the trigger.

Matt saw the man's finger twitch, shoved the barrel as hard as he could to the side as he fired, and while the shot missed, the metal scorched Matt's palm and he had no choice but to let go.

Peterson wasted no time.

He stumbled back a step, put some distance between them, and brought the weapon back around, centered on Matt's chest. "Judgment time, Deputy! Give my best to Ellie!"

Addie came from behind him and jumped on Peterson's back. He twisted slightly, just enough for the shot to go wide—rather than center mass, it grazed Matt's shoulder.

Addie yanked Peterson's head back by his hair, got her fingers around his face, and pressed her long nails into his eyes. The man let out an inhuman screech and tried to buck her off, but she only pressed harder.

Matt grabbed the Colt from Gabby's hand and shot Peterson in the eye. The man dropped, Addie under him.

People were running; some fell trying to get down from the bleachers. Others were at the doors, yanking on the chains and locks as bodies pressed against them from behind, all trying to get out, nobody able to.

Through all of this, Matt had forgotten about Cody Hill, and when he looked over, the boy was busily attempting to reattach the wires of a remote detonator to the explosive vest strapped to his chest.

"Drop it!" Matt shouted, pointing the Colt. "Drop it now!"

He wouldn't. That was Matt's first thought. This kid was ready to die. Ready to take them all with him. The sight of the gun only made Cody's fingers move faster; he'd gotten one wire reattached and was trying to work the screw meant to hold the other with his fingernail.

"Goddamnit, Cody! Now!"

The boy froze.

The remote detonator dangled from his hand for a moment,

then he let it go. It broke into several pieces when it hit the floor. "Okay, Deputy. Okay."

"Take off the vest. Slowly."

"Okay."

He began to work the clasps, his nervous eyes darting around all the faces watching him. His gaze settled on a girl in the fifth row of the bleachers. Matt recognized her—Marcie Holden.

"Marcie!" Cody shouted up at her. He jerked his thumb toward the back corner of the gym. "It's Malcolm Mitchell! He's right there! Do it! Do it now! Before he gets out!"

Matt's mind tried to connect the dots but it wasn't until he saw the Motorola radio in Marcie's hand that he understood. "There's another bomb! Everyone get down!"

Marcie wouldn't do it.

He wanted to believe that.

And when her hand fell to her side, he was certain of it.

Then she twisted some dial on the radio and pressed the button, squeezing her eyes shut as she did.

Matt saw both Addie and Gabby standing there.

He dove, knocked them both to the ground, his body over them.

Matt felt the heat of the blast, but he never heard it. The gym erupted in a ball of flames, the pressure so great, parts of the roof sailed a hundred feet into the air before the entire structure came down around them.

109

BUCK

BUCK STARED IN CONFUSION as Eli McCormick appeared at the edge of the lake, about a foot from Emily.

Then Henry Wilburt, looking stunned and confused.

Stu Peterson came next. He just blinked into existence, like the others. He was gripping a shotgun, and there was nothing but a bloody hole where his left eye should have been. He quickly looked around with his good eye, seemed to realize where he was, and cursed.

The hole in Peterson's head vanished—

Healed

Disappeared

—Buck had no clue. One second it was there, then it wasn't.

A boy appeared after that.

A goddamn boy wearing a bomb on his chest.

Then the cavern filled with voices, so many it was like the entire town was there.

Because they are, you dumb shit, his mind muttered. *Every last one of them*.

Buck remembered his own shotgun, still strapped to his back. He grabbed it, brought it around, and fired at the ice at the edge of the lake.

The boom of the blast echoed all around them, and rather than fade, it grew louder. Buck realized what he'd done when the first stalactite dropped from the roof of the cave and crashed through the ice, breaking it. Another fell after that. Another. The deep rumble of the blast echoed and grew, shaking the cave apart.

"Help me!" he shouted, reaching down, grabbing a chunk of ice and throwing it aside.

Buck reached down into the water, managed to grab the collar of Ellie's shirt, and pulled her up. She let out a loud gasp as she broke the surface, she grabbed at the rocky shore and crawled out, choking out water as she went. He managed to get Evelyn out, too. Fighting the cold and ice, he heaved her out with enough force to toss her to the ground at his side. Mason came out behind her, clawing his way up. Buck was about to reach back in for Emily, *his* Emily, when the other Emily placed a hand on his shoulder.

"I am to remain."

"No way, that's bullshit. You're coming with me!"

"I was always to remain," she said softly before turning to Riley Sanchez. "Both me and her."

Although the cave was coming down around them, the girl looked perfectly calm, at peace. The names written on her arms growing bright enough to light the air around her.

"That is her station," Emily said. "I am to secure those deserving of their place in the lake; she is to console the innocents. Her station and mine, as it always was. As it always will be."

Buck wasn't hearing any of this. Although he couldn't feel his arms anymore, he plunged them back down into the icy water

427

and tried to grab his Emily, but she was too deep, too far down to reach.

Behind him, Ellie managed to say, "Buck. Where are we? What's happening?"

"Get everyone out!" he yelled back at her. He looked around, found Robby. "Show them the way! Get them all out!"

Robby nodded, helped his sister to her feet. He pointed back the way they'd come. "That way! Everyone! That way!"

Ellie understood. She started helping people go in that direction, back toward the hole that would take them out.

Buck turned back to the water, his eyes meeting Emily's. She looked back at him, the sorrow weighing heavily on her face. "I can't leave you again," he told her. "I can't spend another second apart from you. Not now, not ever."

"Your station," the other Emily said softly.

"My station."

"So it shall be."

Buck stood. He kicked off his shoes and stepped into the water.

It was no longer cold.

It was perfect.

From beneath the surface, his Emily smiled up at him, both hands reaching as he stepped forward and sank to her.

Buck never saw Cody Hill bypass the remote trigger on his explosive vest, never saw the boy press the battery directly to the leads attached to his makeshift blasting cap. There was only an incredibly bright light.

110

LOG 10/16/2023 22:16 GMT-4
TRANSCRIPT: AUDIO/VIDEO RECORDING

Sordello: You're dead, Deputy.

Analysis Note: Part of me wondered if the subject's mind went to the blast when she said that. Surely he had no memory of what came after. Or, at the very least, there was a blank spot. Maybe he remembered waking here and nothing else? I don't know. Selfishly, I wish I did. I wanted her to ask him. But she couldn't. There simply wasn't time. Additional soldiers poured into the room, surrounding the Plexiglas booth from all sides, weapons ready. Nobody fired, though. At least five or six voices were shouting in my earpiece, and considering I could only hear the half of it, I can only image what Sordello was listening to. That's probably why she pulled hers out and tossed it on the floor. The subject's vitals were still unresponsive; I did not expect them to return. I was as surprised as all the others when he registered anything at all. He was staring at his hands. Then he turned nervously to the soldiers.

Maro: Are they here to kill me? Why?

Analysis Note: Sordello knew the soldiers would kill *her* if she pressed forward, but she did anyway.

Sordello: You need to read the folders. Start with yours; it's on top. Hurry.

Analysis Note: The subject reluctantly reached forward and removed them all, set them on his lap, and opened his own. The lines on his face grew as he read the text, studied the photographs.

Sordello: You. Are. Dead.

Maro: This can't be…

Sordello: That night, when Gabby Sanchez found you with Addie, she stabbed you six times. Twice in your neck, one of which pierced your jugular. You bled out in under a minute. She then killed Addie Gallagher. The authorities believe she went into shock at that point, because at least thirty minutes went by before she took her own life. You're holding the police reports, newspaper clippings, and interviews with your neighbors and her friends and coworkers. That happened in 1947. Not here, but in Albuquerque.

Maro: I don't understand.

Analysis Note: The soldiers nearest Sordello's door parted, and a man I didn't recognize knelt, pulled some sort of kit from his pocket, and went to work on the lock. Sordello's grip tightened on the gun. She nodded toward all the files.

Sordello: You've been dead for more than seventy-five years, Matt. Not only you, but Stuart Peterson. He committed suicide in 1964. Josh Tatum died of lethal injection in 1992 for killing his wife and children. Arwa Gilmore buried multiple husbands before authorities caught up with her in Atlanta more than thirty years ago. She swallowed cyanide rather than answer for her crimes. Cody Hill blew himself up while attempting to build a bomb in his parents' basement in 2003…the list goes on and on. Nearly every resident of Hollows Bend committed heinous crimes while alive, and we found a record of their deaths with only a few exceptions—

Analysis Note: Sordello located the photograph of Riley Sanchez's arm and held it against the glass.

Sordello: Those listed here appear to be victims.

Maro: Innocents…

Sordello: Innocents. Yes. And all the names on the other girl, the one you called Emily Pridham, are guilty of crimes against others.

Analysis Note: A visible shift appeared in the subject's face. He remembered something.

Maro: Not crimes. Sins. They're guilty of sins.

Analysis Note: Something else clicked, and he looked up at Sordello.

Maro: How did you get a photograph of Riley's arm? Where is she? Did she survive?

Sordello: Riley Sanchez appeared to us in much the same way you did. Three hours ago. We don't know how or why, but she was visible and present for fifty-three minutes before we lost her.

Maro: Lost her?

Analysis Note: Sordello produced a cell phone. She must have snuck it in with the gun. She loaded up a video and held it against the glass. I don't know how she obtained a copy of the footage, but the memory of what happened was still fresh in my mind.

Sordello: She vanished. First her vitals ceased recording, then visibly, she disappeared. She began to fade in and out over the course of five minutes or so, then disappeared altogether.

Analysis Note: I had overheard several people debating this in the hallway before Maro came to us. They felt she "fell out of phase with our visible spectrum." That was how they described it. I don't know any other way to describe it. It began with a slight haze in the air around her in the minutes before she disappeared entirely, and I could see that same haze around Maro. Sordello noticed it, too, because her speech sped up. The man working on the lock also picked up his pace.

Sordello: She's dead. You're dead. All of you are dead. You're in hell, Deputy. More accurately, we believe you are in purgatory and have been for a very long time. The town you know as Hollows Bend doesn't exist in the same reality as the rest of the world. You, and all the other residents, have been dying over and over again. Some horrific repeating cycle.

Maro: That's not possible. I've lived in the Bend for as long as I remember. Most of us have. None of this can be true.

Sordello: I've got satellite images from as recent as three days ago—there was nothing here. We think something tore a hole. Allowed your world to slip into ours. We don't know what. You're trapped here, being punished for the sins you committed in life.

Maro: No. That can't be...

Sordello: Look at your hands. Do you see it?

Analysis Note: The subject was beginning to fade in and out, much like the girl did. I don't know how it looked to him, but he clearly saw something.

Sordello: Your neck. Touch your neck.

Analysis Note: He did, and his fingers came away slick with blood from the wound that had killed him all those years ago. There were stains on his shirt now. They hadn't been there only a few minutes ago.

Sordello: In reality, you and Gabby Sanchez were married and had been for six months when you committed adultery. That was your crime, your sin. The reason you're trapped. Addie coveted a married man. Gabby took her own life. All mortal sins that sentenced you to hell, where you have been ever since. Somehow, your lives have continued there, but it's all part of your punishment. Your personal purgatory. Torture, for lack of a better term.

Analysis Note: The man working the lock made some sort of progress; there was an audible *click*. Sordello fired twice at the glass, striking the lock from the inside. The man fell back, unhurt but frightened. It only bought her a few seconds before he went back to work.

Sordello: [*Speaking faster*] Beneath what you believe to be Hollows Bend, there is a frozen lake. Best we've been able to determine, your souls are there. Trapped indefinitely. Dante described it as the ninth circle of hell. At 6:37 yesterday morning, something punched a hole through to that place. We've since learned it was a large tree. A tree possibly older than time itself. That hole created a tear between the hell in which you exist and our world. *The living world*. We had the area sealed off, thought we had it contained, when a secondary explosion tore it wide open.

Maro: Cody Hill's bomb vest?

Sordello: When that bomb detonated there, the rip between these two realities grew worse. We don't know what will happen if it spills over. We're trying to contain it, and we are failing.

Maro: This is bullshit. People visit Hollows Bend. They come and go all the time. Every weekend, we probably have—

Analysis Note: Shaking her head, Sordello loaded another video on her phone and held it against the glass.

Sordello: We've sent drones through. A handful have managed to transmit video back to us before going down.

Analysis Note: I'd seen the video. I knew what was on it. Much like the girl, cars and people vanished as they drove away from town. Just as crazy were the ones that appeared heading toward Hollows Bend—they blinked into existence on their way into town, filled with unsuspecting strangers. Facial recognition software had managed to identify only a few, but it was clear who they were—they were also guilty of terrible crimes and had died in our world. They were now trapped in their own hell. Every last one of them. Like this man—Virgil Matthew Maro—like all the others.

Sordello: We've tried texting. Some messages get through, others don't. We think Stuart Peterson planted the bugs in the sheriff's house. We don't know why or when, but we've been able to listen to them. What takes place there…changes. It's evolving every time you experience it.

Maro: I don't understand.

Sordello: This isn't the first time you and I have spoken today. It's the third. I know you don't remember, but somehow the events you've experienced in Hollows Bend, what you feel are memories, are repeating. It's like the hell you've been sentenced to is caught in some kind of perpetual loop that changes with each cycle. When that tree fell, something else broke, too, and all of it is getting worse. Last time, you stopped Cody Hill before he could detonate the bombs. This time, you didn't. When you fade from here, we believe you'll go back. You'll be forced to experience it all over again, and whatever happens will be worse than the previous cycle. I need you to do something for me—right now—there's a listening device in the drawer—take it—it's like the others, the ones in the sheriff's house—plant it in Ellie's office. We can use it to monitor your—

Analysis Note: The files slipped from the subject's hands, not because he dropped them, but because his hold on our reality had faded to the point where he could no longer hold them. I watched them pass directly through his fingertips before spilling on the floor. He tried to speak, but the wound in his neck had become more pronounced. Blood gurgled from his lips.

I realized the man picking Sordello's lock had suc-
ceeded a moment before she did, and I won't lie—not
even here—if I had the ability to warn her, I would have.
Unfortunately, she couldn't hear or see me, and by the
time she realized the man had her door open, soldiers
were already streaming in.

I don't believe she meant to kill the first soldier. When
she raised her gun and fired, it was more instinctual; she
wasn't even looking. The first bullet caught the man in
the temple. The second shot, her second kill, was deliberate. She needed to buy time, and although this only got
her a few extra seconds, it was enough for her to say—

Sordello: You need to remember, Matt! You've got to try! You're
the only one who can stop it! Only you! And if you don't, this
world, *the real world*—

Analysis Note: No less than three automatic weapons fired into Sordello's chamber. Her body jerked and
slammed against the back of her chair. Although she
was probably dead instantly, they kept firing until their
magazines were empty. When I glanced over at the other
chamber, the one housing our subject, I realized he was
gone. We had lost Virgil Matthew Maro, again.

END OF REPORT

111

MATT

THE BREEZE COMING DOWN off Mount Washington had a slight edge to it. Just enough to cause Deputy Matt Maro to shiver and remind him that fall and yet another harsh New Hampshire winter were not as far off as they were yesterday. Thanks to a brief cold spell last week, the leaves were putting on a show—all golds, reds, and yellows—so much so half the drivers edging out of town toward Route 112 had their heads in the trees rather than on the road. It was a wonder none had kissed fenders.

Give it time, his mind muttered. *The day has just begun.*

Matt crossed the street and pushed through the door of the Stairway Diner. A bell above the door let out a chime sharp enough to be heard above all the voices, and he stood there a moment taking in the smells of breakfast, long enough to catch Gabby's eye.

"You don't grab your stool, someone else will!" she shouted to him from across the room. "We're on a twenty-minute wait as it is for tables!"

Matt grinned back at her. Her skin was flushed, her uniform

was covered in various stains, and she never looked more radiant. "We're still on for barbecue later, right?"

She gave him a wink before turning back to the large booth holding all eight of the Lockwood family.

Matt made his way through the diner, saying his hellos, and paused when he reached the counter. There was a woman sitting on his favorite stool, the one in the far corner against the wall. Her face was buried in a book, the remnants of an omelet on the plate next to her. She looked vaguely familiar, but Matt couldn't place her. Lucky for him, the stool between her and Roy "Buck" Buxton was still open. When Matt got closer, he saw the sign Gabby had taped in front of it:

RESERVED FOR DEPUTY SHITHEAD

Buck gave him a sideways glance as he balled up the sign and tossed it into the sink behind the counter. "Not my place to meddle in your business, Deputy, but when your woman takes to calling you shithead publicly, it might be time to pack a bag or buy flowers, as circumstances may dictate."

"She's just messing around."

"Uh-huh. Aren't they all."

The fact that Buck then looked across the diner at Addie Gallagher, sitting in a booth by herself, wasn't lost on Matt, but they had something more pressing to talk about.

"You can't keep drinking yourself into a stupor, Buck. You've clocked far too many hours sleeping it off at the station."

Buck pierced a bite of sausage with his fork and stuffed it in his mouth. Said nothing.

"Complaints aside," Matt added, "you're not getting any younger. Your body can't take much more of that."

"My body is doing just fine."

The woman sitting on Matt's favorite stool took out a credit card and set it on the counter. He stole a glance at the name:

Beatrice Sordello

The name didn't ring any bells, but there was something about her he couldn't quite place. He finally just asked. "Excuse me, did you go to UNH? I feel like we've met."

The woman held up one finger to silence him for a moment as her other finger slowly drifted down the text of the page she'd been reading. When she got to the bottom, she looked over at him, studied his face for a moment, then shook her head. "I went to Princeton."

Buck let out a quiet huff and said softly, "Nice try, Romeo. You might want to dial it back; girlfriend number two is on her way over."

Matt looked up.

Addie had risen from her table and started toward them.

Shit.

Gabby had finished with the Lockwoods and was on her way over, too.

Shit. Shit.

Buck stood up. "I'm gonna hit the head."

The woman on his other side had gone back to her book. Many of the pages were folded over, and she'd marked up the one she was on now with several different-colored highlighters. The spine was riddled with so many creases he could barely make out the title:

The Divine Comedy

Matt vaguely remembered the title from somewhere but couldn't recall what it was about.

Behind the counter, Gabby set a stack of plates in the sink's soapy water, ignored the crumpled note floating on top, and scooped up the woman's credit card. "Do you want to see the check before I run this?"

Still reading, the woman gave her a dismissive wave. "No need."

Matt was certain Addie would settle into Buck's seat and set about pissing off Gabby, but instead she gave the woman next to him a nervous glance, pressed something into Matt's palm, and kept walking. She vanished down the hallway and left through the kitchen door.

"What the hell?" Gabby was staring at the note in his palm, her face growing red. "Passing notes? Is this grade school?"

This was not how Matt wanted to start the day.

He unfolded the note, frowned, and showed it to her:

We've got less than twelve hours to set everything right.

Two of the bestselling storytellers of all time have created an unforgettable thriller.

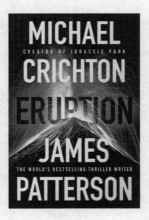

A once-in-a-century volcanic eruption is about to destroy the Big Island of Hawaii.

But a decades-old military secret could turn the volcano into something even more terrifying . . .

Now it's up to a handful of brave individuals to save the island – and the entire world.

Read on for an exclusive extract of the blockbuster thriller of the year . . .

ONE

Rachel Sherrill, thirty years old in a few days, master's degree from Stanford in conservation biology, rising star in her world, still thought of herself as the smartest kid in the class. *Just about any class.*

But today at the Hilo Botanical Gardens, she was trying to be the cool substitute teacher for a restless, wide-eyed bunch of fifth-graders visiting from the mainland.

"Let's face it, Rachel," the general manager of the botanical gardens, Theo Nakamura, had said to her early that morning. "Taking these undersized tourists around is a way for you to put your immaturity to good use."

"Are you saying I act like a ten-year-old?"

"On a good day," Theo said.

Theo was the fearless academic who had hired her when the

park opened last year. As young as Rachel was—and looked—she was very good at what she did, which was serve as the park's chief plant biologist. It was a plum job, and she loved it.

And to be honest, one of her favorite parts of the job was conducting tours for kids.

That morning's walk in the park was with some very lucky and well-heeled schoolkids who had traveled all the way here from Convent and Stuart Hall in San Francisco. Rachel was trying to entertain and educate the kids about the natural world surrounding them.

But as much as she wanted to lecture about what they were observing—orchid gardens; soaring bamboos; coconut palms; jackfruit trees; edible plants like breadfruit, kukui, and red pineapple; dueling hundred-foot-high waterfalls; hibiscus literally everywhere—Rachel had to compete for the children's attention with the two closest of the five volcanoes on the Big Island: Mauna Loa, the largest active volcano in the world, and Mauna Kea, which hadn't erupted in more than four thousand years.

These city kids clearly considered the twin peaks the highlight of their tour, the best sight they'd seen in the picture-postcard wonderland called Hawai'i. What kid wouldn't give anything to watch Mauna Loa erupt and spew out a stream of lava heated to over a thousand degrees?

Rachel was explaining that Hawai'i's volcanic soil was one of the reasons why there was so much natural beauty on the island, a PowerPoint example of the good that had come out of past eruptions, helping Hawai'i grow beans that produced coffee as delicious as any in the world.

"But the volcanoes aren't going to explode today, are they?" a little girl asked, her large brown eyes pinned to the twin peaks.

"If they even *think* about it," Rachel said, "we're going to build a dome over them like we do with those new football stadiums. We'll see how they like *that* next time they try to blow off a little steam."

No response. Crickets. Pacific field crickets, to be exact. Rachel smiled. Sometimes she couldn't help herself.

"What kind of coffee comes from here?" another straight A–student type asked.

"Starbucks," Rachel said.

This time they laughed. *One in a row,* Rachel thought. *Don't forget to tip your waiters.*

But not all the kids were laughing.

"Why is this tree turning black, Ms. Sherrill?" an inquisitive boy with wire-rimmed glasses sliding down his nose called out.

Christopher had wandered away from the group and was standing in front of a small grove of banyan trees about thirty yards across the lawn.

In the next instant, they all heard the jolting crash of what sounded like distant thunder. Rachel wondered, the way newcomers to Hawai'i always wondered, *Is a big storm coming or is this the start of an eruption?*

As most of the children stared up at the sky, Rachel hurried over to the studious, bespectacled boy who was looking at the banyan trees with a concerned expression on his face.

"Now, Christopher," Rachel said when she got to him, "you know I promised to answer every last one of your questions—"

The rest of what she'd been about to say collapsed in her throat. She saw what Christopher was seeing—she just couldn't believe her eyes.

It wasn't just that the three banyan trees closest to her had turned black. Rachel could actually see inky, pimpled blackness spreading like an oil spill, some terrible stain, except that the darkness was climbing *up* the trees. It was like some sort of upside-down lava flow from one of the volcanoes, but the lava was defying gravity, not to mention everything Rachel Sherrill knew about plant and tree diseases.

Maybe she wasn't the smartest kid in the class after all.

TWO

"What the shit—" Rachel began, then stopped herself, realizing that a fragile ten-year-old was standing right next to her.

She bent low to the ground and saw suspicious dark spots leading up to the tree, like the tracks of some mythical round-footed animal. Rachel knelt down and felt the spots. The grass wasn't moist. Actually, the blades felt like the bristles on a wire brush.

None of the blackness had been here yesterday.

She touched the bark of another infected tree. It flaked and turned to dust. She jerked her hand away and saw what looked like a black ink stain on her fingers.

"These trees must have gotten sick," she said. It was the best she could offer young Christopher. She tried another joke. "I might have to send them all home from school today."

The boy didn't laugh.

Even though it was still technically morning, Rachel announced that they were breaking for lunch.

"But it's too early for lunch," the girl with big brown eyes said.

"Not on San Francisco time, it's not," Rachel said.

As she ushered the kids back to the main building, her mind

raced to come up with possible explanations for what she'd just witnessed. But nothing made sense. Rachel had never seen or read about anything like this. It wasn't the result of the vampire bugs that could eat away at banyan trees if left unchecked. Or of Roundup, the herbicide that the groundskeepers used over-zealously on the thirty acres of park that stretched all the way to Hilo Bay. Rachel had always considered herbicides a necessary evil—like first dates.

This was something else. Something dark, maybe even dangerous, a mystery she had to solve.

When the children were in the cafeteria, Rachel ran to her office. She checked in with her boss, then made a phone call to Ted Murray, an ex-boyfriend at Stanford who had recommended her for this job and convinced her to take it and who now worked for the Army Corps of Engineers at the Military Reserve.

"We might have a thing here," Rachel told him.

"A *thing*?" Murray said. "God, you scientists with your fancy words."

She explained what she had seen, knowing she was talking too quickly, her words falling over each other as they came spilling out of her mouth.

"On it," Murray said. "I'll get some people out there as soon as I can. And don't panic. I'm sure there's a good reason for this...*thing*."

"Ted, you know I don't scare very easily."

"Tell me about it," Murray said. "I know from my own personal experience that you're the one usually doing the scaring."

She hung up, knowing she *was* scared, the worst fear of all for her: *not knowing*. While the children continued noisily eating lunch, she put on the running shoes she kept under her desk and ran all the way back to the banyan grove.

There were more blackened trees when she got there, the

stain creeping up from distinctive aerial roots that stretched out like gnarled gray fingers.

Rachel Sherrill tentatively touched one of the trees. It felt like a hot stove. She checked her fingertips to make sure she hadn't singed them.

Ted Murray had said he would send some of his people to investigate as soon as he could assemble a crew. Rachel ran back to the lunchroom and collected her group of fifth-graders from San Francisco. No need for anybody to panic. Not yet, anyway.

Their last stop was a miniature rainforest far from the banyan grove. The tour felt endless to her, but when it was finally over, Rachel said, "I hope you all come back someday."

A thin reed of a girl asked, "Are you going to get a doctor for the sick trees?"

"I'm about to do that right now," Rachel said.

She turned around and once again jogged back toward the banyan trees. She felt as if the entire day had exploded around her, like one of the volcanoes in the distance.

THREE

A voice came crackling over the loudspeakers—Rachel Sherrill's boss, Theo Nakamura, telling visitors to evacuate the botanical gardens immediately.

"This is not a drill," Theo said. "This is for the safety of everyone on the grounds. That includes all park personnel. Everyone, please, out of the park."

Within seconds, park visitors started coming at Rachel hard. The grounds were more crowded than she had thought. Mothers ran as they pushed strollers ahead of them. Children ran ahead of their parents. A teen on a bike swerved to avoid a child, went down, got up cursing, climbed back on his bike, and kept going. Smoke was suddenly everywhere.

"It could be a volcano!" Rachel heard a young woman yell.

Rachel saw two army jeeps parked outside the distant banyan grove. Another jeep roared past her; Ted Murray was at the wheel. She shouted his name but Murray, who probably couldn't hear her over the chaos, didn't turn around.

Murray's jeep stopped, and soldiers jumped out. Murray directed them to form a perimeter around the entrance to the grove and ensure that the park visitors kept moving out.

Rachel ran toward the banyan grove. Another jeep pulled up in front of her and a soldier stepped out.

"You're heading in the wrong direction," the soldier said.

"You—you don't understand," she stammered. "Those—they're my trees."

"I don't want to have to tell you again, ma'am."

Rachel Sherrill heard a chopper engine; she looked up and saw a helicopter come out of the clouds from behind the twin peaks. Saw it touch down and saw its doors open. Men in hazmat suits, tanks strapped to their backs, came out carrying extinguishers labeled COLD FIRE. They pointed them like handguns and ran toward the trees.

Her trees.

Rachel ran toward them and toward the fire.

In that same moment she heard another crash from the sky, and this time she knew for sure it wasn't a coming storm.

Please not today, she thought.

Also By James Patterson

ALEX CROSS NOVELS

Along Came a Spider • Kiss the Girls • Jack and Jill • Cat and
Mouse • Pop Goes the Weasel • Roses are Red • Violets are Blue •
Four Blind Mice • The Big Bad Wolf • London Bridges • Mary,
Mary • Cross • Double Cross • Cross Country • Alex Cross's Trial
(*with Richard DiLallo*) • I, Alex Cross • Cross Fire • Kill Alex Cross •
Merry Christmas, Alex Cross • Alex Cross, Run • Cross My Heart •
Hope to Die • Cross Justice • Cross the Line • The People vs. Alex
Cross • Target: Alex Cross • Criss Cross • Deadly Cross • Fear No
Evil • Triple Cross • Alex Cross Must Die

THE WOMEN'S MURDER CLUB SERIES

1st to Die (*with Andrew Gross*) • 2nd Chance (*with Andrew
Gross*) • 3rd Degree (*with Andrew Gross*) • 4th of July (*with
Maxine Paetro*) • The 5th Horseman (*with Maxine Paetro*) • The
6th Target (*with Maxine Paetro*) • 7th Heaven (*with Maxine
Paetro*) • 8th Confession (*with Maxine Paetro*) • 9th Judgement
(*with Maxine Paetro*) • 10th Anniversary (*with Maxine Paetro*) •
11th Hour (*with Maxine Paetro*) • 12th of Never (*with Maxine
Paetro*) • Unlucky 13 (*with Maxine Paetro*) • 14th Deadly Sin
(*with Maxine Paetro*) • 15th Affair (*with Maxine Paetro*) • 16th
Seduction (*with Maxine Paetro*) • 17th Suspect (*with Maxine
Paetro*) • 18th Abduction (*with Maxine Paetro*) • 19th Christmas
(*with Maxine Paetro*) • 20th Victim (*with Maxine Paetro*) •
21st Birthday (*with Maxine Paetro*) • 22 Seconds (*with
Maxine Paetro*) • 23rd Midnight (*with Maxine Paetro*) •
The 24th Hour (*with Maxine Paetro*)

DETECTIVE MICHAEL BENNETT SERIES

Step on a Crack (*with Michael Ledwidge*) • Run for Your Life
(*with Michael Ledwidge*) • Worst Case (*with Michael Ledwidge*) • Tick
Tock (*with Michael Ledwidge*) • I, Michael Bennett (*with Michael
Ledwidge*) • Gone (*with Michael Ledwidge*) • Burn
(*with Michael Ledwidge*) • Alert (*with Michael Ledwidge*) • Bullseye
(*with Michael Ledwidge*) • Haunted (*with James O. Born*) •

Ambush (*with James O. Born*) • Blindside (*with James O. Born*) •
The Russian (*with James O. Born*) • Shattered (*with James O. Born*) • Obsessed (*with James O. Born*) •
Crosshairs (*with James O. Born*)

PRIVATE NOVELS

Private (*with Maxine Paetro*) • Private London (*with Mark Pearson*) •
Private Games (*with Mark Sullivan*) • Private: No. 1 Suspect (*with Maxine Paetro*) • Private Berlin (*with Mark Sullivan*) • Private Down Under (*with Michael White*) • Private L.A. (*with Mark Sullivan*) •
Private India (*with Ashwin Sanghi*) • Private Vegas (*with Maxine Paetro*) • Private Sydney (*with Kathryn Fox*) • Private Paris (*with Mark Sullivan*) • The Games (*with Mark Sullivan*) • Private Delhi (*with Ashwin Sanghi*) • Private Princess (*with Rees Jones*) • Private Moscow (*with Adam Hamdy*) • Private Rogue (*with Adam Hamdy*) • Private Beijing (*with Adam Hamdy*) • Private Rome (*with Adam Hamdy*) •
Private Monaco (*with Adam Hamdy*)

NYPD RED SERIES

NYPD Red (*with Marshall Karp*) • NYPD Red 2 (*with Marshall Karp*) • NYPD Red 3 (*with Marshall Karp*) • NYPD Red 4 (*with Marshall Karp*) • NYPD Red 5 (*with Marshall Karp*) •
NYPD Red 6 (*with Marshall Karp*)

DETECTIVE HARRIET BLUE SERIES

Never Never (*with Candice Fox*) • Fifty Fifty (*with Candice Fox*) •
Liar Liar (*with Candice Fox*) • Hush Hush (*with Candice Fox*)

INSTINCT SERIES

Instinct (*with Howard Roughan, previously published as Murder Games*) • Killer Instinct (*with Howard Roughan*) •
Steal (*with Howard Roughan*)

THE BLACK BOOK SERIES

The Black Book (*with David Ellis*) • The Red Book (*with David Ellis*) • Escape (*with David Ellis*)

STAND-ALONE THRILLERS

The Thomas Berryman Number • Hide and Seek • Black Market • The Midnight Club • Sail (*with Howard Roughan*) • Swimsuit (*with Maxine Paetro*) • Don't Blink (*with Howard Roughan*) • Postcard Killers (*with Liza Marklund*) • Toys (*with Neil McMahon*) • Now You See Her (*with Michael Ledwidge*) • Kill Me If You Can (*with Marshall Karp*) • Guilty Wives (*with David Ellis*) • Zoo (*with Michael Ledwidge*) • Second Honeymoon (*with Howard Roughan*) • Mistress (*with David Ellis*) • Invisible (*with David Ellis*) • Truth or Die (*with Howard Roughan*) • Murder House (*with David Ellis*) • The Store (*with Richard DiLallo*) • Texas Ranger (*with Andrew Bourelle*) • The President is Missing (*with Bill Clinton*) • Revenge (*with Andrew Holmes*) • Juror No. 3 (*with Nancy Allen*) • The First Lady (*with Brendan DuBois*) • The Chef (*with Max DiLallo*) • Out of Sight (*with Brendan DuBois*) • Unsolved (*with David Ellis*) • The Inn (*with Candice Fox*) • Lost (*with James O. Born*) • Texas Outlaw (*with Andrew Bourelle*) • The Summer House (*with Brendan DuBois*) • 1st Case (*with Chris Tebbetts*) • Cajun Justice (*with Tucker Axum*)• The Midwife Murders (*with Richard DiLallo*) • The Coast-to-Coast Murders (*with J.D. Barker*) • Three Women Disappear (*with Shan Serafin*) • The President's Daughter (*with Bill Clinton*) • The Shadow (*with Brian Sitts*) • The Noise (*with J.D. Barker*) • 2 Sisters Detective Agency (*with Candice Fox*) • Jailhouse Lawyer (*with Nancy Allen*) • The Horsewoman (*with Mike Lupica*) • Run Rose Run (*with Dolly Parton*) • Death of the Black Widow (*with J.D. Barker*) • The Ninth Month (*with Richard DiLallo*) • The Girl in the Castle (*with Emily Raymond*) • Blowback (*with Brendan DuBois*) • The Twelve Topsy-Turvy, Very Messy Days of Christmas (*with Tad Safran*) • The Perfect Assassin (*with Brian Sitts*) • House of Wolves (*with Mike Lupica*) • Countdown (*with Brendan DuBois*) • Cross Down (*with Brendan DuBois*) • Circle of Death (*with Brian Sitts*) • Lion & Lamb (with *Duane Swierczynski*) • 12 Months to Live (*with Mike Lupica*) • Holmes, Margaret and Poe (*with Brian Sitts*) • The No. 1 Lawyer (*with Nancy Allen*) • The Murder Inn (*with Candice Fox*) • Confessions of the Dead (*with J.D. Barker*)

For more information about James Patterson's novels, visit www.penguin.co.uk.